Nephi's Courage

Story of a Bad Mormon

Rory McFarlan

Dedication

To all God's children, my sisters and brothers and siblings. He created each of us as we are. We are all divine. We are all human. We are all flawed. Every single one of us is beautiful.

Trigger Warning: Content in this book contains discussion and portrayal of sexual violence, bullying, mental illness, mental health crisis, family conflict, and hospitalization, which some may find triggering. If you need support at any time, please call the national suicide prevention hotline at 1-800-273-8255.

rorymcfarlan@gmail.com

ISBN: 978-1-7341794-0-8

CHAPTER 1

Four years is a long time to serve in any calling, but four years as executive secretary to the Bishop seemed like an eternity. Try as he might, Nephi Willard couldn't even remember his previous calling. He reflected on the time he spent working with Bishop Thompson over the years, while he waited in the church foyer for the Bishop to arrive. Pacing back and forth, he reviewed the appointment schedule for the evening.

Nephi was tall and thin. Some people, including his mother, would say too thin. His short, golden blond hair was well-styled. A single-breasted suit with jetted pockets hugged his figure. The blend of burgundy, orange and yellow on his narrow tie matched the leaves falling outside. He finished reviewing the agenda, and checked his watch. Bishop Thompson should arrive any time now.

In the Church of Jesus Christ of Latter Day Saints, also known as the LDS Church, or the Mormon Church, there are no paid clergy. A Bishop, a man with no formal religious training and a day job unrelated to the church, leads each ward, or congregation.

The Bishop is called of God by an inspired regional leader called a Stake President. The Bishop calls two counselors, who assist with his duties running the ward. Together, a Bishop and his counselors make up a Bishopric.

The Bishop also calls an executive secretary to keep his calendar - that was Nephi's job. A Bishop serves for about five years before being released, after which, the Stake President calls another Bishop in his place.

In similar fashion, the Bishop calls individual members of the ward to serve in various callings. Callings include positions like Sunday School teachers, music directors, organists, and other posts required to minister to the congregation.

Nephi had served in many church callings in his life, but none as long as this one - four years as executive secretary to Bishop Thompson. As he thought about it, Bishop Thompson walked through the door.

"Good evening, Brother Willard," he said, shaking Nephi's hand. "Thanks for being here on a Thursday night. What do we have lined up?"

"You have a temple recommend interview with Sister Gomez at 6:30, a birthday interview with Ethan Combs at 6:45, and Brother Johnston, a less active member who moved into the ward boundaries about a year ago, requested 30 minutes with you. I scheduled him from 7:00 to 7:30. If you can stay beyond that, I would like to meet with you," replied Nephi.

"Everything okay?" asked Bishop Thompson.

"Yep," said Nephi, "I just have something on my mind."

"Well, alright then. I'm happy to stay. I look forward to our conversation."

Bishop Thompson smiled, and patted Nephi on the shoulder. The Bishop was a portly man with neatly combed brown hair, and a fresh-pressed, well-worn suit. There were visible rub spots just below his knees – the result of countless hours kneeling in prayer. Bishop Thompson turned and headed into his office, while Nephi waited outside to greet people. Sister Gomez soon arrived, and Nephi shook her hand and smiled, an expression ever-present on his face.

"Bishop is ready for you. Go on in," said Nephi.

Sister Gomez was there to renew her temple recommend. A temple recommend is a piece of paper, signed by a member of the Bishopric in the ward and also by a member of the Stake Presidency, the regional leadership arm of the church. The signatures are given at the end of a worthiness interview.

Members may not enter the temple to perform sacred ordinances unless they have a recommend. To meet the worthiness requirements, each member must be faithful in the church, and obey the commandments. This includes honesty in dealings with others, obeying a health law called the Word of Wisdom, paying a full tithe, and obeying the law of chastity, which requires abstinence from sexual relations before marriage and outside of marriage.

Temple recommend interviews take about 15 minutes. During the interview, a member of the Bishopric asks questions to assess worthiness. A similar interview then takes place with a member of the Stake Presidency. Once the two clergymen and the interviewee sign the recommend, it can be used to enter the temple. The recommend is valid for two years, after which it must be renewed through the same process.

While Sister Gomez met with Bishop Thompson, Nephi sat quietly in a soft chair in the foyer and looked up at the large painting of Jesus washing the feet of the apostles that hung on the wall. Nephi thought about how Jesus served others, and the power of the statement he made by washing the feet of each apostle. Nephi loved Jesus and had a testimony of his divine mission as Savior and Redeemer of the world. He also had a firm testimony that the prophet Joseph Smith had seen God and Jesus, and that he restored the fullness of the gospel to the earth under their direction.

Nephi was the kind of Mormon that other Mormons admire. He had never tasted coffee, tea, or alcohol, which are forbidden by the Word of Wisdom, and wasn't even tempted to do so. He was honest, kind, sincere and empathetic. Nephi loved people. He had never broken the law of chastity and despite being thirty years of age, had only ever kissed one girl - his best friend, Stacy.

Nephi read from the Bible and the Book of Mormon every day, and faithfully served in every church calling assigned to him. Despite all of that, Nephi didn't feel like a good Mormon. He had a pit in the bottom of his stomach as he contemplated his upcoming conversation with the Bishop.

Bishop Thompson was a good man. He was earnest and cared about the members of his ward. He did his best to serve them with love and compassion. Nephi had grown up in this ward and lived here almost his entire life, all except for the two years he spent serving as a full-time missionary in Albania. The Thompsons and the Willards were friends. Nephi knew Bishop Thompson and his family, which made him even more uneasy at the thought of their upcoming conversation.

The motion of the door swinging open from outside

interrupted Nephi's discomfort. Ethan Combs arrived with his mother. Ethan just turned fourteen and was there for his annual interview with the Bishop. Every year, a Bishop meets with each member of his ward between the age of 12 and 18. He interviews them for worthiness and approves their advancement within the youth organization. Young men are given the Priesthood, or the authority to act in the name of God, to carry out righteous acts on His behalf.

At 12, they are ordained to the office of Deacon, and given the responsibility to pass the Sacrament to the congregation each Sunday. The Sacrament is like communion in other religions. Each member of the church partakes of bread and water in remembrance of the body and blood of Jesus Christ.

At 14, young men are ordained to the office of Teacher, with the responsibility to prepare the bread and water for the Sacrament, and to teach the members of the ward. They are eligible to be ministering brothers to other members of the church. In this capacity, they visit people in their homes to teach them gospel messages and check on their well-being.

At 16, young men are ordained to the office of Priest, with responsibility to bless the Sacrament, or say the special prayer to consecrate the bread and water before the congregation partakes of it. Priests also have the authority to baptize people.

Young Women between the ages of 12 and 18 are grouped into similar classes, but the Priesthood is not conferred upon them.

Since Ethan had just turned 14, he would discuss worthiness with the Bishop, and then schedule his ordination to the office of Teacher. Sister Combs was beaming with pride as she walked through the door.

"Brother Willard, it's so nice to see you," she said.

"It's great to see you too, Sister Combs," he replied, "Ethan, how are you doing? Are you enjoying school?"

"School is okay, I guess," said Ethan.

"Ethan is first chair Tuba!" his mother added, her voice nearing a shout.

"Wow, that is impressive!" Nephi said, "I don't think I

could even hold an instrument that large for more than five minutes."

Ethan laughed a little under his breath and cracked a smile, revealing new braces on his teeth. He had wavy red hair - not the strawberry kind, more the red Golden Retriever kind. His face was spotted with freckles, and his movement was awkward, not yet having grown into his body. He was tall for his age, with broad shoulders that stretched his shirt. It was no surprise that he played a large instrument.

"Bishop is still in an appointment but should be with you shortly," said Nephi. "Take a seat."

Ethan and Sister Combs sat down on the sofa on the other side of the foyer below the painting. Nephi made small talk with them while they waited for Bishop Thompson to finish with Sister Gomez.

Sister Gomez soon emerged and Bishop welcomed Ethan into his office. Nephi sat back in the soft foyer chair while Sister Combs chatted with Sister Gomez. They were rambling on about an upcoming Relief Society quilting activity. Nephi's mind began to wander.

Relief Society is the women's organization in the church. Each ward has a Relief Society President, who provides leadership to the women in the congregation, and coordinates efforts to enhance the well-being of all ward members. The Relief Society President selects two other women as counselors, and a third as secretary.

Collectively, they are called the Relief Society Presidency. The women in the ward meet in Relief Society meeting every other week, on Sunday, where they teach lessons tailored to their needs. At least once per month, they sponsor an activity on a weeknight that provides an opportunity for fellowshipping, service, fun, and learning.

As Sister Combs and Sister Gomez continued their conversation, Nephi's mind drifted back to his upcoming conversation with Bishop Thompson. Nephi had spoken with the Bishop many times about the topic, and they understood each other. They shared a brotherly bond. Despite that, Nephi was anxious. He worried that their relationship, one he valued, might change after tonight. His mind wavered with second thoughts about the discussion, but ultimately found his conviction and determined to share the things that troubled him, regardless of the consequences.

The door to the Bishop's office opened. Bishop Thompson thanked Ethan and shook his hand.

"I look forward to seeing you set apart on Sunday," the Bishop told Ethan, who re-joined his mother as she was wrapping up her conversation with Sister Gomez.

The trio headed out the door just as Brother Johnston arrived. Brother Johnston was a burly man, balding on top. His sandy hair went almost to his shoulder, and he sported an unruly beard. The length of his hair and his beard were both unusual for a member of the church, which discourages both beards and long hair for men. Such grooming practices are not permitted for full time missionaries or those who attend church-owned colleges and universities. For the church at large, it is not an official rule, but an unspoken one.

"Brother Johnston, I presume?" asked Nephi.

The man nodded and extended his hand. Nephi grasped it, a warm smile on his face.

"I am Brother Willard. I spoke to you on the phone," said Nephi. "It's a pleasure to meet you."

Brother Johnston could tell that Nephi really meant it, from the sincere tone in his voice, and the warmth of his smile. His shoulders relaxed and a hint of a smile found its way to his face.

"Let me introduce you to Bishop Thompson," Nephi said, gesturing toward the Bishop. "He is one of the best men I know."

Bishop Thompson shook Brother Johnston's hand and welcomed him into the office. He closed the door, leaving Nephi alone to his thoughts. Nephi had no idea why Brother Johnston wanted to meet with the Bishop because a Bishop's meetings are confidential. As executive secretary, Nephi scheduled the appointments and sometimes knew the context, especially for routine concerns such as youth birthday interviews and temple recommends. But for most meetings, the purpose was between the individual and the Bishop.

Brother Johnston hadn't been to church in the time he lived in the ward. LDS wards are assigned based on geographic boundaries, as opposed to leaving choice of congregation up to individuals. Unlike churches where parishioners determine the best fit based on personal preference, the ward to which Mormons are assigned is based solely on where they live. In some cases, one could move directly across the street and end up attending an entirely different church building.

Society likes labels. We like to put people in boxes and make assumptions about them based on their box – Republican or Democrat, fat or skinny, rich or poor, etc. The LDS church is no exception. People who are part of the church are called "members" while anyone who is not Mormon is a "non-member". Within the church, members are subdivided into even smaller boxes.

Those who attend church are placed in the "active" box while those who don't are "inactive" or "less active." Someone who is learning about the church is called an "investigator", and a person born in the church but who may or may not attend regularly, and does not follow the rules, is affectionately known as a "jack-Mormon."

Then there are those who were once members of the church but have either been excommunicated or asked to be removed from the records of the church. Depending on their attitude toward the church, they are labeled either "ex-Mormon" or "anti-Mormon".

Like all labels humans give to each other, Mormon labels comes with stereotypes. The more we believe that stereotype, the more we will see the behaviors that we associate with it. We see what we want to see, and our judgements often become self-fulfilling prophesy.

Brother Johnston, who has not attended church since moving to the area, is an "inactive" member. The stereotype that goes along with being an inactive member is that he is someone with a weak testimony of the truthfulness of the gospel, or someone who lacks faith.

Many would assume that he doesn't come to church because he is a sinner who is too proud to repent, or someone who survived on the testimony of his parents as a youngster and never developed his own. Nephi wasn't one to buy into stereotypes. He didn't know why Brother Johnston didn't come to church and didn't much care. He genuinely wanted well for him and would love to see him come back to church, not because he judged him as a sinner, but because he knew that Brother Johnston, like everyone, had much to contribute. Nephi believed that he would be happier if he returned to church.

Nephi's thoughts turned to the upcoming conversation with Bishop Thompson. His stomach churned; it seemed to be tied in knots.

Nephi pondered his concerns, and looked for direction in the same place he always did when he had nowhere else to go. He kneeled on the floor of the foyer, head bowed, and eyes closed. He rested his folded arms on the soft foyer chair as he poured out his heart to God.

"My Dear Father in Heaven," he prayed, "I come before thee with humble heart. Father, I don't know what to do. Thou knows my heart, my intentions, and my deepest desires. Thou knows that I love thee and want to follow thy will. I ask thee to help me understand and accept thy will for me."

"Please, Father, help me know what to say and how to say it when I speak with Bishop Thompson tonight. Please bless my mind with clarity, and bless me with strength and the ability to speak the things that are weighing on my mind and my heart. Bless me with thy spirit. I ask thee to bless Bishop Thompson with inspiration to advise and guide me."

"I love thee and trust thee. Father, I thank thee for sending thy son, Jesus Christ, to atone for my sins, and to take my faults upon Him. Thank you for providing a way for me to return to live with thee through Him. Help me serve in my calling and to do so in a manner pleasing to thee. Father, please help me understand thy will and thy plan for me. I thank thee for the knowledge of the restored gospel, and a testimony of my Savior. I thank thee for the Book of Mormon, and the spirit that I feel when I read it. I thank thee for my many blessings, and I acknowledge thy hand in them. I say these things in the name of Jesus Christ, Amen."

Nephi stayed on his knees after finishing the prayer, and silently pondered and concentrated on his feelings, seeking inspiration. He felt a peace come over his body. His nerves relaxed, and he was assured that he would have the strength to discuss with the Bishop the things that weighed on his mind.

He heard the Bishop's door open and slowly rose to his feet. Brother Johnston and Bishop Thompson returned to the foyer, and Nephi shook Brother Johnston's hand.

"It was truly a pleasure to meet you, Brother Johnston. I hope to get to know you better. Whenever you are at church, you are welcome to sit with me," said Nephi.

"Thanks, Brother Willard. It was nice to meet you, too. I just might take you up on that." With a smile, he turned and left the building.

"Thanks again for being here with me tonight, Brother Willard. Take a seat in my office. Let's have that conversation," said Bishop Thompson as he escorted Nephi into the office and closed the door.

CHAPTER 2

Nephi sat in a chair in front of Bishop Thompson's mahogany desk. A picture of Jesus hung on the wall. The front right corner of the desk housed a small bamboo plant. On the left corner sat a portrait of the Thompson family – Bishop Thompson, his wife Nancy, and their four children. Nephi knew them well. Bishop Thompson took his place behind the desk.

"Thanks for meeting with me, Bishop," said Nephi.

"It is always a pleasure to speak with you, Nephi," Bishop Thompson responded. "Let's start with a prayer."

Nephi nodded in agreement. Bishop rose from his chair and walked to the other side of the desk where he kneeled and bowed his head. Nephi followed his lead, dropping to his knees and folding his arms. Bishop Thompson prayed aloud.

"Our Father who art in Heaven, we come before thee to ask for thy spirit during our meeting. We ask thee to comfort Nephi, and to help us find the answers he seeks. Please bless us with hearts and minds open to thy guidance. Help us understand each other and understand thy will. Bless us with faith, Father, and with willingness to accept thy will. We thank thee for the restored gospel and for our Redeemer, Jesus Christ, who atoned for our sins. Please help us accept Him and allow the atonement to work in our lives. We pray in the name of Jesus Christ, Amen."

"Amen," added Nephi.

Both men returned to their seats. Nephi took a deep breath and then exhaled, preparing for the conversation.

"What's on your mind?" asked Bishop Thompson.

"I have been doing a lot of thinking," explained Nephi. "We have spoken in the past about my feelings and my concerns. I have been reflecting on my standing in the church as a gay man and my state in eternity. Through reflection, I have grown frustrated and I need to talk it out."

"Nephi, I know that you suffer from same sex attraction but you know that having those feelings is not a sin. The sin is in acting on them. You are my executive secretary with good standing in the church. We have been through this. You have nothing to worry about."

Nephi's hands began to tremble. He did his best to steady them. A tear came to his eye as he continued to speak. "The way you say that makes it sound like I have some terrible disease," he said. "Bishop, I do not suffer from anything. I am attracted to men. It is how I am. It is not some health condition I suffer from."

"I'm sorry, Nephi. I didn't mean it like that. I just...," Bishop Thompson started before Nephi interrupted him.

"Can I ask you some questions?"

"Of course, Nephi. Go ahead. I don't pretend to have all the answers, but I'll do my best."

"Do you believe that God made me this way?" asked Nephi.

"I do," returned Bishop Thompson. "The official position of the church also supports that."

"Bishop, do you believe that God makes mistakes?"

"We don't always understand God. The Bible tells us that our ways are not his ways. He seems mysterious at times, but no, Nephi, God does not make mistakes. He is perfect."

"Does God love me?" continued Nephi.

"Yes, he absolutely loves you, Nephi. You are his child. He created you and he loves you," insisted Bishop, a tender look in his eyes.

"I agree, Bishop. I know that I am a son of God and I feel his love for me. He created me just the way I am. That is where my confusion comes from. I love God and I want to return to live with him one day."

"If you continue on your current path, I have no doubt you will return to live with God after this life," said Bishop.

"That's just the thing, Bishop. I'm not so sure about that. To live with God again, we must obtain Exaltation in the Celestial Kingdom, the highest of God's glories. Bishop, what are the requirements for Exaltation?"

"I know that you know this, Nephi, but I'll play along. To

reach Exaltation, you must be baptized in the church, receive ordinances in the temple, and endure to the end, keeping the commandments all of your life," explained Bishop Thompson.

"The part I am confused about, Bishop, is the part about the temple ordinances. There is one temple ordinance that is not available to me as a gay man."

"Temple marriage," said Bishop Thompson. "I see where you are going. You worry that you cannot reach Exaltation because it requires marriage for time and all eternity."

"Am I expected to marry a woman? Should I make a family and live a life contrary to who God made me?" asked Nephi.

"Certainly not. The church has made it clear that gay men should not marry women."

"That is true now," said Nephi, "but it wasn't always the case. The church used to sponsor conversion therapy programs and counsel gay men to marry women in hopes of turning them straight. They eventually realized conversion doesn't work. The church has concluded that God made people the way they are. Even so, church policy does not allow me to marry a man even though God created me to be gay."

"Nephi, I understand your frustration, I really do. I understand that this doesn't seem fair. You know that God values the family as the base unit of society and that God defines marriage as the union between one man and one woman."

Nephi shifted in his seat. He crossed his legs, then uncrossed them. He finally settled in position, digging his fingernails into the arms of the chair with his right knee bouncing up and down.

"That was not always the doctrine proclaimed by the church. Under the direction of Joseph Smith, Brigham Young, and every other prophet through Wilford Woodruff, God defined marriage as the union between one man and one or more women. Until the polygamy manifesto in 1890, marriage to more than one woman was permitted and even encouraged. The definition of marriage changed with the manifesto. I pray that something similar will happen someday to open the door to Exaltation for me."

Bishop Thompson's forehead creased. He appeared deep in thought, not knowing how to respond. After a few moments, he broke the silence.

"Nephi, as your Bishop, I must tell you that those prayers are wasted. God's plan permits marriage between one man and one woman. He declared it in the Proclamation to the World on the Family. It is clear. It is a doctrine that will not change. Sometimes the church creates policies not based on unchangeable underlying doctrine - things like the duration of church meetings on Sunday and the structure of the ministering program. Fundamental doctrine such as the definition of marriage and the role of gender are doctrine and will never change. You should use your energy and your prayers on something else."

Bishop Thompson paused for a moment. Nephi's head dropped into his hands.

The Bishop continued, "As your friend, I need to warn you about the path you are going down. You are walking a dangerous line, Nephi. The brethren have made this clear. If you support and sustain them, as you have acknowledged in your temple recommend interview, you cannot go contrary to the doctrine. Be careful what you say."

Nephi hoped they could have a good philosophical conversation. He hoped to see an inkling of understanding in Bishop Thompson's face. He felt betrayed and defeated. They sat in silence while Nephi gathered his thoughts and composed himself. Once he felt calm enough to reply without an emotional outburst, he responded.

"Bishop Thompson, I have known you for a long time and I respect you. I want you to know that I raise my concerns out of love. I want to foster constructive dialogue. As I said, I have been studying and reflecting a lot. I understand the position of the church, that marriage is only between one man and one woman, and I understand the hard line stating that will never change."

Bishop Thompson nodded as he leaned in and

concentrated on Nephi's face.

Nephi continued, "Church doctrine has changed at various times in the past. In the 1850s, Brigham Young, then prophet, declared that black men of African descent were prohibited from receiving the Priesthood. At the time, black members of the church were not permitted to marry in the temple. Many apostles and prophets until 1978 maintained the policy on black church members as doctrine, claiming it to be God's will, received by revelation. They stated that it would never change. In 1978, Prophet Spencer W. Kimball announced a revelation that all worthy males were eligible to receive the Priesthood, and all worthy members could partake in temple ordinances, including marriage. The church now maintains that the ban on black member participation was not doctrine, but policy made by individual men following societal trends rather than revelation from God. Prior to 1978, however, church leaders were adamant that it was doctrine."

Bishop Thompson appeared deep in thought as Nephi pressed on.

"The practice of polygamy was also declared to be doctrine by the prophets from the time of Joseph Smith until the 1890 manifesto. Marriage between one man and one woman is now the doctrine. The church's position is that polygamy was doctrine prior to 1890 and monogamy has been the doctrine since. Polygamy was not a policy, it was actual doctrine, and that doctrine changed. These are some of the reasons I hold out hope and feel that my prayers are not wasted. In one case, what was once doctrine, is now viewed as a flawed policy of the past. In the other, the accepted doctrine changed. There is precedent for doctrinal changes. Why should I not believe that it could change at some future time, and the current doctrine concerning gay members of the church could give way to a doctrine of acceptance and inclusion?"

Bishop Thompson frowned and the crease on his forehead deepened. A shade of red started at the base of his thick neck and edged up his face until it reached his hairline. He looked like he just returned from a week at the beach.

"Nephi," he said, voice raised, "I want to make this clear so you are certain to understand. The Proclamation to the World regarding the Family is a doctrine that will not change. Got accepts only marriage between one man and one woman. Man invented gay marriage and God does not recognize it. I want you to know that God loves you. He wants you at church. He needs you and values your service, but you are treading on very shaky ground. If you do not fall in line with the prophet and apostles, you will be seen as an apostate, and that could lead to excommunication. I don't want to see that happen to you. Please, Nephi, please see reason."

Nephi thought for a moment. "Let me summarize to make sure I have everything straight. God, who does not make mistakes, created me as a gay man. He created a plan for his children to return to live with him. To reach the highest glory, that plan requires that his children are married for all eternity in the temple. Gay marriage is not recognized by God, so about ten percent of God's children, including myself, are not eligible to live with God again. This is his plan, by design. He intends to exclude ten percent of his children, setting a ceiling on the degree of glory we can achieve. On top of that, church doctrine does not permit us to experience intimate human relationships during this life, a limitation that does not apply to the ninety percent of his children who happen to be straight. Is that about right? Sorry, I just don't believe that a loving God, who is the Father of us all would create so many of his children in a way that ensures their exclusion. Do you believe that is His plan?"

Bishop composed himself and did his best to speak in a concerned and loving tone. "Like I told you, Nephi, I don't have all the answers, but I know this: In Proverbs, the Lord tells us to trust in Him with all of our heart and lean not on our own understanding. His ways are not our ways, Nephi. I don't believe that God wants to exclude you and I don't know exactly how his plan for you works, but I know that you must trust Him. Obey the commandments, put your faith in the Lord, and trust that everything will work out."

This was the answer that Nephi expected, but not what he

hoped. "So God's plan for me is to remain celibate, without an intimate, loving relationship for my entire life. I am to keep all the commandments and take part in the ordinances that the church permits me to participate in and trust that after I die, God will somehow make it up to me and I will enjoy all the same blessings experienced by his straight children?"

"I don't know what to tell you, Nephi. It is obvious that you understand it. I know it frustrates you, and it does not seem fair, but that is the way things are," Bishop explained. "I hope you know that God loves you."

Nephi stood and turned toward the door. He took a step forward and then turned to face Bishop Thompson.

"Bishop, the doctrine does not just seem unfair, it is unfair. I believe that God loves me and that he is just. I don't believe his eternal doctrine would exclude me because of something I can't change. And what of God's children who he created to be Asexual, who have no desire for a sexual relationship? What of his children with a non-conforming gender identity? Certainly God created his children in diverse ways and he loves each of them. The church position also excludes them from salvation. I believe that God loves his children the way that he created them and that he would not exclude any of them solely on the basis of their God-given nature."

"I'm very sorry to hear that," said Bishop. "I don't know where we go from here, but I don't want to leave tonight on this note. Can we pray together before you leave?"

Nephi kneeled and bowed his head. Bishop Thompson joined him. "Will you offer the prayer, Nephi?" asked Bishop. Nephi didn't feel like praying in that moment, but he closed his eyes, cleared his mind, and did his best.

"Dear Heavenly Father, we come before thee to thank thee for our association and our ability to speak to one another regarding topics that concern us. We thank thee for sending our Savior, Jesus Christ, and all that He did for us in the Garden of Gethsemane and on the cross. We thank thee for the gospel and pray that we may feel brotherly love for one another and grow to understand each other. Please bless

Bishop Thompson that he may be guided and inspired in his calling. Bless his family with health and safety. Comfort them while he spends time away from home serving thee. Bless us to arrive home safe this evening. We pray in the name of Jesus Christ, Amen."

"Amen," repeated Bishop Thompson.

Both men stood. Bishop Thompson hugged Nephi, who stood there, arms at his side. Nephi knew Bishop cared, but he wasn't sure quite what might happen next, and he feared it.

"I have a lot of thinking and praying to do," Nephi said.

"As do I, Nephi, as do I," replied Bishop.

Nephi turned and walked out the door. The thumping of his heart echoed in his ears and his mind raced. He wasn't quite sure how he felt about the conversation. It felt good to express his thoughts, even though Bishop Thompson didn't seem to understand them. Exhausted, he climbed into his truck and headed home.

CHAPTER 3

Jolted awake by the harsh blare of his alarm clock, Nephi sat up in bed. He shook his head in an attempt to chase away the fog resting on his mind. Snippets of the conversation with Bishop Thompson played through his head like a movie of thought. This week was a long one for Nephi, and he was glad Friday finally arrived.

Nephi lived alone in a one-bedroom apartment in Pleasant Grove, Utah, a few blocks from the Lindon city boundary. Nephi's parents, Mike and Darla Willard, raised him in Pleasant Grove and they still lived in the split-level house on a cul-de-sac down the road. They were in his ward and he saw them every Sunday at church. He often went to their house afterward for dinner.

Pleasant Grove is exactly like it sounds – pleasant. It sits at the foot of majestic Mt. Timpanogos in beautiful Happy Valley, the Mormon capital of the world. Salt Lake City is home to church headquarters, it's true. Temple Square in downtown Salt Lake is home to the famous Salt Lake Temple, that took Mormon pioneers 40 years to build. The tabernacle and its world-renowned choir are in Salt Lake City, just across from the Conference Center where the Mormon world congregates twice per year to hear the prophet and twelve apostles speak.

Despite everything Salt Lake offers, Happy Valley is the heart of the church for Mormons in the know. It stretches from the city of Lehi, just south of Salt Lake County, and extends through Pleasant Grove, Lindon, Orem and Provo, before ending in Springville, at the base of Hobble Creek Canyon. Happy Valley is where the truest Mormons live.

Nephi strived to fit that mold his entire life. Baptized into the church by his father at eight, the age when all good Mormon children are baptized, Nephi was a regular "Peter-Priesthood". He received the Aaronic priesthood at 12, and the Melchizedek priesthood at 18, before moving to Albania for two years at 19 to serve as a full-time missionary for the church. There, he bore testimony of Jesus Christ and of the restoration of the gospel through the prophet Joseph Smith. He testified of the truthfulness of the Book of Mormon, another testament of Jesus Christ, written by ancient prophets on the American continent, and translated by Joseph Smith by the power of God. Nephi served the Albanian people and learned to love them. He was sad to return home after two years. Nine years later, Nephi still considered those days in Albania among the happiest of his life.

Warm water cascaded from the showerhead onto Nephi's face bringing clarity to his mind. Heated water is not a luxury always available in Albania. Years later, he still felt gratitude for things most take for granted. Nephi prepared for each day the same way, taking time to give his hair a thorough wash and condition with coconut scented shampoo from the salon. He would then moisturize his face with a mild cleansing cream and cold water before applying moisturizer under his eyes and to the spot on his forehead that tends to crease when he becomes anxious or concentrates on something.

He dressed for work in slacks and a well pressed button-up shirt – the business casual dress code required by the call center where he worked. Nephi then kneeled in prayer, thanking God for his blessings and for sending Jesus to save him, and asking for direction and safety during the day. After morning prayers, Nephi read the Book of Mormon in the app on his phone and pondered the things he read. Nearly ready for the day, he ate a breakfast of wheat toast and scrambled egg whites accompanied by a piping hot cup of Pero. Pero is a hot drink made from barley, enjoyed by Mormons in the morning, since they don't drink coffee. Nephi grew up watching his father drink Pero, and acquired the taste for it. After eating, Nephi brushed his teeth and headed out the door.

Fall leaves painted the trees red, orange, and yellow. Crisp fall air inflated Nephi's lungs as he drew a deep breath. He walked along the sidewalk toward the covered parking space that protected his truck from the weather. The 1996 Chevy 1500 4x4 showed signs of rust just above the tires and on the roof of the standard cab. Nephi preferred to think rust gave it character.

It wasn't perfect, but he owned it outright, having earned every penny of the five thousand dollar price tag. The truck was white with a tuxedo blue interior, and sported custom saddle blanket seat covers that Nephi ordered on the internet. Despite its age, the immaculate interior gave the truck a modern appearance. A 5.7 liter Vortec V8 engine made her purr like a tiger, and her manual transmission allowed Nephi to control the acceleration. He loved driving that truck. It wasn't fancy, but it was his. At least it wasn't a Ford, so he wouldn't need to wonder if it would start each morning.

Nephi climbed into the truck and turned the key. The roar of the engine did his heart good. Falling leaves waved to him as he pulled out of the parking lot and guided his rig toward work. He drove along State Street and made a right on 1600 North, following it to the Brower Hotels reservation center where he was a day shift manager. Brower assigned shifts on a bidding system. Over the past nine years, Nephi worked his way up the seniority ladder. Fresh off of his mission, he started as a customer service agent.

Empathy came naturally to Nephi, and he excelled in customer service. God blessed him with the ability to connect with people, and that served him well in the hospitality industry. Through the years, he progressed from customer service agent to reservations team lead, escalation supervisor, and now to shift manager. Nephi's seniority placed him high in shift bidding priority, landing him the day shift that he preferred – seven in the morning until four in the afternoon.

Nephi pulled into the parking lot and made his way to his usual spot at the back. He could not achieve ten thousand steps without intention, and parking at the back of the lot gave him a better chance to meet his goal. The conversation from last night returned to his mind as he walked toward the door. He couldn't wait to discuss it with Stacy during their weekly Friday lunch date. Stacy had been Nephi's best friend for as long as he could remember, and he valued her opinion.

A stream of cars entered the parking lot, a sign that the

seven o'clock shift was about to begin. Nephi scanned his badge at the door and went inside. The night shift reservations agents looked relieved at Nephi's arrival. They would soon badge out and go home to sleep. Fatigued faces turned toward the clock as Nephi went to his office and sat down at the computer to check the statistics from night shift.

'Time to Answer' at 4.7 seconds and 'Abandon Rate' under five percent. Not bad. Day shift never did quite so well because of higher call volume. Call handling time was 6.4 minutes, which was high, even for night shift. The agents may have been completing work typically done after the call, while the customer was still on the phone, because the increased call handling time corresponded to a reduction in 'Idle Time'. Monica, the night shift manager, must have been coaching her team.

Nephi had learned that people always perform according to how they are measured. If you want to change behavior, simply change the way you measure people and they will fall in line. Emphasis on 'Idle Time' reduction by a manager could easily lead to the unintended consequence of increasing call handling time. Then again, Monica may have intentionally made the tradeoff. Mark, the call center General Manager, had emphasized 'Idle Time' in the last leadership meeting. After analyzing the data for several minutes, Nephi walked next door to Monica's office.

Monica sat in a mesh-back office chair, eyes glued to her monitor. She was a slender brunette with stunning brown eyes. Four years back, while a freshman at BYU, Monica hired on as a reservations agent. After graduating with a Bachelor degree in Hospitality Management last month, they promoted her to shift manager on the night crew.

"Good morning," said Nephi.

"Is it?" asked Monica. "I've been stuck here all night, I wouldn't know."

"A beautiful fall morning," stated Nephi. "Take some time to enjoy the colorful leaves on your way home. The snow will be here before you know it."

"I suppose," she said. "Brock and Angela from your shift called off again. My guess is that they partied all night and called in just before crashing."

"That's the third time this month," said Nephi. "I just don't understand it. This job isn't that hard. I guess they are overdue for a difficult conversation."

"Good luck with that."

"Your stats from last night look great. I can tell you have been emphasizing 'Idle Time' with your team," Nephi said with a smile.

"Thanks for noticing, Nephi. I hope that Mark will notice, too. He doesn't seem too fond of me. I bet the only thing he will notice is that 'Call Handling Time' went up."

"Well, I have noticed how hard you are working and the night crew isn't easy to motivate. I'll find an opportunity to point it out to Mark when he gets in," offered Nephi.

"I appreciate it. Well, look at the time. I'm going to wrap things up and get out of here," she said, cueing Nephi to let her work.

"I'll leave you to it," he said, turning to walk the floor.

Nephi roamed the maze of cubicles. Night shift had all but cleared out, and most of his team had already logged in. Everyone was present except Brock and Angela. They had been nothing but trouble from the beginning. Having started in the same orientation group, they became fast friends and started dating after a week. Ever since then, they were inseparable. Sitting next to each other with shoes off and playing footsies was their thing.

They spent every break making out, unable to keep their hands off of each other. Those two didn't know the meaning of discretion. Nephi had told them time and again to be discreet, but they didn't get it. For the past month, he made them sit in different areas while on the phone, to help them concentrate on customers, but Nephi wasn't sure it was helping. Their 'Time to Answer' was the highest on the team, as was their 'Abandon Rate' and 'Transfer Rate'. A hard conversation was, indeed, overdue. Discipline was the part of the job that Nephi disliked. But it was necessary, especially when employees behaved like Brock and Angela, treating customers as if they don't matter.

Every phone was lit up and chatter filled the room. Nephi knew they must already have a hold queue. He retreated to his office to monitor the team and to prepare for escalations. Although his role was to motivate and supervise, Nephi often took calls when it was busy. He enjoyed speaking with customers and he was good at it. A fresh batch of new hires recently graduated from training and this was their first week taking live calls. Inexperienced employees, many fresh out of high school, provided ample coaching opportunity for the managers. Busy or not, Nephi needed to get a feel for their performance and correct any bad habits before it was too late. He first monitored Ben, one of the new training graduates.

"Thank you for calling Brower Hotel reservations," stated Ben. "How may I assist you?"

"Nice", thought Nephi, "he followed the script perfectly so far." Nephi jotted notes as Ben helped the customer change a reservation for a business trip to Vancouver, BC. Ben did well, following the script for the most part. He missed some upsell opportunities and Nephi made a note for their one-on-one coaching session next week. Ben scored 77 out of 100 on the monitor. Not bad for a newbie. Nephi monitored four more new hires, and took two escalations before Mark arrived.

Mark stood straight and entered the building in measured steps, making his way to the corner office. The office was large, with windows on two sides, allowing plenty of light. Gray streaks accented his neatly combed dark hair. He was a handsome man, who carried an air of authority. Even though Brower had a business casual dress code, Mark wore a full suit and tie. Nephi entered Mark's office, met by a humorless stare. The men knew each other well outside of work before Nephi even started working at Brower. Before Nephi served a mission, Mark was his Bishop, and he now served as second counselor in the Stake Presidency.

"Good morning, Mark. How are you today?" asked Nephi.

"I'm well. Thanks for asking. How are things so far today?"

"So far, so good, although it is still early enough for that to change," noted Nephi with a smile.

Noticing that Mark did not find the humor in his lighthearted comment, Nephi turned to a more serious note.

"I went over the numbers from last night and Idle Time is really improving. Monica is doing a great job with the night shift. They are a tough bunch."

"Yes, I see that," said Mark, "but look at this 'Handling Time' number. It's up. I need to have her focus on that."

"It makes sense for that number to come up if the agents are extending the call to allow them to take care of post-call work to keep the 'Idle Time' down. I think it is important to acknowledge the wins. It is motivating. Night shift numbers are starting to look even better than evening shift," observed Nephi.

"That is true, but on evening shift, Steve deals with much higher call volume than Monica does. It is easier for Monica to have good numbers. Besides, I don't really want to get my hopes up with her. I was hesitant to promote her in the first place."

"Why? Monica is fantastic. She is hard-working, motivated, and really cares about customers. You know as well as I do that it is difficult to find people like that in this business," said Nephi.

"I know, but you know how those BYU girls are. She works hard now, but as soon as she gets pregnant or her husband graduates from Law school, she will be out of here as fast as you can blink, and then we will be in a world of hurt."

"With all due respect, Mark, it is not fair to assume what Monica might or might not do when her husband graduates. It is also not right to speculate about her family planning choices and how they might affect her career. Not to mention the fact that it is illegal to discriminate on the basis…."

"Whoa, hold on there," interrupted Mark, "no one said anything about discriminating against anyone. You seem to be the one who is jumping to conclusions. Let's end this conversation right here."

"All I know is that Monica works hard. She is good at her job, and that is the only factor that should go into the way you evaluate her."

The eyebrows on Nephi's head turned upward, which made him worry about the crease beginning to form in the center of his forehead. He forced himself to remain calm to let his moisturizer do its job, despite his disbelief at Mark's line of thinking.

"I best get back monitoring," Nephi said before returning to his small, windowless office.

The conversation annoyed Nephi, but he had several monitors left to do before lunch, so he pushed it out of his mind and concentrated on work. Before long, ten score sheets laid before him. While he reviewed them one by one, Nephi thought about his lunch date with Stacy. She had canceled on him a week earlier, and it felt like forever since they talked. 77, 64, 68, 72, 81, 76, 84, 67, 92, and 88. Ten monitor evaluations in one morning. Not bad at all. Nephi admired his handiwork. He would have been very pleased with himself had he not just created a heap of coaching sessions to schedule. After filing away the evaluation forms, Nephi put on his jacket and headed out.

The white truck rumbled down State Street toward the Purple Turtle, Nephi's favorite lunch destination. One of Pleasant Grove's oldest local eating establishments, the Purple Turtle offers burgers, hot dogs, chicken strips, salads and sides. Most of the time, Nephi would choose a salad but today, that just wouldn't do. He needed comfort, and few things soothed his nerves like the fish and chips from the Purple Turtle. Unlike most hamburger restaurants, the Purple Turtle prepared everything fresh. They hand-breaded the fish and onion rings and the English chips were to die for. Nephi looked forward to the food almost as much as the conversation with Stacy.

The beak of the turtle on the restaurant's sign smiled at Nephi as he pulled into the parking lot. The aroma of fried fish and onion rings hit him as he opened the truck door. No matter how many times he visited this place, the smell never got old. Stacy waited for him inside. Her light brown hair came almost to her shoulder and her round face greeted him with a loving grin. Nephi opened his arms wide and embraced her. Warmth washed over him as he squeezed his friend. Stacy gave the best hugs.

"Thanks, sister. I needed that," he said.

"It's so good to see you," she exclaimed. "It seems like forever since we got together."

"I know, it has been way too long. Where are the kids?"

Stacy, and her husband, Roger, got married five years ago. They now had two children – three-year-old Chloe, and adorable baby Wyatt. "Wyatt is napping at my mom's house," she replied, "and Chloe is hiding over there in that booth."

Her finger pointed toward a booth in the corner that appeared empty. A small head popped up. "Boo!" Chloe screamed out before falling back to the bench in a fit of giggles.

Nephi walked over and picked her up. Curly locks of golden hair jumped from her head like coiled springs from a click pen. Blue eyes, wide with wonder, stared up at Nephi. The ruffles on her pink A-line dress waved.

"How is my little Chloe Bear today?" he asked as he swung her up to give her a hug.

"I'm great, Uncle Nephi!" she boldly declared while returning his embrace. She called him 'Uncle' even though they weren't actually related.

"Chloe, what do you want for lunch?" asked Stacy who had joined them at the booth.

"Grilled cheese with tater gems, please!"

They approached the counter. Stacy ordered the grilled cheese kid's meal for Chloe and the Amigo Burger for herself. She loved the way the salsa blended with the Swiss cheese in her mouth. Nephi ordered a three piece halibut with English chips. Stacy added three small pumpkin shakes to their order. The Purple Turtle has the best ice cream in town, and pumpkin was in season. Stacy knew that Nephi wouldn't order one for himself and from the way his arms lingered when they hugged, she could tell he needed it.

"Okay, now spill!" Stacy insisted. "What's on your mind?"

Nephi collected the lunch tray and carried it to the booth while Chloe clung to her mother's finger. Silent while gathering his thoughts, Nephi took a bite of halibut. Finally ready, he started to speak.

"Last night, I met with Bishop Thompson and shared some of my concerns about church policy regarding gay church members. I told him that I hope for a different future."

"You didn't!" exclaimed Stacy, wide eyes glued to Nephi from the other side of the table. "What did he say?"

Details of the conversation were difficult to push through his lips. Tears came to Nephi's eyes as he recalled the finer points of the discussion. He paused, choked back the tears, and continued.

"I could see the disappointment on Bishop's face. He said that I am walking the fine line of apostasy and I better fall in line and support the Brethren. I didn't feel heard or understood. I love Bishop Thompson, but empathy is not something that comes easily to the man, and he sees this in black and white." Nephi gazed down at his food, lost in thought.

"Most church leaders I have known see that way," said Stacy. "The church needs less black and white and a little more rainbow," she grinned in an attempt to cheer him up.

Nephi cracked a smile and shot Stacy a glance that said he was glad to have her in his life. Stacy sipped on her pumpkin shake while Chloe picked at tater gems.

"It's just so unfair," said Nephi. "I feel so lonely. The church accepts gay members in good standing, but only if we remain celibate for life. And even then, we cannot receive the same degree of eternal salvation as God's straight children. I could live a perfect life, obeying every commandment and remaining celibate and lonely and then what? I just don't believe that a loving Heavenly Mother and Father would be so cruel as to create children in a way that precludes them from returning home to live with them again. I feel their love and I believe they want me to be happy. The Book of Mormon says that God placed us on earth to have joy. Why are the rules different for his straight children?"

Frustration came through in Nephi's voice, bordering on desperation. Stacy had known Nephi for as long as she could remember but had never seen him like this. The inner part of her eyebrows turned downward. Placing her finger below his chin, she raised his head until their eyes locked.

"Nephi," she said, "I need you to know that I love you and I know that God loves you. He wants you to be happy. I have no doubt of that. He wants you to return to live with Him again. You are the best person I know, and if you can't make it to heaven, I don't know how anyone can. God doesn't hate you for the way he made you. I won't pretend to understand everything or have all the eternal answers, but I do know that God created you just the way you are, and he loves you that way."

"Thanks, girl," he replied. "You are too sweet. I don't know what I would ever do without you."

Stacy smiled, continuing to look Nephi in the eye. Her tender tone comforted him. She took him by the hand. "You call me anytime you need to talk, day or night."

"Thanks, I appreciate your concern. Stacy, I haven't talked to anyone about this, but I am thinking about giving dating a go. You are still the only person I have ever kissed, and we both know how that went. I know doing so will shake up my life, and my relationship with the church, and most likely my family. It might even change our…"

"No," interrupted Stacy, "nothing you do will change our relationship, Nephi. I love you unconditionally and I mean that in every sense of the word. That won't change. I want you to be happy. If you go down that road, come hell or high water, I have your back."

Contemplating the weight of his feelings, Nephi squeezed Stacy's hand tighter and smiled. Tears filled his eyes as they sat in silence.

"What's wrong, Uncle Nephi?" asked little Chloe.

Chloe disappeared under the table for a few seconds before popping up on the other side and giving Nephi a Chloe-sized hug. He laughed and hugged her back.

"Nothing is wrong, Chloe," he said. "In this moment, everything is just perfect. I love you both. I really needed this today, but I've gotta run or Mark will have my head."

Nephi placed one last spoonful of pumpkin shake in his mouth, and then gave Stacy and Chloe another hug before heading back to work.

Tears proved difficult to hold back on the short drive. Nephi turned his mind to work in an effort to let his cheeks dry before walking into the office. By the time he stopped at the back of the parking lot, he seemed collected enough to work. He badged in, walked past reception and moved toward his office. As he passed by Mark's office, the sound of his name changed his course.

"Nephi," Mark called out, "come in here for a moment. I need to chat with you." Confused at the request, Nephi wiped his eyes, double-checking they were dry before entering.

"Please close the door and take a seat," Mark requested.

The door swung closed and Nephi heard the click of the latch before sitting down in a soft, upholstered chair that was much nicer than the chairs in his own office.

"How can I help you?" asked Nephi.

"Your eyes are red and puffy. Is everything okay, Nephi?"

"Everything is fine. It's just my allergies acting up," said Nephi, hoping Mark was dumb enough to believe it.

"I see. You should take something for that. It's not a good look," said Mark before continuing. "I have some business to discuss with you."

"Okay. I'm all ears. What's up, Mark?"

"Nephi, please address me as President Stone during this meeting. I called you in here in my capacity as a member of the Stake Presidency, not as General Manager of the call center."

"President Stone," replied Nephi, "I am happy to meet with you at the Stake Center after work today. We don't need to meet on the company's time."

"Nonsense," stated Mark, "I have the time now and I want to speak with you. President Miller called me during lunch after he got off the phone with Bishop Thompson. I understand that you are questioning some things related to the church."

"President Stone, I do have questions. I think everyone in the church has questions about something or other. President Miller relayed some of my concerns to you, I assume. Do you have answers for me about what the afterlife holds for a faithful gay man who remains celibate for life?" asked Nephi.

"The church has been very clear. Those who suffer from same sex attraction can remain in good standing in the church and should trust in God to take care of them in the next world. I have nothing further to say about that. I called you in to extend you a release," said President Stone.

"A release? You are releasing me from my calling as executive secretary? Why so sudden?" asked Nephi.

"After discussing it with President Miller, Bishop Thompson felt it best to release you. We thank you for your service."

"President Stone, I have served as executive secretary to Bishop Thompson for four years, longer than I served in any other calling. The calling has been challenging, and I have grown a lot during that time. I enjoyed it. I understand it is time for a release, although I can't say I'm not disappointed about the way it is happening, and what I suspect are the reasons. Nevertheless, I thank you for the opportunity to serve and I look forward to my next calling, whatever that might be,"

"The recommendation from the Stake Presidency is that you spend time in the Gospel Principles class while you work on repentance, and figure some things out," said President Stone.

Gospel Principles is the introductory Sunday School class. The class for new members of the church to learn the basics. Nephi loved the class. He found the basic principles of the gospel beautiful. God is our Father. Jesus Christ is our Savior. Love your neighbor as yourself. Show faith in Christ. He wouldn't mind taking part in the class, although a direct assignment to Gospel Principles from the Stake Presidency was a passive aggressive slap to the face.

"I see," replied Nephi. "Well, I guess that's it then. Is there anything else you would like to discuss?"

"I am curious, Nephi." said President Stone. "Your questions for Bishop Thompson are bordering on apostasy. What brought them about? Are you seeing someone?"

"If you are asking if I have engaged in intimate relations with anyone, the answer is no… not that it's your business. I have never even held a man's hand. But I have questions, President Stone - questions about God's plan for me, one of his children who he created different than he created you," replied Nephi.

"I don't believe that God created you that way," replied President Stone. "He wouldn't do that. He created us male and female in his image. Each gender has a divinely assigned role and you are choosing not to follow that role."

Pressure built up in Nephi's core. Several years back, such a comment would make him explode. He had worked on remaining calm and patient, and had become good at remaining civil. President Stone tested his limits. Swallowing his building anger, Nephi forced a tempered, deliberate tone.

"Believe me when I say this, President Stone. If I could choose my sexuality, I would not have chosen a path that subjected me to ridicule my entire life, a path that causes the church that I believe in with my whole heart to reject me. I am gay and I have always been gay. It is not a choice I made, it is the way God made me. You may want to have a conversation with church leaders. While they once declared the way you think as doctrine, that is no longer the case. The position of the church is that God created me this way, and as long as I don't act on my natural feelings, I remain in good standing. President, do you believe that God makes mistakes?"

"God does not make mistakes," he replied. "It is you who made the mistake when you chose perversion rather than God's way."

"This conversation is going nowhere. Let's agree to

disagree, and carry on with the work day," said Nephi.

He stood and walked out of Mark's office, retreating to his own. Door closed, Nephi rested his head on the desk and sobbed. Good thing Nephi was so productive this morning, because the rest of the day was shot. Nephi's eyes scanned the daily stats on his monitor, but his mind did not process any of it. All focus was on the conversations from the past two days. Nephi's feelings during the conversation with Stacy stood in stark contrast to those elicited by Bishop Thompson and President Stone.

The afternoon hours dragged on while Nephi did his best to get some work done, despite his anxiety. Four o'clock was approaching, and Nephi did one last floor pass to check whether any of his agents needed him before he left. Steve, the evening shift manager, arrived at the office.

Steve stood about 5 feet 9 inches. He sported dark spiky hair, brown eyes, and a fake smile. Steve graduated from Utah Valley University five years back with a four-year degree in Hospitality Management. UVU is the largest university in Utah by student population. It sits in Orem, a few miles down the road from BYU. Although Nephi had the most seniority of the shift managers, he was the only one without a college education, which made Steve feel superior.

Together, they reviewed the day shift statistics and talked about the new upsell goals for next week. Steve gave Nephi a hard time about a week over week slip in 'Handle Time'. Mark typically stopped by around this time to supervise the shift hand off but he was nowhere to be found. Nephi wished Steve luck and headed home.

Tired from a long day, yet full of anxiety, Nephi compelled himself to hit the treadmill in the apartment complex gym. He ran hard for an hour, completing six miles at a three degree incline. The exercise made him feel better. After a shower, he called Stacy.

Most days Nephi avoided calling Stacy at night. She had Roger and the kids at home and he didn't like to disturb her family life. Tonight, though, he needed to talk, and didn't feel comfortable discussing this with anyone else. The phone hadn't finished the first ring when Stacy picked up.

"Hey, Nephi, What's up?"

"The second half of my day was pretty rough, and I need to talk. Is this a good time?"

"I'll always make time for you," she said. "Hold on just a second."

She put the phone down, and Nephi could hear her talking to Roger in the background. She asked him to keep an eye on Chloe and Wyatt so she could talk.

"Okay, I'm back," she said. "Tell me about your day."

Gratitude for his friend filled Nephi's heart. It was nice to have someone willing to listen. He walked her through the meeting in Mark's office.

"Please tell me you're kidding," she said. "He really did that at work?"

"Sure did."

"The nerve and arrogance of that man never cease to astound me. I'm glad we moved to American Fork so I don't have to deal with him anymore."

"How do you like your ward there?" Nephi asked.

"I really love it. Just like nay ward, there are plenty of the stuffy, militant Relief Society types who seem to think I'm evil if I don't attend every weekly activity. But, I have a lot of good friends here," she said.

"I'm glad you're happy there."

"You should move closer to me," she suggested. "Did I tell you that Roger was just called as second counselor in the Bishopric?"

"You didn't mention that," he said. "Good for him. He will do great in that calling. As for me, I don't think moving is the solution. I have a feeling that my sort of problems will follow me wherever I go."

"Nephi, I'm really sorry about everything. Life really isn't fair. I wish there was something I could do to fix it all for you. Just remember that I have your back."

"Thanks, Stace," he replied. "I really appreciate you taking my call. You always make me feel better."

"That's what I'm here for," she replied.

"It's getting late, I'll let you get back to Roger and the kids."

"I'll give you a call tomorrow," she said. "Goodnight."

The connection ended and Nephi sat alone on his sofa, contemplating the day. So many thoughts flowed through his mind. He would deal with all that tomorrow. For now, he needed sleep. He opened the scripture app on his phone and read two chapters in the Book of Mormon before kneeling in prayer. He thanked God for his blessings and plead for guidance. Exhausted, he crawled into bed and slept.

CHAPTER 4

Prior to the resurrection of Jesus, the Sabbath was observed on the seventh day. Jesus overcame death when he rose from the tomb on Sunday. From that time forward, Christians recognized the first day of the week as the Lord's Day, and observed it as the Sabbath.

Sabbath day observance is an important element of faith in the Church of Jesus Christ of Latter Day Saints. Sunday is a holy day when Mormons attend church for two hours, visit with loved ones, and rest from worldly cares such as work, shopping, house chores, and worldly entertainment.

Because Mormons dedicate the Sabbath day to God, they use Saturday as a day of preparation. It is a day to do the housework and shopping, gas up the car, and prepare spiritually for Sunday. For Nephi, it was no different.

The day started the same as every other day, with prayer and scripture study. Every Saturday morning, Nephi followed up his scripture study with a trip to the Mt. Timpanogos temple in American Fork. The temple is a sacred building where Mormons feel closest to God. It is a place to make promises to God, and to pray. The temple is also at the center of one of the most beautiful LDS practices – completing ordinances for the dead. Mormons believe that God, being just, offers the opportunity for salvation to each of his children, whether or not they accepted the gospel of Jesus Christ in this life. Ordinances, such as baptism, can be performed for them posthumously, allowing them to accept the gospel in the afterlife.

Nephi attended the temple every week to set himself right. The temple is where he felt most at peace. After scripture study, Nephi dressed in his suit and tie, grabbed his temple bag, and directed his truck toward the temple. Few scenes offer the beauty of the Mt. Timpanogos temple. The white granite exterior and bronze doors stood against a mountain backdrop adorned in the colors of the bright autumn leaves. Nephi gazed up at the artistic windows and the spire that towered over him.

He admired the golden statue of Angel Moroni standing on top of the spire blowing a trumpet.

A similar statue tops most LDS temples. Moroni is a prophet from the Book of Mormon. The book is named for his father, Mormon. Mormon compiled the writings of the prophets among his people, the Nephites, and abridged their historical records, combining them into what is now the Book of Mormon. Moroni inherited the book when his father died. The last of his people, Moroni roamed the American continent, adding to his father's book and avoiding the enemy of his people – the Lamanites.

Before his death, Moroni buried the book, which was written on gold plates. Centuries later, Moroni, now an angel, appeared to Joseph Smith, a young farm boy living in upstate New York. Moroni showed Joseph the plates and Joseph translated the book by the power of God. It provides another testament of Jesus Christ. Along with the Bible, the Book of Mormon is scripture. The golden statue you see on top of LDS temples is the angel Moroni, blowing his trumpet to announce the second coming of Jesus Christ.

Nephi took in the temple's beauty on a crisp fall morning before continuing inside. He completed ordinances for his fifth great grandfather who died in Cambridgeshire, England in 1810. Working for the salvation of his ancestors always brought a smile to Nephi's face. It made him feel connected to them. After completing ordinance work, Nephi remained in the temple to pray.

He kneeled and prayed for over an hour, pleading with the Lord for guidance and direction and asked the Lord for help to understand His will. He sought to know his place in God's plan. Speaking with God just like he speaks to a friend, he laid bare his soul, praying for the comforting influence of the Holy Ghost. While pouring out his heart in prayer, a peace came over Nephi. The warm sensation started in his chest and spread outward until it consumed his entire body. Deep inside, he knew that God loved him, and felt that everything would be okay. Nephi thanked God for His love and comfort.

Rejuvenated, Nephi left the temple and climbed into his truck. The Lord would not abandon him during his time of distress. Pondering upon the experience in the temple, Nephi drove home. He changed into grubbies, the word his family had always used for worn-out clothes you don't mind getting dirty, and cleaned his apartment. This was his Saturday ritual since he learned to walk.

Growing up, his mother directed the work. Nephi and his siblings would change into grubbies on Saturday morning and do the chores. Nephi hated chores as a kid and mowing the lawn was the worst. He always tried to pawn it off on his brother, Ammon. Now an adult, Saturday morning cleaning, continued to be part of Nephi's routine. He even enjoyed it, well, except for the bathroom. He wasn't especially fond of scrubbing toilets, but someone had to do it. He lived alone, so he was that someone. At least in the apartment, there was no lawn to mow.

While cleaning the house, Nephi worked up an appetite. He made peanut butter and jelly sandwiches that hit the spot and brought a sense of nostalgia. Many a Saturday afternoon in his childhood, Nephi enjoyed peanut butter sandwiches after a long morning of chores. The sandwiches washed down nicely with a glass of milk. Tired from a long week, Nephi lay down for a nap.

The exhaustion took over his body, and by the time he woke up, it was almost seven o'clock. A red light flashing on his phone alerted him to a missed call from Stacy. She left a voicemail saying that she hoped he felt better. After his temple trip and a good nap, he did. Aware that she was likely eating dinner with her family, Nephi didn't return the call. Instead, he called to speak with Bishop Thompson.

The phone rang four times before Bishop Thompson answered. "Hi Nephi, what can I do for you?"

"I spoke with President Stone yesterday and he informed me of my release. I would like to speak with you about it, and follow up on our last conversation."

"That sounds good, Nephi. I was planning to schedule

something with you. I'm busy this evening, but speak with Brother Hanson tomorrow at church. He is making my appointments until we call your replacement."

"Thanks, Bishop. I'll see you tomorrow."

"Don't bother coming to Ward Council meeting in the morning. Just come in time for Sacrament meeting. I'll see you then, Nephi. Goodbye."

"Bye," replied Nephi before ending the call.

In every case Nephi could remember, a new executive secretary was called at the same time that the previous one was released. He found it strange that they would release him so abruptly. Despite the comfort he felt in the temple that morning, the way they handled this bothered him. Dis-inviting him to Ward Council was like a release before the official release, which gave Nephi a bad taste in his mouth. Brother Hanson, who served as the ward membership clerk, would be in Ward Council meeting, so he would be at Sacrament meeting early. Nephi would catch him in the chapel before it started to set an appointment with Bishop.

Nephi spent the rest of the night binge watching Gilmore Girls on DVD while eating a microwaved bean and cheese burrito. He preferred his old school DVD player to the newfangled streaming services. There was no need to pay for cable or fork out money every month for a streaming service. Plus, used DVDs were dirt cheap. Gilmore Girls was his favorite show. He loved the wit and banter, and understood the small town charm. Though he had watched the series dozens of times and knew almost every word by heart, he never tired of watching it.

Around eleven thirty, Nephi read a chapter in the Book of Mormon and said his prayers before retiring to bed for the night.

Warm covers on a cool morning dampened Nephi's will to get out of bed. He was glad to snooze his alarm, since he was not invited to Ward Council meeting. Arms drawn against his chest, he nestled into the blanket for an extra hour before finally shaking the cobwebs from his head, and falling to his knees for morning prayers. The feeling of the cold floor through his pajamas helped wake him. Now alert, he hopped in the shower to begin his morning routine. Nephi took his time getting dressed and prepared mentally for the day. Today was Fast Sunday, which is typically the first Sunday of every month. Today was September 29th. Fast Sunday was a week early because the following week was General Conference.

On Fast Sunday, Mormons go without food for two meals and donate the money that they would otherwise spend on food to feed the needy. They also pray for specific blessings while fasting because fasting magnifies the power of prayer. Today Nephi was fasting to understand God's will for him.

On Fast Sunday, rather than prepared talks given by members of the ward during Sacrament meeting, Fast and Testimony meeting is held. You can think of it as open mic church. During the testimony portion of the meeting, anyone who wishes to bear testimony can stand at the pulpit to speak. It is intended for members to share convictions with one another and to strengthen each other. The counsel of church leadership is to keep it simple, and focus on testimony of gospel topics. Despite that, many use it as an opportunity to share a travel log, or a rant on their topic of choice. Testimony meeting was Nephi's favorite Sunday of the month.

General Conference is a meeting held twice per year on the first weekend of October and April. The prophet and twelve apostles that lead the church speak to church membership during five two-hour sessions that span Saturday and Sunday. Regular church meetings are not held that weekend, so Fast Sunday is moved to either the week before or after General Conference.

Nephi skipped breakfast since he was fasting. He put on a dress coat over his suit and headed to church at eight thirty to make sure he had time to talk to Brother Hanson about an appointment with Bishop Thompson. Only two blocks from his apartment complex, Nephi enjoyed the walk to and from church each week. This morning was unusually cold for September, and puffs of white breath floated into the air as he exhaled. Bright golden leaves covered the sidewalk, forming a yellow brick road that led to the church. For the first Sunday in as long as he could remember, Nephi didn't have a set agenda, which was nice, but the change left him uneasy.

He arrived at church and entered the chapel. The chapel is the most sacred room in an LDS church building. Sacrament meeting, the one meeting per week that includes the entire congregation, is held there. During that meeting, the congregation partakes of blessed bread and water in remembrance of the body and blood of Christ. In doing so, they renew the covenants, or promises, that they made with God at baptism.

The chapel is a large room with pews extending from the front all the way to the back. Hymnals are located on the back of each pew. At the front of the room is a rostrum that most members refer to as "the stand." The Bishopric sits on the stand, looking down on the congregation. A piano and organ are also on the stand. In addition to the Bishopric, the organist, chorister, and speakers for the day sit there.

In the center of the stand is a podium with a microphone where speakers present talks on gospel topics. The speakers change each week and are selected from members of the congregation. The Bishop does not speak every week. Because of Fast Sunday, no speakers would be assigned today, and anyone in the congregation who felt inspired to address the group would have the opportunity to do so.

Brother Hanson sat on the third pew back from the stand with his family. Sister Hanson was at his side, and their eighteen-year-old son, Bradley, sat next to her. His thirteen-year-old brother, Todd, was with the other deacons on the bench, at the far left side of the chapel where the priests would bless the bread and water for the Sacrament during the meeting.

Their other six children, who ranged in age from eleven to one, filled the rest of the row. Sister Hanson home-schooled all of them, worried that public school would corrupt them with teachings of evolution and climate change. Nephi approached Brother Hanson, whose broad shoulders took the space of two average-sized people. His unkempt hair covered most of his ears and Nephi could see the large bald spot on the crown of his head from behind.

"Good morning, Brother Hanson," said Nephi, extending his hand.

Brother Hanson stood and looked down at Nephi, who was a good foot shorter. He hesitantly extended his hand and seemed almost repulsed when their hands touched. Nephi grasped his hand and shook it firmly for a second before Brother Hanson's arm quickly retreated.

"I understand that you own the Bishop's agenda until they call someone else," Nephi said. "I need to meet with him today."

"He gave me a heads up this morning. How does one thirty this afternoon work?"

"That's perfect. I'll be there."

Nephi turned to go find a seat on the bench in the middle of the congregation, where he sat with his parents almost every week.

"Hold on a second, Nephi," called Brother Hanson. "There I something that has been bothering me that I would like to ask you."

Nephi turned to face Brother Hanson and looked upward, his bright blue eyes expressing curiosity, as they locked with Brother Hanson's coal black pupils.

"What is it?" asked Nephi.

"I just don't get it, Nephi," Brother Hanson explained. "Why do you even bother coming to church? You clearly don't believe in the doctrine. You don't follow the brethren. All you do is question. If you are going to come here, you need to have faith and fall in line with the Brethren. We don't need the doubting. It spreads and causes people to fall away."

Nephi was flabbergasted and hurt. His gaze shifted downward momentarily before raising back up and locking on Brother Hanson's eyes. Nephi's face showed an intensity that Brother Hanson had not seen before.

"Brother Hanson, we have worked side by side for a long time, but you do not know me. You have no idea what is going on inside my head. I can assure you that I have a testimony of Jesus Christ and His role as my Savior and Redeemer. I have faith in the restored gospel of Jesus Christ. I believe the doctrine. Sure, I have questions; lots of people do. That doesn't mean that there is no place for me here. God's church is for all of His children."

Nephi continued, "There are areas where I am strong, and others where I am weak, just like all of God's children. Believe me, I try hard to improve on my faults and to show love and kindness to all of God's children. Some make it harder than others. Please don't judge me because I sin differently than you do. And don't assume that you know my sins. Remember that God will judge us the same way that we judge others. Keep your eyes on your own actions, and leave the judging to God. I apologize if I am coming across harshly, but I feel strongly about this. I love you, and respect you, and hope that we can stay on good terms."

As Nephi was speaking, Bishop Thompson approached. He could hear the conversation from across the room and was worried that it might escalate in front of the congregation that was growing in numbers as the nine o'clock hour drew near.

"How are you brethren doing?" asked Bishop.

"Just fine," said Nephi, before turning to take a place next to his mother a few rows back.

Convinced he de-escalated the situation, Bishop Thompson took his place on the stand. Nephi forced his attention to the sweet sound of the organ that piped prelude music into the chapel. The music calmed him and prepared his mind for Sacrament meeting as he squeezed his mom's hand.

The prelude music stopped as Bishop Thompson stood and walked to the podium.

"Good morning, Brothers and Sisters. Welcome to Sacrament meeting. As a reminder, today is Fast and Testimony meeting because General Conference is next week. We encourage all to attend all sessions on Saturday and Sunday.

Prepare your minds and hearts this week to receive the words of the prophets. We will now sing hymn number 2, "The Spirit of God," after which Sister Worthington will offer the invocation."

Music from the organ filled the room as Bishop Thompson took his seat. Hymn books in hand, the congregation sang praise to God with exuberance. Nephi loved this hymn. He sang loudly, his voice blending with his mother's in harmony. Following the hymn, Sister Worthington walked to the stand and offered a prayer to open the meeting. The prayer finished, and Bishop Thompson returned to the podium.

"We'd like to thank Sister Brown and Sister Layton for the beautiful music. I will now turn the time over to Brother Peters from the Stake High Council for some stake business, after which, we will prepare to partake of the Sacrament by singing hymn number 172, "In Humility, Our Savior."

Bishop Thompson returned to his seat, while Brother Peters came to the podium. Brother Peters served on the High Council in the stake. A Stake is made up of multiple wards, or congregations, in the LDS church. Each ward is led by a Bishopric and the Stake is led by a Stake Presidency. The Stake President calls twelve additional men to assist with the leadership of the Stake. These twelve men are called the High Council. Every member of a Stake Presidency, Bishopric, and High Council must be ordained to the office of High Priest, a higher calling in the priesthood. One responsibility of the High Council is to bring Stake business to the wards, and this is the reason that Brother Peters stood at the podium.

"Good morning, Brothers and Sisters," he said. "We have some releases and callings for positions in the Stake. The following individuals have been released from their callings in the Stake. Brother Simon James from the third ward as the Stake sports coordinator. Sister Julie Mayhew from the seventh ward as the Stake young women's secretary. Brother Nephi Willard from the ninth ward as the ward executive secretary. All those who wish to give these individuals a vote of thanks for their service, please do so by the uplifted hand."

Everyone in the congregation raised their right hand, signifying their gratitude for the service provided. Brother Peters continued.

"The following individuals have been called to positions in the Stake. If you are present, please stand when I read your name. Brother Richard Wahlstrom of the ninth ward has been called as the Stake sports coordinator. Sister Sarah Cahill has been called as the Stake Young Women's secretary. All those in favor, please signify by the uplifted hand." All hands were raised.

"Any opposed, by the same sign," he continued. No hands were raised. "Thank you," he concluded.

Brother Peters took his seat on the stand and the organ began to play. The congregation sang to prepare their minds and hearts to partake of the Sacrament. It was unusual to release an executive secretary without calling another one, and Nephi thought, despite what anyone said, his release directly resulted from his earlier discussion with Bishop Thompson.

As he sang, Nephi pushed those thoughts out of his mind and concentrated on Jesus. He thought of the earthly ministry of Christ, and of his atoning sacrifice. When the hymn ended, one of the priests blessed the bread and the young deacons passed it to the congregation. After everyone had partaken of the bread, they blessed and passed the water.

Bishop Thompson stood and thanked the young men of the Aaronic Priesthood for their service in blessing and passing the Sacrament and then bore his testimony. It is customary, at the beginning of Fast and Testimony meeting, for the member of the Bishopric who is conducting Sacrament meeting that month to share their testimony. At the conclusion of his testimony, he invited any who wished to bear testimony to stand.

The first to make her way to the stand was Maddie McIntyre, a six-year-old fireball with wild bright red hair to match her personality. She escaped the pew while Sister McIntyre was wrestling Maddie's three-year-old brother, Michael. Maddie's testimony was a monthly occurrence.

Through the years, the church has given direction from time to time regarding young children sharing testimonies in Sacrament meeting. The guidance usually instructs church members to give children opportunities to bear testimony in primary class, and in the home and discourages them from doing so in Sacrament meeting. But it still continues, mostly to the delight of the congregation.

Brother Baker, the first counselor in the Bishopric, scooted a carpeted block against the podium, allowing Maddie to reach the microphone. She stepped onto it, and grasped the mic, pulling it close to her face. Maddie's mouth breathing echoed through the chapel.

"Brothers and Sisters," she said directly into the microphone, a bit too loud for the comfort of the congregation. Brother Baker adjusted the PA volume downward. "I'd like to bury my testimony."

Low chuckles echoed through the congregation at the thought of the child placing her testimony in a hole in the ground.

Little Maddie continued, "I know the church is true. I love my mommy and daddy, and I know that they love me. I know that Jesus loves me even when I don't share with Michael. In the name of Jesus Christ, Amen."

Maddie climbed down and ran back to her seat next to Sister McIntyre, leaving the congregation smiling. Sister McIntyre put her arm around Maddie and gave her a kiss on the forehead. Emboldened by Maddie's success, three more primary children headed to the stand and shared short, sweet testimonies.

Sister Allred was next. She never failed to speak on Fast Sunday. Sharing the details of her visit to her daughter's family in Gilbert, Arizona earlier in the month, she bore testimony of missionary work and bragged of her grandson who would leave for a mission to Arkansas within the month. Nephi felt impressed to stand while listening to Sister Allred. He stood and walked to the stand, taking a seat behind Bishop Thompson, while he waited for Sister Allred to finish.

Bishop turned to look at Nephi, shooting him a stern glare as if to warn him against spreading doubts to the congregation. Annoyed at the lack of trust, Nephi smiled and nodded. Once Sister Allred said "Amen" and walked toward her pew, Nephi went to the podium. Standing tall and wearing that ever-present smile, Nephi spoke.

"Good morning, my siblings in the Lord. I would like to bear my testimony today. My heart is full of gratitude for the opportunity that I have had to serve you as executive secretary for the past four years. I learned and grew in my calling. I am especially thankful that I got to know so many of you so well. I want you to know that I know that Jesus Christ is our Savior, and that He lives. He suffered for our sins so that we may repent and return to live with God again. I know that each of us is a child of God. He created us and he loves us just the way we are. When we have faith in Him, and seek His guidance, He will direct us and help us grow. I know that Joseph Smith was a prophet of God, and that he translated the Book of Mormon by the power of God. I know that book is true, and that it contains the full gospel of Jesus Christ. I know that this is God's church. I love you, Brothers and Sisters, and I love my Heavenly Father and his son, Jesus Christ. I am so thankful for the atonement of Christ. It is a great blessing in my life. I say these things in the name of Jesus Christ, Amen."

Nephi smiled and returned to the pew next to his mom. Despite the turmoil of the past few days, and the mal-intent he felt was directed his way, he had a testimony of the gospel and knowledge that God loved him. He was glad for the opportunity to share that testimony with his family, and with the members of his ward. He looked forward to speaking with Bishop Thompson.

Several members of the congregation stood to bear testimony of Jesus Christ and various principles of the gospel until the end of the hour. The meeting closed with hymn number 5, "High on the Mountain Top," and a prayer by Brother Bennet. The congregation then dismissed for Sunday School classes.

Although Bishop had not asked Nephi to attend Gospel Principles class, after his conversation with President Stone, he knew that was the intention, so he went straight to that class. He was glad to be in a smaller class with the full-time missionaries, and members of the ward who were either newly baptized or less active. Rumors fly fast in an LDS ward, and are followed by judgment and awkward stares. Nephi could avoid all of that in Gospel Principles class. The topic for the day was honesty - a straight forward topic that Nephi was glad to discuss. If Nephi was anything, he was honest. He enjoyed the discussion.

Nearly every Sunday, Nephi went directly to his parents' house after church to visit for the day. When Sunday School was over, he told his mom and dad about his one thirty appointment with Bishop Thompson, letting them know that he would be over later.

He hugged them and followed the yellow brick road back to his apartment, where he prayed for guidance during his discussion with Bishop. He watched a Tabernacle Choir concert DVD, enjoying the sound of their well-blended voices. The concert ended, and Nephi prayed again, seeking to understand God's will for him, as he continued to fast. One thirty approached, and he headed back down the golden leaf path toward the church building.

Once Nephi arrived, he walked through the doors and into the foyer where he found Brother Hanson waiting. It felt strange to see someone else managing Bishop Thompson's agenda.

"Bishop is still in a meeting," said Brother Hanson. "He should be with you soon."

Nephi sat in a chair with his head in his hands. Brother Hanson's tone was friendly, almost as if their heated exchange before Sacrament meeting hadn't happened, but Nephi didn't feel like talking to him. He remained silent until Bishop Thompson emerged from his office.

"Come on in, Nephi," Bishop Thompson called out. Nephi shook Bishop's hand on the way into his office and sat in the chair opposite Bishop's desk.

"Let's begin with a prayer," suggested Bishop Thompson. "Will you please offer it, Nephi?"

The men kneeled before proceeding to fold their arms, bow their heads and close their eyes. Nephi prayed aloud.

"Our Father in Heaven, we come before thee in fasting and prayer, and ask for thy spirit to be with us while we meet. We ask thee to bless us with guidance and direction. Please help us understand one another, and to understand thy will for us. We ask thee for strength and for discernment. Bless us with those things that we fast for today, and bless those who are in need. We thank thee for the gospel of Jesus Christ and for His atonement. We thank thee for the opportunity we have to come to earth. Please help us follow thy commandments and to do the things necessary to return to thee. We ask and pray for these things in the name of Jesus Christ, Amen."

"Amen," repeated Bishop, before returning to his seat. "Nephi, I have some things to discuss with you, but first, tell me what's on your mind."

"Bishop, I appreciate you hearing me out the other night. I felt that we discussed some serious things and concerns that have been wearing on me."

Bishop Thompson nodded, eyes locked on Nephi.

Nephi continued, "I was surprised and taken back when President Stone called me in to release me the following day, and I was alarmed by the abruptness of everything."

"Nephi, that is what I want to talk to you about. First, I hope you know that I love you, and want what is best for you. The truth is that your questions were very concerning to me. I called President Miller after I met with you, and he shared my concerns. To be frank, Nephi, your beliefs and prayers for God to accept a homosexual relationship are contrary to the doctrine of the church."

"Bishop…" Nephi started, before being interrupted by Bishop Thompson.

"Nephi," he scolded, "Let me finish. In the temple recommend interview, you are asked if you sustain the prophet as the only person on the earth who can exercise all priesthood keys and speak for God. You are also asked if you have any beliefs that are not in harmony with the teachings of the church. Your comments during our conversation make it clear that you cannot answer those questions affirmatively. I have been asked to take your temple recommend. I must also ask you to attend the Gospel Principles Sunday School class. I encourage you to study the scriptures, pray about this, and seek guidance from Heavenly Father. If you repent, and come back in harmony with the teachings of the church, and fully sustain the prophet, then you will be able to interview for a temple recommend again. Until that time, you will not have that privilege."

Nephi was dumbfounded. Bishop Thompson's words rendered him speechless. He sat there in silence, fighting to hold back tears. In his view, he had done nothing to warrant the loss of his temple recommend. He loved to attend the temple every week to commune with God. Try as he might, Nephi couldn't get his head around what he was hearing.

"Nephi, what are your thoughts?"

Thinking carefully before speaking, Nephi said, "I don't know what to think, Bishop Thompson. I have tried my entire life to do what the Lord wants me to do. I make it a priority to obey His commandments. Today I am fasting for God to help me understand His will. The church asks me to live a lonely life and when I have questions about why God would require that of me, because I am struggling to make sense of it, my ability to attend the temple is taken away. When you ask me what I am thinking, I have a hard time putting it into words. I am confused and disappointed."

"Maybe this is the answer to your prayer today, Nephi. God is letting you know His will for you. He wants you in His church and He needs you to accept the guidance from His prophet," said Bishop Thompson.

"Maybe," said Nephi. "I have a lot of thinking and praying to do, Bishop Thompson - a lot of searching for where I fit in the big picture."

"I suppose you do," said Bishop. "Nephi, I really need you to understand that this is not a punishment. We are doing this out of love. Allowing you to continue attending the temple while you carry such dangerous doubts puts you in spiritual danger. I want you to fully participate, but you need to repent first. You can continue to take part in all church meetings and take the Sacrament, but you need to make some changes before you can attend the temple again."

"Okay," said Nephi before standing and pulling his temple recommend from his wallet. He placed it gently on the Bishop's desk, and turned to leave.

"Hold on, Nephi. Let's pray before you go," said Bishop. Nephi kneeled and Bishop Thompson prayed. His head spinning, Nephi didn't hear a word of the prayer. After Bishop Thompson concluded the prayer, Nephi stood and shook his hand before walking out of the office, exiting the church, and walking back to his apartment. Nephi was shaken. He felt that his entire world had been torn apart, and he didn't know how to feel. A stream of tears flowed down his cheeks as he made his way home, leaves crunching beneath his feet.

Once at his apartment, Nephi dried his eyes and changed into jeans and a comfortable light blue cardigan sweater. Nephi didn't feel like going to dinner at his parents' house but his siblings and their families were coming to break the fast together as a family and he didn't want to disappoint them. So, he followed a routine he knew well. He swallowed his feelings, put on his big boy pants, faked a smile, and walked out the door.

CHAPTER 5

Memories from Nephi's childhood played in his head as he strolled through the neighborhood where he grew up. The children there were all good friends and played together almost every day, until the streetlights came on, signaling it was time to go home. He remembered those times fondly, and wondered what became of those kids.

After reminiscing for a few blocks, he approached his parents' home at the end of the cul-de-sac. It was a split story home with yellow aluminum siding and a white door. The driveway sloped downward to the two-car garage at a steep angle. The silver Mercedes SUV told Nephi that his sister, Tiffany, and her husband Rob were inside. Tiffany was seven months pregnant with her first child and Nephi wasn't sure whether she would make it for dinner. His brothers, Jacob and Ammon, had not yet arrived.

Nephi walked through the unlocked door and removed his jacket while he stood on the landing. The six by six landing connected to the stairs. One flight descended into the basement where there was a family room, a bedroom, and a half bath. The other flight of stairs extended upward into the main part of the house with a living room, kitchen, full bathroom, and three bedrooms. The house was about 1600 square feet in total. The Willards purchased the home in 1975 for sixty thousand dollars. By now it was paid for, and they owned it outright. It wasn't much, but it was theirs.

Nephi placed his jacket on the coatrack that stood next to him on the landing, and started to climb the stairs toward the kitchen. He could hear Tiffany talking to their mother. She smiled when she saw him and waddled over to give him a hug.

"It's so good to see you," she exclaimed.

"I'm glad to see you too, Tiff. It has been too long."

Tiffany stood tall at five feet, ten inches. Her naturally blonde hair was colored a deep shade of auburn and it fell to the middle of her back. It was well styled with one side down and the other in a double braid. She wore designer maternity jeans and an oversized yellow cable-knit sweater. Her beautiful face was perfectly made up without overdoing it. She looked great, even at 30 weeks pregnant. Tiffany was the baby of the family.

"Where did Rob and Dad run off to?" asked Nephi.

"They went downstairs to chat," said their mother, Darla.

"I suspect they are doing more football watching than chatting," added Tiffany.

Nephi gave his mom a hug and kissed her on the cheek. Darla and Tiffany were busy making chicken enchiladas. They were rolling the mixture of shredded chicken, sour cream, and cream of chicken soup into soft flour tortillas and topping it with more soup and shredded cheese. Nephi turned on the oven at 350 degrees, and started preparing the avocado lime salad. While Nephi lived nearby and spent nearly every Sunday evening with his parents, his siblings lived further away, and only visited once per month on Fast Sunday.

Tiffany and Rob lived in Draper, just past the Point of the Mountain, at the south end of Salt Lake County. Rob worked as an executive for the MLM company that his dad started. They lived in a 4000 square foot mini mansion, high on the hill, on the east side. In his thirty years, Nephi had discovered that there are different types of wealthy people.

There are those like Rob's dad, who put in the work and the sweat to build something and understand its value. Then there are those like Rob, who are spoon-fed everything by their parents, and never have to worry about what it is like to choose between the rent payment and having enough food. Rob was a nice enough guy, but his coddled upbringing left him with a sense of entitlement. The ready executive position in his daddy's company didn't teach him to work for anything. Despite that, Nephi was glad that Tiffany had the things she needed, especially with a baby on the way.

The title of uncle sounded sweet to Nephi's ears. Between his brothers, Jacob and Ammon, he already had two nieces and one nephew. Tiffany's new addition would make four. The thought of it made Nephi smile. He loved holding babies, and no one was better at singing them to sleep. Nephi longed for a family of his own, but that was a dream he dared not entertain because, within the church, it could only end in disappointment.

With the salad made and chilling in the fridge, Nephi helped load the baking pans stuffed with enchiladas into the oven. The front door burst open and the pitter patter of little feet stormed up the stairs like a herd of stampeding chinchillas. Three small humans grasped at Nephi's legs, competing for the first hug.

"Uncle Nephi, Uncle Nephi," squealed their high-pitched voices as he bent down to embrace them all at once.

"Look, it's my favorite nieces and nephew," he exclaimed.

The children giggled while he tickled them. Laughter filled the house, bringing warmth on a cold September evening. Now on his knees, near eye-level with the children, Nephi asked them how they were doing.

"Crystal, my little angel," he said to the youngest, "what did you do this week?"

Crystal, an energetic toddler with straight brown hair and bright blue eyes, stood tall and proceeded to give a report in the biggest voice her three-year-old body could muster. "I made dinner with Mommy and played games on her phone," she said.

"That sounds like fun," said Nephi. "I don't have any games on my phone. I need you to show me the best ones."

He turned toward Crystal's brother, Dallin, who was almost five-years-old. "What about you, Super Boy? How was your week?"

"Well," said Dallin, "I watched lots of hero movies and I picked a new book at school." His light brown hair and wide brown eyes gazed lovingly at Nephi.

"You know what? Grandma has a whole shelf full of books in the bedroom downstairs. I'll have to read one of them to you after dinner," said Nephi.

Dallin and Crystal were Jacob's kids. Jacob was the oldest of the Willards. He married his wife, Camille, within six months of returning from his mission to the Philippines. They struggled to have children for several years, but eventually had Dallin after many rounds of fertility treatment. Crystal came as a bonus surprise about a year and a half later. They lived in Herriman, on the southwest end of Salt Lake County, on the other side of the valley from Tiffany.

Next, Nephi turned toward Sophie, the daughter of his Brother Ammon, who was two years younger than Nephi. He married his wife, Chelsea, when he was twenty-three. Sophie was born almost exactly a year later. She recently turned four. Ammon's family lived in Eagle Mountain, a newer sprawling community on the west side of Utah Lake. With golden blonde hair and stunning hazel eyes, Sophie was a spitting image of her mother.

"What have you been up to, Princess Sophie?" asked Nephi.

"Uncle Nephi, I got a new baby doll for my birthday," she said, holding it up proudly on display.

Nephi took the doll from her outstretched arms and rocked it gently in his arms. He sang it a sweet lullaby before lowering it back into Sophie's grasp.

"Shh," he said, "she's asleep."

Sophie smiled, pressing her index finger to her lips. Nephi spoke to the children like they were adults. When they spoke, he listened and responded in a tone of acknowledgement. He really saw them and they could feel it. That's what made him their favorite.

Their conversation was interrupted when the rest of the crew entered the kitchen. Jacob, Camille, Ammon, and Chelsea came to deliver their potluck assignments. Camille placed a bag of dinner rolls on the table, and Ammon laid Chelsea's famous "better than sex cake" on the counter. Being a virgin, Nephi couldn't be confident about the comparison, but the cake was so sinfully delicious that he didn't doubt it.

"Come on, kids," said Jacob. "Let's go play downstairs while Grandma finishes making dinner." The children raced down the stairs to the bedroom that had been stocked with toys, puzzles, and books. Jacob and Ammon followed them while Nephi and the women stayed upstairs to set the table and spread the food buffet-style on the kitchen island. When the enchiladas had finished cooking, Darla called for everyone to come upstairs to break their fast. Mike, Rob, Jacob, Ammon and the children rushed to the kitchen.

Mike, the patriarch of the home, called on Jacob to offer a blessing on the food. Everyone folded their arms, bowed their heads, and closed their eyes while Jacob prayed.

"Heavenly Father, we thank thee for this day and for all the blessings which thou has bestowed upon us. We thank thee for the food and ask thee to bless the hands that prepared it. Please bless it to give nourishment and strength. As we break our fast, we pray that thou will bless us with those things we have been fasting for, and bless the needy that they will have sufficient for their needs. We thank thee for our family, and the opportunity we have to be together this evening. We pray for these things in the name of Jesus Christ, Amen."

Amens echoed in agreement.

"Ammon and Jacob, please help your children make their plates first and then the adults can dig in," said Darla.

With the help of their fathers, the children filled their plates and then moved to the kiddie table that was set up in the living room. Darla and Mike, along with Nephi's siblings and their spouses, squeezed around the eight place settings at the kitchen table while Nephi took his dinner to the kiddie table in the living room.

He loved his siblings, but preferred the company of their children and the kitchen was crowded, anyway. Nephi learned all about the latest episodes of popular children's shows and enjoyed the world from the viewpoint a child while he ended his fast with his mother's enchiladas. From a child's perspective, the world is magical and glorious. Too bad we all have to grow up.

After dinner, everyone enjoyed a slice of Chelsea's "better than sex cake" before retiring to the family room in the basement for a combined Family Home Evening. Once per week, Mormon families spend a night together discussing a gospel topic, playing games, cooking together, or otherwise having fun as a family. Traditionally, Family Home Evening is held on Monday night although recently, church leadership has indicated that families should do it on whichever night best fits their schedule. While Nephi's siblings all conducted Family Home Evening in their own homes, they held a joint FHE once per month when they broke the fast.

The lesson fell to Ammon's family this month. They started FHE with an opening prayer, offered by Sophie with help from Chelsea. They then watched a Bible video about a scripture in the first chapter of James. It spoke of being meek and slow to wrath and being doers of the word and not hearers only. After the video, Ammon led a conversation on the topic with the family. They then sang hymn number 237 from the LDS hymn book, "Do What is Right", and finished with a closing prayer by Dallin.

As soon as FHE ended, the children hurried back to the play room while the adults remained in the family room to catch up.

"Dad, how has work been going lately?" asked Jacob. Mike thought for a moment before responding. He was a gruff man with short reddish-brown hair and a mustache. His face had aged beyond his years. Outside of a single suit that he wore to church each week, his wardrobe consisted of thrift store jeans and flannel shirts. Mike worked as a foreman on a local building construction crew which demanded long hours and a tough demeanor.

"Work is work," he said. "There's a lot of construction in the valley, so we aren't hurting for jobs. It pays the bills."

Work ethic was engrained in Mike. He took pride in a job well done, and had done his best to teach his children to do the same. He was hard on them growing up, the same way his father was hard on him. It was the only way he knew, and hard work had made him the man he was.

"What about you, Jacob?" asked Mike. "How are things going at that computer web factory of yours?"

"It's called a software startup, Dad, and it's going great. Three of our apps are on the Top 100 list!"

Jacob and some of his college buddies started a mobile app company. They leased space in a collocation building where multiple startups had dedicated working space, while sharing common resources like a reception desk, conference rooms, and printers. The business already created several well-known apps despite their small size. Jacob was smart, and he knew it. He was proud of it, and took every opportunity to make sure that everyone else knew it, too. Being the first member of the Willard family to graduate from college in generations, he felt that he had something to prove.

Jacob was not popular growing up. In high school, he wore thick glasses, was overweight, and had terrible acne. The acne scars still remained. By now, he had traded his glasses for contacts. He was bald on top and kept the sides shaved short. He served as the Elders Quorum president in his ward in Herriman. Despite his lack of popularity, Jacob had always been confident, if not arrogant. He excelled at work, and in the church, and for as long as Nephi could remember. There was no convincing him he was wrong about anything. Camille stayed home with Dallin and Crystal.

"We are about to launch an app that will have the venture capital firms salivating," Jacob continued.

"Good for you," said Mike. "We're real proud. Ammon, what have you been up to?"

"Mostly just trying to keep up with Sophie," said Ammon. "She really keeps us on our toes."

Ammon was much the opposite of Jacob. Beautiful curly brown hair topped his head. His handsome face had a chiseled jawline, and he didn't have a single wrinkle. Ammon was muscular and had always been popular. Everyone he knew was drawn to his outgoing personality allowing him to make friends easily. Ammon worked as a salesperson for a wholesale produce company and he was good at it. Chelsea was a hair stylist at a small salon in Saratoga Springs. Chelsea and Ammon both served as nursery leaders in their ward, teaching the three and four year old children.

"Between Sophie and work, we really don't have time for much else," said Ammon. Mike nodded his head in understanding and then turned to face Nephi, who sat in a chair across the room.

"Nephi, how is Brower treating you these days?"

"This week was interesting," explained Nephi. "Mark Stone called me into his office on Friday to inform me that I would be released from my church calling. The conversation was awkward."

"How so?" asked Darla.

"I had a conversation with Bishop Thompson on Thursday and brought up some concerns that I have, and I was released the next day. The timing of everything was strange, and it felt odd to have a meeting about church when I was at work," said Nephi.

"You have been in that calling for four years," said Jacob. "That is a long time and you were due to be released. Don't assume the worst in people."

"I'm not assuming the worst," replied Nephi. "I may have been due for release anyway, but I know that my conversation with Bishop caused my release. I just talked with him about it this afternoon. He even took away my temple recommend."

"Why? What did you do?" asked Jacob in an accusatory tone.

"I asked questions," replied Nephi.

"Questions," interrupted Jacob before he could continue, "are not enough to get your temple recommend taken away. You're not giving us the whole story. You seriously need to stop acting so gay, Nephi. Come on, just tone it down a bit. If you wouldn't throw it in everyone's face, then you wouldn't have to worry about issues at church or at work."

"Excuse me?" said Nephi, reaching the point of exasperation. "I am who I am, and I don't throw anything in anyone's face. Yes, I am attracted to men, but I have never even been on a date. How dare you assume anything about a situation you know nothing about?"

"Oh, I know all about it," said Jacob. "I grew up with you, remember? I know how you are and I can imagine what led to this. Nephi, you just need to humble yourself, repent, and stop flaunting your gayness. Think about the family for once. Think about Mom and Dad, who go to the same ward as you. Imagine what people are saying."

Nephi did his best to calm himself before speaking. Jacob had always been embarrassed of Nephi, more so since he came out. Nephi and his brothers were all named after prophets in the Book of Mormon and Jacob always felt that he was best at living up to the name. Nephi began to open his mouth to speak before being interrupted by Darla.

"Jacob Nehemiah Willard!" she yelled. "Don't you dare speak to your brother that way. I am proud of him, and I don't care what in the heck anyone at church thinks or says about me, or any of my children. People talk. Ain't no stoppin' it. What we can control is the way we respond. I'm proud of all of you, and you should stick up for each other, not tear each other down. Now, I won't listen to another word of this."

When Darla put her foot down, that was that. End of conversation. Everyone sat in awkward silence with their mother staring them down, one by one, forcing their glance to the ground. She had a stare that could burn right through you and one could only bear it for so long.

The uncomfortable moment was interrupted by laughter as Dallin, Crystal, and Sophie returned to the room carrying a story book. "This one, Uncle Nephi," said Dallin. "Read this one."

Nephi took the book, and the children sat on the floor in front of him. He turned the book around so they could see the pictures while he read. They were captivated as he played every character in a perfect voice.

After story time, Nephi's siblings all said they needed to get going. Nephi gave everyone hugs, even Jacob, and they went on their way. Nephi was left alone with his mom and dad.

"You know, Nephi," said Darla, "your brother doesn't really mean it."

"Oh, he means it, Mom," said Nephi.

"Well, Jacob has a point on some things," Mike interjected.

Darla gave him a light jab with her elbow and shot him an angry glare.

"He's a smart boy," she said, "but he doesn't know everything. He doesn't understand people like Nephi does."

"Nephi," she continued, "your father and I love you just the way you are. Do you know that?"

"Yes, Mom," he replied. "I best get going, too. I have an early morning."

Nephi hugged Darla tightly, and then gave Mike a quick side hug before heading out the door and walking home. While he walked, he thought about the conversation with Jacob. He was frustrated and hurt by Jacob's words, but he didn't really expect more from him. The night had grown dark, and the golden leaves on the ground appeared dull in the streetlight. After arriving home, Nephi brushed his teeth, said a prayer, read a chapter from the Book of Mormon, and went to sleep.

CHAPTER 6

Darkness still cloaked the sky when Nephi arrived at work. He didn't look forward to the coming winter months when he could count the daylight hours outside of work on one hand. Shift change brought a buzz to the office, and Nephi smiled at his coworkers as he passed them on the way to his office. After reviewing the nightly reports, he entered Monica's office.

"How was last night?" he asked.

"Same as usual," she replied. "How was your weekend?"

"Interesting, to say the least. I've been wanting to talk to you. I had a conversation with Mark on Friday after you left, and just want to give you a heads up."

"I'm listening," she answered, leaning toward him.

"I told Mark what a great job I think you are doing, and he said some things that bothered me - some misogynistic things about women in the workplace, and how a lot of BYU grads tend to leave the workplace when their husbands get a better job or when they get pregnant. I just wanted you to know he has these thoughts in his head, and that if you ever feel you are being passed over for a promotion, or not getting the opportunities you deserve, I have your back. It is probably a good idea to document any interactions you have, and talk to a lawyer if you feel the need."

"Thanks, Nephi. I wish I could say that I am surprised, but that is common in Utah County. Utah as a whole is dead last in gender pay equality. It's not right, and I feel like I always need to be perfect and outperform men because the deck is stacked against me. I appreciate the information and the support."

"I just thought you should know," he said. "I'll let you wrap up and get out of here."

He walked the floor, interrupting a long kiss between Angela and Brock, to invite them to his office for a discussion. Brock wiped his lips with the back of his hand, rubbing it back and forth to clear the lipstick before grabbing Angela by the hand, and following Nephi into his office.

"Please take a seat," he offered, as he sat behind the desk.

They sat down in the two chairs opposite Nephi's desk, still holding hands.

"We have discussed the need to remain discreet in the office," Nephi said. "Making out on the floor, and in the break room, is distracting for your coworkers. I am also concerned about your absences. Last month, you both called in sick three times, always on the same day."

"We can't help it if we get sick at the same time. I mean, we are always together, so it makes sense that we are exposed to the same germs," retorted Brock.

"Look," said Nephi, "I like both of you. When you focus, you are among the best agents in the call center, but your performance has slipped lately. Your monitor scores are down and your statistics have regressed across the board. I need to see improvement. This is a verbal warning. The next time we meet, you will receive a written warning. When you are at work, you must focus on work. You can do whatever you like on your own time."

"Yes, sir!" said Brock, exaggerating a salute.

"Angela, I need you to acknowledge that you understand," said Nephi.

"I understand," she said with a nod.

"Good, now both of you get to work, and please remember to be discreet. Everyone doesn't need to see you with your tongues in each other's throats."

Brock and Angela made their way toward the call center floor, hand in hand, while Nephi documented the conversation.

Even though Utah is an at-will employment state and employers can fire employees at any time for any reason, Nephi had to document all conversations carefully for HR and legal. He hoped that Brock and Angela would take the coaching well and it wouldn't come to that. The at-will laws stack the deck against employees, but don't prevent them from suing for wrongful termination. While such lawsuits are rare, documentation makes it easier for the company if the occur.

Brower required managers to meticulously document any disciplinary action.

Nephi resumed his daily routine after filing away the verbal warning documents for Brock and Angela. He took a couple of escalation calls, and conducted coaching sessions for Millard and Whitney, two relatively new employees with low scores on their last monitor. While making rounds on the floor, Nephi's phone dinged. He looked down to see a text from Stacy.

"Taco truck, 20 mins," it read.

Fifteen minutes later, Nephi found himself in his truck rumbling down 1600 North toward the taco truck permanently affixed in the parking lot on the corner. It wasn't much to look at, but the tacos were incredible and the flan, oh, the flan! Nephi didn't even like flan, but this flan was so sweet and fluffy that angels must have made it.

Nephi recognized Stacy's beige car in the parking lot with child seats in back. He parked next to her, and she waved as he got out of the truck. "I already have food," she called through the rolled down passenger window. "Get in."

He sat in the front seat, while Stacy rolled up the window and handed him a box containing a chicken taco and caramel drizzled flan. Fresh cilantro, mixed with salsa and grilled chicken, filled the car with a pleasant aroma. Glancing in the back seat, Nephi could see that Wyatt was asleep and Chloe's smiling mouth was stuffed with a taco.

"You didn't answer my call over the weekend, and I just needed to see you to make sure you're okay," she explained.

Nephi enjoyed a few bites of his taco before responding, "Thanks. It was a crazy weekend. I spent Saturday morning in the temple praying and getting my head straight. On Sunday, they released me. I bore my testimony, and it felt good. After church I met with Bishop Thompson, who took away my temple recommend."

"He what?" asked Stacy in disbelief. "No, he wouldn't…"

"He certainly did. He wants me to repent and prove that I align with the brethren before I get it back. After I met with him, I went to dinner with my family to break the fast, and got into it with Jacob. He wants me to act less gay, but it's not like I try to act in any certain way. I just am who I am, and I don't understand why I don't fit anywhere."

"Nephi, you do fit. You follow all of God's commandments better than any other Mormon I know. You are a really, truly good Mormon. I can't think of anyone who fits better."

"But I don't fit. On Sunday, Brother Hanson asked why I bother coming to church at all. Between the conversation with him and Bishop Thompson taking my temple recommend, it is hard to understand how I fit in. I am struggling with it. I have been doing a lot of thinking this weekend."

"You know I love you, don't you?" asked Stacy.

"Yes, I know. I'll always have you and my mother," he replied.

"After thinking and praying over the weekend, where is your head?" she asked.

"Honestly, Stacy, I am frustrated and sad and don't know quite what to do. What I have been doing is obviously not working. I am ready to shake things up a bit. I am tired of being so lonely all the time. I think I am ready to start dating, but I have no idea how to get started. How do I even meet guys around here?"

"Good question," she said. "I'm not an expert, and your options might be limited in Utah County. Some of my friends have had good luck with online dating. Maybe you should give it a try."

"I've thought about it, but I don't really know anything about it. I am totally clueless."

"My sister, Cindy, met her boyfriend on the Snuzzle app," said Stacy as she pulled out her phone and browsed the app store. "It looks like there is a two week free trial. You should download it."

Stacy reached over and grabbed Nephi's phone and handed it back 30 seconds later.

"There," she said, "I installed Snuzzle. Set up your profile today and see how you like it. Happy hunting!"

"Um, thanks?" replied Nephi. "I guess I'll get my Snuzzle on."

They chatted while finishing lunch in Stacy's car. Nephi took his time, and enjoyed every bite of flan. His nerves felt like fire from his heightened anxiety. He didn't know whether to cry or shout for joy. Managing to swallow the anxiety with the last bit of flan, Nephi leaned over and hugged Stacy. He thanked her for listening, and for her suggestions and wondered how he would navigate this new direction. With a blown kiss and a wave to Chloe, Nephi returned to his truck and went back to work.

The office felt cold, which had nothing to do with the temperature. Nephi hadn't changed his routine or the interactions with his team, but there was a different dynamic with Mark. The friendly watercooler conversations were absent. The only time Mark acknowledged Nephi was during a meeting. Mark wasn't outwardly hostile or aggressive toward him, but Nephi sensed hostility just the same, and he didn't like it.

Doing his best to ignore the cold wave emanating from Mark's office, Nephi focused on his work. He told himself if he worked hard and his team's numbers were good, things with Mark would surely return to normal.

As shift change drew near, Nephi made the rounds, checking on each agent to make sure they were on task and asking if they needed anything from him. Seeing that everything was good, he wrapped up his work for the day and headed home to hit the treadmill.

Nephi had a lot going on in his head and in his heart and running always helped him work it out. He bumped the incline to five to get his heart really pumping, and allowed his mind to process his thoughts and feelings. The feelings overwhelmed him and he increased the speed to eight in an attempt to shift some emotional burden to the machine. It didn't work. Nephi gradually slowed the treadmill to a halt and sat on the end, head in hands. He had a good cry, all alone, in the small apartment complex fitness room. Conflict raged inside him. Faith and testimony engrained themselves on Nephi's heart from a young age. They were part of him, yet they collided with who he was. God created him a gay man, and the church told him that was wrong and unnatural. Try as he might, Nephi could not reconcile the two sides of him, and the tears flowed.

All cried out, Nephi returned to his apartment for a shower before trying to learn what Snuzzle was all about. He opened the internet browser on his phone and searched videos about how to use the app. His search turned up more videos than he could possibly watch. There were reviews, walkthroughs and rants. One video featured a girl rambling on about her ten terrible Snuzzle dates and how they refused to refund her money after three months unlucky in love. The video was horrible, but somehow intriguing, and he couldn't look away. By the end, Nephi realized that he would never get that half hour of his life back, and decided that his search for 'Snuzzle' had returned too much garbage. He tried 'Snuzzle tutorial' and the results seemed more promising.

The top video featured a handsome guy in his mid-twenties walking through the Snuzzle account creation process and showed how to identify potential dates. Butterflies churned in Nephi's stomach at the thought of putting himself out there. He wasn't sure if the feeling was uneasiness or excitement.

Following the instructions in the video, Nephi opened the Snuzzle app on his phone and followed the prompts to create an account.

Name you want others to see: Nephi
I am a: Male
I am looking for a: Long term relationship
With a: Male
Hair color: Blond
Eye color: Blue
Body type: Slender
Occupation: Call Center Manager
Education: High School
Religion: LDS

Race: Caucasian
Children: Someday

Nephi continued completing the long profile, specifying his hobbies, favorite music, and movies. He then described his ideal date, and added a bio describing himself as an honest, caring gay Mormon who came out several years ago, but has never been in a relationship. He wrapped it up by snapping a selfie for a profile pic. The hard work was done, now the Snuzzle magic could find him a man.

A host of pictures now flooded his phone screen - all gay men looking for love in Utah. Nephi never knew so many existed. The tutorial video showed that he should swipe right if he was interested in the person and swipe left if he wasn't interested. Others on the app would do the same when they saw him and before he knew it, he should have a date.

As Nephi swiped through the parade of pictures, he built a pool of guys he found attractive that he just might hit it off with. He would have to just wait to see if any of them had mutual interest. Browsing through profiles, a lot of the descriptions confused him. "Mature bear seeking bears and otters. No pups," read one profile.

"What on earth? Is this a dating app or a zoo?" thought Nephi, realizing he knew nothing about the world he was stepping into.

Ding! A notification lit up Nephi's phone. "You've been Snuzzled," it read. "Snuzzled?" he thought, as he continued to read the message. Evan, one guy that Nephi swiped right on, had also swiped him. His mind raced, and his heart fluttered in anticipation of a real connection. Although Nephi had come out years ago, he didn't really have any gay friends. He had built his social structure entirely around church, work, family, and Stacy. Pushing down his nerves, he looked through Evan's profile. Evan was cute. From his picture he seemed to have an average build. He had dark brown hair that curled in the middle of his forehead. Gorgeous brown eyes, and a cleft chin highlighted his handsome face. Nephi was excited.

He continued reading through Evan's profile. He lived in Murray, up in Salt Lake County. His bio sounded interesting. "Hey, everyone. I'm a well-educated, confident guy who's always down to Netflix and chill. Looking for like-minded people. Hit me up!" While Nephi preferred his DVDs to a streaming service, he loved to curl up and watch a good movie. Maybe Netflix has Gilmore Girls. That sounded like fun. He sent a PM to Evan.

"Evan, my name is Nephi. I'm kind of new to this, but I would love to get to know you better. I am pretty low key and would love to Netflix and chill with you. I get off work by 4:30 and can be in Salt Lake by 6:00. I am free any night this week. Let me know what works. I look forward to getting to know you better," wrote Nephi.

Almost instantly, Nephi received a reply. "Cool, my place, Friday, 9pm," it read, with Evan's address added at the end. The reply seemed short, but Nephi was excited. His first date - only a few days away. There was so much to do. He needed to get a haircut and find the perfect thing to wear.

The week at the office dragged on. Nephi tried to focus on work, while thinking constantly about his date. Mark continued to give him the cold shoulder. Brock and Angela still couldn't keep their hands off of each other, but Nephi could tell they were trying because their call performance improved. He hoped they would stay consistent and not fall back into bad habits. For most of the work week, Nephi was on cruise control.

On Wednesday evening, he made a trip to the mall to find something to wear on Friday. Since he had never been on a date, he wasn't sure where to start, but some light internet searching gave him a few ideas. He ended up with slim-fit, gray wool dress pants, a form-fitting sunrise orange polo shirt, a pair of light brown suede slip-on sneakers, and a black leather jacket. Standing in front of the dressing room mirror with everything put together put a smile on his face. He looked good and would kill it on this date.

After a long week of anticipation, Friday finally arrived.

Nephi went to work and stayed busy monitoring calls and coaching reservations agents, watching the clock all the while. Shift change couldn't come soon enough. Toward the end of the shift, he rushed all the reports and handed off to Steve before driving home to get ready for his date.

Arriving at the apartment complex, Nephi hit the fitness room for a quick run on the treadmill, and then showered and dressed in his new slacks, polo, sneakers and the leather jacket. He looked good and felt good. Nephi wanted to make a good impression, but wasn't sure about dating etiquette.

Finding himself fully ready by 6:30, Nephi didn't know how to kill time. He was hungry, but wasn't sure if they would go eat on the date, so he didn't want to eat anything heavy. He made a light tomato salad and then decided he better run the truck through a car wash and vacuum it out in case Evan wanted him to drive. After hitting the car wash, Nephi went to a local flower shop. Flowers might be just the thing to make a good impression.

Nephi entered the flower shop and looked around. The floral scent filled his nostrils, and the sweetness made him smile. He would sure love to get flowers, and he hoped that Evan appreciated them, too. He didn't see anyone working the counter, so he dinged the bell. A young woman emerged from the back. She had long black hair pulled back in a ponytail. Her forest green polo with the store logo went well with her khaki pants. Emily was the name on her tag.

"Hi Emily, I would like to buy some flowers," said Nephi.

"Is this for a special occasion?" she asked.

"A first date."

"That's very romantic. We don't sell many first date flowers anymore."

"Oh," he replied, "do you think it's too much?"

"Not at all," she said. "I think it's very sweet. What are you thinking?"

"I'm new at this and I'm not really sure. What do you suggest?"

"Well, for a first date, you don't want to go too big.

Something simple will do. How about an orchid bouquet accented with lavender and baby's breath?" she asked.

"I love the smell of lavender," said Nephi. "That sounds perfect."

Emily handpicked the flowers and put together a bouquet.

"Would you like a vase?" she asked.

"Yes, please. I'm not sure if he will already have one," said Nephi.

"He?" she asked.

"Yes, my date. Evan."

"I see," she replied. "It's a good thing my mom isn't out here, or she would refuse to sell them to you. We had a big wedding order this summer, and when she found out the couple was gay, she refused to take their business. If you ever come here when she is around, you shouldn't mention who they are for."

The excitement fled from Nephi's face as he glanced down at the floor. "Listen," he said gently, "for most of my life, I have been hiding part of me and I'm not doing it any more. If you don't want my business because I am gay, I will not hide who I am just so you will accept me. I respect your religious views, and if you don't want to sell me flowers, then that is fine. But if that is the case, I would rather buy them from someone who wants my money."

"You're right," she replied. "I don't agree with what my mother did. Here, take the flowers. They are on the house. I hope you have fun on your date, and I understand if you choose another flower shop next time."

With a nod of gratitude, Nephi took the flowers and headed out the door. He tucked the vase between the truck seats and wrapped the middle seatbelt around them to be certain they wouldn't spill on the way. The engine roared with the turn of the key and he headed north toward Murray.

The sun was setting on the other side of Utah Lake as Nephi drove on I-15, painting the sky orange and pink. He couldn't help but notice all the business that had popped up along the freeway in recent years. He hardly recognized the place. A tech boom hit the valley bringing outside investment, and causing home prices to skyrocket. He drove past the corn maze, pumpkin patch, and Thanksgiving Point in Lehi, home to the Museum of Ancient Life where he liked to take his nieces and nephew. He hoped to one day share the museum with children of his own. Before long, Nephi noticed the windmills on his left, signaling the end of Utah County.

After reaching the Point of the Mountain, he began the descent into Salt Lake County. It wouldn't be long now. Less than a mile from the 54th South exit, Nephi began to move into the right lane before a BMW cut him off, swerving from the far left lane all the way to the right without a hint of a signal.

Laying on the horn, Nephi blasted the inattentive driver with a loud warning, while applying the brakes. Why doesn't anyone use their blinker in this state? It drove Nephi crazy. After forcing his heart from his throat back down into his chest, Nephi put on his blinker and moved into the right lane in time to make the exit. Heading east off the exit, Nephi passed the hospital and arrived at Evan's apartment complex on State Street.

The clock read 8:27, and it was five minutes fast. He was too early. Nephi calmed himself, bowed his head, and said a prayer. He prayed that God would help him know what to do and that he could make friends and learn how to accept all the parts of him. After praying, he turned on the radio and listened to a local pop station, while mentally preparing for the date. When the clock read 8:55, he straightened his hair in the rear-view mirror, gathered the flowers, and went to find Evan's apartment.

Nephi climbed the stairs to the second story of the apartment complex and navigated to 18B. Holding the flowers in front of him with a smile on his face, Nephi knocked on the door. The sound of his heart thumping was like a mallet on a bass drum. The door swung open suddenly, and there stood Evan, shirtless in a pair of jeans. His broad, hairless chest excited Nephi. He was beautiful. Nephi introduced himself, extending the flowers.

"Wow, flowers, huh? Interesting. Well, come on in and take a seat," said Evan, while taking the flowers from Nephi and setting them on the table.

Evan had decorated the open layout apartment beautifully. The living room had a salmon colored European style sofa on one side and two cream colored modern arm chairs on the other. A large area rug under the coffee table tied the whole room together. Lighted sconces hung on the wall providing a warm atmosphere and a vanilla scented candle burned in the middle of the coffee table, emanating an inviting glow and a smell that was perfectly yummy. Nephi admired the furnishings as he sat on the sofa.

"I love your apartment," said Nephi. "When you finish getting ready, do you want to grab a bite to eat? I can drive."

"I ate earlier, and plan on staying in," said Evan. "I am ready. Would you like a glass of wine?"

"No, thank you. I don't drink," replied Nephi.

"That's too bad," said Evan. "I have a very nice Pinot Noir. Would you like anything else to drink?"

"No, thank you. I'm good for now. I'm really looking forward to getting to know you," said Nephi.

Evan poured himself a glass of wine, and sat next to Nephi on the sofa. He crossed his legs and took a sip. Being this close to a beautiful shirtless man raised Nephi's pulse. It turned him on and that made him nervous.

"So, uh, what do you want to do tonight? I love Gilmore Girls," said Nephi awkwardly.

"Well," said Evan, "I was thinking we could start real slow, build up fast, go a few rounds, and if all goes well, we can have breakfast in the morning."

Evan leaned in toward Nephi, placing his hand on Nephi's knee and crawling it up his leg while leaning in for a kiss. Nephi jumped up off of the sofa.

"Wait, what are you doing? We don't even know each other yet. Let's talk a while. I'm not ready for a kiss," he said.

"Not ready for a kiss?" replied Evan. "What the hell is wrong with you?" What did you expect to happen tonight?"

Confused, Nephi just stared at him. He didn't know how to respond. He thought through their exchange of Snuzzle messages. He must have missed something.

"I don't know. I thought maybe we would get to know each other, have a nice date, and maybe watch a movie. Didn't you read my profile?" he asked.

"I never read profiles. I only look at the picture and swipe it if I like what I see. Besides, my profile makes it clear that you shouldn't meet up with me if you aren't DTF and I promise you won't be disappointed. I am quite the artiste," said Evan.

"I don't know what DTF means," said Nephi. "Your profile said you like Netflix. I'm confused. And I definitely can't be staying up all night, I need to be up for General Conference in the morning."

"Ok, pup, it's obvious we both made a big mistake. What century are you from?" asked Evan. "I don't have the time for this but let me give you a little education. DTF means down to f…"

Nephi interrupted him mid-sentence, with a startled look on his face. "Please stop right there. I get the gist. Swearing really offends me. Please don't swear around me. There is no need for it. Can't we just start over and try to get to know each other? We can Netflix and chill like your profile said."

"Where do you get the nerve to come into my place and tell me what I can and cannot say?" asked Evan. "And sweetheart, Netflix and chill had nothing to do with Netflix and everything to do with being DTF, so if you aren't DTF, you can march your scrawny, self-righteous little ass out that door."

"I'm sorry," said Nephi. "I didn't mean to come across that way. I am new to all of this. This is my first date and I know nothing about online dating."

"That's obvious," replied Evan. "I really don't know what you were expecting. You might want to learn something about the internet, and dating, and the community, before you jump in like this."

"Maybe Bishop was right," Nephi muttered to himself

under his breath.

"Wait, what?" asked Evan. "Did you say Bishop? Are you a practicing Mormon?"

"Yes, I am," replied Nephi.

"Asshole!" yelled Evan. "You are an asshole. Get the hell out of my apartment."

"Hold on, just because of my religion?" asked Nephi.

"Don't you dare think that I'm the asshole," said Evan. "It is people like you who are the problem. Do you have any idea how many friends of mine committed suicide because they couldn't live up to the expectations of their parents or their bishop?"

"I'm so sorry about your friends," said Nephi. "I didn't know."

"Of course you didn't know. The truth is that you will never live up to the expectations of that church. They reject who you are at the core and tell you that you can only get to heaven if you deny your very nature. When you finally realize that, it won't end well. The church hates you. They hate all of us," said Evan.

"I get what you are saying and I have seen my share of hate from members of the church, but there are a lot of good people in the church, too. And there is truth in the church. I have felt it. I feel it every day when I read the Book of Mormon," Nephi explained.

"There might be people who pretend to care, but deep down, they hate you. You cannot be who you are and expect the church to accept you. I have seen it a hundred times and have seen so many take their lives when they can't deal with it. It needs to stop. Please explain to me why you keep going to a church that doesn't want you. You don't fit in there and you never will. Why try? Just embrace who you are. Despite what they tell you, there is nothing wrong with you," said Evan.

"I know there is nothing wrong with me. I feel that God made me this way. I have come to accept it. I keep going to church because I feel spiritual power there. I feel the Spirit when I read the Bible and the Book of Mormon and when I pray to God. I have doubts and questions and struggles, but underneath it all, I know there is truth and I feel peace. I don't really know how to explain it, but it is part of who I am. Yes, I am gay, but I am also Mormon. You are right, I must embrace the gay side of me. I have suppressed it my whole life and I realize that isn't healthy. At the same time, I can't cut off the Mormon part of me. It is an equal part of my identity," explained Nephi.

"See, that is just the problem," said Evan. "Those two parts of your identity don't agree with each other. They never will. It is those who try the hardest to bring them in harmony that end up killing themselves, and I am fed up with it. I just can't see it anymore. When you perpetuate the idea that those two sides can coexist, the problem continues. Look, Nephi, I know you are dealing with some shit right now and you need to work it out, but I have been down that road before and I just can't deal with it. I can't go through it again. I wish you the best, I really do, but you need to leave. This conversation isn't good for my heart."

"I get it," said Nephi. "Tonight was definitely not what I expected, but it opened my eyes to a lot of things. I'll get out of your way."

Evan approached Nephi with open his arms. Nephi moved into his embrace. They hugged tightly for a moment. Confusion, anger, love, compassion, and sadness all coursed through Nephi's body. He felt emotional overload. He left the apartment and drove back to Pleasant Grove with a lot on his mind. At least tomorrow was General Conference. Hopefully the messages from the prophets and apostles would provide him with answers.

CHAPTER 7

Nephi awoke in the morning, excited to face the day. He circled October 5th on his calendar the day he bought it. Twice per year, the leaders of The Church of Jesus Christ of Latter Day Saints speak to the general membership in a meeting known as General Conference. It takes place the first weekend of October and April. They broadcast it on television, and via the church website and mobile apps so that all church members can hear it.

His routine for preparing his mind for conference was always the same for Nephi. Waking at 7:00, he kneeled at his bedside to pray, asking God to open his mind and heart to receive the messages of conference. He then put steel-cut oatmeal in his crockpot to cook while he read the scriptures. Most Mormon families make a special breakfast with waffles, pancakes, or French toast. In Nephi's family growing up, Darla always made fresh cinnamon rolls, but Nephi loved steel cut oatmeal, and that became his tradition ever since he moved into his own apartment.

With the crockpot going, Nephi read scriptures for an hour, giving equal time to the Book of Mormon and the Bible. He then went to the fitness room for a good, hard run to clear his head. After a shower, the oatmeal was ready. He enjoyed it with a spoonful of brown sugar, a splash of almond milk, and a half cup of crushed pecans. It was the perfect breakfast.

After eating, Nephi brushed his teeth and retrieved his notepad from the nightstand. He took notes during each talk of every General Conference. Ready with his notebook, he reviewed the notes from the April conference and prayed again to prepare his mind to receive the messages from the prophet and the apostles.

The President of the LDS church is recognized as the Prophet, the only person on earth with authority to receive revelation from God on behalf of the entire earth. Individuals can receive personal revelation for themselves, and their families. Bishops can receive revelation for their ward, but only the Prophet can receive revelation for the entire church, and for the world.

The Prophet calls two counselors to assist him. The three men make up the First Presidency of the church. They also call twelve apostles, just like Jesus did when he was on the earth. The fifteen men that make up the Quorum of Twelve Apostles and the First Presidency are recognized as prophets, seers, and revelators. These men, along with other men and women who make up the general leadership of the church, speak in General Conference.

Nephi watched General Conference at home so he could concentrate on the words being spoken, and on his feelings. He always felt the Holy Spirit during conference and received impressions to direct his life. Today, he felt the need for guidance more than ever, and wanted to be in the right state of mind and spirit to receive inspiration.

Right before conference, they always showed Music and the Spoken word – the weekly Tabernacle Choir program. Nephi loved the choir. He often felt the Spirit and received inspiration through music. He listened and prepared his heart while he enjoyed the music. Once the choir's program was complete, it was time for General Conference to begin.

Familiar organ music played while a man's voice announced that the General Conference of the Church of Jesus Christ of Latter Day Saints was beginning. The choir sang "We Thank Thee O God for a Prophet," and the meeting started.

President James E. Snead, second counselor in the First Presidency, who conducted the Saturday morning session, stood at the pulpit. He announced another song by the choir, "Praise to the Man," and an opening prayer, after which, the Prophet would address the congregation. Nephi always loved to hear the Prophet speak. The choir sang a lovely rendition of the hymn. The prayer was a bit flowery for Nephi's taste, but he appreciated the sentiment. Then came time for the Prophet to speak.

President Maxwell L. Johannson, the President and Prophet at the church made his way to the pulpit. He was an elderly man, ninety-six years-old with snow white hair and intense blue eyes. A cane assisted him as he walked. Despite his age, President Johannson had a sharp mind and strong voice. He welcomed the congregation with a warm smile, and announced that six new temples would be built. Nephi always loved to hear about new temples. He wished he had the time and means to visit them all.

President Johannson spoke about personal revelation. He told the members of the church that if they lived worthy enough to be in tune with the Holy Ghost, God would provide inspiration in their lives through the Spirit. It was a short talk, but powerful. It touched Nephi's heart as he fervently took notes. He needed direction from God right now, and he knew that He would provide it if he prayed with a pure heart and real intent, just like President Johannson said.

Sister Michelle Blackburn, first counselor in the general Relief Society Presidency spoke next. There is typically one or two token women speakers in each conference session. Nephi loved to hear them speak and wished they gave women more opportunities to speak. He always watched the women's session since the speakers in that session are mostly women.

Sister Blackburn spoke about loving our neighbor as ourselves, and finding opportunities to serve others. Service and love for others was a topic that Nephi was passionate about, and he enjoyed the talk as he took notes.

The conference session progressed with talks from two members of the Quorum of Seventy, and two from the Quorum of the Twelve Apostles. Nephi took notes of every talk and felt uplifted. The last speaker of the session was President Michael B. Westover, first counselor in the First Presidency.

President Westover began his speech talking about love for our fellow man. He shared stories of Jesus showing love to others, like sharing the stories of Christ feeding the multitude, healing the blind man, and blessing the Nephite children. He talked about His love for others and compared it to the way we should treat each other. President Westover then focused his talk specifically on the LGBTQ community. Nephi was glad to hear a leader of the church paying attention to his concerns. He had prayed for this.

President Westover instructed the members of the church to show kindness, love, and compassion to members of the LGBTQ community. He scolded them for mistreatment of their LGBTQ brothers and sisters, and told them to be loving and accepting of everyone. Nephi was beaming as he continued to take notes. He began to tear up as an apostle of the Lord instructed church members to be kind and accepting. As the talk continued, President Westover turned his focus to the Proclamation on the Family.

"While we must show love and acceptance to all people," he said, "we cannot allow ourselves to accept their sin. There are many who wish us to declare that because we obey the laws of the land, we will accept those laws even when they are contrary to God's commandments. God decreed from the beginning of time that marriage is between man and woman. It is not in the power of men who are God's prophets and apostles to change his eternal law."

"While governments may recognize marriage between same-sex couples, such marriages are not recognized by God and those who enter such a marriage are in violation of God's law of chastity, just like a heterosexual couple who engages in premarital relations. God's law of chastity is eternal. Marriage between man and woman is also an eternal concept essential to God's plan. God created his children as male and female with traits and identities according to their gender. No man can change that."

"While we must all show love and respect to our LGBTQ brothers and sisters, we cannot accept an ideology that flies in the face of God's eternal laws. To my LGBTQ brothers and sisters, I want to tell you that God loves you. He wishes you to keep his commandments and return to live with him again. If you keep all of his commandments, including the law of chastity, I can tell you that you will enjoy the same eternal blessings that all God's children may enjoy."

"I must say that I don't understand how everything will work in the hereafter. I don't know the exact details of the nature of family relationships after this life for our LGBTQ brothers and sisters, but I know that if you follow God's commandments, you will be full participants in his blessings. You must trust in the Lord with all your heart, as the writer of Proverbs instructs, and lean not unto your own understanding. Follow the commandments and trust in the Lord, brothers and sisters, and you will be blessed."

President Westover carried on but Nephi's note taking trailed off. Deep in thought, tears were streaming down his face, but not for the same reasons as before. It felt like a backhanded compliment, a passive aggressive slap to the face. Doctrine-wise, nothing had changed. The church has maintained for a long time that gay individuals can be in good standing in the church as long as they remain celibate. But to start the talk by giving Nephi hope, by scolding church members for their treatment of the LGBTQ community and then to turn it around by giving more fuel to their fire rubbed him the wrong way.

Nephi knew the church's position. He understood it. He accepted it, and lived by it for years. He had accepted that to return to live with God, he would need to live a lonely, celibate life with no spouse or children. He wished for as long as he could remember that the church would at least recognize his sacrifice. That they would acknowledge that what they ask of the LGBTQ community is a hard thing – that it isn't fair. No such acknowledgement ever seems to come.

They offer glimmers of hope. They support measures to prevent discrimination in housing and employment based on sexual orientation, but then they turn around and fight a bill that would ban conversion therapy and fight hard against same-sex marriage, which is the very mechanism by which many rights are secured. There isn't another mechanism in our society that ensures health care benefits to same-sex partners, or rights of survivorship. Nephi could understand the opposition to religious marriage, but why must it apply to civil union? Why so many mixed messages from church leadership?

Depressed and confused, Nephi didn't even listen to the final number by the choir. Instead, he kneeled and prayed. He sought guidance from Heavenly Father, the guidance that President Johannson said that he could receive. He needed it now more than ever.

After praying, his mind turned to the conversation with Evan last night. He wondered if Evan was right. Could he ever reconcile the two sides of himself? He was Mormon, and he was gay. President Westover's talk gave him a lot more to think about.

The train of thought was interrupted by the ring of his phone. He really didn't feel like talking to anyone. Glancing down, he saw that Stacy was calling and he picked up.

"Hey, Stace, what's up?" he asked.

"I just finished watching the first session of conference and felt like you might need to talk," she said.

"Honestly, I'm struggling with it. I mean, nothing he said is new, but every time I hear it, it gets me all over again."

"I know. I'm worried about you. You know that I love you no matter what, right?"

"Of course I do. After my date last night, I just have a lot on my mind."

"Wait! What? Date? You never told me you had a date. Tell me everything."

"Yeah, I guess I haven't talked to you since Monday. I met a guy on Snuzzle and went over to his apartment last night. We had planned to watch Netflix and chill but it wasn't what I expected," said Nephi.

Stacy began laughing uncontrollably. Nephi was annoyed at the laughter. "Netflix and chill," she said. "You had no idea what that meant until last night, did you?" She continued laughing.

"Ha, ha, ha. Very funny," said Nephi. "I assumed we would watch a movie and you know, maybe cuddle a little, but he had something else in mind."

"You can be so naïve sometimes, Nephi. Maybe if you

would get on social media more, you would know about these things. I swear you were born in the wrong decade."

"Social media just never appealed to me," he replied. "I mean, I really don't get it. Why would I want to know what the bullies from high school had for lunch or where they are spending their fabulous vacations? You know that half the stuff you see on there is exaggerated, and the rest is flat out made up, right?"

"I know, I know, but you do have to admit that you could have saved yourself some embarrassment if you knew what Netflix and chill meant," she retorted with amusement in her voice.

"Well, maybe. I'm still not ready for social media, but I should probably at least run my dates by you before meeting up with anyone else."

"You definitely should, and we need to talk about basic online safety. You don't just go over to some random guy's place without meeting him first. You need to voice verify to make sure you aren't getting catfished and your first meeting should always be in a public place. Don't you know anything?" she asked.

"Apparently not. The more I see lately, the more I understand that I know absolutely nothing. When it comes to dating, that is the honest truth, and apparently it's the same for the church, too. Not to mention being gay. I know nothing."

"Well I'm not sure I can help you know anything about being gay, but I'm sure you will figure it out, and you have me to help you with dating stuff," said Stacy.

"Stace, I don't know what I would ever do without you," he said. "Thanks for calling. I feel better already."

"Hey, would you like to watch the afternoon session of conference and the women's session with me and Roger? His famous chili is cooking in the crock pot, and I'm making grilled cheese sandwiches. I know you like to watch it alone, but we would love to have you."

"I would love to come over. I honestly don't really feel like watching conference at all right now, and seeing you and the kids will give me something to look forward to."

"Great!" she said. "We will see you a little before 2:00."

"Sound good. I'll see you then."

The short drive to American Fork gave Nephi time to think. He loved the church and believed it to be true, and also knew that God created him just the way he was. He believed that God did so for a reason, and that a loving God would not exclude so many children from salvation. God must have a plan for him. Trust in the Lord, he thought. That's good advice. God is the Father of us all. He created each of us the way we are, and he loves us.

Thoughts and questions circled in Nephi's head until his truck rolled into Stacy's driveway. She lived in an old red-brick home with one floor at street level and a basement. The fallen leaves from two mature trees in the front yard had blanketed everything in color. A patchwork quilt of orange, red, and gold covered the ground. Nephi made his way onto the porch, opened the screen door, and knocked on the wooden front door.

"Welcome! Come on in," said Stacy, giving Nephi a hug. He walked through the door, which opened directly into the living room. Roger sat in the rocking chair holding Wyatt while Chloe played with princess toys on the floor. When she saw Nephi, she ran over to him. He scooped her up and gave her a hug. College football was on TV. Roger was a fanatic. He loved BYU football. Although they don't play on Conference Saturday, he was keeping tabs on the other teams. Nephi didn't care for sports. He was reasonably athletic for his size, and enjoyed running, but watching other people run around a field chasing a ball didn't appeal to him.

"Roger, it's almost time for conference," said Stacy. "Let's change to the conference channel." Roger picked up the remote and reluctantly changed the channel. A church documentary was just ending. It told of the humanitarian efforts of the church in response to a recent hurricane. Nephi looked around the room, noticing that Stacy had just decorated for Halloween. She was a sucker for craft projects. Little wooden ghosts, goblins, and witches adorned the mantle, end tables, and walls. "I love your cute decorations," he said. "What is this year's addition?"

"I'm painting those flower pots," she said, pointing to a stack of ceramic pots in the corner. "When they are all painted and glued together, they will make an adorable wizard for the front porch. I haven't had time to finish him yet."

"She always has at least one unfinished project," added Roger. "Sometimes I think she will never finish them."

"Just look around, Sweetie," she said. "I don't see many of these projects that are unfinished, do you?" That seemed to shut him up. He ignored her and turned up the volume on the TV. Satisfied, she smiled and nodded. The house smelled of chili. Nephi could tell it had been cooking all day. He also noticed a hint of pumpkin spice and realized that Stacy had potpourri boiling on the stove. The house was small, but it was warm, cozy, and full of love.

Nephi sat on the couch with Stacy next to him. She took a piece of paper from the end table and handed it to Chloe along with a box of crayons. "Chloe, here is your General Conference coloring page. Whenever you hear them discussing a topic, you can color the picture that goes with it," she explained.

"I know how to do it, Mommy," exclaimed Chloe, snatching the paper from her hand. Nephi smiled. Children were so sweet and innocent. He loved spending time with them, and the feeling seemed to be mutual. Children were drawn to Nephi.

Chloe happily colored while the adults watched General Conference. The Saturday afternoon session started with the sustaining of the General Authorities and other officers of the church and featured talks about prayer, the Book of Mormon, faith, fasting, temple work, gratitude, and service. All the speakers were men. Nephi enjoyed the messages, even though it was difficult to keep his mind from President Westover's talk in the morning session.

After the session, they enjoyed Roger's chili and grilled

cheese sandwiches, while Roger watched football. Nephi filled Stacy in on all the juicy details from his date with Evan. He spoke to her about his growing concerns about his place in the world, in general, and his place in the church, in particular. Recent events didn't sit well with him, and praying wasn't bringing him as much peace as it had in the past. He struggled to find contentment in his loneliness.

"Do you have any new Snuzzle connections?" asked Stacy.

"I don't know, I haven't checked it in a couple of days," he replied.

"Can I see your phone?" she asked. He gave it to her. She opened the Snuzzle app and checked his messages. "It looks like you have a connection from a cute guy."

"Shut up, I do not," he protested.

"I'm not kidding. This one looks promising. After your experience with Evan, you need to be very open about who you are and what you're looking for, and you really should talk to him on the phone before meeting in person."

"Don't worry. I've learned my lesson. I definitely won't go jump right into meeting someone blindly this time. Now give me the phone." He took the phone from her and looked at the new Snuzzle connection.

Alex was his name. He was shorter than Nephi, about 5 feet, 7 inches with dark curly hair and deep olive skin. His big brown eyes drew Nephi in right away, and his arms seemed muscular as far as Nephi could tell from the pictures. The smile on his face was inviting.

"It looks like someone is smitten," said Stacy, noticing Nephi's grin. Nephi blushed. "Send him a message," she prodded. "Get the ball rolling."

Nephi decided that he would do just that. "My name is Nephi," he wrote. "It looks like we have a connection on Snuzzle, and I would like to get to know you better. I am new to this and want to take things slow. I'm not the Netflix and chill kind of guy, if you know what that is. I am just a guy who wants to get to know you and see where things go."

He handed the phone to Stacy for approval. She read his

message and nodded. Nephi hit send. He was excited to hear back. He hoped it would go better than the Evan fiasco. He really just wanted someone to talk to, someone who could relate. He wasn't sure if it would lead to love, or even if he wanted it to, but he no longer wanted to be lonely. Nephi craved connection on a human level. Stacy was awesome, but she had her own family and he needed more.

After dinner, Stacy and Nephi watched the women's session of General Conference in the living room, while Stacy fed Wyatt. He was wide awake and ready to play. Roger watched football in the bedroom, and Chloe played a game on Stacy's phone. Every talk in the women's session was given by a woman except for the last three by the First Presidency. Nephi really enjoyed the session. He spent the last half hour holding little Wyatt, rocking him to sleep in his arms. After he fell asleep, Stacy moved him into the crib.

After conference, Nephi thanked Stacy and Roger for inviting him, gave everyone hugs, and headed home. Once home, he read scriptures and prayed and then checked his phone before going to bed. No message yet. He really felt something while looking through Alex's profile, and he hoped they would hit it off. He checked Snuzzle every ten minutes until he finally fell asleep.

In the morning, Nephi checked his phone first thing. Snuzzle notified him of a new message. He quickly opened it to find a note from Alex. "Nephi, I'd love to chat. I work an evening shift from 3:00 to 11:00 PM. I am available any day during the morning and I have Wednesday and Thursday off. Let me know what works best for you. I look forward to meeting you."

Nephi immediately responded. "I am a call center manager on day shift. I work from 7:00 to 4:00 so it looks like we have opposite work schedules. I have Saturday and Sunday off. I can't wait to talk to you. Snuzzle messages seem impersonal, so let's talk on the phone. Give me a call when you have time." Nephi ended the message with his phone number. He couldn't wait for Alex to call.

He began his day as usual with scripture study, a prayer, and a shower before polishing off the rest of yesterday's oatmeal batch. By 10:00, he was ready for the Sunday morning General Conference session. The music for this session was provided from a choir of missionaries from the Missionary Training Center in Provo. As soon as they started singing, Nephi's phone rang. It was an 801 number that he didn't recognize. It must be either a car warranty scam or Alex. As tired as Nephi was of the scammers, he was willing to take the risk. He paused General Conference. "Hello, this Nephi," he answered.

"Well, hello there, Nephi, this is Alex," said the high pitched, breathy voice on the other end. "It's nice to meet you. Tell me all about yourself."

Nephi felt his heart skip a beat at the sound of Alex's name. He was glad to be starting this conversation over the phone rather than in front of a shirtless man.

"I don't even know where to start," he said. "What do you want to know?"

"For starters, where are you from? What do you do for work? What do you do for fun? You know, the basic stuff," Alex replied.

"Okay," said Nephi. "I was born and raised in Pleasant Grove. I have lived there almost my entire life, except for two years that I spent in Albania as a missionary. I am a supervisor at the Brower Hotels central reservation center, where I have worked for almost nine years. Outside of work, I don't do much lately, but I like to read and listen to music. I like to run, and I love hiking. You should also know that I am Mormon. I hope that isn't a problem for you."

"It's not a problem for me," said Alex, "but maybe it should be for you. Let's not dwell on that for now. Let's get to know each other first. When did you come out?"

"After returning from my mission, it took me a few years to come out to myself. I was raised to believe that it is unnatural and wrong to be gay and I had a hard time accepting myself. I was in denial. I think everyone close to me acknowledged it before I did. Looking back on it, I think that even my high school bullies knew before I did. They tortured me mercilessly, and I denied it hard. About seven years ago, I finally admitted it to myself, and I came out to my family about two years later."

"How did they take it?" asked Alex.

"Better than I expected. My mom and my best friend, Stacy, have never shown anything but love. They both told me they already knew and they loved me. Most other people seemed okay with it except for my brother, Jacob, and my dad. Jacob has always been embarrassed of me, and always tells me to tone it down and pretend to be someone I'm not. My dad has never come right out and said it, but our relationship changed after I came out. We haven't been as close. I can feel his disappointment. I have been talking this whole time," he said. "Tell me about you, Alex."

"My story isn't very exciting," he said. "I was born and raised in Jensen, Utah just outside of Vernal. It's a tiny town and I'm sure you can imagine how a gay Mexican kid fit in. I moved to Salt Lake at seventeen, working in several fast-food restaurants before moving to a diner where I learned to cook. I worked my way through culinary school and now I am the chef at La Bambolina, an Italian restaurant downtown. For fun, I love going to concerts and movies and binge watching shows. I hate running, but I like to work out. Strength training is my thing at the gym."

"When did you come out?" asked Nephi.

"Honey, I was always out. Even if I want to, I couldn't hide it. In a town of less than five hundred, there weren't a lot of kids, but every one of them was a bully. I came out to my parents as a teenager," he said.

"And how did they take it?" asked Nephi.

"That, my new friend, is a topic for another day. Tell me more about you. What are you looking for in a relationship? I just got out of a two year relationship, and I'm honestly not ready to dive in hard to a new one. Taking it slow, and seeing where it goes, sounds good to me."

"Well," said Nephi, "I have never been in a relationship.

To be honest, I have never even kissed a guy. I had one Snuzzle date, and it was a disaster. I'm looking for someone I can talk to. I am looking for friendship first, romance second. Even though I am gay, I really have no gay friends, and I know nothing about being gay. I am so confused by most of the Snuzzle profiles. I don't understand terms like twink, circuit boy, bear, wolf, and daddy. I am honestly so confused. I feel lost."

Nephi could hear laughter on the other end of the line. He really wasn't amused. "What's so funny?" he asked.

"It's just my luck to sign up for Snuzzle against my better judgement, and end up with a baby gay," he said. "Most guys on there are looking to hit it and forget it. My first match is with a damn thirty-year-old baby gay. Sorry, I'm not laughing at you, I'm laughing at myself. I'll tell you what, I'm not necessarily looking for a romantic relationship, least of all with a virgin pup, but it sounds like we could both use a friend right now. I'll help you understand things going on in the community and get started in dating, and we can be friends, and only friends. Does that work for you?"

"Sounds perfect to me," said Nephi. "I do have a favor to ask though. Swearing is really offensive to me. Will you please not swear around me?"

"Damn, you're offended by me saying damn? Damn! Well, I will try my best not to swear around you, but I can't promise that one won't slip out now and then. I have to warn you, though, without swearing I lose half my charm."

"Don't flatter yourself," said Nephi in a playful tone, "you're not that charming to begin with."

"Oh, that's cold," replied Alex, "I knew I liked you. Now dish the dirt on your disaster of a Snuzzle date."

Nephi described every embarrassing detail of his date with Evan, which left Alex doubled over in laughter. They talked about life, family, work, and everything else. Nephi couldn't remember the last time his soul felt this light. Before Nephi knew it, it was 12:30. They had talked all the way through the morning session of conference and beyond.

"Well, unfortunately, I need to take care of some things before work so I've gotta run," said Alex. "I enjoyed our chat and would love to talk again."

"I would love to meet up. Can we meet on Wednesday evening?" asked Nephi.

"I would love that. How about we meet half way between Salt Lake and Pleasant Grove? There's an amazing Mexican café right across from South Town Mall on 106th South and State. It's called Los Cucos. Meet me there at 5:30. We can grab a table."

"I'll be there," said Nephi.

With that, they hung up. Nephi couldn't contain his excitement. He called Stacy and told her about the conversation with Alex. He was glad to have a new friend, someone that could really understand him.

Nephi spent the rest of the day watching the morning and afternoon sessions of conference online. The weekend was an emotional rollercoaster, but it ended on a high note. Nephi was optimistic about the possibilities ahead.

CHAPTER 8

By now, every work day seemed the same. Badge in, run reports, walk the floor, monitor, coach, run more reports, and badge out. After you have been in a job long enough, even the complex seems mundane. Nephi was good at his job. He knew the ins and outs and could almost coast through every day. The thing about call centers is that turnover is always high. People are always coming and going. With new people come new challenges. Of everything the Brower job offered, Nephi enjoyed the people the most.

With the dawn of a new week, Nephi badged in and began to make his way back to his office. As he passed the break room, he noticed Brock sitting in a chair with Angela on his lap. Their faces were attached like a car wash vacuum to a minivan seat full of cheerios. Nephi wasn't sure if they would ever come apart. If Angela had any cheerios, they almost certainly belonged to Brock now.

"Be discreet!" he called out as he walked by. After pulling reports, he completed shift handoff with Monica and settled into his daily routine.

Mark stopped by Nephi's office just before noon. He stood in the doorway, a smug grin spread across his face. "How was your weekend, Nephi?" he asked.

"I had a great weekend, Mark," he replied. "How about you?"

"I always enjoy conference weekend," he replied. "I assume you heard President Westover's talk?"

"I sure did, along with all the other conference talks. I look forward to every General Conference."

"I'm glad to hear it. I just want to let you know that I love you and I'm glad that you come to church."

"Um, thanks, Mark. I'm guess I'm glad that you go to church too. We all need the Savior in our lives. Is there anything I can help you with?" asked Nephi, trying to bring an end to the awkward conversation.

"No," replied Mark, "I just wanted to let you know that

you are loved. Carry on with your work."

As a member of the Stake Presidency, Mark had to set an example for others. Nephi could tell that he was trying extra hard to follow the counsel from the conference talks and since Nephi was probably the only gay person he knew, he made sure to reach out in what he believed was love and brotherhood. Nephi just wished that Mark understood boundaries, especially in the workplace.

When Mark left, Nephi pulled out the peanut butter sandwiches he had brought from home and checked his phone while he ate. No new Snuzzle messages or texts from Alex. He really looked forward to seeing him on Wednesday evening. With a few minutes to kill while eating, he texted Stacy to fill her in on the developments with Alex. She would be excited for him and there wasn't anyone else with whom he felt comfortable sharing. The kids were probably keeping her busy and she didn't text back right away.

Nephi kept thinking about Wednesday night while he coasted through the rest of the work day. The next two days brought more of the same. The call metrics for Nephi's team had improved week over week, despite him being on cruise control. The tone of his interactions with Mark improved, though they were no less awkward. During lunch on Wednesday, he spoke with Stacy on the phone. She was excited for him and wished him luck with Alex. Nephi was glad they both agreed to be friends. He wanted more conversation with someone who could understand him.

Shift change on Wednesday arrived, and Nephi completed the hand off meeting with Steve before heading home to shower and change. He wore the same outfit he bought for his date with Evan, but skipped the flowers this time. As he made the drive over the Point of the Mountain, he became cognizant of the fact that he felt fantastic. He couldn't remember the last time he felt that way.

Before long, the white truck pulled into the Los Cucos parking lot. Nephi recognized Alex standing near the entrance. He looked almost exactly like his profile picture, except in the profile picture, he was clean shaven, and he now sported a neatly trimmed beard. Pulling into a parking space near the entrance, Nephi climbed down out of the truck.

"Alex, it's nice to meet you in person," he said, extending his hand.

"Oh, hell no," replied Alex. "Please tell me this truck is not yours. Do you have any idea how much carbon that thing spits out?"

"Language, please," said Nephi. "Have you forgotten already? And yes, this is my truck. I own her outright, and I love her. You will too, once you get to know her. I know she's not the most fuel-efficient vehicle, but we've been through a lot together, and she can do things that a hybrid just can't do."

"Well then, I can see that this is a discussion we will need to continue at a later time. Come on, let's grab a table."

Alex grabbed him by the hand, and led him into the restaurant. The touch of his hand surprised Nephi, but he liked it. The restaurant wasn't very busy yet, and the host seated them right away.

The host left menus while they waited for the server. "Everything is good here," explained Alex, "but my personal favorite is the stuffed avocados. They are to die for."

Nephi looked over the menu. It was one of those menus that is so large, that you have a hard time deciding what to eat. You want to try a bit of everything, but have to force yourself to choose. He always loved Fajitas, and the seafood enchiladas sounded amazing, but the stuffed avocados that Alex recommended also looked good.

The server arrived at the table with water. "Hi, my name is Gabby and I will be your server tonight. What can I get you to drink?"

"I'll have a glass of merlot," said Alex.

"Water is good for me," added Nephi.

"Very good," she replied. "Are you ready to order, or would you like more time with the menu?"

"I think we need more time to decide on entrees," said Alex, "but please bring us some fresh guacamole with the chips and salsa."

Gabby nodded and walked back toward the kitchen. Nephi made up his mind, and laid the menu on the table.

"Well, what did you decide?" asked Alex

"I'll try the seafood stuffed avocado."

"Excellent choice. You won't be disappointed. I'm going with the veggie stuffed avocado myself."

Gabby soon returned with chips and salsa, and Alex's glass of merlot. Someone from the kitchen was with her, and he prepared the guacamole in front of them at the table. He cut the avocados, and scooped them out of the shell. He then mixed them with pico de gallo and seasoning. Nephi had never seen guacamole made, and he enjoyed it. Gabby took their order, and removed the menus, leaving them alone to talk.

"Ok," said Nephi, "so you have to tell me the deal with the bears and wolves and such in the Snuzzle profiles. They have me thoroughly confused."

Alex chuckled. "Well, you know how in high school, kids like to label each other. You have jocks, nerds, goths, and on and on. Each of them has a stereotype. When you get to know people, you see that they don't actually fit the stereotype, but it carries on, anyway?"

"Yes, I totally get that," said Nephi.

"Well, it's kind of the same thing. You have jocks, which are your fit, athletic types, who are into sports. They usually wear the jersey of their favorite sportsball team, and they pride themselves on the fact that you would never guess they are gay. Then you have your bears, big guys with beards and body hair. They look tough, but they are mostly big cuddly teddy bears. You have your twinks, skinny young effeminate guys with little body hair. Then you have show queens, who are super into show tunes and …"

"And what about wolves?" asked Nephi. "Is that like a bear, or something else entirely?

"Please keep in mind that these are stereotypes, and you shouldn't really put stock into it. You should know that humans are complicated, and don't fit into a simple bucket," said Alex.

Nephi nodded.

"Okay," continued Alex, "wolves are only like bears in the sense that they have body hair, but they are mysterious and well, not as cuddly. The list goes on and on. Circuit boys are muscular guys, who wax everywhere, and I mean everywhere. They like to hit the clubs. Oh, and I almost forgot about daddies. A daddy is an older guy, usually with gray hair. There are also daddy chasers. That one is self-explanatory. There are probably dozens of other buckets and stereotypes, but you will just have to learn the rest on your own. It's not like anyone fits a strict stereotype, anyway."

"Wow," said Nephi. "I'm really getting an education here. I can't thank you enough for filling me in. Maybe I won't feel so lost while I'm roaming around Snuzzle. How would you categorize me?"

"You're really putting me on the spot, aren't you?" asked Alex. "Well, let's see. You definitely seem twink-ish but you are getting close to aging out of that bucket. I don't know you very well yet, but if I had to guess, I would say you are a show queen."

"You're good," said Nephi. "I do love my show tunes. I can't get enough of Rent, and I could sing the full score of Dreamgirls all day long."

"What can I say? I am good at judging people based on nothing but their appearance and mannerisms. I'm just that shallow. It's a gift. That's all that matters anyway, right?" laughed Alex.

Nephi laughed. "Okay, so what about you? I'm digging your beard. Are you some sort of cross between a circuit boy and a bear? A wolf maybe?"

"I'm not nearly mysterious enough to be a wolf, and I can tell you I'm most certainly not a circuit boy. Clubbing isn't my thing, and I wouldn't be caught dead waxing downstairs. Mind you, I'm always well groomed, but waxing? Can you say ouch? No thanks, sister," said Alex. "Bears are typically bigger than I am, though I do like to cuddle. I really hate these stereotypes, but if I am forced into a label, some might call me an otter."

"An otter?" asked Nephi. "I haven't heard that one yet. What on earth is an otter?"

"You can think of it as a skinny ass bear with muscles," replied Alex.

"Language!" protested Nephi. "I'm not kidding when I say it offends me. Please don't use that language around me."

"Sorry, man. I forgot. I told you I can't make any guarantees. Cussing really is half my charm. At least half."

"Okay, so what should this show queen discuss next with the handsome otter across the table?" asked Nephi.

"First, let's eat," he replied, as their food arrived from the kitchen. Nephi was so enthralled in their conversation, that he hadn't even tried the fresh guacamole. He ate a couple of chips with guac before starting in on the stuffed avocado.

The fresh cilantro in the guacamole made it pop in his mouth. It tasted like heaven. He then took a forkful of stuffed avocado. They filled it with seafood and cheese, and then breaded and fried it. The bright green color contrasted nicely with the white filling. The way the seafood and cheese blended with the rich texture of the avocado delighted his mouth in a way he didn't expect. It was really amazing. He had been enjoying the conversation, but he now couldn't get his mind off the food. It was new and wonderful.

Alex must have noticed the mix of disbelief and satisfaction on his face. He grinned from ear to ear. "It's good, right?" he asked.

"I mean, you said I wouldn't be disappointed, which is typically a set up for disappointment, so I tempered my expectations, but you are right - this is amazing," said Nephi.

"If you think this is good, you should try my food. I'll have to cook for you sometime."

"I would love that. Just name the place and time, and I'll be there. I can't wait."

The conversation fell off a bit while they enjoyed the meal. Nephi savored every bite. The avocado was more filling than expected, and he was full before he could finish it. Pushing the plate aside, he asked Alex about what type of guy to look for.

"Well, that's up to you," said Alex. "What do you like in a guy? What type of person would you like to date?"

"I really don't know. I'm new to this, and I've never been in a relationship, but I kind of think I'm into otters," he said, a longing look in his eyes.

"No, no, no, no," said Alex. "Don't get any ideas. I already told you I'm not a babysitter. I'm not going to break in a fresh, baby gay. I'll help you learn the ropes so you know what's what, but you and I can't happen."

"Understood," said Nephi. "I get the friends thing, and I know it's a good idea. How do I go about meeting someone? Do you think I'll have any luck on Snuzzle?"

"I'm new to Snuzzle myself and I really hope that it works for both of us. Outside of that, you can hit the clubs and bars, if you're into that scene."

"I don't really think that is my thing. I don't drink, and I'm not much of a dancer, unless you want a good laugh," said Nephi.

"You could volunteer at the Pride Center and get involved in community events. That's a great way to meet people. A few times a year, there is a speed dating event that's good for entertainment, if nothing else," said Alex. "There's really no magic bullet. If there was, I wouldn't be single myself."

"Thanks," replied Nephi. "That gives me some good ideas to go on. I hadn't thought about volunteering. That's a good suggestion. Hopefully I'll have luck on Snuzzle too."

With dinner finished, Alex asked for separate checks. Nephi protested, offering to pay for dinner. Alex reminded him that this wasn't a date. Nephi agreed, and they paid separate checks and walked out together.

"I'm really enjoying our conversation," said Nephi. "Would you like to sit in my truck for a while and chat?"

"We still need to have that conversation about your truck sometime, and I'm not even sure I could climb up into that thing, but I would love to chat more. Let's sit in my car," proposed Alex.

"Works for me," replied Nephi, following Alex across the parking lot to a silver Toyota Prius.

"It certainly is more fuel efficient than my truck," noted Nephi as they got in.

"Tell me more about you," Alex said. "Other than show tunes, what kind of music do you like?"

"I like a bit of everything. I like P!nk, and I am crazy for Christina Aguilera. She's a Goddess. Honestly though, my favorite singer was also my first crush. Tommy Page," said Nephi, his eyes gazing off in the distance.

"I'm sorry, I don't even know who that is. Is he new?"

"No," replied Nephi. "He's been around since the 80s. He is the most beautiful human I have ever seen in my life. Great style, perfect hair, and dreamy eyes. Not to mention, the voice of an angel. It broke my heart to read that he passed away. It devastated me."

"I am very sorry to hear that," said Alex. "Sometimes losing a celebrity almost feels like losing family."

"It truly felt that way. He has been a part of my life for as long as I can remember. His songs connect with me, and have become a part of me. The lyrics feel so real when he sings. It felt like he was my friend. I guess he still is. When I was a kid, my mom took me to a charity benefit concert where he performed. I promise you, I was screaming louder than every last one of the teenage girls there."

"Tell me more about his music. What genre is it, and what does he sing about?"

"His style is mostly pop with some synth, especially in his earlier stuff. He has some amazing dance tunes as well. He's a true romantic, and wrote incredible love songs. He also wrote songs about places, and the memories connected to them, like a street, or a sunset in Africa. What he created is more than music, it's art. One of the last things he recorded was a remake of one of his older songs called "I break down." It is slower than the original, and so beautiful. It's about putting up a front of strength in order to be there for someone else, but dealing with your own demons and weaknesses beneath it all, and breaking down. I feel like that sometimes, and listening to the song makes me feel better. His first album is my favorite. For the life of me, I can't understand why it didn't get more radio play. My favorite song, "A Shoulder to Cry On" is on that album. I connected with Tommy the first time I heard it. Do you mind if I play you a few songs from the album?"

"I would love to hear it. Do you have it with you now?"

"I have all of his songs on my phone," Nephi proudly declared. He proceeded to play songs for Alex. He started with "A Zillion Kisses." Alex was digging it, and dancing as best as he could while seated in the car.

"Are you serious? I can't believe he recorded this in the 80s. It's great. This would still play well in the club. This song is brilliant."

Next, Nephi played "A Shoulder to Cry On," and sang along with Tommy.

"Nephi, you have a beautiful voice. Are you sure that call center manager is your calling? I can see why you like this song. It's sweet."

"Thanks," said Nephi. "You are too kind. I love to sing, but I don't have what it takes to make it my day job."

"Well it's better than I could do. I am completely tone-deaf and can't sing worth a da… worth a lick," replied Alex.

"Thanks for catching the swear. Okay, I have to sing you one more," said Nephi. He played "Turning Me On" from Tommy Page's first album. The synth charged rhythm had Alex smiling and laughing right off the bat. Nephi really got into it as he sang along, pretending to hold a microphone, dancing with his hands, and gyrating his hips as best as he could in the seat of a car. Nephi was seriously into it, and Alex couldn't contain his laughter, doubled over in the driver's seat. The song ended and Nephi took a bow.

"You are telling me that this is your favorite artist, and you are just now starting to date guys? I mean, come on, if that song isn't the embodiment of being gay, I don't know what is. You should have jumped in the deep end long ago, my queen," said Alex with a laugh.

"Maybe you're right. He has been my favorite artist since I was a kid. A lot of kids teased me, and told me I shouldn't like him because his music was just for girls, but I didn't care. The man's voice is beautiful," insisted Nephi. "Okay, enough about my obsession. What kind of music are you into?"

"Music is my life. I listen to many genres depending on my mood. Music gets me through the tough times, and provides a soundtrack for the good times. I really can't think of words to express how important it is to me," he replied.

"Tell me about some of your favorite artists and songs."

"I'm a big fan of many of your fellow Mormons and ex-Mormons. Neon Trees, Imagine Dragons, Panic! At the Disco, The Killers, and Arcade Fire are all incredible. Lately I have been on a talented ladies kick. Lucius, Kitten, and Muna have been rocking my world. I've also been grooving on NF lately. Like I said, my taste is kind of all over the place."

"To be honest, I haven't heard of most of those bands, but I would love to listen to them together with you. Who are your favorites?" asked Nephi.

"That's not fair," replied Alex. "It's like trying to choose your favorite child. You just can't. I have always enjoyed Counting Crows, the lyrics are real, and I never get tired of listening to Blue October. Their music is amazing, and I don't think there's a band that gives a better live performance. It is a life-changing experience. Most of all, I love them because their music literally saved my life.

There was a point where I found myself in a deep depression. I was in complete despair, not knowing what to do. I heard the song "Into the Ocean," and it just clicked with my soul. I was like "what is this?" because I had heard nothing like it before. I related to it. I bought all of their albums, and binged. I wasn't just listening, I was breathing it all in. It told the story of my depression and pain. Feeling the real connection in that music made me feel like I wasn't alone, and helped pull me out of it. And their newer stuff just blows my mind."

"Sounds to me like Blue October is your favorite child,"

said Nephi, a smirk on his face.

"You might be right," Alex laughed. "Sorry Counting Crows and Muna, you're not the favorite, but don't worry, there is plenty of love in papa's heart to go around."

"I haven't heard Blue October before. Why don't you play some for me?"

Alex opened the music streaming app on his phone, and started the Blue October playlist. The first song on the list was "Fear". Nephi loved the song and its message. It made him feel strong, like he could face the pressure he was feeling from all sides.

"Thanks for playing that," he said, "it gave me the chills in a good way. Let me hear more."

Alex continued the playlist. "Into the Ocean" was next, followed by "I Hope You're Happy". That one reminded Nephi of Stacy.

"Alright, it's getting late and we probably better get going. I just want to play one more," said Alex. "This is another one that got me through a tough time."

Alex played "Should be Loved," and Nephi was mesmerized. "I love this," he said. "I need to check this band out."

"Okay," replied Alex, "but be careful. As one so sensitive to language, if you listen to Blue October too much, your ears might burn off."

"Thanks for the heads up, and for a wonderful evening. I have enjoyed it more than you know. When can we meet up again? Are you open tomorrow?"

"Tomorrow I have a thing, but text me and we'll set something up. Be safe going home, and good luck with Snuzzle," said Alex.

Nephi leaned over and hugged Alex across the seat, and then walked back to his truck and drove home. He couldn't remember ever having a conversation that made him feel so good. Lonely was all he had known for so long, and now he didn't feel so isolated. He was refreshed and ready to pull back the covers, and explore this new world of people like him.

CHAPTER 9

The positive energy from the evening with Alex carried over to Nephi's work life. Outwardly, Nephi was already happy, always smiling. His new positive outlook spread his outward smile through his body, making it more than a cosmetic decoration.

His cheery disposition radiated from his core, and became contagious. People responded differently to him. Monica grew genuinely appreciative of his interest, and less sarcastic, and Steve seemed friendlier. Even Brock and Angela appeared to exhibit more discretion, at least when Nephi was around.

Nephi wasn't sure if the people around him were different, or if the change was all in his perception. He didn't know if it even mattered, but he found that the more he accepted himself, the more he felt in harmony with those around him. The change showed in his team's numbers, too. Over the next two weeks, 'Time to Answer', 'Abandon Rate', and 'Call Handling Time' steadily improved. Monitor scores were up, and his team needed fewer coaching sessions.

At church, things were different since Nephi had no calling. He had a lot more time to himself on Sunday, with his meeting load cut in half, and despite the way they handled it, he enjoyed Gospel Principles class. Somehow, discussions on basic gospel topics were refreshing.

Outside of work and church, Alex, Stacy, and Snuzzle kept Nephi plenty busy. He continued his weekly Friday lunches with Stacy, filling her in on everything in his life, and listening to her talk about Roger and the kids. He texted Alex nearly every day, and talked to him on the phone for about an hour several times per week. They hadn't met again in person since Los Cucos, but their friendship grew through their chats. They updated each other on Snuzzle connections, and shared advice.

Snuzzle had made three connections for Nephi, and he had been chatting with each of them. Gary worked as an accountant at a consulting firm in Provo. Brent was a salesperson for a medical device company in Draper, and Kevin wrote software for a video game startup in Salt Lake. All of them seemed nice so far, and he enjoyed talking with them. He wanted to give dating another go, but was nervous. He was up front with all of them about being inexperienced, and wanting to take it slow, which hadn't scared any of them off just yet.

After work on the Thursday before Halloween, Nephi got a Snuzzle message from Kevin.

"What r ur plans on Sat?"

"No big plans. You?"

"Wanna meet 4 coffee?"

"I'd love to meet, but I don't drink coffee."

"U can have cocoa. Java Springs Eternal on 33rd at 10am?"

"Sounds good. See you there."

It was all set. A date. The first real date since the Evan debacle. Despite a touch of anxiety, Nephi felt ready. He was excited to meet a guy he might have a real relationship with, and hoped it would go better than last time.

After Nephi's regular Saturday morning routine, he gassed up the truck, and directed it toward Salt Lake. He took I-15 through American Fork and Lehi, and then over the Point of the Mountain. Over the past few weeks, he had made that drive more times than in the previous year combined. The Point of the Mountain is an invisible barrier. People who live in Utah County rarely drive north into Salt Lake County, and those in Salt Lake County almost never travel south of the Point of the Mountain. Not that the distance is far, it is more of an ideological boundary, a mental schism between two worlds.

When speaking of going to Salt Lake, those in Happy Valley, say that they are going "up north" as if Salt Lake is some far-off distant land. If a person from Salt Lake must go to Provo for some reason, they just don't speak of it. Separated by mere miles, they are worlds apart, with different politics and ways of living.

Nephi made his way through the suburbs south of Salt Lake, taking the 33rd South exit, and heading west toward State Street, where he found Java Springs Eternal. Having never been inside a coffee shop before, it felt strange, somehow sinful. He walked through the doors and scanned the room for Kevin, hoping to recognize him from the Snuzzle profile picture.

Not recognizing anyone, he took a seat at an empty table and waited. Five minutes passed, and then ten, with no sign of Kevin. Nephi started to worry, wondering if Kevin stood him up. He pulled out his phone to message Kevin when he heard a bell ring, as someone walked in.

Casting his gaze toward the door, Nephi saw a man. He was younger than Nephi, with brown hair, and brown eyes. Nephi recognized him from the Snuzzle photo. It was Kevin. Tall, thin, and handsome, with smooth skin and no facial hair, he appeared to fit the twink stereotype, as far as Nephi understood it. If it weren't for their difference in hair and eye color, Nephi might as well be staring in a mirror. He waved to get Kevin's attention. Kevin smiled and made his way to the table where Nephi sat.

"Nephi, it's good to meet you in person," he said. "I'm glad to see that you look just like your picture. Shall we grab a coffee?"

They walked to the counter. "I'll have a grosso caramel frappuccino with extra caramel," said Kevin. "And whatever he wants," he continued, pointing at Nephi.

"I want a hot chocolate with whipped cream, please."

"Ok, would you like piccolo, medio, or grosso?" asked the barista behind the counter.

"I'm sorry, I don't know what that means."

"She is asking what size you want," Kevin clarified. "Piccolo is the smallest size, then medio. Grosso is the largest cup size."

"I see, then I guess I'll have a medio hot chocolate with whipped cream."

Kevin paid for both of them, and Nephi watched as the barista made the hot cocoa. She put milk into a machine that steamed it, and combined it with the chocolate in a cup. It left a pattern of milk at the top of the cocoa in the shape of a leaf. A smile of amazement came to Nephi's face.

"That's incredible! How do they do that?" he wondered aloud.

Kevin laughed at Nephi's excitement over such a small, everyday thing. Nephi almost hated to see them top it off with whipped cream, covering the milky leaf.

With drinks in hand, they returned to the table to chat. Seated, they sipped while staring into each other's eyes. The hot chocolate was rich and creamy, not like the powder packet cocoa Nephi was used to.

"A damn fine cup of coffee," blurted out Kevin. "How's the cocoa?"

"Just about the best I have ever had. I'm really impressed. There is something you should know about me though. Swearing offends me, and I would appreciate it if you refrain from saying cuss words around me."

"Wait, are you for real? You're offended by the word "damn"? You sound just like those hyper-sensitive Mormons," replied Kevin.

"I don't mean to be oversensitive, but I am Mormon, and the words are offensive to me. I am just trying to be honest and up front with you."

"I see. Would it make you feel better if I call it a darn fine cup of coffee, or a dang fine cup of coffee?"

"Yes, I feel a lot better about that. It says the same thing without being offensive."

"Give me a break, man. You Mormons and your fake cuss words. Do you really think God gets angry if you say damn but darn is perfectly okay? Or that saying hell is bad but heck is fine? All day long, I hear Mormons say things like 'That's a bunch of bull shiz' or 'no effin way, dude' or 'Judy is such a witch' or 'Bob is a total A-Hole'. Are you trying to tell me that God cares more about the actual word than the intent? From where I'm sitting, one doesn't sound any different from the other, and if you are going to say it, you might as well just say the real thing."

At this point, Kevin was in full rant mode, and Nephi didn't dare interrupt. He thought it best to just let him finish. He carried on about "fetch" and "flippin", "eff that" and "shiz". It was true that a lot of Mormons liked to swear without really swearing. Nephi was taken back by Kevin's rant, but also somewhat amused.

"I'm sorry, Nephi, but if you say 'son of a bishop' or 'what the shiz', it does not make you a 'Bad-A', it makes you a dumbass. I really don't see that there is a damn bit of difference between the real swears and the fake ones, and I don't imagine that your God does either."

"I think you are probably right," Nephi chuckled. "I don't use fake swear words, or real ones. I mean, I suppose I have been known to say heck and darn every now and again, but those other ones just sound ridiculous. Swearing offends me just the same. Can you hold back when you are around me?"

"I don't know, man. I mean, it's part of my personality and shit. I am trying to figure you out. You're gay and you're looking to have a relationship, but you are also Mormon, and offended by cussing. Explain that to me. Where do you draw the line? Because I'm not sure if you know this, but you can't get too far as a gay man if you follow the Mormon rules."

"I hate trying to explain this all the time. I know it makes little sense to you, but the Mormon part of me is as real as the gay part of me. Both of them are important to me. I have always tried my hardest to be a good Mormon, and now I am exploring my gay side. I am starting to date, and trying to figure it out. I'm hoping you can help me do that, and I would appreciate it if you can hold back on the swearing while you do it."

"Hold on, I'm still trying to understand. Let's say that we date. I understand you want to take it slow, but hypothetically, say we really hit it off, and we have been dating for three months, and want to take it to the next level. Since all gay sex is a sin in Mormonland, where do we take it? I have heard of BYU students who are into insertion with no movement. They call it soaking, or marinating, or something like that. They actually believe that God is okay with that if they don't get off. I've also heard of them saying things like 'oral is moral'. Will you try to justify yourself like that? Because I'm pretty sure the church isn't okay with that either."

"No," replied Nephi, "I have heard that type of thing too. Soaking and oral are obviously just as sinful as going all the way. I know the church will see gay sex as a sin no matter what, but I want to hold myself to the same standard as straight church members. By that, I mean only kissing before marriage - no sex until after marriage."

Kevin started laughing in disbelief, shaking his head as he shot Nephi a look that said he couldn't believe what he was hearing.

"What's so funny?" asked Nephi. "Why can't I follow the same rules as everyone else? It only seems fair."

"I find it funny that the only Mormon I have every met who seems to want to follow all the rules, is gay. As far as why you can't follow the rules just like everyone else, that isn't a question for me. You should ask the church. You sound perfectly reasonable. The problem is that the church doesn't see it that way. Even if you wait until after marriage, sex for you is a sin. The church won't even recognize your marriage. And while a breeder couple can have sex before marriage, and then get married and "repent" to be in good standing with the church, the only way you can "repent" will be to deny who you are, get a divorce, and never have sex again. If fair is what you are looking for, Nephi, I suggest you look somewhere other than the Mormon Church."

Kevin's words hit Nephi like a punch to the gut. Nephi already knew the truth in what he said, but he was in denial because he didn't want to believe it.

"You're right," said Nephi. "I know you're right but despite all of that, I want to wait until marriage. That has been my plan all of my life, and I don't see it changing, even if it doesn't make sense to anyone but me."

"Ok, I get it, but I need to be honest with you, too. I'm not one who will just jump into marriage. I have to date a guy for a couple of years, and then live with him for several more before I can consider making a permanent commitment. I'm not willing to wait until marriage, not for anyone. Right now, I am looking for a serious relationship, and you are clearly not what I am looking for. You seem like a nice enough guy, and I hope you find what you are looking for, but I'm not it, and it's probably best if we don't waste each other's time."

"I can't say I'm not disappointed," replied Nephi, "but I appreciate your honesty, and I have enjoyed meeting you, even if it gave me a reality check. You are a handsome guy. I'm sure you won't be on the market for long."

They finished their drinks, and wished each other well. Nephi got back in his truck and turned it back down south. As he drove, he wondered if he would ever find someone willing to wait for him. He didn't want to waste his own time, or anyone else's, so he figured he owed Gary and Brent a very frank conversation about what he was looking for. He worried about rejection, but he had to be himself, and he wouldn't compromise his values.

The stereo in Nephi's truck had a cassette tape deck, and Nephi still had a case full of cassette tapes. A Tommy Page cassette was already in the stereo. Nephi turned it up loud and sang along the entire way home. It helped him clear his head and gain perspective. By the time he arrived home, he felt strong.

He sent messages to both Brent and Gary, letting them know that he is both gay and Mormon, and that both parts of him are equally important. He informed them of his intention to wait until marriage to make love, and his intention to continue attending church, and to observe the word of wisdom, abstaining from alcohol and coffee. "While I understand if this is too much for you to handle," he wrote, "I must be true to myself and who I am. I hope you are open to continuing our relationship, but no hard feelings if you're not." After sending the messages, Nephi made soup for lunch, and then called Alex so he could share the details of his date with Kevin before Alex's shift at the restaurant.

Nephi recounted every detail, while Alex listened patiently. He told of Kevin's critique of fake Mormon swearing, and of his own realization that the LDS standards of chastity were a tough sell in the gay community.

He wondered aloud if he could ever find someone willing to pursue a relationship with him, given his commitment to obeying the commandments of God. After listening to Nephi ramble on about his romantic pursuits, including the messages he just sent Brent and Gary, Alex thought carefully before replying.

"Nephi, I'm not sure what to tell you. To be honest, I'm not sure if you will find someone willing to go along with your fantasy of blending two worlds that don't mesh. It's like trying to mix water with oil. They both stand fine on their own, but no matter how hard you try, they remain separate. Believe me, I don't fault you for trying. I understand that you are who you are. I just worry that you are setting yourself up for disappointment. I mean, Kevin has a point. Even if you are perfect, and never drink alcohol or coffee, and you are kind and generous - even if you are perfectly honest, and even if you practice abstinence until marriage, you will still be a sinner in the eyes of the church. The same rules that apply to straight Mormons, don't apply to you. You are gay, and their rules for you are different. The sooner you come to grips with that, the better."

Nephi sat in silence while Alex's words sunk in. There had to be a way to make it work. Surely, loving Heavenly Parents would not create him into an existence destined for sadness. Certainly, they would not apply a different standard to their straight children. Nephi believed that they loved him just as much as all of their children. He believed that they created him for a purpose, and that they wanted him to be happy. In the deepest depths of his soul, he believed that if he kept the commandments, the blessings for him would be the same as those afforded to his straight counterparts. It is the only thing that made sense. Loving eternal beings, the parents of his soul, would surely be fair.

"Nephi?" asked Alex. "Are you still there? Sorry to lay something so heavy on you. I'm just trying to help."

"I know you are, and I appreciate the advice. I have been doing a lot of thinking lately, and there are things that I need to figure out on my own. But hey, there is something else I want to ask you. Thursday is Halloween, and my ward is doing a Trunk or Treat for the kids. We all park our cars in the church parking lot and decorate our trunks for Halloween. The kids go from car to car for candy. There is a chili cook off and games. It's fun. Will you come with me? We can dress up."

"I don't know about that. Me and church activities don't go well together. I doubt they'd welcome me. You go ahead. You can call me afterward, and let me know how it went. Besides, I don't have a costume."

"Don't worry about that. I have a closet full of them. Please come. You'll be my guest, and I don't really care what anyone else thinks. You can even make some chili for the cook off."

"Well, I do make a mean black bean chili. I guess I can come, but you better not leave my side the whole time. It's torture being alone with church people."

"Don't worry. I won't leave you alone. I'll text you my address. Meet me at my apartment at 5:00, and we'll get your costume sorted before we head over to the church."

"Sounds good," replied Alex. "It will be an interesting night."

Alex had to get ready for work, so they said their goodbyes. Nephi's next call was to Stacy. He filled her in on all the developments in his life. While they were talking, he received a message from Gary, who thanked him for his honesty, and indicated that he was an ex-Mormon himself so he understood how difficult it can be to find a new normal, but he wasn't up for the drama. Nephi was glad he had Alex and Stacy. He didn't know what he would do without them. Stacy told Nephi all about Sophie and Wyatt's Halloween costumes. Sophie would dress as a princess, and they found a little onesie tiger costume for Wyatt. She texted Nephi a picture, and he found it absolutely adorable. The conversation wound down, and they said goodbye.

Nephi spent the evening reading scriptures and praying, searching for answers from God about his place. When he read, he felt a warm burning inside. He knew that God loved him, and despite his doubt and confusion, he held his convictions, and felt good about his direction.

CHAPTER 10

The next few days went by quickly. Church and dinner with his parents on Sunday, and then into the work week. Despite no progress on the relationship front, and still no reply from Brent, Nephi carried his new found confidence forward. For the first time that he could remember, he knew who he was, and felt comfortable with himself. Accepting all parts of himself, he was happy at work, at church, and in his personal life. Everything was far from perfect, but that didn't matter so much anymore, because he was comfortable in his own skin.

Before he knew it, Thursday arrived. Ever since he was a young boy, Nephi loved Halloween. Although he wasn't into horror movies, he loved the decorations and costumes. Every year at work, they held a costume competition, and Nephi was all in. He won the contest the first three years he worked there, forcing Brower to make a rule that the same person couldn't win two years in a row. When he became a manager, they changed the rules again, making managers ineligible to win. Despite the fact that he had no prospect of a prize, Nephi always had the best costume, and this year was no exception.

The level of detail in the paint on Nephi's face took it to a new level. He painted a perfect Calavera – a Day of the Dead sugar skull. A white paint base coated his entire face. He framed his eyes with black flowers, highlighted with red edges. The web painted on his forehead was home to a small, black spider, and if you looked close enough, you could see its evil grin.

Nephi painted his lips red, the same shade as the trim on the flowers around his eyes, with thin black lines extending onto his cheeks, mimicking the teeth on a skull. His upper cheeks and temples sported green vines, with small flowers budding from the stalk. Both sides of his nose were painted black, with a narrow white crack separating them. He topped it off with a pinstripe suit, and matching fedora. The costume was exquisite.

Knowing that no costume would compare to Nephi's, Mark designated him as the judge for this year's competition. The office was abuzz as clowns, vampires, fairies, princesses, and monsters occupied each cubicle. Speaking with Monica, dressed as a mummy, he learned that Jimmy Haslam won the night shift competition, and the $50 gift card. He dressed as a werewolf, using face paint, a wig, and patches of hair, rather than a mask. It was fantastic, and even rivaled Nephi's costume.

Today, Nephi's rounds expanded beyond his own team area so he could examine the costumes throughout the call center. Judging would not be easy. There were too many good costumes. Brock and Angela dressed as conjoined twins, connected at the hip. Very fitting. Nephi laughed when he saw them, knowing he had been beat. He couldn't very well force them to sit apart, or it would ruin their costume. As he made the rounds, Nephi took pictures of each contestant, and made notes about creativity, effort level, and visual impact.

Mark arrived at the office dressed in jeans with holes in the knees, and a dirty white t-shirt topped with an open flannel shirt. He was wearing gloves with the fingers cut off exposing filthy fingers. His mussed hair sat above a smudged face. Around his neck hung a cardboard sign that read, "Why lie? I need beer money." Nephi was taken back.

"Hey there, Mark, what are you supposed to be?" asked Nephi, afraid of the answer.

"Isn't it obvious? I'm one of those lazy bums that beg on the streets up north."

"Cute," replied Nephi. "I can't even begin to describe the levels on which I find that offensive."

"Don't tell me that you're one of those triggered, snowflake libtards that's offended by everything. Come on, Nephi, where's your sense of humor?"

"Mark, believe me, it takes a lot to offend me. Congratulations, you've managed to do it. And if you find human beings living on the street, struggling to survive, to be humorous, then you may be right, I must not have a sense of humor."

"Come on, Nephi, it's not like that. It's just a Halloween costume. Lighten up."

Nephi managed to muster a half smile. He patted Mark on the shoulder before walking away, returning to his judging duties. He had known Mark for a long time, and had respected him on many levels, but all of that just went out the window. It's funny how you can know someone for so long, but at the same time not really know them at all. It's sad when people give you a glimpse of what lies under their skin, and it leaves a bad taste in your mouth; the taste of disappointment.

Nephi walked the call center, making sure the candy bowl at the end of each aisle was full, and that hot cocoa wasn't running low in the break room. He collected all the data required to choose the winning Halloween costume, and retired to his office to deliberate. After much internal debate, he whittled the list down to three. Each would receive a gift card, $20 for third place, $25 for second, and $50 for first, but who should be the winner?

Paul was a zombie that was nearly good enough to be in a movie. He wore torn pants, and a shredded jacket that exposed a rubber rib cage. He had painted his face white, and fake skin hung from his cheeks. He walked with a convincing limp, dragging his right leg dramatically.

Abram dressed as a very convincing luchador, complete with mask and cape. The royal blue mask had bright orange flames going up the side of the head, and wrapping around the back. The eye holes were accented in shiny gold trim. He wore a muscle shirt, giving his stocky body the appearance of abs, and his blue cape extended almost to the floor. The speedo-covered leotard was a nice touch.

Kara was a porcelain doll, who was truly creepy. With a black and white striped dress that came almost to her knees, and torn thigh-high stockings, she painted her face white with a black streak forming a crack in the center of her forehead. The fake smile painted on her face made the costume. If ever there was a haunted doll, Kara personified it.

The decision was difficult, and Nephi went back and forth, before finalizing his decision. Third place would go to Abram, the fantastic luchador. Second prize belonged to the terrifying zombie, and he awarded the $50 gift card to Kara, the haunted doll from Hades. Nephi enjoyed distributing the prizes, and posting the pictures in the break room for all to see. With work winding down, he couldn't wait for the Trunk or Treat.

Shift change came, and Nephi filled Steve in on the happenings of the day, and wished him luck with the evening shift. He then headed home to give his apartment a once-over before Alex arrived. The place was already spotless, but Nephi wiped down everything in the kitchen, and ran the vacuum over the carpet just to be sure. A few minutes after 5:00, he heard a knock on the door. He half walked, half skipped to the door, and invited Alex in.

"Wow, your costume is incredible," noted Alex. "You really went all out, didn't you?"

"Thank you! Any trouble finding the place?"

"Not at all, I drove right to it. I knew I was in the right place when I saw that ugly truck of yours in the parking lot."

"Hey, careful now, you might hurt my beautiful girl's feelings."

They both laughed and Nephi took Alex's coat and hung it on the rack near the door.

"Welcome to my humble abode," he said. "Have a seat on the couch while I gather your costume options."

Nephi disappeared behind the closet door while Alex examined the small apartment. He found it clean, and well decorated, unlike the apartment of most single men. Nephi emerged from the closet, carrying three hangers, each holding a neatly pressed costume.

"First, we have a pirate," he said, holding a costume out for display, and moving his extended hand from the top of the costume to the bottom and back up again. "What do you think?"

"Definitely no pirates," replied Alex. "I am so over the butt pirate jokes."

"Got it," said Nephi, laying the pirate costume aside. "Next we have a hippie costume. I think it suits you nicely."

Alex shook his head. "I'm just not feeling it. Do we really have to go to this thing? We could just hang out here tonight, and watch something. I see you have quite the Gilmore Girls collection over there. Besides, I'm not really comfortable going to a church."

"Oh, I do love me some Gilmore Girls, but tempting as that is, I already signed us up for the chili competition, and I need to make sure that the young men and the primary kids don't tear apart the decorations. Besides, I love to see all the kids in their costumes. Don't worry, you'll be fine. I'll stay right next to you all night."

"Okay, fine," replied Alex. "What's option number three?"

"Option number three," said Nephi, "is a cowboy. I have some chaps, a button-up western shirt with a leather vest, and a cowboy hat. It's perfect for you."

"I guess it will do. Give it here," said Alex, as he removed his shirt and reached for the costume. Alex was well built, with a fair bit of definition to his biceps, triceps, and chest. Nephi couldn't help but smile and blush watching him change into the costume.

Both ready, Nephi grabbed a bowl of candy, and they headed out the door. Alex offered to drive since the crock pot full of black bean chili was already in his car. Besides, riding in a gas guzzling truck like Nephi's went against his convictions. Nephi directed him the few blocks to the church building.

They pulled into the parking lot, and backed into a parking space along the sidewalk where the children would Trunk or Treat. They walked toward the building. The activities would kick off in the cultural hall, a big room in the church with a basketball court and stage, where they hold ward events. Once at the building entrance, Alex stopped for a moment, and took a deep breath.

Nephi opened the door, and Alex hesitantly followed him through the foyer, into the cultural hall. The large room had a hardwood floor covered in round tables, where people could eat. Several long rectangular tables sat at the front of the room, and people busily placed food on them. Some people brought rolls or cornbread, and others brought chili and toppings. Nephi and Alex made their way to the buffet tables where Nephi placed Alex's crock pot. He took the number 15 sticker from a sheet, and placed it on the crock pot. They provided numbered stickers for people to cast their chili vote.

With the chili in place, they took a seat on the far side of the room near the doors. A few minutes later, Mike and Darla walked in and approached their table. Nephi stood and gave Darla a hug.

"Hi, Mom and Dad," he said. "This is my friend, Alex." He motioned toward Alex, who stood and extended his hand.

"It's a pleasure to meet you," said Alex.

"The pleasure is ours," replied Darla, shaking his hand.

Mike then shook Alex's hand, while giving Nephi a sideway glance. "So we're doing this, are we?" he asked, still staring at Nephi.

"Doing what, Dad? Introducing you to my friend? I'm not sure exactly what is going through your head, but whatever it is, just stop."

The squeal of the microphone signaled them to take a seat. Darla sat next to Nephi, with Mike at her side, as Bishop Thompson started the program.

"I'd like to welcome you all to our annual Trunk or Treat activity and chili cook off," he announced. "Brother Mace will offer the opening prayer, then help yourselves to the food. The young men have set up a spook alley on the stage, and there are activities for the little ones in the back. Please remember to vote for your favorite chili. At 6:30, we will announce the winner of the chili cook off, and move outside for Trunk or Treating."

Brother Mace then took the microphone. He said a prayer

to ask a blessing on the food, and for safety during the activity. By the time he said "Amen," there was already a line at the buffet table.

The adults conversed at the tables while they ate, and the children, decked out in Halloween costumes, ran wild through the gym. The youth of the ward had set up games for them, including bobbing for apples, the spook alley, corn hole, and a fish pond with Halloween themed prizes. Darla made polite conversation with Alex about his work while Mike checked the football score on his phone.

Nephi enjoyed watching the joy on the children's faces as they played. Dressed as super heroes, and their favorite cartoon characters, they were really in their element. He remembered what it was like to be that age, so carefree. At times like this, he wished he could go back, if just for a moment, but that time had long passed.

Nephi stole Alex away from Darla, and they both helped clean tables, while the indoor activities wound down. Before long, it was time to announce the winners of the chili cook off. Bishop Thompson returned to the microphone.

"We had many good entries this year," he said. "More votes were submitted than any year since I was called as Bishop. We will announce the top three chili chefs, and ask each of them to stand as we give them a round of applause. I'm sorry to say that the only prize is bragging rights for the next year. Without further ado, the second runner up in the chili cook off, is number 2, Brother Pike with his white chicken chili."

Brother Pike stood, a proud look on his face, while everyone clapped and cheered. He took a bow, and raised his hands in the air as if he had just brought down the house in a Broadway production.

Bishop Thompson continued, "Our first runner up is chili number 17, a fine chili con carne cooked up by my good wife, Sister Sally Thompson."

Sister Thompson stood and nodded while everyone clapped. Red-faced, she sat down quickly, and the applause died down.

"And the big winner of the Pleasant Grove ninth ward chili cook off is number 15, the delicious black bean chili from Brother Nephi Willard."

Nephi grabbed Alex by the arm and pulled him up. They both stood while everyone clapped.

"I'm honestly not that good of a cook," said Nephi in a loud voice, "and I can't claim any credit for that delicious chili. It was made by my friend, Alex, who is with me tonight. He is the amazing chef."

The clapping slowed and then stopped as the pair sat down. Bishop Thompson invited everyone to move outside for the Trunk or Treat portion of the activity, as whispers spread from table to table, and the children gathered their treat buckets and bags in preparation for the candy.

Nephi grabbed Alex's empty crock pot and washed it out in the kitchen sink on their way outside. He placed it on the floor of the backseat, and retrieved the candy bowl for the kids who were already roaming from car to car, asking for candy. This was always Nephi's favorite part of Halloween. He enjoyed seeing each costume, and loved to see their little faces light up as he placed candy in their bag.

Alex and Nephi chatted while they watched the trick-or-treaters make their way toward the Prius. The night was clear, and the darkness brought cold. Neither of their costumes stood up to the elements, and they shivered. Nephi smiled seeing Alex by his side. In prior years, he was either on his own, or sharing a trunk with his parents. Having a friend next to him somehow made him feel warmer. As the children moved closer, Nephi noticed child after child take candy from the Wilson family car to one side of him, skip the Prius altogether, and proceed to the car on the other side. A perplexed look made its way to Nephi's face as the trend continued.

"I'm not sure what's going on. I've never seen anything like this. I always bring the best candy," said Nephi.

Alex stared at the ground. "I'm sorry, Nephi, it probably

has everything to do with me being here."

"Don't be ridiculous. I'm not sure what is going on, but I'll get to the bottom of it," replied Nephi.

Little Billy Mason was passing by in a superhero costume, holding his dad's hand. The Masons lived next door to Nephi's parents, and he knew Billy well.

"Hi, Billy," he called out. "I've got plenty of candy over here." He held out the bowl, filled to the top with premium brand candy.

Billy started to run toward Nephi before being pulled back by Brother Mason, and redirected to the next car. Brother Mason turned to follow him.

"Hold up, Brother Mason," Nephi said. "What's going on? Why won't you let Billy take candy from me?"

Brother Mason slowly walked over to Nephi. A cowboy hat sat atop his head, covering his growing bald spot. He wore a button-up shirt with suspenders that held up his oversized jeans on his large belly. His ensemble was capped off by the worn cowboy boots on his feet. Unlike Alex, he wasn't wearing a costume.

He walked up to Nephi, and leaned in close. In a low voice, he explained, "Look, Nephi, I like you, I really do. But the thing is, we don't want our kids hanging around you and your faggot friends. We don't need you influencing them, and making them think people like you are normal. They need to know that isn't God's way."

As Brother Mason turned to walk away, Nephi felt pressure build in his toes that gradually made its way to the top of his head. With clenched fists, he forced himself to breathe. He bit his lip, trying not to cry. It didn't work, and tears started flowing down his face. Never in his life had he felt so rejected, and so belittled. He felt like less than a person. Alex embraced him, and he continued crying on his shoulder.

"Come on, let's get out of here," offered Alex. "We can go back to your place and just chill for a while."

Nephi's voice wasn't strong enough to speak, but he

nodded in agreement. As he was getting into the car, he heard someone call his name. "Nephi! Nephi, wait up." Looking around to see who was calling him, he saw a familiar form approaching.

The tall, broad-shouldered figure ran toward him in the dark. As he drew closer, Nephi could make out his well-groomed brown hair, and a sadness in his face. His eyes were red from crying. It was Bradley Hanson, the eighteen-year-old son of Brother Hanson, the ward clerk.

"Bradley, what's wrong?"

He had a hard time getting the words out. Nephi could see that he was shaken. He put his hand on Bradley's shoulder. "Just calm down. Take a moment to compose yourself, and tell me what's going on."

After a few moments, and some deep inhaling followed by stuttered exhales, Bradley had composed himself enough to speak.

"My parents and I had a big fight," he explained. "I turn nineteen in a couple of months and they have been concerned that I am not on a mission, and haven't even started filling out my papers. My dad sat me down, and told me that I need to either turn in my mission papers within the next week, or move out."

"Ouch, that's harsh," said Nephi. "I'm sorry. I served a mission myself, and I can tell you that it is one of the best decisions I ever made, but a mission isn't for everyone. Your dad knows that a mission isn't required for salvation, right?"

"He demands perfection. He always has, and I have never measured up to his standards. But it doesn't end there. You see, I've been hiding a secret from everyone. I'm gay. My dad is the most homophobic person I have ever met. Somehow in the heat of the moment, I found the courage to come out to him. I told him that I will not serve a mission and that I'm gay. He grew so angry. He drew back his fist, and I was sure he was going to kill me. Instead, he directed the punch toward the wall, and put a hole straight through it. I have never heard him yell so loud before. He told me that I am no longer his son, and he kicked me out on the spot. I have nothing but the clothes on my back. I didn't know where else to go."

"Oh, Bradley, I'm so sorry," said Nephi. "Come here."

Bradley collapsed into his arms. Nephi held and consoled him, much like Alex had done for him only moments earlier. Alex, who had listened to the entire exchange, said, "Both of you, get in. Let's head back to Nephi's apartment and figure things out from there."

Bradley climbed in the backseat, next to the bowl of candy, and Nephi rode in the front with Alex. They sat in silence as they traveled the few blocks to Nephi's apartment.

Once inside, Nephi made hot cocoa, and Alex changed out of the cowboy costume before they sat in the kitchen to talk. Now able to speak, Bradley recounted the day's events. In that moment, the thing that Bradley needed most was to be heard, so they just listened. After he finished, Alex and Nephi each gave him a hug.

Alex then looked Bradley directly in the eye, and began to speak. "One thing I have learned is that those we love can cause us the most pain. We expect prejudice and hate from random people, so we are able to shake it off, but we expect more from those we love. We expect better of them. We expect them to love us. Even when we are at our worst, they are the ones who should support us, and when someone we love shows us hatred or rejection, it goes against our expectations, and hurts so much more. Bradley, you didn't deserve what happened today. No one deserves that. I'm sorry it happened, but we will help you move forward."

"I have known your family and worked with your dad in my church calling for a long time," Nephi added. "I am shocked to hear about what happened, but at the same time, I can't say that I'm surprised. Your dad doesn't understand. He is under the flawed impression that being gay is a choice; that you somehow intentionally rejected your straight nature in pursuit of a path he believes to be perverse. He doesn't understand that God made you the way you are. I wish I could snap my fingers and make him understand. I wish I could take away your pain. I can't do that, but you are welcome to stay with me for as long as you need to. You're not alone."

"I really appreciate your support," replied Bradley. "I honestly don't know what I would do if you weren't at the church tonight. I have nowhere else to go. My family hates me."

"I'm sure they don't hate you, and I really hope they come around," said Nephi.

"I wish I shared your faith in Bradley's family," countered Alex, "but I have seen enough hate to know that all people don't have good intentions, or a desire to understand. Some don't have the capacity to feel empathy, and their hearts are filled with hate. I don't know your family, Bradley, and I hope that Nephi is right, and they come around, but prepare yourself in case they don't. It can be a bitter pill to swallow."

"Bradley, the bed is all yours. It has fresh linens and blankets and it's ready for you," offered Nephi.

"No, I can't take your bed. I am fine on the couch."

"I usually fall asleep on the couch while watching TV anyway," Nephi lied. "I insist, you sleep on the bed."

Bradley thanked him, and lay down. Tired from the emotional toll of the day, he fell asleep within minutes.

"Do you really sleep on the couch?" asked Alex.

"No, but I thought he could use a good night's sleep, and I can fall asleep anywhere. It's not a big deal. Thanks for your help tonight, Alex. I don't know what I would have done without you."

"People can be cruel. The more open you are about who you are, the more you will see it. Thanks for inviting me. There was a lot going on tonight, but I'm glad I was here. I better get going now."

Alex hugged Nephi, and headed out the door. Nephi changed and showered to wash off the face paint. Clean and in pajamas, he popped in a Gilmore Girls DVD, and curled up on the couch. Before long, he was asleep.

CHAPTER 11

A new day brought the sun, and a fresh perspective. Nephi awoke to the sound of the alarm on his phone. The glow of the TV, and the soft imitation leather against his face, reminded him that Bradley Hanson was in his bed. He showered, and made a breakfast of scrambled egg whites and toast. Today, he cooked for two.

The smell of breakfast cooking was enough to wake Bradley, who soon joined Nephi at the table. "Thanks again for letting me stay here. Don't worry, I'll get out of your hair before long. I just need to figure out what to do next."

"I am serious when I say that you can stay as long as you need to. It's just me here, and I'm gone most of the time, anyway. What's mine is yours, Bradley. I know what it's like to live in a world where nobody understands you. It's lonely and painful. We can get through it together."

"Thanks. I really appreciate it," replied Bradley. "Thanks for breakfast. My head is much clearer today."

"So what have you been up to since you graduated in the spring? Are you going to school or working?"

"I've been working at my dad's shop, saving money for the mission that he wanted me to go on. I guess I'm not sure where that job stands now. I've spent nearly every day with him since I finished home-school."

Brother Hanson ran an auto body shop on State Street. He inherited the business from his father.

"What are your plans for today? I've got to leave for work in about thirty minutes, but I am happy to give you a ride somewhere if you need it. I get off around 4:00, and I'm available for whatever you need after that."

"Thanks. I don't need a ride this morning. I think I'll walk home to see if this whole thing sticks after everyone has calmed down. At the very least, I can get some of my things. Then I'll go down to the shop to see where I stand with work."

"Do you want me to go with you? If you wait until I get off, I can give you a lift, and then you won't have to face them alone."

"No, thanks. I think I can handle it on my own. Let me get your number. I'll call you and let you know how it goes."

Nephi took Bradley's phone and entered his phone number in the contacts app, and then retrieved a spare key from a hook on the kitchen wall.

"Here, take a key so you can get back into the apartment if you need to. If everything works out, you can give it back to me on Sunday. Text me your number, so I have it, in case I need to get a hold of you."

"Thanks," said Bradley, as he took the key.

"No problem. Help yourself to anything you want in the apartment, and feel free to use the shower, and help yourself to any of my product. Just make yourself at home. I need to go, but I'll talk to you later today."

With that, Nephi headed out the door and drove to work. Halloween turned into a long, emotionally draining day, and he was glad that today was Friday. The prospect of a weekend with nothing to do gave him something to look forward to.

While Nephi worked, Bradley finished breakfast, and enjoyed a nice, long shower. At his house, showers ran on a timer. Sister Hanson managed the schedule, and he only had five minutes. His mother programmed his entire day. She woke him at 6:00 for family prayer and scripture study. 6:30 was time for his personal scripture study. Breakfast was at 7:00, and she assigned him the 7:20 shower slot. The rest of his day was planned to the minute. Being alone in Nephi's apartment with unlimited time to shower was a luxury, and he took the time to enjoy it.

After the shower, he put on yesterday's clothes, because he had nothing else to wear. Now ready, he placed Nephi's key in his pocket, and headed out the door toward home. Last night was the first time Bradley ever slept away from home. He shared a room with two brothers, and it seemed strange waking up in a different place, even if it was only two blocks away. Nerves grew in his belly as he got closer to home. Not knowing what to expect, his mind gravitated to the darkest alternatives, but he forced himself onward.

He opened the front door and walked inside. Sister Hanson was a homemaker and home-school teacher and Bradley knew she would be home with all of his siblings. His father should already be at work.

"Mom?" he called out.

"Bradley!" exclaimed his towheaded, four-year-old sister, Brook, as she ran to him, hugging his leg.

Bradley patted her on the head and told her he was glad to see her. He called out again for his mother.

Moments later, Sister Hanson emerged from the hallway. The plump woman wore a dress and apron. Her graying hair was pulled back in a ponytail. The stern look on her face didn't suggest she had missed Bradley in the least.

"What are you doing here?" she asked matter-of-factly.

"I came to see you. To work through things with you and Dad."

"Are you prepared to repent and give up your perversions?"

"If you are asking if I am somehow magically straight now, then no. I am gay, Mom. It isn't something I chose, it is just the way I am."

"Don't use such language in front of your sister!" she demanded. "If you are not ready to repent, you are not part of this family. Please be on your way."

"Mom, I love you. Please try to understand…"

"Please be on your way!" she reiterated, voice raised.

"Okay, Mom," he replied. "I just need to get a few of my things."

"You don't have any things. Your father and I provided everything for you. You are no longer welcome to it, since you are not part of our family. We will not tolerate your perversion here."

A tear rolling down his cheek, Bradley bent down and kissed Brook on the forehead, and then turned and walked out. He made it a block and a half before breaking down into a sob, and asking God why he allowed such cruelty. With no answer, he continued to walk toward his father's shop.

While he walked, he choked back the tears, and gathered himself. He would speak with his father man to man. By the time he arrived at the shop, he built up his nerve. He entered, and asked to speak with his father privately. Brother Hanson invited Bradley in to his office and closed the door.

"What do you have to say for yourself?" asked Brother Hanson.

"I have come to work."

"Work? Are you ready to repent of your perversion?"

"Dad, being attracted to men does not make me perverse. It is who I am."

"Then you no longer have a job here."

"Please try to understand," he begged.

"You best be on your way."

"Fine, just give me the money from my account, and I will be out of your hair for good."

"What money?"

"The money I have been earning while working in the shop for the past five months. I have almost six thousand dollars saved."

"That money is for your mission, and it is in an account in my name. Unless you serve a mission, it belongs to me. When you come to your senses, repent of your sins, and serve the Lord, it will be waiting for you."

"That's not fair!" cried Bradley. "I worked hard to earn that money. It's mine."

"The Lord doesn't bless sinners, Bradley. Unless you repent, it all belongs to me. And one more thing, hand over your phone. I pay the bill and it is also mine."

Heart broken, Bradley took the phone from his pocket and threw it against the wall, before storming out of the office and away from the shop. Phoneless and coatless, with nowhere else to go, Bradley followed State Street for a mile in the brisk fall air until he arrived back at the apartment. There, he sat, and waited for Nephi to return.

Nephi wrapped things up at work after a routine day, and

headed home. He hadn't received a call or text from Bradley, and wondered how things turned out with his parents. When he arrived home, he walked through the door to find Bradley sitting on the couch, head down, gazing intensely at the floor.

"Bradley, what's going on? Is everything okay?"

He didn't answer, but just continued staring at the floor in silence. Nephi grew concerned and sat next to him on the couch, trying again to get his attention by waving his hands in front of Bradley's face. Silence was the only answer. Not knowing what else to do, Nephi kneeled on the floor, rested his folded arms on the couch, and began to pray aloud.

"Dear Heavenly Father, please bless Bradley with thy Spirit. Please comfort him and help him in his time of…."

Bradley interrupted him mid-sentence. "Don't do that."

"Don't do what?" asked Nephi, looking up at Bradley.

"Don't pray for me. It doesn't work."

"Prayer has always helped me."

"Listen, Nephi, I prayed half the night, and all morning, that I could make things right with my parents. I prayed for guidance and comfort, and to know what to say to them. Today, I spoke to both of them and neither of them acknowledges I am their son. I have nothing but the clothes I am wearing. They took my clothes, my money, my phone, everything.

I have nowhere to go, and no way to take care of myself. Where is God? Why didn't he help me? If he is all knowing and all powerful, and he loves me, then why did he abandon me, and leave me with nothing? I don't want to hear your prayers."

Nephi hugged him. Bradley hugged Nephi back and cried. They stayed that way for several minutes with Bradley's tears flowing freely onto Nephi's shirt, leaving a large wet spot on his shoulder.

Bradley slowly turned his head toward Nephi's and kissed him gently on the lips. It took Nephi by surprise. and confusion spread across his face while they held the kiss for a few brief seconds before Nephi pulled back.

"We can't," said Nephi.

"Because of Alex?"

Nephi laughed. "No, not because of Alex. We're just friends."

"Could have fooled me," replied Bradley, "but if it's not because of Alex, then why?"

"Don't get me wrong, I like you, and I'm honored that you were my first kiss, but I feel kind of weird about our age difference, and how well our families know each other, and all. Plus, with all the emotion of today, it just doesn't feel right."

"Your first kiss, what? You have got to be kidding."

"Well, I kissed my best friend Stacy once, but this is the only time I have kissed a guy."

"It was my first kiss too. What did you think?"

"It was nice," smiled Nephi, "but that's not the point. We should both take our time, and do things for the right reasons."

"You're probably right."

"Like I told you earlier, you are welcome to stay here as long as you need. Don't worry. We'll find you a job, and clothes won't be an issue. My brother Ammon is about your size, and my parents still have a lot of his old clothes at their house. Let's head over there now and get you a few things, and then I'll take you shopping for something new. It will all work out."

Grateful to be in Nephi's apartment instead of on the street, Bradley followed Nephi outside to the truck, and they paid a visit to Mike and Darla. Darla greeted them as they came through the door. Nephi explained that they were there for some of Ammon's old clothes, without going into all the details about Bradley's parents. She gathered up a pair of jeans, a pair of slacks, five shirts, and a coat, and gave them to Bradley, who thanked her and gave her a hug.

The pair then headed to the mall, where Nephi bought Bradley two pairs of slacks, and three polo style shirts. He also bought a button-up shirt, and neck tie that Bradley could use for job interviews. Nephi enjoyed putting together outfits, and had fun shopping. Bradley had never owned anything that didn't come from the thrift shop, and it felt good to have something new, but he was mostly thankful just to have a few things to call his own. After purchasing the clothes, they picked up a prepaid burner phone for Bradley at an electronics store so prospective employers could get in touch with him.

Shopping bags in hand, they climbed back in the truck, stopping at a drive through for dinner on their way home. In the past day, Bradley had lost everything he knew. Before today, he took many things for granted - a roof over his head, clothes on his back, and food on the table. He now felt gratitude for those things, but the thing he appreciated the most was Nephi's friendship.

Back at the apartment, they ate and talked. They talked about family, the church, sexuality, and friends. Twelve years separated them, but they shared a real connection. They grew up in the same ward, and shared similar experiences. They understood each other.

After conversing for three hours, the conversation turned to Bradley's job search.

"Have you thought about what you want to do for work?" asked Nephi.

"I'm worried about that. I don't really have any marketable skills. I mean, I can do a bit of car body work, and general office tasks, but that's about it. I don't even know where to start."

"Tomorrow you can use my laptop to search the classifieds. There are a lot of jobs out there. Restaurants around here are always hiring, and there are several call centers nearby. If you are interested, I can see when the next group is due to start at Brower."

"Thanks for letting me use the laptop, and I would really appreciate it if you check for any positions available at work."

"Ok, I will. Don't worry, you'll find something."

They continued chatting until late. Once again, Nephi slept on the sofa, giving up the bed to Bradley. Completely spent, they dozed off quickly, and slept late into Saturday morning.

Nephi helped Bradley put together a resume, and he searched for jobs online while Nephi ran on the treadmill. Alone in the fitness room, Nephi called both Stacy and Alex to fill them in on the situation, and to get their advice. Stacy encouraged him to continue being there for Bradley, and to show him love and kindness while he figured things out. Alex agreed with that, but also cautioned Nephi against letting him become too dependent. Based on his own experience, he felt that Bradley needed to get a job soon, and learn to support himself.

"The biggest contributor to success as an adult is self-reliance, which you can't develop when you depend on others for everything," he counseled. "Bradley needs all the help he can get now, but he must develop the ability to be independent if he is going to make it, especially with no family behind him."

"I agree that independence is important," replied Nephi, "but genetics alone don't make someone family. His biological parents disowned him, but he still has us – we are his family."

Alex agreed. After catching them up, Nephi returned to the apartment and chatted with Bradley over a bowl of hot tomato soup. The soup warmed them from the inside on a chilly day. Bradley was upset, having a difficult time keeping his mind off of home. Nephi suggested they pray together, but Bradley declined. To get his mind off of things, Nephi introduced him to Gilmore Girls. They laughed and cried together while binge watching the first season until they both fell asleep on the couch.

In the morning, Nephi got ready for church. He invited Bradley, but he didn't want to go. He preferred not to see his family and besides, he was angry at God for failing to answer his prayers, and allowing him to be in this situation. He was also angry that God would send him to a family that would not accept who he was. He stayed at the apartment, and continued his job search, while Nephi went to church.

Nephi received an icy reception at church. People he thought to be friends gave him the cold shoulder. Seeing him with a male friend at the Trunk or Treat activity had apparently set something in motion that he did not anticipate. The rumor mill had churned, spreading disinformation throughout the ward, and the fruits of the campaign were making their way back to Nephi. He sat in the middle of the row next to his parents, and noticed the rest of the pew was vacant. People chose to sit on the hard chairs at the back, rather than on the soft bench next to Nephi.

Brother Baker conducted Sacrament meeting. Today was the first Sunday of November - Fast Sunday. Brother and Sister Hanson sat two pews ahead of the Willard family. Their son Todd sat with the other deacons, ready to pass the Sacrament while their remaining six children sat next to them. After the congregation sang hymns, and partook of the Sacrament, Todd joined his siblings on the bench.

Melanie Jameson, a fourteen-year-old young woman in the ward kicked off testimony meeting talking about choosing uplifting music, books, and movies. Next, Sister Hanson made her way to the pulpit to speak. Nephi wondered if she would mention her son. She spoke on the topic of charity, not the giving to the poor kind of charity, but the charity spoken of by Paul in the Bible, and by the prophet Moroni in the Book of Mormon. She spoke of the kind of charity that embodies kindness and love, like that showed by Jesus Christ when he walked the earth.

She recounted the story from John, chapter eight, where the Pharisees brought to Jesus a woman taken in adultery, and asked him whether they should stone her according to the Law of Moses. He asked for any without sin to cast the first stone. Everyone left, leaving Jesus alone with the adulteress. Jesus told her he did not condemn her, and to go, and sin no more. Sister Hanson offered it as an example of the pure love of Christ - charity. She admonished the congregation to show that same love for others.

Nephi squirmed in his seat as she spoke, in disbelief that she could speak those words with a straight face, after kicking her gay son out on the street penniless, with no place to go. He was still trying to process it when she finished speaking. After she sat down, several other ward members took the stand to bear testimony. Nephi loved Fast and Testimony meeting but he couldn't enjoy it today, his mind preoccupied with Sister

Hanson's hypocrisy.

As Sacrament meeting wound down, Brother Hanson approached the podium. His wrinkled shirt and mussed hair usually distracted Nephi, but today, he didn't even notice them. Instead, he studied the man's face, searching for any evidence of humanity. His stony eyes showed no sign of warmth as he spoke.

"The scriptures tell us that the Lord cannot look upon sin with the least degree of allowance. Think about that, Brothers and Sisters, the least degree. That means that sinners cannot co-exist with God. He must cast them out of his presence. Thankfully, Jesus Christ fills that gap for us, and if we repent, change our ways, and choose righteousness, there is a path back to Him."

"Just as God cannot allow any sin," he continued, "we must shut all sin out of our life. Whenever we become aware of sin, we must shun it, cut it off. God will not look favorably upon us if we allow it to remain. When it comes down to it, we must choose. Like Joshua, we must choose today whom we will serve. We can serve God, or we can serve the devil. If we choose God, we must evict all earthly desire, and perversion from our lives."

He continued the discourse in similar fashion. It became clear to Nephi that Bradley's chances of a happy reunion with his family were slim. He felt bad for him, and racked his brain for anything he might do to rectify the situation. Nothing came to mind.

Brother Hanson finished speaking, and sat down, as the congregation sang the closing hymn, and bowed their heads while Sister Simpson offered the closing prayer.

At the conclusion of the meeting, Nephi moved forward two pews. He felt compelled to say something to Brother Hanson.

"Brother Hanson," he said. "I listened closely to your testimony. I have to say, I'm not sure that kicking your son out on the street is what Heavenly Father had in mind when he said that he can't look upon sin. Your wife made some great points that you might want to go back and study."

"What do you know about Bradley?"

"I assumed he told you. He has been staying with me since you kicked him out."

"You are playing a dangerous game, harboring a runaway boy. Butt out of this, and mind your own business."

"That runaway boy is a man, who is almost nineteen years old, and he didn't run away, you forced him out on the street. Where did you think he would go?"

"You need to stay out of this. Bradley needs to be on his own, so God can humble him unto repentance. Once he abandons his perversions, and decides to serve a mission, he can come back home."

"Exactly what do you expect him to repent of? He has done nothing wrong. You can't change who he is. You can't pray the gay away, or turn him straight with the power of the priesthood. That has never worked, and it never will. If that is what you are holding out for, you are only setting yourself up for disappointment. God created Bradley the way he is – an intelligent, kind, wonderful, gay man. Why don't you try to accept your son for who he is, and love him just because he is your son?"

"As long as he continues in sin, he is not my son, and I will not love a sinner, especially one like him."

Realizing that banging his head against a wall would be more productive, Nephi excused himself. Not in the mood for gospel discussion, he walked right past the Gospel Principles room, and out the door. He found Bradley at home, browsing classified ads.

"Any luck?" he asked.

"There are a couple of fast food jobs nearby, and a call center customer service job. Most of the jobs are too far away without a car."

"You can also check the bus schedules and find something near a stop on the bus route, or work somewhere within walking distance, and save money for a car. It will take some time, but you can do it. You don't need to worry about covering rent while you're with me."

"That's a good point, and I really appreciate that. How was church?"

"You know, same old routine. Nothing exciting," replied Nephi, not wanting to upset him with the ugly details.

"I guess I didn't miss much."

"Believe me, today you didn't miss anything. Just know that you are always welcome to come with me, and if you aren't feeling it with your family there, you can always attend the singles ward that meets at noon. I'll go with you if you want."

"Thanks, Nephi, but I've had my fill of church for a lifetime, and I think a Mormon singles ward would feel awkward for me as a gay man. I don't see myself going back."

"I get it, but if you ever change your mind, you have a place next to me. Do you have any plans for the rest of the day?"

The question made Bradley laugh out loud. "Where would I go?" he asked. "This apartment is my world right now."

"Then let's expand your world view. We have dinner with my family at 6:00. Every Fast Sunday, we have a get together with the whole crew."

"I can't say that it makes me feel good seeing your loving, accepting parents. I can't help but contrast them to mine, but I've never been one to turn down Darla's cooking," replied Bradley.

"Honestly, my relationship with them hasn't been the same since I came out, especially my dad, but your family takes it to an absurd level, and I can't tell you how sorry I am about that. In this life, you have to accept kindness where you can find it. As you know, it isn't an abundant resource."

"Ok, I'm in. You talked me into it."

"Perfect. Feel free to ignore anything Jacob says. He has nothing on your parents, but he suffers from a nasty case of acute homophobia."

"Thanks for the notice."

Nephi changed out of his church clothes, and the two of them binged half of Gilmore Girls, season two, before it was time to head over to Mike and Darla's place for dinner.

The entire Willard clan was already at the house when Nephi arrived with Bradley in tow. Dallin, Sophie, and Crystal clamored with delight when he came through the door, and stampeded down the stairs to attack him with hugs.

Nephi hugged them back, and asked how they were doing. That led to a ten minute conversation about the pandas at the zoo, the latest crime fighting adventures of the Hero Battalion, and everything he ever wanted to know about raising a baby doll.

Nephi sent them downstairs to play, while he and Bradley proceeded into the kitchen, where they found Darla, Chelsea, Rob, and Camille.

He greeted them and introduced his siblings-in-law to Bradley.

"You two sure have been hanging out a lot, lately," observed Darla.

"Well," said Nephi, "Bradley will be staying with me for a while."

"Oh, you two are living together? Are you like, a thing?" asked Rob.

"No, it's not like that," replied Bradley. "I came out to my parents, and they kicked me out of the house. I had nowhere else to go, and Nephi was kind enough to take me in."

"Oh, no, they didn't," sighed Darla. "I knew your mother was uptight, and your father can be overbearing, but I never pegged them for the kind that would cast out a child."

"Apparently, they are that kind," whispered Bradley, as his gaze fell to the floor.

"You are always welcome here," said Darla, stepping forward to give Bradley a hug.

Bradley hadn't realized how much he needed a hug from a mother, even if she wasn't his own. A tear streamed down his check as he embraced her.

"Nephi, why don't you take Bradley downstairs to the family room? Dad is down there with Jacob, Ammon, and Tiffany. They are having a little family chat while this bunch helps me with dinner. Nephi noticed the serving bowls full of meat, chili, green onions, shredded cheese, tomatoes and sour cream.

"Potato bar?" he asked.

"I thought we could do both potatoes and tacos tonight. The baked potatoes are in the oven, and I am warming tortillas in the microwave," replied Darla. "It should be ready in about ten minutes."

Nephi and Bradley descended the stairs to the family room, where they found Mike chatting with the other Willard kids.

"Bradley is with you again, huh?" said Mike. "Are we doing this now? Are you guys an item?"

Before Nephi could speak, Jacob interjected, "Dad tells us you brought a date to the Trunk or Treat, and now you bring another one to family dinner? What's going on? Are you going full blown gay?"

"First," replied Nephi, "I'm not sure what full blown gay even means. You already know that I am gay, and as far as I know, there is no tool to measure how gay someone is. Second, I don't know why the four of you feel you need to have a family meeting about my relationship status, but it is none of your business."

"We are just concerned about you," added Tiffany.

"You don't need to be," said Nephi. "Whatever all of this is," he continued while moving his hands in a circle, "you need to stop. Just stop."

"You all have the wrong idea," said Bradley. "Nephi and Alex are just friends, and I'm nothing more than a house guest."

"That's not true, you are my friend," countered Nephi. "And you don't need to justify anything to them. It's not any of their business."

Nephi hadn't placed himself in the middle of their romantic relationships, and he didn't appreciate them getting in the middle of his, even if there was no relationship to get in the middle of.

Bradley then recounted the events of the week to Mike, Jacob, Ammon, and Tiffany. Tiffany's jaw dropped as he explained the details of his eviction.

The sound of Darla's high pitched voice, calling the family for dinner, interrupted the story. Nephi gathered the children from the playroom, and everyone headed upstairs for tacos and baked potatoes. It seemed an odd combination to Bradley, but he was glad to have something to eat, and to be with people who seemed to have drama of their own.

The rest of the night was uneventful, other than the entertainment factor of little Dallin trying to cheat at Go Fish. Bradley enjoyed watching the interactions between members of another Mormon family. He sensed the tension between some of them, but they were much more relaxed than his family.

After dinner and card games, Nephi excused himself and Bradley. He gave everyone hugs, and told them he loved them, and he and Bradley returned to the apartment for the night.

They squeezed in two more episodes of Gilmore Girls before bed, and then Nephi crashed on the sofa, while insisting that Bradley sleep in the bed. Bradley wasn't sure what the new week would bring. He was devastated by the actions of his own family, and intrigued by Nephi's. He felt uneducated about life, and ill-equipped to face it. One thing he knew, is that he needed a job. His search would continue in the morning.

CHAPTER 12

While Nephi worked the next day, Bradley continued the job search. He submitted dozens of resumes, and waited for a call. With nothing else to do, he watched DVDs, and spent a lot of time thinking and worrying. He had never been on his own before, or without a strict routine. His newfound freedom was exhilarating, but also terrifying.

While Bradley sat at the apartment, doing his best to stave off anxiety, Nephi went about his day at Brower. Hotel reservations really pick up right after Halloween, as people start thinking about travel for Thanksgiving and Christmas. Even staffing the call center with more agents didn't keep the hold queue at an acceptable level, and it impacted their numbers. 'Time to Answer' was through the roof. Even the managers took calls in an attempt to keep up.

Despite the busy day, Nephi took a break to pay a visit to Mark's office. He knocked on Mark's open door.

"Come in," said Mark, motioning inward with his hand.

Nephi entered his office and took a seat.

"I would like to talk to you about Bradley Hanson," said Nephi.

"Oh, yes. Bishop Thompson filled the Stake Presidency in on the Hanson family. It seems they are dealing with some things right now."

"I should say so," replied Nephi. "Anyway, Bradley has been staying with me since his parents kicked him out last week, and I am trying to help him get on his feet. He needs a job, and since we are so busy this time of year, I think it is a good opportunity to get someone who is eager to learn. I think he would be a great reservations agent."

"I'm sorry, Nephi, but I can't hire Bradley Hanson."

"Why not? We must have a new group starting training soon, anyway."

"Yes, a week from today."

"That's perfect. Let's add him to that group."

"I told you, I will not do that. Bradley Hanson needs to

learn that the Lord will only bless him if he obeys the commandments. If he does not honor his father and mother, and disregards the commandment to serve a mission, he will have no such blessings."

"That makes no sense. Are you making that judgement on the Lord's behalf? Withholding blessings because you judge it to be right?"

"I don't feel impressed to offer him a job right now. And my advice to you is to stop helping the boy. If he has nowhere to go, he will be humble, and will honor his parents. Your actions are blocking his blessings."

"That is the most convoluted logic I have ever heard. I'm sorry, I will not abandon someone in need after he was forced out by no fault of his own. Bradley has done nothing but be honest about who he is. He is much braver than I was at his age, and I admire that. At that age, I couldn't even admit it to myself."

"Suit yourself, but be careful. You don't want the Lord's judgement to fall on you, too."

"I'll take my chances, and I will help Bradley find a job and get on his feet, even if it's not here."

Upset, Nephi left Mark's office, and returned to the call center floor. The thick cloud of judgement that hung in the air over Pleasant Grove seemed contagious, and he was desperate to find a cure.

Redirecting his mind back to work, Nephi took several customer calls until it was time for lunch. With a guest at home, his routine was thrown off, and he forgot to bring food, so he grabbed a protein shake from the vending machine in the break room, and drank it in his office while he called Alex.

"How was the rest of the weekend?" asked Alex.

"Bradley's parents both spoke in church. The entire time his dad was using scripture to justify disowning his own son, and his mom was either in denial, or is a total hypocrite. I tried talking some sense into his dad, but that turned out to be just as productive as conversion therapy."

"That's the problem with scripture, there are so many ways

to interpret it, you can use it to justify just about anything. Look at all the wars people fought throughout history in the name of God," said Alex.

"I know. It was infuriating. Then we had dinner with my family last night. When we arrived, my father was leading a family meeting about me and my romantic relationships, which are a figment of his imagination. Unless you count the short kiss with Bradley, that is."

"Wait, what? You kissed Bradley?"

"Not exactly. On Friday, he was upset, and I consoled him. In the heat of the moment, he kissed me. It only lasted a few seconds before I pulled away and told him it can't happen."

"Wow, how does it feel to break out of the virgin lips club?"

"The kiss was nice, but he's way too young for me, and the history with his family in the ward would make it super awkward. Besides, I like Bradley, but I'm not really into him in that way."

"I get that. Either way, congratulations on taking a step. Even if it wasn't intended, that's no small thing."

"True. I thought it would make me feel guilty. Maybe it was the moment, and the way it happened, but it felt natural. Next time I don't think I'll be as hesitant as I have been in the past."

"Baby steps. I think you're smart to take it slow. You're a complicated man."

"I'm not sure how to take that."

"How are things progressing with Brent and Gary?"

"They're not. After confessing my Mormonhood, Gary cut it off and I haven't heard a thing from Brent in a week."

"Oh man," laughed Alex, "he's totally ghosting you."

"Ghosting me?"

"You know, completely ignoring you. He disappeared like a ghost, and eventually you'll have no idea if he was real, or just a figment of your imagination. Consider yourself lucky. At least he isn't breadcrumbing you."

"Breadcrumbing?"

"Don't you know anything? It means stringing you along,

sending little flirty messages, with no intention of carrying it forward, but not having the guts to cut it off. They both suck, but I would rather be ghosted, than breadcrumbed. What can I say? Snuzzle can be a cruel place."

"Why don't I know any of this?"

"You are new to dating apps, and you're not on social media. I don't know how you expect to keep up with the world."

"I don't know, maybe I'm a lost cause, but hey, I wanted to ask if you are free sometime this week. I still owe you an environmental debate about my gas guzzling beauty."

"I'm looking forward to it. How about Wednesday night? I can make dinner for you and Bradley at your apartment."

"Wednesday works. I've been wanting to try more of your cooking ever since I tasted your chili."

"Alright, we're on for Wednesday then. I'll be there around 6:00."

With that, they said goodbye. Nephi finished out his shift by monitoring calls and running reports. On his last pass through the call center he noticed that Brock and Angela had migrated back together, and were playing footsies while taking calls.

"Be discreet," he whispered as he walked by. "I don't want to see you sitting together tomorrow."

Brock grinned sheepishly, knowing that they had taken advantage of a busy day to pull one over on Nephi. They continued with the footsies as he walked away.

Steve arrived, and Nephi reviewed reports with him, and completed shift handoff before heading home.

Bradley had been submitting resumes all day. In all, he submitted over fifty, but had yet to hear back from a single one, which left him discouraged.

Nephi told him, "It can take a while to get through the resume filter and get a human to look at it, and a lot of the local places don't even list jobs online. Tomorrow, you should walk around and ask places if they are hiring."

"Just walk in off the street and ask for a job? That sounds

strange. I'm not sure if I would be comfortable doing it."

"You need to get out of your comfort zone to grow. It seems awkward at first, but once you get over that, and push through the discomfort, good things will happen, and you will grow. After a while, it might not seem so awkward."

"Okay, I'll give it a try tomorrow. Did you have time to see if anything is open at your work?"

Nephi hesitated and looked away, not sure how to answer. After thinking for a few seconds, he said, "Yeah, I looked into it, but it seems we don't have anything right now. I'll ask around and see if anyone else knows of something. I'll check with Stacy and my family, too."

"Thanks for checking. I appreciate it. I just hope I find something soon."

"So do I. Hey, Alex is coming over on Wednesday night to cook for us, and chat about my truck and world issues."

"Sounds like fun. I guess I have something to look forward to," said Bradley.

Work filled the next two days for Nephi while Bradley continued the job search. In the afternoon, Nephi taught him how to use the machines in the fitness room, and they both spent the evening continuing the DVD binge. Nephi liked having company at the apartment. Each night didn't seem so lonely. Bradley felt lost ever since his parents turned his world on its head, but he was glad for somewhere safe to stay, and for a listening ear.

On Wednesday after work, Nephi returned home quickly. He showered, changed into fresh clothes, and put on a splash of his favorite cologne. Then he watched out the window in anticipation of Alex's arrival.

"Wow, you're really into this guy, aren't you?" asked Bradley.

"You know we're just friends."

"You keep saying that, but since I have been staying here, this is the first time you have dolled yourself up right after work, and the way you are staring out that window reminds me of the way my dog stares at a bully stick before he devours it."

"Don't be ridiculous. My work day was just long, and I needed a shower. It's not that uncommon, and I'm just interested to know when Alex arrives. He should be here any minute now," replied Nephi, beginning to pace as he continued staring out the window.

Excitement grew in Nephi's belly when he saw the Prius pull into the parking lot and settle into an empty space. Alex got out of the car, and walked around the back, removing two paper grocery bags from the hatchback. Nephi moved to the bathroom, and ran a comb through his hair, double checking the mirror to make sure it was just right.

When the knock came at the door, Nephi asked Bradley to answer, while he sat casually on the couch, as if he had been there the entire time. Bradley rolled his eyes as he opened the door and invited Alex inside.

Nephi stood up from his place on the sofa and took the grocery bags from Alex, setting them on the kitchen counter. He gave Alex a hug and welcomed him.

"Okay," said Alex, "For the next hour, the kitchen belongs to me. I have a little surprise for you, and I will need you to stay out of my way so I can get everything done right."

"Don't worry, we'll stay on the couch," replied Nephi. "I can't wait to see what you cook up."

Alex pulled ingredients out of the bags, followed by some circular ceramic dishes, which he rested on the counter. Nephi could see meat, spinach, eggs, rice, cheese, and seasonings. There were several other ingredients that he couldn't quite make out. He wanted to help in the kitchen, but Alex made it clear that he owned the place, so Nephi thought better of it, and continued his binge-fest on the couch with Bradley.

Pots and pans clanged in the kitchen while Alex worked away. Before they knew it, Alex joined them in the living room.

"Dinner's in the oven," he said, "In about 30 minutes, we eat."

Nephi scooted over to make room next to him for Alex.

"Gilmore Girls, huh?"

"I never get tired of it," Nephi commented, "but our

conversation has been on the back burner for far too long."

He turned off the TV, and turned to face Alex. "Ok, now tell me what's so offensive about my truck."

"For starters, the carbon dioxide in the earth's atmosphere is the highest it has been in three million years, and the average temperature of the earth is trending upward at an alarming rate. Almost fifteen percent of global greenhouse emissions come from cars and trucks, and that little gas hog of yours spits out more than its share of carbon. What's offends me, is that it isn't good for the future of the planet. If we each do our part to reduce our carbon footprint, it can make a huge difference."

"My dad says that climate change is a hoax invented by the left wing libtards to scare people into investing in their clean energy companies," said Bradley.

"Well, your dad is a moron. The facts are based on science. Glaciers in the Antarctic have broken apart, wildfire seasons are longer, coral reefs are bleached, mosquito territory is expanding, and humans are the cause. We burn fossil fuels, and destroy rain forests in the name of progress and technology."

"You could have stopped at 'my dad is a moron'. On that point, there's no argument from me."

"I'm not going to argue with you about climate change," replied Nephi. "I understand that it's a problem. I have read the science, and believe that humans are contributing to the problem, and I do things to help, but my truck can do things that your Prius can't. It serves many purposes."

"Please explain exactly why you think you need such a big, gas guzzling truck, as a manager at a call center," said Alex.

"I am often asked to help family and friends move things like furniture that wouldn't fit in a smaller vehicle."

"And if you didn't have a truck, they wouldn't ask you. They would have to find another solution, like a short term truck rental, which would leave fewer trucks on the road overall."

"True, but it also has four wheel drive, which is useful when we get heavy snow in the winter."

"There are smaller vehicles with four wheel drive that are

more fuel efficient."

"Also true, but I spend a lot of time in the mountains, and the smaller four-wheel-drive vehicles don't have high enough tire clearance for much of the terrain."

"What do you do in the mountains?"

"A bit of everything. Hiking, fishing, hunting. I need the truck to get to off-road recreation areas that aren't accessible to a car. I'll concede that I really only need a truck during those times, but I can't afford to purchase or insure a second vehicle, so a truck is practical for me. Technology is changing quickly, and trucks that are more fuel efficient are on the way - even electric trucks, but they are not affordable, and my truck fits all of my needs."

"Wait, what? I didn't figure you for the outdoorsy type. I mean, you don't look like you would enjoy that at all, and hunting? Like, with guns?"

"Guns, bows, muzzleloaders… I have done it all. Growing up, my dad took us all hunting every year. I love target shooting, and I'm good at it. I'm more accurate than anyone I know, especially with a rifle."

"Wow, I don't know what to say. I'm genuinely horrified. What do you hunt and how many animals have you killed?"

"My favorite thing to hunt is elk but I also go deer hunting on occasion. I don't suppose you could call me a good hunter, though. Honestly, in all my years of hunting, I have never killed an animal. Not to say that I wouldn't, if I had the right opportunity. I'm not after a trophy, mind you, just good meat. An elk can feed an average family for half a year. I see animals every time I go, but the permits are restrictive. In some areas, you can only take a spike elk, for example. If you see a big bull or a cow, you just admire the majesty of it, and take pictures, but you can't shoot. When I have a spike only permit, I only see bulls, and when I have a bull permit, I only see cows. Shooting an animal isn't the only reason I go. I love camping, hiking, and enjoying the outdoors, and it doesn't get any better than Utah."

"Interesting. I never would have guessed. When do you

hunt?"

"You have to choose between archery and rifle hunting. You can't do both in the same year. The archery hunt runs from mid-August to the beginning of September. The rifle hunt is the first two weeks in October, and the muzzleloader hunt is going on right now. It wraps up in about a week. I haven't gone hunting yet this year, but I drew a late season cow elk tag. That hunt begins later this month, after muzzleloader season ends. You should come with me."

"Me? Hunting? I don't think so. I've never even been camping, and it doesn't sound like the type of thing I would enjoy. Besides, I'm terrified of guns, and I could never kill anything."

"Guns are scary because you don't know the rules, or how to use them. I'll take you to the range and teach you. It will be fun. Besides, you won't be carrying a gun when we hunt, anyway, since you don't have a permit. Bradley, you should come too. I know you've been hunting before."

"No thanks," asserted Bradley. "Hunting is my dad's thing, and I want nothing to do with the things he likes. He and I are very different people. I always hated camping, anyway. I can't stand getting dirty, and it's no fun sleeping in the cold."

"Don't worry, I have a nice canvas tent with a stove, you'll keep plenty warm."

"Thanks, but I'm out," replied Bradley. "Besides, I need to focus on finding a job."

"What about you, Alex? I promise we'll have fun."

"When are you going?" asked Alex.

"The weekend before Thanksgiving. I need to be back before church on Sunday, so I am planning to drive up to set up camp on Wednesday, and hunt Thursday, Friday, and Saturday morning. I will break down camp in the afternoon, and be back Saturday night."

"I'm both intrigued and terrified," said Alex. "Let me think about it and see if I can get someone to cover for me at work for a couple of days."

"Sounds good. I would love for you to come with me."

"So you drive a truck, shoot guns, and go hunting," observed Alex. "If I didn't know any better, I would say you're a redneck."

"The evidence certainly suggests it," laughed Nephi. "I proudly come from a long line of rednecks, but I'm more cosmopolitan at heart. I guess you could call me a half breed. What about you, farm boy? You grew up in Jensen."

"I'm not anywhere near ready to get into that right now. Let's save my upbringing for another time. I'm curious though, you're gay and you're Mormon, most would say that's an oxymoron. Most Mormon's I have met are die hard Republicans, and most in the community are staunch Democrats. Where do your political views fall?"

"We're diving right into politics and religion, are we?" asked Nephi. "Well okay then, let's get into it. I'm not one to shy away from controversy. Despite the church insisting that it is politically neutral, most Mormons seem to think that one party is anointed by God."

"That's true," added Bradley. "My dad says that God founded the Republican Party and Satan leads the Democrats."

Alex laughed out loud, taken back by Bradley's matter-of-factness.

Nephi continued, "I don't see things so black and white. Lately, politics has become so divisive, and people have grown bitter. Society seems to believe that we can only be friends with people who share our political views. The founders built this country on freedom of thought and speech. If I pick any random person, I am confident that I can find many areas where we disagree, but I am just as confident that there are things we agree on. Rather than tear each other down because of our differences, we should build on our similarities. I know people with views across the political spectrum, and I respect their right to believe the way they do, and I don't hate them just because they disagree with me."

"Interesting," said Alex. "Tell me more."

"For example, I am a hunter. I enjoy using firearms, and believe they are an effective tool that can be used for protection, and other practical purposes. I don't agree with those who believe guns should be banned, but, I respect their right to believe so. I am a reasonable person, and I can find common ground with them. For example, I support universal background checks and education requirements for gun purchases. I acknowledge that there are bad people out there who should not own firearms. Education, training, and background checks can be effective measures to curtail the mass shooting epidemic that has haunted our country for too long."

"That makes sense. What other issues do you feel strongly about?"

"Health care is an issue that is important to me. So many people in Utah decry Obamacare as an ugly socialist agenda, yet the United States has the highest infant mortality rate of any industrialized nation, and we have people declaring bankruptcy every day because they are buried in medical debt."

"Our system is broken," he continued, "yet people are not open to reasonable alternatives. If insurance companies had their way, they would deny all pre-existing conditions, and leave people in need of medical care with no way to get it. I am in favor of universal healthcare, and believe that there are ways we can find common ground there, too."

"Why do we not hear debate about a hybrid system where there is a base level of universal care, provided to everyone by the government, with optional health insurance for elective procedures? It could work. The government could pay medical school tuition for doctors, in exchange for their work in government medical facilities for the first five or ten years of their career, after which, they could go into private practice. I'm not saying I have all the answers, but I am tired of our political leaders constantly fighting, and stonewalling when they could find common ground, compromising, and finding effective solutions that work for both sides of the political divide."

"Wow," replied Alex. "I didn't expect a response with so much thought behind it."

"Hey, even us Rednecks can think. Imagine that," chuckled Nephi. "Anyway, I could go on and on. I support environmental regulation, and the preservation of our lands. I believe in common sense, compassionate immigration reform that views immigrants as people, and not some enemy without human rights. I support conservation. In fact, I bet most people don't realize how much hunting funds conservation. Money for hunting permits goes to restore habitat for animals. From the early 1900s to now, the elk population has grown from 41,000 to more than a million because of hunting money."

He continued, "Because of wetland restoration efforts funded by hunting, there are over 40 million ducks. Deer, turkey, pronghorn, and more species have boomed because of hunting dollars. I'm proud of my contribution to that. I support gender equality, gay rights, transgender rights, and equal treatment for all. On these and every other issue, I believe there is common ground and room for agreement, if politicians would be open to discussion. Sorry, I guess my answer was more long-winded than you were expecting. To sum it up, I guess you could say that I have views that fall on the right, and views that fall on the left. Overall, I am left of center but I respect the right of everyone to hold their own views, and I won't decline to be someone's friend only because we don't agree on some political issue. People are more complicated than that."

"You are an interesting man, Nephi. Based on our prior interactions, I wouldn't have pegged you for such a deep thinker. I respect that."

Ding! Ding! Ding! The oven timer alerted them that dinner was ready. Lost in discussion, they had almost forgotten about it. Alex excused himself to remove the food from the oven and finish preparing the meal.

When he opened the oven, a distinct aroma filled the apartment. It invaded Nephi's nostrils, and brought a memory from the deep recesses of his mind to the surface.

"Is that? No, it can't be…"

By now, the smell permeated everything. There was no mistaking that smell. It was Tavë Kosi, an Albanian lamb and yogurt dish that Nephi hadn't tasted since his mission. His mouth watered, and his mind returned to the old world, where he spent two years of early adulthood. He smiled from ear to ear as he walked over to the kitchen.

"Tavë Kosi?" he asked. "But how?"

"You mentioned that you were a missionary in Albania, so I pulled out my book on dishes around the world from culinary school, and learned how to make some Albanian food. I wanted to make something special. I made Tavë Kosi, and Byrek me Djathë dhe Spinaq, a spinach and cheese pie."

"I could kiss you right now," declared Nephi as he inhaled the memories.

Pleased at Nephi's reaction, a smug grin came to Alex's face. He cut the spinach pie, and placed a slice on each of three small plates, while he waited for the round ceramic bowls that held the lamb and yogurt dish to cool enough so he could place them on the table. After bringing the food to the table, he opened the fridge and removed a pitcher of Bozë, an Albanian drink made with corn and wheat flour, sugar, and water.

"Everything is perfect," declared Nephi as they sat at the table. "Let's have a blessing on the food."

Bradley and Alex nodded and Nephi offered a prayer of thanks for the food. In his prayer, he also asked God to bless Bradley in his job search, and to bless Alex that he would travel home safely.

After blessing the food, Nephi raised his glass of Bozë. "Gezuar," he said aloud, extending his glass toward Alex.

"Gezuar," Alex replied as their glasses clinked together.

"Cheers," added Bradley, touching glasses with his newfound friends.

The lamb was so tender, and the way it's flavor blended with the yogurt, rice, and spices excited Nephi's taste buds. Alex and Bradley also enjoyed the meal. The spinach pie crust was so light and flaky. Alex definitely had skills in the kitchen.

"It's incredible how authentic this is. How many times did

you practice it?"

"Practice?" replied Alex. "This is my first time making any of this, but the recipe in my book is very detailed, and I had a great Mediterranean instructor in school. I can tell you right now, this won't be the last time I make it. It's delicious. Someone should open an Albanian restaurant around here."

"Maybe you should do it," suggested Bradley.

"I'm happy at La Bambolina now, but you never know what the future holds, I guess."

The three continued eating and talking for a couple of hours, and then washed the dishes before Alex had to go. Nephi helped him out to the car with his ceramic dishes and utensils. After giving him a long, warm embrace, he reminded Alex to wear his seatbelt and to drive safe. Nephi then returned to the apartment where he slept on the sofa while Bradley snored away in the bed.

CHAPTER 13

The rest of the workweek was busy, but otherwise uneventful for Nephi. Bradley followed Nephi's suggestion and visited several businesses within walking distance to ask about job openings. He managed to line up an interview at the ice cream shop on the corner for Tuesday. An ice cream shop may not sound like a great place to work in the winter, but Utah is funny about ice cream. It's not just for summer. They eat it all year round. Winter flavors like eggnog, pumpkin, and peppermint keep the shop busy. It's not uncommon to see someone walking down the street, eating an ice cream cone in the snow.

Bradly grinned when he broke the news of the interview to Nephi. It seems a little thing, but he hadn't been excited about anything in a long time, and it was a big deal to him. Nephi congratulated him, and wished him luck.

Saturday morning, Nephi spoke to Alex on the phone. The thought of hunting with Nephi intrigued Alex, and he took off the Friday and Saturday before Thanksgiving. That would give them four days to hunt. If they returned home Saturday, Alex would be back for his Sunday evening shift.

Nephi arranged a lane at the indoor shooting range for them on Thursday afternoon, and a lane at the outdoor range on Saturday morning. He figured Alex better have some instruction and exposure to firearms before they get out in the field. It also gave him an excuse to spend more time with Alex.

Between planning the range excursion and entertaining a house guest, he didn't have any time for Snuzzle connections, and he wasn't sure dating apps were for him, anyway. After all, his track record wasn't good with Snuzzle dates, and Brent was still ghosting him.

Church on Sunday morning brought more sideway glances and cold shoulders for Nephi. He shrugged it off and enjoyed Sacrament meeting and Elders Quorum. He reasoned that he didn't attend church for the people, anyway. He attended for God and for himself, and those are the only opinions that mattered. He skipped dinner with Mike and Darla that evening and made crockpot corn chowder at home for Bradley. They ate, chatted, and continued the Gilmore Girls DVD binge, finishing the fourth season.

Bradley and Alex met the new week with excitement and hope of new beginnings. Sometimes the anticipation of change is just as good as change itself. Tuesday morning, Bradley went into his interview, ready to start anew. His kind, soft spoken personality made a good impression on Gene, the owner of the ice cream shop, and he hired Bradley on the spot. He would start the following Monday. Bradley thanked the gray-haired man, and half walked, half skipped out of the shop with the prospect of income and independence on the horizon.

When Nephi returned home from work, he treated Bradley to dinner at a local steakhouse to celebrate the job offer, and a fresh start. Bradley couldn't wait to start his job. While they ate, Nephi's mind wandered as he thought of his own fresh start. He was excited to see Alex on Thursday. His mind snapped back to Bradley when the server interrupted to ask if they would like to see a dessert menu. Nephi figured that Bradley's new job warranted dessert as much as anything, and they split a chocolate eruption cake.

The next day passed quickly, and before Nephi knew it, Alex was pulling in to his apartment complex, ready for his first trip to a gun range. Nephi hopped into the Prius and navigated Alex to his parents' house where his family stored the guns.

"My dad keeps my firearms in his safe," he explained. "I don't really have room for them at the apartment and don't have money for an expensive safe, either."

They entered the house and Nephi said a quick hello to Darla on their way to the gun safe in the garage. The safe was larger than Alex expected. It stood about seven feet tall, and was four feet wide, and about three feet deep. Nephi pulled a backpack off of a rack on the wall.

"These are our eyes and ears," he said. "Whenever you use firearms, it is important to use eye and hearing protection."

He pulled the plastic goggles and the earmuffs from the bag, showing them to Alex.

"Before we get the guns and ammo, I will go over some safety rules with you. I'll review them again at the gun range, but it gets loud there, so I am going over them here to make sure we are clear."

Alex nodded.

"First, you always store guns and ammo separately. Notice that the gun safe has only guns, and no ammunition. There is a separate lock box in my dad's closet where he stores the ammunition."

"Got it," replied Alex.

"Okay, next, it is very important that whenever you handle a gun, assume it is loaded even if you think it isn't."

"Makes sense."

"Good. The next gun rule is that you should never place your finger in the trigger guard, or on the trigger, until you are ready to fire."

Nephi typed the combination into the gun safe, turned the wheel, and pulled it open. He took a small rifle from the shelf.

"See, here is the trigger guard. When I hold the gun, I extend my pointer finger here, above the trigger guard, keeping it away from the trigger."

"Thanks for the demonstration. I get it now."

"Rule number four, never point a gun at anything that you are not willing to destroy. And finally, know your target, what is in front of it, and what is behind it. A bullet will pass through your target and move on to whatever is behind it, so you must know both what is in front and what is behind."

"I understand."

"Awesome, we are almost ready. Not that you would, but never, ever handle a firearm while you are using alcohol, or drugs of any kind. That is a deadly combination."

Nephi pulled a second rifle from the safe. He pulled back the action and locked it open.

"Today we will be shooting .22 caliber rifles, he explained. These are both semi-automatic rifles. Once loaded, you don't need to take any action such as cocking a lever or cycling a bolt to make the gun ready to fire again. The force from the round you fire cycles the action, and loads the next round for you, so you just need to pull the trigger again to fire."

"Do they kick hard?" asked Alex.

".22s have a very slight kick, but it isn't bad. It is a good caliber to learn to shoot with, and to practice fundamentals, but don't make the mistake of assuming that means they aren't dangerous. A .22 caliber rifle can kill just as well as any other firearm, and it is critical that you follow the safety rules at all times, no matter what firearm you are holding."

"It is a lot to process, and I'm kind of nervous, but I think I understand."

"Don't be nervous. As long as you follow the rules, a gun can be an effective tool. Every gun accident that I have ever heard of resulted from someone breaking the basic safety rules. If you follow the rules, you will be safe."

Nephi handed a rifle to Alex, and showed him how to hold it, and how to aim.

"These rifles have open sights. To aim, you want to line up the post at the end of the barrel, with the notch at the back of the barrel. The top of the post should be level with the top of the notch, and the post should be directly in the center. You want to place your target immediately above the post, so it looks like it is resting on the post. You will leave your index finger extended above the trigger guard until you have your target lined up, and understand what is behind it. Once you are lined up and ready to fire, you will move your finger carefully down into the trigger guard. Hold your breath either right after you inhale, or right after you exhale, whichever is more comfortable, and then squeeze the trigger gently. Don't pull a trigger, squeeze it in a way that you're not sure when it will fire."

"Okay, I think I've got it," stated Alex.

"Alright, I think we're ready. Let's get the ammo box and head to the range."

They proceeded up the stairs and took a locked ammo box labeled ".22 LR" from the closet. They went out to the car where Nephi opened the hatchback and placed the rifles in the back, before placing the ammo box on the floor of the back seat.

Nephi acted as navigator, while Alex drove a few exits down the freeway to the indoor shooting range.

"Hi, Nephi," called out a man behind the counter as they entered.

"How's it going, Bill?" replied Nephi.

"Not bad. We've got lane twelve all ready for you. Do you need any targets?"

"Yes, please give me two self-painting targets."

Turning to Alex, he explained, "The self-painting targets make it easier to see where you hit at a distance."

Alex nodded.

"This is my friend, Alex," Nephi told Bill. "It's his first time shooting."

"Welcome," said Bill. "You've got yourself a good instructor here. I hope you have a good time."

"So do I," mumbled Alex under his breath.

Alex could tell by their familiarity with each other, that Nephi was a frequent visitor to the range.

Nephi paid for the targets and handed Alex goggles and earmuffs. "Put on your eyes and ears now," he said.

With protection for both eyes and ears, they walked through double doors that led to the range. Others were already there shooting, and Alex could hear their shots through the earmuffs, but he could tell they were doing their job. Nephi led him to lane twelve, where he pressed a switch that brought the target toward them. It hung on a mechanized line, connected to a pulley system, that allowed the shooters to easily send and retrieve their targets, without going out onto the range.

Alex observed that the other shooters were following the rules that Nephi had explained to him, keeping their finger out of the trigger guard until they were ready to fire.

Nephi stapled a target onto the hanging target holder and then sent it out on the range by flipping the switch in the other direction. Alex watched as it glided past the distance markers on the wall. It zoomed past 10, 20, and 30, eventually coming to rest at the far end of the range at the 50 yard marker.

Nephi pointed to a sign on the wall with numbered rules. It read, "1. Treat all firearms as if they are loaded. 2. Never point a firearm at anyone, or anything you are not willing to destroy. 3. Keep your finger off the trigger and out of the trigger guard until you are ready to fire. 4. Know your target and what is behind it."

Alex read over the rules and nodded in acknowledgement. Nephi opened the ammo lockbox and loaded the rifle. The magazine was a small cartridge that held ten shells. Once full, Nephi placed the magazine in the rifle, and pulled back on the action, letting it snap closed.

Nephi told Alex to watch as he raised the butt of the rifle to his shoulder, resting his cheek on the stock while he lined up the target directly above the post centered in the notch. Now ready to fire, he crept his finger from its extended position down into the trigger guard, and gently squeezed. Alex heard a pop, and looked down at the target to see a hole about an inch above the bullseye.

Nephi rested the rifle on the shooting bench, keeping it pointed downrange, and motioned for Alex to take it. Hesitant, Alex picked up the rifle. He carefully raised it to his shoulder and rested his extended index finger above the trigger guard, while he lined up the sights as Nephi had instructed. When he felt ready, he moved his finger to the trigger and began to squeeze. Expecting a bit of recoil, he flinched a bit, as he jerked back on the trigger. The bullet hit the target, but was about six inches high, and to the left of the bullseye.

"You started off just right," explained Nephi, "but you anticipated the shot and flinched. You can't do that. You need to stay right in there on the target the entire time, and squeeze slowly so you don't know when the gun will fire. Don't anticipate it, just hold that breath, stay on target, and squeeze gently until it fires."

Alex nodded and tried again, remembering Nephi's instructions. He lined up the target, took a breath and then held it on the exhale while he moved his finger into the trigger guard and gently squeezed. He was surprised when the rifle fired, and even more surprised, and delighted, to find that he had hit the bullseye. His shot was even closer than Nephi's.

Excited, he continued shooting while Nephi loaded up a few more magazines. After about fifty shots, there wasn't much left of the bullseye, and Nephi flipped the switch to bring the target back in. He removed it and asked Alex to mount the new target.

Alex stapled the second target to the board and flipped the switch to send it out to the 50 yard marker. This time, Alex loaded the shells into the magazines, and then resumed shooting. By the time they finished, both targets had shredded bullseyes, with a few stray holes here and there. Alex had done the bulk of the shooting, and admired his handiwork as he held the targets in his hands.

Nephi double checked the rifle to make sure it wasn't loaded, and locked the action open before sealing the ammo box, and exiting the range. Once in the lobby, they removed eyes and ears, and Nephi showed Alex to the washing station.

"After shooting at the range, it is important to wash with cold water because the bullets have lead in them. The cold water closes your pores, so that lead particles don't get in. The soap here also helps with lead removal. Don't eat or drink anything until you wash thoroughly," Nephi explained.

They both washed up and returned to Alex's Prius.

"Well, what did you think?" asked Nephi.

"At first, the thought of shooting a gun terrified me, but I actually ended up having a lot of fun. I didn't expect to enjoy it that much. Thanks for taking me."

"I'm glad you liked it. On Saturday morning, we are going to an outdoor range. The indoor range is only 50 yards, and the maximum caliber is .223, which isn't a big enough caliber for hunting elk. The outdoor range goes out to 300 yards, but we will shoot on the 100 yard range. The guns we will use have scopes instead of open sights, and they are bolt action, so you have to cycle the action before each shot. I will use the 30-06 that I use for elk hunting to sight it in, and I will bring a .243 for you to shoot. It is bigger than the .22 we used today, but it still doesn't kick too badly, and the mechanics are the same. I'm impressed with your shooting. You're a natural."

"I didn't think I would ever say this, but I'm looking forward to it," replied Alex.

"Do you want to grab a bite to eat before you head back to Salt Lake?" asked Nephi.

"I would love to. Why don't we get the guns back in your dad's safe and swing by to pick up Bradley?"

Nephi was enjoying his alone time with Alex, and didn't want it to stop, but didn't like the thought of Bradley all alone in the apartment, either. After cleaning the guns and putting everything away, they picked up Bradley, and headed to Arctic Circle, a Utah based fast-food restaurant with fresh, high quality burgers, chicken, and salads.

Nephi ordered a taco salad, Alex a fish sandwich, and Bradley got a kid's meal with a cheeseburger. Growing up, his family never went out to eat, and he was jealous of the kids that got kids meal toys. He was almost nineteen, but he was still excited for the toy. They enjoyed the meal while they chatted about the range, and the upcoming hunting trip. Bradley played with his toy as they talked.

"Won't I need some hunting clothes and camping supplies?" asked Alex.

"Don't worry about any of that. We have more camping supplies that you could imagine, and my dad saves all the hunting clothes we have ever bought, hoping that the grandkids will use them some day. Some of Jacob's old things should fit you, or maybe some of Tiffany's stuff."

"Your sister hunts too?"

"She sure does. She's good at it, too. I have personally never taken and animal, but Tiff has taken at least ten. I think she brought home more meat for the family than my brothers combined."

"Impressive," replied Alex. "What about food. What will we need for the trip?"

"I'll bring a backpacking stove and a percolator to boil water. We'll eat mostly freeze dried meals that we rehydrate with the boiled water. Most of them are better than you would expect."

"It sounds like you have it all planned out,"

"When you have hunted as much as I have, or with my lack of success, maybe we should just call it camping, much of the preparation is routine. It's almost automatic."

The conversation shifted to Bradley's job search, and Bradley shared his good news with Alex, who congratulated him.

After dinner, Alex dropped off Nephi and Bradley at the apartment before returning to Salt Lake. He enjoyed the shooting range and the two Mormon gay greenies were growing on him. He looked forward to seeing them again on Saturday, and was eager to see what the hunt would bring.

Friday came and went, and Saturday arrived, bringing with it a chill in the air. Twenty degrees Fahrenheit would make for a frigid morning at the range, but it would be good practice, too. Hunting weather might be even colder, and it would likely snow.

Alex arrived, and they went to Mike and Darla's garage to retrieve the rifles and ammunition. Nephi demonstrated how to cycle a bolt, and reviewed the safety rules again, making Alex repeat them.

They loaded the guns in back of the car, and drove up Provo Canyon to the outdoor shooting range. On such a cold morning, there weren't many people at the range, but a couple of lanes were in use. There was a range safety officer, or RSO, there, running the range and directing traffic. When they pulled up, Alex noticed a red flag hung on the range.

"It looks like the range is hot," said Nephi. "That means that people are actively shooting. I'll check with the range safety officer, but we should be able to get set up now."

Nephi exited the car and spoke with the RSO before they touched the guns. He confirmed that the range was hot, and they were safe to set up their firearms. Nephi carried his 30-06 and the ammunition box, while Alex carried the .243. As soon as they finished setting up the guns, the RSO called a ceasefire, and declared the range cold. Everyone stopped shooting and moved behind the yellow line unless they were setting up or checking targets.

Nephi and Alex stapled their targets onto wooden target stands, and walked them out to the 100 yard marker, while another man swapped out his target. Once they returned, the RSO declared the range hot. With eyes and ears in place, Nephi showed Alex how to load the .243 magazine, and stayed next to him while he fired the first four rounds, all on target.

Giving Alex a thumbs up, Nephi moved over to his bench where he shot his 100 yard target with the 30-06. Alex could tell that it was louder than the .243 that he was shooting, and looking over as Nephi took a shot, he could also tell that it kicked harder.

Both of them continued shooting until they had each spent a twenty round box. Nephi pulled another 20 round box for each of them before the RSO called the next ceasefire. With the range cold, a man who just arrived set up his target. The range hot again, the man set up on the bench next to Alex, whose shooting was interrupted by an ear breaking boom. Even with ear muffs on, the shot was loud. It startled Alex, causing his round to miss the target.

While finishing the remainder of his ammo box, Alex thought it best to wait until the man took a shot to take his own, so the booming noise wouldn't throw him off. By the next ceasefire, Nephi and Alex had each polished off two full boxes of ammunition. They collected their targets, both had tight groupings around the bullseye.

When the RSO declared the range hot, they moved the rifles to the car, and headed back to Mike and Darla's place.

"What kind of gun was that guy next to me shooting?" asked Alex. "Even with ear muffs, it was way too loud."

"It was a .30 caliber rifle similar to mine," replied Nephi, "but he had a muzzle brake."

"What's that?"

"He installed a muzzle brake at the end of the barrel. It redirects a lot of the gases released by the round to the sides rather than straight out the end of the barrel. It reduces recoil and muzzle rise, but the bang is much louder."

"I figured that part out. It threw off one of my shots."

"One of mine too," confessed Nephi. "Did you have fun?"

"I had a lot of fun but honestly, I think I prefer shooting the .22 at the indoor range."

"I can't blame you. Plinking with a .22 is a lot of fun. I always enjoy it."

Back at Mike and Darla's, they cleaned the guns and locked them back in the safe. They went into Nephi's old bedroom where plastic bins full of hunting clothes sat in the closet. Alex tried them on, and found three pair of camouflage pants that fit him nicely, along with four shirts, a coat, and two orange vests.

"Don't forget wool socks, and thermal long-johns," said Nephi. "And you'll need some gloves and a hat." Nephi gathered them and put them in a bag.

"Long underwear?" asked Alex.

"It is freezing up there, believe me, you want them. Oh, and you'll need some good boots. What size do you wear?"

"Size nine."

"Some of my old ones should fit you just fine." Nephi dug through the closet until he found them. "Here you are."

With clothes gathered, they visited with Darla for a bit, while enjoying some of her famous homemade cinnamon rolls. Mike was at work, and she was there alone. She had been baking all morning, and was happy for someone with whom she could share the spoils of her labor.

After warming themselves and filling up on sweet, gooey goodness, they thanked her. Nephi gave her a big hug before they headed out. Alex had to get back to Salt Lake to prepare for work, and Nephi spent the day hanging out with Bradley. This time of year, Bradley missed baking and decorating holiday sugar cookies with his mother, so they went to the grocery store and bought everything they needed to bake pilgrim and turkey shaped sugar cookies.

Once the cookies cooled, they frosted them. Bradley enjoyed it, but it wasn't the same as baking with his mom. He was very grateful for Nephi, but he missed his family, especially his mom and his siblings. The forced separation was necessary though, at home he wasn't free to be himself. He looked forward to a job, and a new start.

On Sunday, Bradley once again declined Nephi's invitation to church, but tagged along with him for dinner at Mike and Darla's afterward. He brought them a plate of holiday cookies, which Mike seemed very thankful for.

Monday finally arrived, and for the first time, Nephi and Bradley had to coordinate showers in the morning. Nephi had to be to work at 7:00 and Bradley was to report to the ice cream shop at 8:00, for four hours of training before the shop opened at noon.

Gene, the shop owner, was happy for some help. He showed Bradley how they made the ice cream, and gave him a sample of each of the twenty flavors, so he could give proper recommendations to customers. He enjoyed eggnog and bubblegum, but mint chocolate chip was his favorite. Gene schooled Bradley on the sizes and the specialty desserts. Once he had a good grasp on the product, Gene trained him to use the cash register, and showed him how to clean the dining area and the back.

The work was harder than Bradley thought it would be, but he enjoyed it, and was excited for them to open. Noon arrived without a customer in sight, which isn't what Bradley had envisioned.

"We don't get many customers this early," said Gene. "A few people will stop in for a cup or a cone on their way back from lunch, and we'll get a small rush in the afternoon, and a bigger one after dinner in the evening, but you won't be here that late today."

"I guess that makes sense," replied Bradley. "Thanks again for offering me the job. I really need it right now."

"I'm happy to have you."

Just like Gene predicted, several customers came through the door between 12:30 and 1:30, and Bradley happily scooped their ice cream and handed it to them with a smile. Gene was pleased to see how good he was with the customers, and how hard he worked. Most of the teenagers he hired in the past had no work ethic, but Bradley was different. He took pride in the work and did it right. After helping a customer, he was quick to wipe down the counter with a towel, and he cleaned each table as soon as a customer left it vacant.

By the end of the day, Gene was satisfied he made a good hire, and Bradley was proud of the job he did. It wasn't the most exciting work, but he liked it, and he was good at it. Gene made him feel valued, which is really all anyone can hope for in a job.

At the end of his shift, he walked home a new man, believing he could make this work. He sensed that he would be okay on his own, finally able to be himself.

CHAPTER 14

More than a week passed, and Bradley had really hit his stride at work. Gene had him on the opening shift, working from 11:00 to 7:30, Tuesday through Saturday. He enjoyed the job, especially greeting customers.

Work was moving along normally for Nephi as the time for the hunt drew near. His shift ended on Tuesday, and he headed to his parents' house, to load up the truck for the hunt. He opened the garage and placed tarps, the canvas tent, foldable cots, sleeping bags, and water jugs in the bed of the truck. He placed his rifle on the gun rack that hung in his back window, with the ammunition locked in a box behind the seat.

He gathered his backpack, which held the small one-burner stove, hunting knives, binoculars, and a spotting scope. He loaded it into the truck, along with the box of camp pots and pans. Food storage lined the back wall of the garage, and included buckets full of single serving, freeze dried meals. He collected enough for himself and Alex.

Biscuits and gravy and omelets for breakfast, chicken rice and protein bars for lunch, and an assortment of dinners including chicken teriyaki, lasagna, beefy macaroni, and taco casserole. Having reviewed the checklist on his phone to verify he didn't forget anything, Nephi went inside to thank Mike and Darla for everything.

"Bring back some meat for the freezer," said Mike, in a voice dripping with doubt.

"I'll do my best," replied Nephi, with a smile.

He hugged them both, before heading back to the apartment to spend one more night on the comfy sofa. For the rest of the week, he would sleep on a cot in the cold. He made sure food was stocked for Bradley, who would have the place to himself until Saturday night. The two of them curled up on the couch, and finished the seventh and final season of Gilmore Girls, before going to sleep.

Nephi wanted to get an early start since he had to pick up Alex in Salt Lake before driving all the way to camp, and they would need enough daylight to set up the tent. He woke up at 6:30 and got ready for the day. He had already packed the truck with everything but his hunting clothes. He threw them in a bag, and woke Bradley at 7:30 to say goodbye.

"I will be out of cell phone range most of the time I'm gone, but I left my mom's phone number on the fridge. Please don't hesitate to call her if you need anything. I let her know that you might call."

"Thanks. I really appreciate it. I am so thankful for everything you have done for me, Nephi. I honestly don't know what I would have done these last few weeks without you."

"I'm happy to have you, man. I'm only gone for four days. I'll see you Saturday night," said Nephi.

Bradley gave him a big bear hug, squeezing him so tight he thought it might crack a rib. It evicted all the air from Nephi's lungs. Taking a deep breath to gain some needed space, Nephi patted him gently on the back. Bradley released his grip and gave Nephi a kiss on the cheek before he turned and headed out the door for the elk hunt.

Nephi stuffed his clothes under the truck bench and climbed in. He set off for Alex's apartment in Salt Lake, making the now familiar drive over the Point of the Mountain, and past Draper, Sandy, Midvale and Murray. He took the 21st South Freeway to the east side, where Alex lived. Following the GPS, he found the apartment complex. Alex was waiting for him in the parking lot, with bags in hand.

Nephi opened the truck bed cover, and they tucked Alex's bags between the tent and the cots, before closing the cover, and climbing into the truck.

"Do you mind if I say a prayer before we leave?" asked Nephi.

"I'm not much of one for praying, but go ahead."

Nephi bowed his head, closed his eyes, and offered a prayer to God for their safety, and thanked him for the opportunity they had to spend time together. He closed the prayer in the name of Jesus Christ. Alex sat respectfully while he prayed. After the prayer, they buckled their seat belts and hit the road.

"Alright," exclaimed Alex, "we're really "redneckin' it" now!"

"Redneckin' it?" asked Nephi.

"Heading into the mountains in a pickup truck with a gun in the window, I would definitely say we are "redneckin' it." All we need now is some real country boy music. I think I might have Cotton Eye Joe on my phone," replied Alex.

"As much as I love Cotton Eye Joe, it hardly qualifies as country music."

"What are you talking about? The name of the band is literally Rednex."

"Ha, ha, ha," laughed Nephi. "We'll just have to agree to disagree. Below your seat, there are some country music cassettes though. Since I'm the only one in the family that still has a cassette deck, I inherited all the tapes, including all my mom's 80s country jams. I've got Dan Seals, Dwight Yoakam, Reba, Hank Williams Jr, Randy Travis, George Strait, Alabama, Kenny Rogers, you name it…"

Alex reached below his seat and retrieved the zipper case full of old cassette tapes.

"Which one do you want to listen to first?" asked Alex.

"Your choice. They remind me of my childhood, and I like them all."

"Well, I can't say that I know any of them," replied Alex. "Eenie, Meenie, Meinie, Mo." He grabbed one from the middle of the case. "Dan Seals, "Won't Be Blue Anymore" it is," he said as he ejected the Tommy Page tape from the stereo, and replaced it with Dan Seals. "Now this is full-on "redneckin' it!"

"I guess I have to agree with you," said Nephi.

Alex cranked the stereo as they made their way to I-80 and drove through Parley's Canyon.

"I really like this one," said Alex, as the third song on the album played.

"It's one of my favorites," replied Nephi, singing along.

"Where are we headed, anyway?"

"My permit is for the South Slope of the Uinta Mountains. I checked this morning, and Wolf Creek Pass is still open, so we will go that way, and turn left at the road to Lightning Ridge. There is some good elk country up there. Hopefully we will see some animals."

"I'm not sure exactly where that is, but I guess I have no choice but to trust you."

They continued jamming to the country tunes until they reached Parley's Summit, where Nephi pulled off for gas. It was nearing lunch time, so he pulled out some sack lunches he had made for them - turkey sandwiches with chips, and granola bars. They ate in the truck while Nephi took Highway 189 until the Kamas turn off, and then headed south to Francis where he connected with Highway 35, which would take them through Wolf Creek Pass.

Three inches of snow blanketed the small town of Francis. The white-dusted landscape glistened in the sun and surprised Alex with its beauty. The trees had not fully shed their leaves, and the bright red, yellow, and orange foliage stood out against the sparkling snow. As they drove further into the canyon, green and yellow pines replaced the colorful leaves. It looked like a scene out of a painting.

Spending all of his time in the city, Alex wondered what other natural treasures he was missing out on. The truck rumbled up the canyon, and passed several lakes and campgrounds before they approached a smaller dirt road on the left. Nephi turned off, and began to climb the road. There were about four inches of snow on the ground now, and Alex could feel the cold outside as he touched his hand to the window. He replaced Dan Seals with Kenny Rogers, and Nephi popped into four wheel drive, as their redneck adventure continued.

The truck rounded a sharp corner, where an RV had pulled off to camp. Its lights were on, and Alex could see the shadows of people moving inside. Nephi's rig continued up a steep section of icy dirt road, and it slid backward a few feet. Nephi downshifted to 4LO, and they slowly crawled up the slope. Moving back into 4WD, they descended the other side, and drove through several large meadows.

Nephi followed signs toward an LDS girl's camp, before turning right, and following a rocky road through a thick section of forest. About half way down the road, he pulled off into a small clearing, and the truck came to a stop.

"We'll set up camp here," he said.

They got out of the truck and stretched their legs. After the long drive, they really had to go, so they each found a tree to water. Nephi then opened the truck bed cover and grabbed two large tarps. Alex helped him spread them on the ground in a nice, flat spot, where they could set up the tent. The weight of the canvas surprised Alex, and he wondered how Nephi managed to load everything into the truck by himself. He must be stronger than he looks, he thought. They built the tent frame, and then draped the canvas over the top, and set the guy lines.

With the tent nearly complete, Nephi brought a thermal mat from the truck, and placed it on the floor of the tent. He asked Alex to help him carry the wood-burning stove into the tent, and they placed it on the mat. They assembled the stove pipe, and ran it through the stove jack in the roof to vent the smoke.

The cots came next. They were the nice, wide Alaskan Guide cots that support up to 400 pounds. They laid inflatable pads on top of the cots, followed by cold weather mummy bags. Nephi unloaded bundles of firewood from the truck, and placed them next to the stove. He brought in their clothes and backpacks, and then closed the truck bed cover.

Alex breathed deep, noting the way the pine-scented mountain air refreshed his lungs. With about an hour of daylight remaining, they took a walk to get familiar with their surroundings. Alex pulled out his phone to check his email.

"I'm not getting any bars here."

Nephi laughed. "Yep, I must have forgot to tell you. There is no cell phone reception here. We will be without our phones until Saturday evening."

"What if we get lost or hurt, and need some help?"

"I brought a beacon with me. In the case of an emergency, I can press a button to send a 911 request with our GPS location. My mom got it for me a few years back, because she worried when I went hunting by myself. Fortunately, I haven't had to use it yet."

"That makes me feel better, but hopefully we won't need it."

"We should be fine. We just need to use common sense, and follow basic safety rules."

Alex enjoyed their walk. The snow-covered trees were beautiful. During the short stroll, they saw several squirrels, and a couple of deer, both does. Alex was amazed to see them up close. They didn't even seem to be alarmed by the humans staring at them through the trees, and just stood there, and continued to eat the grass that was poking up through the snow.

As darkness fell, they looked up and admired the night sky. They could see more stars than are visible from the city. The quarter moon was bright enough to cast light on the snow, as they made their way back to the tent. By the time they returned, Alex noticed the cold toes inside his boots. Nephi built a fire in the stove, and they both changed into long thermal underwear, and sat in folding chairs in front of the fire.

Nephi boiled water and made hot cocoa, and used the rest of the boiling water to prepare their freeze dried dinners. Alex chose chicken and dumplings, and Nephi had teriyaki chicken. After ten minutes, they were fully hydrated and ready to eat. It didn't taste as bad as Alex feared. Maybe it was all the walking, or the exertion put into setting up the tent, but the chicken and dumplings tasted good, and warmed him from the inside. The fire felt good on his hands and toes.

After dinner, Nephi pulled some foot warmers out of his backpack, and suggested that Alex put them in the bottom of his sleeping bag to keep his feet warm at night. They lay in their sleeping bags talking about the morning hunt to the glow of the fire. To Alex, getting back to nature felt primitive, but somehow natural. Sleeping in the tent next to the glowing fire in the stove, somehow seemed magical.

It didn't take long for them to fall asleep, and Alex slept much better than he expected. There is something about how a warm sleeping bag separates a person from the cold air that deepens one's sleep, and rejuvenates the body. When Nephi's alarm sounded at 4:30 in the morning, they both felt refreshed and ready to face the day. If Alex wasn't awake before stretching his arms outside the sleeping bag, he certainly was when the frozen air touched his skin. He sat up, and noticed that Nephi was already dressed in camo, and building a fire in the stove.

"Good morning, sunshine," exclaimed Nephi.

Alex croaked, "Good morning," as he blinked, trying to bring his eyes into focus.

"We'll hike out in about 20 minutes. Get dressed. I should have hot cocoa ready by the time you're ready."

"I don't suppose you have any coffee on hand?"

Nephi smiled and shook his head.

"Oh yeah… Mormon… of course you don't," said Alex.

Alex pulled two pair of wool socks over his feet, and climbed into Tiffany's sherpa-lined pants, which he borrowed from Mike and Darla's place. He pulled a long sleeve camo shirt over his head, and slipped his arms into the warm coat.

Once ready, he walked over to the stove where Nephi handed him a steaming cup of cocoa. It warmed him as he sipped. He thought how nice it would be to stay inside the tent next to the fire, but he knew that Nephi was excited to hunt, and he was curious what it was all about.

"We will follow the game trail about 20 yards above camp through the trees for about half a mile, and then we'll climb up the mountain. Do your best to be quiet, but with the snow on the ground, there's no stopping our steps from crunching. That's okay though, elk make a lot of noise when they walk through the forest, so the sound of snow crunching won't alarm them. Just be sure not to talk. The sound of human voices will send them running."

"Okay, got it, but it's pitch black outside. How do you plan to hike in the darkness?"

"That's what the headlamps are for," replied Nephi. "Now, when we get to the top of the ridge, we will move slowly. Just follow me. Move as slow as you can, and when you start to feel like a snail, slow it down some more. There are no rewards for getting there fast, and we don't want to spook the animals."

"Honey, I'm not exactly known for my speed. Slow shouldn't be a problem."

"Good. Patience is the name of the game."

"I'm not exactly known for my patience either, so that one might be a problem," said Alex.

"Just follow me and we'll be fine. Once we come over the other side of the ridge, we will stop for a while. From there, we will see the opposite ridge about 200 yards away. There is a stream there where the elk sometimes drink, and a big clearing where grass should still come through the snow. We'll sit there and be quiet, and glass for a while."

"What if I don't know how to glass? What if I don't even know what that is?"

"It just means that we'll use our binoculars to watch the hill on the other side for any sign of animals."

"Ok, why didn't you just say that? I think that's something I can handle."

"Shooting light isn't until 7:25, so we'll be sitting in the dark for a while. Put some hand warmers in your pockets, so your hands won't freeze."

About now, Alex was wondering what he got himself into. He was still intrigued, but questioning whether he was cut out for this.

With cocoa cups empty, they put on the blaze orange vests over their coats, strapped on binoculars, and pulled on hats and gloves. They walked out of the tent into the cold, dark morning air. Nephi made his way to the truck, and took his rifle from the gun rack. He placed four rounds in the magazine and clipped it into the gun.

"I have the magazine in the rifle, but I don't load one in the chamber until I am ready to fire," he explained. "It is dangerous to walk with a loaded rifle, especially since we must climb over fallen trees. Never climb over anything with a loaded firearm."

"Makes sense to me," replied Alex.

Nephi threw the gun over his shoulder, and switched on his headlamp. The light was stronger than Alex expected. It illuminated the path for almost 100 yards. He followed, as Nephi led the way up to the game trail that hugged the mountain through the trees. The trail climbed the mountain gradually. The snow was frozen over, and it crunched with each step. Alex wondered how they would sneak up on anything with all the noise their feet were making in the snow. As they continued to walk, Nephi stopped and held his arms out, signaling Alex to stop with him.

Directing his headlamp to the ground, he pointed. "Fresh elk tracks and droppings," he whispered.

Alex could see a pile of droppings on top of the snow. Each dropping was about twice the size of an almond, and steam was coming off of them. The tracks were about four inches long, and just as wide, with two rounded sections at the back that went into two open toes that were more pointed. The tracks fueled their excitement as they continued to follow the trail in the dark.

They reached the split in the trail that heads to the ridge, and began to ascend toward the peak. The steep terrain grew more difficult to navigate. Nephi led on, while Alex followed. Alex began to feel the burning in his legs as they climbed. The hard work and movement of their bodies kept them warm, but they were moving slow enough to avoid breaking a sweat.

CHAPTER 15

In time, they reached the top of the trail, and took a moment to rest and catch their breath before moving onward. They walked along the ridge, still guided by the light of the headlamp. Nephi loved it here. It made him feel like he was on top of the world. He couldn't wait for the sun to come up to reveal what had become one of his favorite views - the snow-covered peaks in the background, fronted by a mountain stream, in a valley surrounded by flocked trees.

They reached the lookout spot, and Nephi pulled two folding stools from his backpack, and set them on the ground. The two friends turned off their headlamps, and sat there in silence, surrounded by the snowy forest. It was a serene morning, and they felt a sense of reverence for nature. Alex couldn't remember the last time he felt so calm.

Light slowly filled the small valley below them, revealing the stream that meandered through the snow-covered meadow. Not quite light enough for glassing, they took it in with the naked eye. The bugle of an elk in the distance broke the silence. To Nephi, there was no sound more beautiful in all the world. He could hear his heart beat faster as the bugle echoed through the air.

Elk were Nephi's favorite animal. Beautiful and majestic, he saw them as the rulers of the forest. He loved their powerful legs, and the way a bull's thick brown neck hair contrasted against its light colored body. He didn't think anything on earth was quite as lovely, as a big bull elk. This was their country, and he was their guest. This time of morning, right before the sun came up over the mountains, was his favorite time. He took a deep breath, inhaling the fresh, cold mountain air, and thought about how wonderful it was to be alive and to enjoy God's creations.

About 7:20, it was light enough to see, and Nephi raised his binoculars and began to glass the length of the hill on the other side of the valley. Alex followed suit. Nephi noticed movement to one side, and zeroed his binoculars in on the spot. He saw three cow elk, wandering through the trees. They were beautiful. He tapped Alex on the knee, and pointed in the direction of the elk. It took a few moments, but Alex managed to find them. He was excited to see animals in the wild.

Nephi raised the rifle to his shoulder, and lined up a cow in his scope. His rifle followed her as she walked. After all his years of hunting, this would be his first elk. His father would be so proud of him, and happy to have a freezer full of meat.

Glancing back at Alex for a moment, he noticed a look of horror on his face. After loading a round into the chamber, Nephi returned to the elk in his scope. He followed her into a clearing, where he had a perfect broadside shot. He confirmed his target and what was behind it. All clear. He exhaled and held his breath while he crawled his finger onto the trigger. All ready to squeeze, he thought about the great time he was having with Alex. The cow stopped to eat some grass.

He had never had such a perfect opportunity. At about 150 yards, the shot was easy for Nephi. Once he squeezed that trigger, he would have to clean the elk, and pack out the meat. As he contemplated it, he realized that all the fun would be over as soon as the bullet left the barrel, and he wasn't ready for his time with Alex to end. Nephi eased his finger back out of the trigger guard, removed his magazine, and ejected the round from the rifle.

Alex exhaled in relief, as a confused expression came to his face. "What happened?" he asked. "Why didn't you shoot it?"

"It was a bit too far away to get a good shot," said Nephi. "Besides, we might come across a bigger one later."

"It looked pretty big to me," replied Alex.

"Keep your eyes peeled. More elk are bound to come through."

They sat there and glassed until the sun fully came up over the mountain, casting warmth on their backs. Sitting had caused their bodies to cool, and the sun felt good. After another hour of glassing proved unfruitful, Nephi led them along the ridge back toward the direction of camp. They made their way down through the trees, and Nephi pointed out elk tracks and droppings everywhere.

More fresh tracks and droppings told them that an elk herd had been through there last night. Elk are mostly nocturnal animals, moving and feeding at night, especially during hunting season. The best chance to see them is first thing in the morning, and right before sundown. Alex and Nephi hiked through the forest, moving slowly. Moving so slow proved a bigger challenge than Alex expected. He used muscles in ways that didn't feel natural, and grew sore. Several rabbits and a fox crossed their path, making the slow, painful process worth it. Alex didn't realize how much he would enjoy seeing wildlife like this.

At about 10:00, figuring that their chances of seeing elk were slimmer this time of day, Nephi led the way back to camp, where they built a fire in the stove to warm up and make breakfast. Nephi's favorite freeze-dried breakfast meal was biscuits and gravy, and he boiled some water to make a pouch for each of them.

They sat and talked while they ate, and soaked up the warmth of the stove.

"What did you think of the elk?" asked Nephi.

"It was incredible to see such large animals in the wild. It's freezing up here, but so beautiful. It's worth it. I loved seeing the rabbits and the fox, too. Thanks for dragging me up here."

"I love it up here. I have since I was a kid. I have great memories of coming here with my family."

"Your family seems nice."

"They are, mostly. My dad is a blue-collar guy with a blue-collar job, and a strong work ethic. He is down to earth, and I think at least some of that rubbed off on all of us."

"Not all blue-collar families are down to earth. Some can be downright mean," replied Alex.

"I suppose you're right. Bradley's dad, for example. He puts off a bad vibe, more so recently, but my family isn't like that… except maybe my brother Jacob, to some extent."

"What's the deal with Jacob, anyway?"

"I don't really know. He has always been one of those holier-than-thou types, and has always been embarrassed of me, even before I came out. I think I always acted a bit too feminine for his taste, and he didn't know how to handle it. He just takes his frustrations out on me."

"That's too bad. I hate it when people act like that," said Alex.

"My other brother, Ammon, has always been supportive, and so has Tiffany. My relationship with Dad hasn't quite been the same since I came out, though. I don't know how to explain it, but it's different. I feel like he's disappointed in me. It really hurt when they were all talking about me before I arrived at the last family dinner. Like my relationship choices are any of their business…"

"Fathers can be difficult. I have seen that a lot. So many in the community struggle with that relationship. I think some men have a hard time comprehending how someone could be gay, so they shun it. What about Darla?"

"Mom has shown nothing but love and compassion. I think on some level, she is disappointed in me, but she has never said so. I don't know what I would do without her."

"I'm happy for you. You're lucky to have such a great family. Most don't."

"You know about my family, my job, my obsession with Tommy Page, my living arrangements, my religious beliefs, and my political beliefs, but I know almost nothing about you, except that you come from Jensen, love to cook, and love Blue October and Counting Crows. Tell me about you. What's your family like?"

"I'll tell you anything else about me, but I'm still not ready to get into my family with you. Don't be offended, I don't talk about it with anyone. Maybe someday that will change, but today is not that day."

"Okay then, tell me something about you that I don't already know."

"I'm a simple person, Nephi. I love to cook and I'm good at it. I love music, and like to sing along even though I'm tone deaf, and it sounds terrible. I enjoy watching movies, and I'm on the far left of the political spectrum."

"I already knew all of that. Tell me something else."

"Okay, I'll tell you something I didn't know myself until today. I enjoy spending time outdoors. The snow, the trees, the animals… It is all amazing, and sitting here with you, next to the warm stove is just what I needed to recharge."

They polished off the biscuits and gravy, and drank one more cup of cocoa, before heading back into the snowy wilderness. The hike lasted until late in the afternoon. They saw several deer, but no elk. Sitting at the edge of a clearing, they took time to hydrate and eat a protein bar while remaining quiet, and watching for elk. They then made their way back up to the top of the ridge to glass the stream and the slope on the opposite side as evening fell, and shooting light faded. By the time the sun disappeared behind the opposite slope, they still hadn't seen any more elk, and they turned back toward camp by the light of their headlamps.

Tired and wet, they built a new fire in the stove, and fashioned a clothesline above it from a rope. They removed their wet clothes, and hung them over the stove to dry while they sat in front of it in their long-johns, and warmed their feet.

Nephi boiled water for dinner. He selected freeze dried lasagna, while Alex opted for beef stew. After a long day in the snow, it really hit the spot. They burned the packaging in the stove, and added more wood to the fire.

"I wish I could listen to music right now," said Alex.

"Why don't you pull out your phone and play something?" asked Nephi.

"There's no data service up here for me to stream."

"I have tons of mp3s on my phone. I have all of Tommy Page's albums, of course, and after we talked about music, I even bought a Blue October album, if you want to listen to it."

"Wow, I thought there was no longer a need to download physical music files, but I guess this is the perfect situation for it. To be honest, I thought you were living in the wrong decade, honey, but you proved me wrong. Which album do you have?"

"I bought the "Sway" album, but I haven't listened to it yet."

"I can't think of a better time. It's not like you have anything better to do."

"You have a good point," replied Nephi as he retrieved the phone from his backpack.

After browsing to the album in the music app, he pressed play. The first track on the album was an instrumental introduction. Next up was the title track of the album, "Sway". Alex smiled, and his head perked up as it began to play.

"I love this song," he said. "Let's dance."

Alex stood and took Nephi by the hand, pulling him up out of the chair. They folded the chairs, and leaned them against the tent wall to make space. Nephi wrapped his arms around Alex's waist, while Alex hugged Nephi around the neck. They followed the song's suggestion, and swayed to the music, while staring into each other's eyes. Nephi had waited for a moment like this. Alex's strong arms wrapped around him, making Nephi feel safe.

He enjoyed the dance so much that he almost didn't mind when he heard an f-bomb drop in the middle of the song.

"Sorry," said Alex, "I forgot that one was in there."

Nephi laughed it off and hugged Alex tighter, as they continued the slow dance on the tent floor in their long-johns. They moved to the music as they watched the fire light cast shadows on the tent wall. The shadows seemed to dance along with them. Nephi felt a real connection, and though he had been fighting it for quite some time, so did Alex.

The song neared its end, and being caught up in the moment, their heads moved close toward each other. Nephi's bosom burned as their lips touched in a sweet, gentle kiss. They continued to kiss while the album played. Alex's lips moved down Nephi's cheek to his neck, unleashing a course of fire through Nephi's body. Their lips reconnected, and they explored each other's mouths with their tongues. They moved to the cot while continuing to kiss. Lying next to each other, they made out passionately.

Alex reached down and touched Nephi's thigh. Nephi withdrew from him.

"I'm not ready for that," said Nephi.

"Just kissing?"

"Yes, for now, just kissing."

"I can work with that," smiled Alex.

They continued making out on the cot in front of the stove. Warmed by the fire and the passion, Nephi pulled back again.

"Alex, I need to stop. I can't tell you how bad I want this, but I'm not ready to go any further, and if I don't stop now, I don't know if I'll be able to stop at all."

Fighting his own desire, and respecting Nephi's wishes, Alex moved to his own cot, and climbed into his sleeping bag. They both bridled their passions, and slept, while dreaming of each other's touch all night.

Morning came early, and with it, what sounded like pine needles constantly dropping onto the roof of the tent. Nephi opened the tent door to reveal large snowflakes falling quickly form the sky. He started the fire and crawled onto Alex's cot and lay there, holding him through the sleeping bag for several minutes until he woke up. Nephi just wanted to be close to him.

Now fully awake, Alex poked his head out of the sleeping bag, and kissed Nephi on the forehead, before sitting up. After making their way out into the falling snow to pee, they returned to the warm tent, and made a breakfast of freeze dried omelets and hot cocoa. They dressed in the clothes hanging over the stove that were now warm and dry, and made their way toward the ridge.

Like the previous day, the arrived in their perch before daylight, and glassed the valley below, and the opposite ridge, as the sun rose over the mountain. As Nephi gazed high upon the ridge through his binoculars, he felt frantic tapping on his shoulder. He turned to see Alex, clearly excited and pointing toward the stream.

Moving his binoculars slowly down toward the watering

hole at the base of the valley, Nephi understood why Alex was so excited. A monster, 6 x 7 bull elk stood there drinking from the stream. It was massive. Nephi had never seen anything as beautiful as that bull. They both sat and watched it through their binoculars, as best they could in the falling snow, as it drank from the stream, and dug its face down into the snow to find the grass that grew underneath.

They observed in awe, as it made its way up the hill on the opposite side, and over the ridge. Exhilarated by the shared experience, they hugged each other as the snow continued to fall, and then made their way back to camp to warm up.

"The snow hasn't stopped falling," observed Nephi. "If it doesn't let up, we could get stuck up here. I think it's best if we break down camp after we warm up, and head back home before it's too late."

"I don't want to get stuck up here, and I trust your judgement," replied Alex.

"That settles it. Let's warm up and eat something, and then we'll make our way home."

They didn't' want to light a fire in the stove, because it would complicate camp tear down, so Nephi started the truck and they sat in the cab with the heater, and ate protein bars. The heat felt good on their hands and their feet, and before long, they were ready to take everything down.

They cleared the inside of the tent, moving everything to its place in the truck bed, before taking down the tent. The job was difficult because of the snow. Nephi used a broom to raise the tent ceiling from the inside, causing the snow to slide off. They removed the canvas from the frame and folded it. It is never good to put a tent away wet, but they didn't have a choice. Nephi would need to dry it out in his parents' garage when he got home. They took down the frame, placing each piece in the truck, and then double checked the camp site, before getting in the truck and allowing the heater to warm them again before pulling out.

"I don't know that there are many things more fun than "redneckin' it," said Alex as he placed the Alabama cassette tape in the stereo. "Yee Haw!"

Nephi chuckled, "We should redneck it more often." He tried to drive forward, but the wheels just spun, so he got out and placed some pine boughs both in front of the tires, and behind them. He had trouble moving forward, and shifted into 4LO, and then into reverse where he had better luck. The truck backed out of the campsite onto the dirt road, now covered in more than a foot of snow.

Nephi stayed in 4LO, and slowly crawled the road until they reached the highway. Shifting into 4WD, he steered the truck back toward Francis, doing his best to avoid sliding off the slushy mountain road.

CHAPTER 16

Bradley gave Nephi a big bear hug, squeezing him so tight he thought it might crack a rib. It evicted all the air from Nephi's lungs. Taking a deep breath to gain some needed space, Nephi patted him gently on the back. Bradley released his grip and gave Nephi a kiss on the cheek before he turned and headed out the door for the elk hunt.

With Nephi gone, Bradley found himself alone in the apartment. Living away from his family was a big change, and he was nervous at the thought of spending the night alone. He took a nice, long shower, made himself pancakes and eggs for breakfast, and prepared for his shift at the ice cream shop. With about twenty minutes until the beginning of his shift, he locked up the apartment, and walked to the shop.

Gene was glad to see him. Bradley proved to be an exemplary employee, and the customers loved him.

"I need some help to move the ice cream from the back into the display freezer," said Gene.

"No problem, I'm on it," replied Bradley.

Bradley brought two fresh ice cream pans at a time from the back of the shop to the display case in the front, until all twenty slots were filled.

At noon, he unlocked the shop, and flipped the sign in the window from 'Closed' to 'Open'. All ready to serve customers, he took his place behind the counter in anticipation of the day's first guest. Thirty slow minutes passed before the first customer walked through the door, a regular named Tabatha.

"The usual?" asked Bradley.

"I think I might change it up today with Thanksgiving coming up. Why don't you give me a two-scoop cup of pumpkin, with white chocolate chips, and whipped cream on top?"

"Excellent choice, Madame," he said, as he scooped the ice cream into a cup, and added her toppings. She sat at the table in the corner, and happily enjoyed her treat before heading back to work.

More customers filed in, and Bradley handled the lunch rush by himself, while Gene did paperwork in his office in the back. It had been quite some time since Gene had an employee he could trust to run the store without close supervision.

Customers came and went until 3:00 when Jodie arrived. She would close the store today. Their shifts overlapped by a few hours so they could both support the dinner rush, the busiest time of the day.

Jodie was a sophomore at UVU. She had short red hair, and brown eyes. She was outgoing. She enjoyed working with Bradley. They were both personable, which made them good with customers.

Jodie had been encouraging Bradley to apply for admission to UVU, and find something he was passionate about to study. He wanted to attend school, but didn't know where to start, and worried that his home-school education wasn't sufficient to prepare him for university. Jodie assured him he would do just fine.

Bradley worked hard to clean the restaurant before the dinner rush, while Jodie covered the cash register. With all the tables and the floor spotless, he returned to the counter in time for the rush of customers that hit around 6:00.

About twenty minutes into the dinner rush, with a lobby full of customers, Bradley turned to help the next customer and shuddered at the sight of his parents with all of his siblings in tow.

"Um, what can I get for you?" he stuttered, surprised to see his parents, who never spent money on things like this.

"Ouch," said his father, while staring at the menu. "How does this place even stay in business with prices this high?"

Jodie chimed in, "Can I help you?"

"Yes, please. I would like to see your manager," said Brother Hanson.

Gene overheard him as he emerged from the back. "Hello sir, I'm Gene. I own the place."

"Hi Gene, I am Bradley's father."

"I'm pleased to meet you. Your son is one of my best employees. How can I help you?"

"I heard talk of my son working here, and had to come see it for myself. I just thought you should know that your employee entertains wicked perversions. Did you know that he is gay?"

"Well, I suspected, but didn't really know, but that makes no difference to me. He comes here every day and does his job well. I value him as an employee, and I don't appreciate what you are doing here. I have to ask you to leave."

"You would deny business to a family of nine, and take the side of this pervert?" asked Brother Hanson in an accusatory tone.

"Sir, your son is a fantastic employee, and a wonderful person, and I can say with confidence that I don't want business from someone like you, no matter how much ice cream you buy."

"Well, I never…" exclaimed Sister Hanson.

Little Brook pulled on Sister Hanson's dress. "Mama, can I have some ice cream?" she asked.

"Absolutely not, we will never support a business like this." She stormed out of the ice cream parlor in a huff, while the shop full of customers stared in astonishment.

"Come on kids, let's go," demanded Brother Hanson as he followed his wife out the door, a line of children following.

Bradley ran to the back of the store in tears while Gene addressed the customers.

"Sorry about all the commotion, folks. I have a wonderful, hardworking employee, who just so happens to be gay. If any of you have a problem with that, you can follow the bigot parade right out the door. Otherwise, Jodie here, will be happy to get you whatever you want at a ten percent discount."

He then went to the back of the store, where he found Bradley crying in the mop closet.

"I'm so sorry," said Bradley. "I can't believe my family made a scene like that in your store."

"Son, after meeting your father, I'm honestly not sure how

you turned out as well as you did. You're so kind and compassionate, everything that he's not. I want you to know that I'm not concerned one bit about those horrible people making a scene in my shop. I'm glad you're here. I value you as an employee and as a friend."

"Thanks," Bradley managed to say through the tears.

"Now you go home and get some rest. Your shift is almost over, anyway. I'll see you in the morning."

Gene patted him on the shoulder, and went back to the front of the store. Happy customers filled every table. Not one customer had followed the Hanson family out the door. Jodie went into the back to check on Bradley.

"That was crazy, man. I'm so sorry that your dad is such an asshole. I thought my dad was bad, but that is another level."

Bradley laughed through the tears, causing tears and snot to splatter all over the font of his apron. He wiped himself with a tissue.

"I guess I'll head home," he said.

"I think that's best," said Jodie. "Try to ignore the awful things your dad said. You're awesome, and we appreciate you here. I'll see you tomorrow."

Bradley left the store, and walked back to the apartment. He didn't feel like eating, and just lay on the bed thinking about the events of the evening, and crying. He felt lost, angry, and alone. The actions of his mother and father completely embarrassed him. He wished Nephi was home. He might know what to do. Eventually, he fell asleep, but spent a restless night, tossing and turning in bed.

Sometimes sleep is all it takes to clear one's head and set the world right. This was not one of those times. Bradley woke up in the morning, hopping mad about his family's stunt at the ice cream shop. He knew he should eat, but felt sick to his stomach, and couldn't bring himself to force anything down.

Thinking exercise might help, he went to the fitness room, and ran on the treadmill until he couldn't run anymore. Exhausted and drenched in sweat, he returned to the apartment and took a shower. He didn't know where to turn, and considered calling Darla Willard, but thought this problem was probably more than she bargained for, and decided against it. He went to the apartment complex laundromat, and washed his work clothes. By the time the dryer cycle finished, it was almost time for work.

He changed into his work clothes and walked to the ice cream parlor, where Gene greeted him with a smile. Glad to be at work, Bradley got to cleaning and stocking right away.

"I'm glad to see you back to yourself," said Gene.

Bradley wasn't feeling "back to himself" just yet, but he smiled. "I'm glad to be here."

With everything prepared, Bradley unlocked the door, and flipped the sign, while he awaited today's customers.

Bradley saw customers approaching the door, and put on his best smile, before he noticed that they weren't customers, but his family. They were marching in a circle in front of the door, pumping signs up and down in the air. He moved closer to get a better look. Sister Hanson carried a sign that read, "Repent or Perish". Todd's sign said, "Shop elsewhere. Don't support Satan." Bradley couldn't believe what he was seeing.

He read each sign as it passed the window. "Choose Jesus", "God Hates Gays", "Repent of Perversion", "Only Straight Families are Forever." Even little Brook carried a sign that said, "Repent and Choose the Right." It was a blow to Bradley. They started chanting in unison, "Repent or Perish". Tears again came to his face, and he called for Gene, who came running to the front of the store to see what the commotion was all about.

"Go in the back while I call the police," he said.

Bradley had seen enough, and didn't follow Gene's instructions. Instead, he walked out the front door, and confronted his father.

"What is wrong with you?" he yelled. "I'm not hurting you. I'm not hurting anyone. Just leave, and let me go on with my life. Focus on your other children, and leave me alone."

"I can't leave it alone," replied Brother Hanson. "You are ruining our eternal family. If you don't repent of your perversion, and return to God's ways, our family can't be together forever, and that is all because of you."

"Get it out of your head. I'm not coming back. I will never go on a mission, and nothing you can say or do will change the fact that I'm gay."

"You wicked child, you destroyed our eternal family. It would be better if you died as a child, instead of growing up to be gay. Your mother and I don't deserve this. I command you in the name of Jesus Christ to humble yourself, and repent."

The words cut to Bradley's core like a knife, taking his breath, and his will to fight. Everything in him wanted to scream at his father to leave, but the words wouldn't come out. He collapsed to the ground. As his father barked in his ear, calling him to repentance, a police car arrived, and two policemen approached the protesting family.

"What's going on here, folks?" asked an officer.

"Just a peaceful protest," replied Sister Hanson. "We're exercising our rights of free speech."

"This is private property," replied the officer. "If you are not welcome, you are trespassing. And if this was public land, you would need a protest permit. Do you have one of those?"

"Don't worry, officer, we were just leaving," said Brother Hanson, as he motioned the others to follow him to their van.

They got in the van and drove away, leaving Bradley there on the ground. Gene ran out of the store and helped him to his feet.

"Are you okay, son?" asked the officer.

"I think so," squeaked Bradley.

Though he was fine physically, he felt as if his soul had been gutted. He didn't know what to do, or how to make sense of it. The family who raised him would rather see him dead than acknowledge who he really was. The thought destroyed him.

"I saw how aggressive he was with you. Do you want to press charges against him?"

"No," replied Bradley, head down, eyes focused on the sidewalk.

"And would you like to press trespassing charges?" the officer asked Gene.

"Bradley?" asked Gene.

"No, no charges," came the reply.

"I guess not, officer. Thank you for coming out."

"If you need anything else, just give us a call."

"Will do," said Gene before the officers returned to their car. Gene gave Bradley a hug. They returned to the store and went about the work day. The rest of the day was thankfully, uneventful. Jodie was furious to hear what happened.

She gave Bradley a long hug. Since she was there to cover the counter, Gene told Bradley to go home and rest, and to forget about all the trouble with his family.

Bradley left the store in a daze, his head spinning while his father's words echoed in his mind. He hadn't slept well, and hadn't eaten in almost two days. He felt depleted. He needed to recharge and forget about his horrible family for a while. He wanted it all to go away and needed some good sleep.

Bradley stopped at the drugstore he passed every day on the way home, and bought a bottle of pills to help him sleep, and then returned to the apartment. With his father's words haunting his mind and not wanting to deal with his emotions, he took a double dose of the sleeping pills, and crashed on the bed.

Bradley awoke the next morning in a fog and realized he had slept fourteen straight hours. Fourteen straight, blissful hours, with no emotions tugging at his insides, tearing him apart. His head was cloudy, and he wasn't thinking straight. Bradley wanted to feel numb. Feeling nothing at all was so much nicer than feeling the constant pain of a broken heart, and a tormented soul.

Seeking relief from his emotions, Bradley opened the pill bottle and emptied it into his mouth, before washing it down with a bottle of water. He lay back on the bed, and drifted peacefully off to sleep, with a smile on his face.

CHAPTER 17

Loaded with hunting gear and two men, the white truck thundered slowly down a snow-packed Highway 35, while the best country music the 80s had to offer blasted on the stereo. As they approached the town of Francis, Nephi spelled out his plan for the day.

"I'll drop you off in Salt Lake, and then head to my parents' house to unload the gear and dry out the tent."

Now that they were out of the snow, Alex unbuckled his seatbelt and slid over into the middle seat. He fastened the middle belt around his waist, and placed Nephi's hand in his.

"I'm in no rush. I wasn't planning to be back until tomorrow night. Let's just head to Pleasant Grove. I can help you unpack and clean everything up. Besides, I'm not ready to leave your side just yet."

Nephi smiled and squeezed Alex's hand tighter. Rather than turning right toward Kamas, he continued straight through Francis, and made a left toward Heber. They drove through Heber, making a right on Highway 189 which took them around Deer Creek, and into Provo Canyon.

Descending the canyon, they passed Bridal Veil Falls, which provided a spectacular view backed by the colorful fall foliage. They continued past the outdoor shooting range, which reminded Alex of the terribly loud rifle with the muzzle break.

Holding hands the entire time, they drove through Provo and Orem, where they connected to I-15, and navigated north to Pleasant Grove. There, they exited the freeway, and made their way into town.

"Let's hit my parents' house first," said Nephi. "We can unload all of this gear, lock up the gun in the safe, and set the tent out to dry in the garage."

"Listen, honey," replied Alex. "We've been in the woods for two days. I'm cold, stinky, and filthy. Before I do anything else, I need a shower."

"Fine, we'll head to my apartment for a shower and a

change of clothes first, and then we'll unload."

"Much better plan, darling," replied Alex.

Nephi continued home, and pulled into the apartment complex parking lot.

"Bradley should be at work by now, so we should have the place to ourselves," he said.

"Good, I can't wait to get you alone behind closed doors," responded Alex, as he slapped Nephi on the butt.

They locked the truck and ran up the stairs to the apartment. Nephi opened the door and walked in. Thirsty from the long drive, Alex went to the sink to get some water, while Nephi removed his coat.

"Oh, shit!" exclaimed Alex, in a panicked voice.

"Language, mister!"

"Nephi, there's an empty bottle of sleeping pills on the counter. Is Bradley here?"

The small, one bedroom apartment, was mostly one big, open room. The bedroom was separated from the rest of the apartment only by a short hallway that passed by the bathroom. Nephi darted into the bathroom first. Finding it empty, he proceeded to the bedroom, where he found Bradley, lying on the bed.

Nephi rushed to him, as Alex joined them in the room. His body was warm, but he couldn't feel a pulse.

"Call 911," yelled Nephi.

His eagle scout training kicked in, and he began chest compressions, while Alex dialed 911. An ambulance arrived within minutes, and the paramedics took over the life saving efforts, while Nephi began to cry.

"I have a pulse," declared the paramedic, "but it's weak."

They moved Bradley to a stretcher, and carried him out of the apartment, and loaded him in the back of the ambulance.

"Where are you taking him?" asked Nephi.

"We're taking him to American Fork Hospital."

"We'll follow you over," said Nephi.

"Hold on, Son. You won't be able to see him until he is stable, and you might want to clean up a bit first," said the paramedic, pointing toward Nephi's muddy boots, and orange vest.

"I guess you're right. We'll clean up quickly and be over."

The ambulance sped away, siren blaring, while Alex and Nephi ran back into the apartment. They alternated taking quick showers, and changed into fresh clothes, before hopping in the truck and speeding to the hospital as quickly as traffic would permit.

They went straight to the information desk, and asked about Bradley. The woman at the desk indicated that he was in the ER, and could not have any visitors, but they were welcome to wait for news in the lobby.

Nephi's leg nervously bounced up and down while he sat. Alex sat next to him, with his hand on Nephi's shoulder. Nephi took the phone from his pocket and called Darla.

"Mom," he said, his voice agitated, "We came home early from hunting and found Bradley unconscious in my apartment. The ambulance brought him to American Fork Hospital with a weak pulse. Alex and I are waiting in the ER lobby, and I'm not sure what to do. Will you call his parents, and let them know what happened?"

"Of course, I will, sweetheart. I'll give Sister Hanson a call right now, and then I'll come to the hospital to wait with you."

They hung up, and Darla made the call. Not knowing where else to direct his nervous energy, Nephi called the ice cream shop to let them know what happened. Gene answered the phone, and Nephi explained what happened.

"That poor, sweet boy," cried Gene. "Those bastards did it to him. It's all their fault!"

"All whose fault?" asked Nephi. "What happened?"

Gene told Nephi all about the disturbance the Hanson family caused in the shop on Wednesday, and the picketing on Thursday. He explained how Bradley had collapsed to the ground after his father told him he would be better off dead, and that he seemed distraught for the rest of the day. Not knowing what else to do, Gene had sent him home early. He tried calling when Bradley didn't show up for his shift, and worried that something had happened, but didn't know who else to call.

"I'm closing the shop and coming there to wait with you," offered Gene.

"That's very kind of you. I'll see you soon."

Nephi's knee resumed bouncing as he waited impatiently for any news of Bradley's condition. Before long, Darla joined them in the waiting room, immediately followed by Gene.

"Were you able to get in touch with Bradley's parents?" asked Nephi.

"They weren't answering the phone, so I went over and knocked on the door and interrupted home-school. I spoke with Sister Hanson, and explained what happened, and offered to drive her to the hospital. At first, she appeared upset, and I thought she would come with me, but then the look on her face changed to that intense, stern expression that she always wears. She told me that God's will would be done, and to let her know of any further developments. She then closed the door. I knocked again to talk some sense into her, but there was no answer, so I came straight here."

Gene recounted the events of the past two days to all of them. Tears filled Darla's eyes as she listened, jaw dropped.

"The monsters!" she exclaimed. "I knew they were strict and uppity, but I never thought them capable of that."

Gene hugged her tightly while her fists clinched at her side. She turned, took Nephi by the hand, and looked him directly in the eye.

"Son," she said, "I need you to understand that I love you no matter what. I am your mother, and nothing you could ever say or do could change my love for you. I accept you, and love you for who you are, and even in the darkest times, you can always come to me."

"I know, Mom."

He embraced her, and they both stood there, crying in each other's arms. Alex and Gene were both crying, as they observed the loving embrace.

Nephi pulled back and sat down. He dropped his head and

confessed, "This is all my fault. I should have never left him to go hunting. If I had been home, I could have consoled him, and helped him see things clearly."

"Nonsense," said Darla. "That boy has demons that you can't cast out. If fault lies anywhere, it's with his parents. I will never understand how anyone could treat their own child like that. Don't think for a second that this is on you. Bradley needs some professional help to cope with all of this."

"Listen to your mom," added Alex. "None of this is your fault. You even offered Bradley a chance to come with us to the mountains. We both wish he would have come with us, but hindsight is twenty-twenty. We can't change the past. What has happened, has happened. All we can do is move forward from where we are, in the best way we know how."

Alex leaned over and gave Nephi a hug. Nephi truly felt terrible, and assigned himself blame, despite the wise words of his mother and Alex.

The moment was interrupted when Jodie joined them.

"Thanks for calling me, Gene," she said. "Any news?"

"Nothing yet."

Gene introduced Jodie to the group. She explained how she and Bradley became fast friends, and how horrified she was when his family showed up at the ice cream parlor to traumatized him.

Nephi suggested that they pray for Bradley. They all kneeled there in the waiting room, and Nephi prayed aloud, asking God to heal Bradley. The five then sat in silence, and waited for news from the Emergency Room. After some time, a doctor approached them.

"Are you Bradley's family?" she asked.

"Yes," Nephi instinctively answered, "I mean, we aren't blood relatives, but we are the closest thing to family he's got."

"I'm sorry," replied the doctor. "I'm only at liberty to discuss his condition with family. Can you find an immediate family member?"

"Yes, I can," replied Darla. "Wait right here, I'll be back."

She rushed out of the hospital while the rest of them waited anxiously, worried about Bradley's condition.

Darla drove straight to the Hanson home and pounded on the door. Todd answered, and Darla demanded to speak with his mother.

"Audrey," she said, "you need to come with me to the hospital right now. They have some news and they will only discuss it with immediate family members."

"I can't," she replied. "My husband wouldn't like it."

"I don't much care what he would like. All I know is that there is a group of people at that hospital who love your son, people who will be there for him, and support him through this, and they can't do it without you. I'm not leaving until you get in the car!"

Sister Hanson reluctantly followed Darla to the car, and got in. They sat in silence the entire way to the hospital, and Sister Hanson followed Darla into the waiting room, where a host of concerned faces greeted her, trying their best to suppress their anger.

Darla let the desk know that Bradley's mother was present, and the doctor soon came out.

"Are you Bradley's family?" she asked.

"I'm his mother," she stated.

"Would you like to speak in private?"

She looked around at all the anxious faces, waiting for news of her son.

"No," she replied. "You can say whatever you have to say in front of them."

"Your son took too many sleeping pills," she explained. "It caused his heart rate and breathing to slow, and he had a seizure. We were able to restore his heart rate, and he is now breathing with help from a machine, but there isn't any brain activity. He is essentially in a coma, and there is a possibility that he won't wake up. We need to run more tests but you are welcome to see him now."

"Thank you, doctor," replied Sister Hanson. "But I don't want to see him."

The doctor gave her a puzzled look.

"But," she continued, "I want you to let these people visit him. Lately, they have acted more like his family than I have. May the Lord's will be done."

With that, she turned to Darla. "Take me home?" she asked.

Darla nodded, and the two of them left the hospital. The rest of the group was astonished. Maybe deep down inside, that woman had a fragment of a heart after all.

"Bradley can only have two visitors at a time," explained the doctor.

"You two should go first," said Gene, pointing to Nephi and Alex.

They followed the doctor back through a corridor, and around the corner to room 215. There, they found Bradley, unconscious in bed, tubes attached everywhere, his chest rising and falling to the billowy sound of the breathing machine.

Nephi ran his fingers through Bradley's hair while Alex squeezed his hand.

Nephi pleaded with him, "Wake up. Please, wake up. I'm so sorry, man. I never should have left. You needed me, and I wasn't there. I hope someday you can forgive me. Please open your eyes. I need you."

Leaning over, Nephi maneuvered around the tubes to kiss him gently on the forehead. Alex pulled the visitor chairs closer, and they sat next to the bed, Nephi clutching Bradley with one hand, the other interlocking fingers with Alex.

Not knowing whether he could hear them, they told Bradley all about their hunting trip. They talked of the beautiful snow flocked trees, the elk, and their dance to the glow of the fire in the tent. They told him how they hoped to share many more moments like that with him after he woke up.

After visiting for a while, they promised to be back, and left the room to give Gene and Jodie a chance to visit. In the waiting room, they discovered that Darla had returned. They sat and visited with her while Gene and Jodie followed a nurse to room 215.

Gene and Jodie spoke to Bradley, telling him that they

valued him as a coworker, but loved him even more as a friend. Gene told him how good he was with customers, and how difficult it is to find someone with his work ethic, and that he could even manage the shop someday.

Jodie told him all about UVU, and that she was confident he would excel there, and could become whatever he wanted. They both squeezed his hand gently, before making an exit. In the waiting room, they wished Nephi, Alex, and Darla well, and excused themselves for the day.

Darla then visited Bradley together with Nephi, while Alex stayed in the waiting room. Then, Darla, too, excused herself for the night. She traded keys with Nephi, and drove his truck home, so she and Mike could clean and put away the hunting gear, allowing Nephi to focus on Bradley.

Alex and Nephi sat next to Bradley's bed and talked to him, and to each other.

"Thanksgiving is less than a week away," observed Nephi. "Are you going home to Jensen for the holiday?"

"No, I haven't been back in a while. I'm not much of one to celebrate holidays. I'll most likely just hang out at home, and binge watch whatever strikes my fancy."

"There's not a chance I will let you spend this holiday alone. Come to Thanksgiving dinner with my family. Hopefully Bradley will be well enough to join us, too. Nobody puts on a Thanksgiving like my mom. Her turkey is moist, and she uses real potatoes with butter, and her secret ingredient – cream cheese. Oh, and her pies, her pies are unbelievable! You have to come."

"Okay, honey, you can stop now. You sold me already. I'll be there."

"Perfect. Come to my apartment around 11:00, and we can hang out for a bit, and then head over together."

"It's a date," replied Alex.

A date. Nephi liked the sound of that. He wasn't sure exactly what their relationship was, but he knew that it was something more than it was at this time last week, and he was happy about that.

The pair of them stayed by Bradley's side until visiting hours were over, and the hospital made them leave. Since it was late, Alex crashed at Nephi's place. They were physically and emotionally exhausted. Nephi gave Alex the bed, while he slept on the sofa. Alex protested, suggesting that they both sleep on the bed, but Nephi wasn't ready to take that step, even if they were just sleeping. Besides, he had grown accustomed to sleeping in the living room.

They slept soundly through the night, and woke up late in the morning. Nephi awoke to the smell of eggs, and looked up from the sofa to see Alex in the kitchen, making breakfast. His omelets were much better than the freeze dried variety that sustained them at camp. They enjoyed breakfast together, and then returned to the hospital to visit Bradley. His condition hadn't changed. They sat next to his comatose body, and talked to him, begging him to wake up.

They visited for several hours, with no apparent change to his condition, and then left to get some lunch, and take Alex home, because he had to work the following day. Still driving Darla's car, Nephi drove to Alex's Salt Lake apartment. They shared a long kiss across the center console in the front seat before Alex disappeared inside, and Nephi made the long drive back to Pleasant Grove, going directly to his parents' house. He didn't want to be alone, and besides, he had to get his truck.

He pulled in the driveway to find everything put away, and his truck clean, inside and out. He was thankful for that gesture of love. Darla greeted him as he walked inside. She gave him a big hug and told him how sorry she was about everything that happened with Bradley.

Mike joined them in the living room, and they chatted about Bradley and his family, and about Alex and the hunt.

"So you didn't manage to bring me any meat?" asked Mike.

"Nope, we saw a few cows, but I just didn't have the right shot," replied Nephi, not revealing the whole truth.

"With everything that happened, it's just as well. If you had returned any later, that Hanson boy wouldn't have had any chance," observed Mike.

"I guess you're right. We have become good friends. I really hope he wakes up and makes a full recovery," said Nephi.

"We hope so too," said Darla.

After visiting for a while, Nephi swapped keys with his mom, and drove his truck over to the hospital, where he sat alone in Bradley's room, praying for a miracle.

The same doctor from the previous day walked in the room to find Nephi on his knees, arms folded, on Bradley's bed, praying for him to wake up. She waited for him to finish the prayer before speaking.

"Are you Nephi Willard?"

"I am," he said.

"Bradley's mother gave me permission to give you updates on his condition."

"She came to visit?" he asked.

"No, you and your friend have been his only visitors today, but I spoke with her on the phone."

"Oh, how is Bradley doing?"

"Pretty much the same as yesterday. We ran some additional tests. His body is healthy but there is no sign of brain activity. I'm afraid the prognosis isn't good."

"Is there any chance he will wake up?"

"There is always a chance, but less than three percent of patients in this condition ever regain consciousness, and of those that do, over fifty percent suffer permanent brain damage. We will continue to observe and test Bradley's condition, but you shouldn't get your hopes up."

Visibly shaken and crying, Nephi struggled to say, "Thanks, doctor."

"I'm sorry about your friend," she said. "I hope I'm wrong and he makes a full recovery."

She turned and walked out of the room. Nephi sat at Bradley's side, and took his hand.

"Come on, Bradley. I really need you to pull through."

Visiting hours ended, and they again forced Nephi to leave the hospital. Sad and alone, he returned to his empty apartment. It had been nice having someone to share the place with. Reserving the bed for Bradley when he woke up, Nephi slept on the sofa.

The following day, the ward held a special fast for Bradley, fasting and praying for his recovery. As soon as church ended, Nephi went to the hospital, and stayed with Bradley all day. Mike and Darla joined him for a few hours. Still no change to Bradley's condition.

The days were long as the week moved forward. Nephi went to work each day, spending the evenings in the hospital at Bradley's side, holding his hand, and praying for a miracle.

Alex joined him at the hospital on Wednesday afternoon, and the two of them stayed until the end of visiting hours. Thanksgiving being the following day, Alex stayed at Nephi's place to avoid making the drive home, only to return in the morning. They rented a movie from the grocery store kiosk, and watched it together. Before the movie ended, they had fallen asleep on the couch in each other's arms, and found themselves in the same position when they woke up on Thanksgiving morning.

Nephi leaned over and kissed Alex, and thanked him for being there.

"Mom will put on a king's feast today," he said. "We better have a light breakfast."

He made a batch of steel-cut oats, and they ate, while they watched the Thanksgiving parade on TV. The parade was one of Nephi's favorite things about Thanksgiving. He loved seeing the large cartoon character balloons fly through the streets, and the floats pass by as people on the street cheered. He especially loved the musical performances.

After finishing their oatmeal, they cuddled together on the couch, watching the parade. Around noon, they each took a shower and got ready for the day, before going to Mike and Darla's place for Thanksgiving dinner.

They arrived to a house already in chaos, with children flying around, and Darla frantically trying to put the finishing touches on dinner. The commotion was unfamiliar to Alex, who hadn't experienced a family Thanksgiving in a very long time. He was a little overwhelmed, as Nephi brought him upstairs and introduced him to the family.

"This is my friend, Alex, everyone."

"Welcome, Alex," said Darla, giving him a hug.

"I'm so sorry about what happened to Bradley Hanson," said Tiffany, before hugging both Nephi and Alex.

"How are you holding up, bro?" asked Ammon.

"As well as can be expected, I guess. I just keep praying that he will wake up."

"We've all been praying for him," said Jacob. "I'm sure he will make a full recovery if it's God's will."

They caught up on each other's lives until the turkey was ready. Darla spread everything out, buffet style, on the kitchen island Mike carved the turkey, and then asked Jacob to offer the blessing on the food. They all bowed their heads, and folded their arms while he prayed.

"Our Dear Father in heaven, on this Thanksgiving Day, we are thankful for all of our blessings. We thank thee for this beautiful country in which we live, and the freedom that we enjoy. We thank thee for one another, and the love we share, and we thank thee for this food, and for those who prepared it. Please bless that it will do our bodies good, and provide us with strength. We thank thee for the opportunity to be together as family and friends. We ask a special blessing on Bradley Hanson at this time. Please bless him that he may recover, and be well, if it be according to thy will. Please bless him with a desire to choose the right, and follow thy ways after he recovers, and please bless each of us here with a desire to obey all of thy commandments, even if it is hard for us. We thank thee for the gospel, and our Savior, Jesus Christ, and for our knowledge of the truth. Help us to always remember Him and to follow His ways. In the name of Jesus Christ, Amen."

Overall, it was a beautiful prayer, but the passive aggressive undertones were not lost on Nephi, or on Alex. Ammon and Chelsea offered to sit at the smaller table with the children to make room for Nephi and Alex at the big table. While Nephi would have preferred to eat with the children, he was thankful for his brother's gesture and accepted the offer to eat at the table with his parents and other siblings.

"As a chef, I am interested to know your opinion on the food," Darla said to Alex.

"Ma'am, this is the most delicious bird I have ever tasted, and your mashed potatoes are divine. And I'm not just saying that. Everything I have tried is excellent."

Satisfied, Darla smiled, and continued eating as the meal and the conversation carried on. They discussed Jacob's job, and Tiffany's pregnancy. The baby was now past due, and if it didn't come on its own by Monday, here obstetrician would induce labor. Enjoying the conversation, Alex leaned over and rested his head against Nephi's shoulder, while Nephi extended his arm around Alex.

Annoyed, Jacob stood, and shot a disgusted glare in Nephi's direction.

"Why do you always have to throw the gay in my face?" he shouted.

Alex pulled away and sat up straight in his chair.

"What are you talking about? I'm not throwing anything in your face, or anyone else's."

"You said that you and Alex weren't a thing the last time we talked, and now you're snuggling with him at the dinner table?"

"At the time, we weren't a thing, but a lot has happened and we're, well, I'm honestly not sure what we are, but we're not… not a 'thing'."

"We're a thing," countered Alex.

"We're a thing? Okay, I guess we're a thing," said Nephi.

"Well, I don't have to put up with this. They say "love the sinner, and hate the sin," but you make that awfully difficult when you throw around your gayness at the dinner table," protested Jacob.

"You cuddle with Camille in front of me all the time. How is this any different? And how can you love the sinner, and hate the sin, if you think the very essence of who I am is a sin? I don't see any way you can love me," said Nephi.

"It's completely different. When I cuddle with Camille, it's totally natural, and accepted in the sight of God."

"And putting my arm around Alex is what?"

"It's… it's unnatural."

"I wish you would understand that God made me this way. It is my nature. It isn't something I chose, it is just who I am, something I have no control over. How is it unnatural to be who God made me?"

"You're impossible, you know that?"

Darla interrupted them, "That's enough boys. I will not allow you to ruin Thanksgiving with your arguing. Jacob, sit down! Your brother has been through a lot in the last week, and this conversation isn't healthy."

"I will not sit down, and I'm not dealing with Nephi's blatant sin, and flouting of God's law. I'm done! Camille, let's go. We're leaving."

Jacob abruptly stood, and grabbed Camille by the hand, pulling her away from the table. They went to the children's table, picked up Dallin and Crystal, and carried them toward the door, kicking and screaming.

"I will not have you set an example of perversion for my children," said Jacob as they exited through the front door, slamming it closed behind them.

Their minivan sped away, while everyone else sat there, shocked. The silence was broken by Darla, who yelled, "Ammon and Chelsea, please bring Sophie in here. Bring your plates. There's plenty of room at the table. What we need now, is some pie."

"Mom, I'm sorry," started Nephi.

"Nephi, let's drop this. You have nothing to be sorry for, and I will not have this Thanksgiving ruined any more than it already has been. Mike, please slice the pie."

Mike did as he was told, and soon everyone was eating pie and chatting. Sophie's plate held more whipped cream than pie.

Holidays always seem to bring out the worst in a family, especially adult siblings. Sometimes, sharing a childhood together is the longest they can bear being civil to one another.

Once they are adults, and no longer fully intimidated by mother's guilt trips, and corrective glare, their claws come out, and their true selves are revealed.

Nephi was sad about the way it ended, and embarrassed that it happened in front of Alex, but at least he had given Alex some warning about Jacob's nature.

With Jacob gone, the rest of the day was pleasantly peaceful, full of good food, and good company.

After they left, Nephi apologized to Alex for the incident.

"Don't worry about it," he replied. "That's the best Thanksgiving I've had in as long as I can remember. I love your family, and of all the things I'm grateful for, having you in my life is at the top of the list."

"Aww, look at you, you sweet man." Nephi leaned in and kissed him, and then gave him a big hug. "I feel the same way. So, we're a thing, huh?"

"I didn't intend for it to happen, and truthfully, I never thought it would turn into this, but we are definitely a thing."

They returned to Nephi's apartment building, where Alex gave Nephi one more kiss before getting in his Prius and heading out. In all, it had been a great day, but he had to work on Friday, and needed to get home.

After he left, Nephi went inside. On his knees, he thanked God for sending Alex into his life, and prayed again for Bradley to recover. If anything, Thanksgiving had been eventful. Nephi was thankful for his many blessings, and hoped that the future held good things.

CHAPTER 18

Friday morning, Nephi woke up feeling unusually anxious. He finished the steel-cut oats he had made Thanksgiving morning, and ran on the treadmill to calm his nerves. He then prayed for Bradley's health. Long overdue for a talk with Stacy, he texted her, asking if they could meet for lunch.

Fully ready for the day, he went to the office. After shift hand-off with Monica, he started daily rounds and monitors. Keeping his mind on work was difficult, with his friend still in a coma, but he did his best to have a reasonably productive morning, given the circumstances.

Stacy returned his text, confirming she was good to meet for lunch. She would wait for him inside the Purple Turtle. When lunch time arrived, he quickly headed to their meeting place. Both Chloe and Wyatt were there with Stacy. Wyatt lay in the car seat, and sucked on his binky while they ate and talked.

Nephi went into detail about Bradley, the hunting trip, Thanksgiving, and his budding relationship with Alex. It was a lot to take in. She was so excited for him on the Alex front. If anyone was deserving of a happy relationship, it was Nephi. She was more than angered by the actions of Bradley's family, and those of Jacob at Thanksgiving, and she was heartbroken about Bradley.

"Don't you dare go so long without telling me big things ever again," she scolded. "I love you and I'm here for you through everything. Let me do that."

"I'm sorry. Things have been so crazy lately, and everything happened so quickly. I have been so busy attending to Bradley and trying to hold it together, that I just didn't make the time."

She hugged him and told him that everything would be alright. The ringing of Nephi's phone cut the hug short. It was Sister Hanson. She wanted Nephi to meet her at the hospital right away.

"I have to get to the hospital," he said.

"I'm coming with you," insisted Stacy.

Nephi drove toward the hospital, while Stacy followed. On the way from the parking lot to the waiting room, he called Mark and let him know there was an emergency, and he might not be back in the office.

Once inside, Sister Hanson approached him, while Stacy stared her down with a soul-piercing glare. If Stacy had super powers, it would have burned a hole right through the woman. Sister Hanson reached Nephi, and took him by the hand.

"The hospital called me this morning. They want to talk about Bradley, and I thought you should be here. He needs you, and I think I need you, too."

"What about Brother Hanson?"

"He refuses to come. He's not acknowledging Bradley's existence at the moment."

"Okay, I'll do anything I can for Bradley. Where do we go?"

"The doctor is waiting for us in a consultation room around the corner."

Stacy stayed in waiting room with the kids while Nephi followed Sister Hanson to the room where the doctor waited.

"Thank you for meeting with me," she said.

"We have been constantly monitoring Bradley's condition, and it has not changed. The machine is breathing for him, and he has a strong heartbeat, but there is no brain activity. I'm afraid that the most likely outcome is that he will remain in a persistent vegetative state."

Tears began flowing down Nephi's face as he listened.

"Are either of you aware of whether Bradley has an advance directive in place?"

"Not that I'm aware of," Nephi choked out.

"I don't believe so," replied Sister Hanson.

"In that case, as his mother, I will leave the decision to you, about how to proceed. I strongly believe that his condition will not change. If we turn off the machine, there is a chance that he will breathe on his own for some time, but the most likely outcome is that he will pass away quickly. I want you to think about it for as long as you need, and let me know what you would like to do."

Sister Hanson lowered her head in thought. Uncomfortable silence permeated the room. She was at a loss for words. She turned to Nephi.

"What do you think?"

"Sister Hanson, this has to be your decision. I love Bradley and would give anything to have him back. In this situation, I just can't, the decision is yours."

"I haven't been a very good mother lately," she confessed, "When I think of him, I still see my sweet little boy. If you were in his place, what would you want?"

Nephi considered it carefully before replying, "I wouldn't want to stay like that forever, lying helpless in bed, unable to move or enjoy life."

"I agree," said Sister Hanson. She turned to the doctor. "Let's unplug the machine, and leave him in the Lord's hands."

"Alright," said the doctor. "Would you like to say goodbye?"

"Yes," replied Nephi. "I want to be with him until the end."

"I want to remember him as my sweet little boy," said Sister Hanson. "I don't want to see him stuffed with tubes like that."

"I understand," said the doctor while giving Sister Hanson some paperwork to sign.

She signed the papers, and headed out to the waiting room to await the outcome.

"Please follow me, Nephi," directed the doctor.

Nephi followed her into Bradley's room. He kissed Bradley on the forehead and took his hand.

"Ready?" asked the doctor.

Nephi nodded. The doctor turned the breathing machine off, and removed the tube from his nose and mouth. Bradley's chest continued moving up and down for a few moments, and then slowed, as Nephi observed the numbers on the monitor drop, eventually resting at zero. The machine unleashed a continuous monotone beep before the doctor turned it off. She checked his pulse.

"He's gone," she said. "I'm sorry for your loss."

Nephi continued holding his hand as he sobbed. Bradley's passing devastated him, but he was glad to be there, so his friend did not walk into the next life alone.

"God be with you until we meet again," he whispered.

"Whenever you are ready," said the doctor.

"I'm ready," replied Nephi.

He released Bradley's hand, and gave him one last kiss on the forehead, before following the doctor back out to the lobby, where she informed Sister Hanson of her son's passing. A single tear glistened in Sister Hanson's eye. She shook the doctor's hand, and thanked her for her help, and gave Nephi a nod before walking out of the hospital.

Stacy embraced Nephi as he sobbed on her shoulder.

"I'm so sorry, Nephi. There aren't any words."

He continued sobbing while she held him. He eventually collected himself.

"Come to my place," she suggested. "You shouldn't be alone right now."

"Maybe you're right," he agreed.

He followed her to her house, a quarter mile away, having difficulty remaining composed enough to drive. Once at her house, they watched a movie while Chloe colored at his feet, and Stacy nursed Wyatt. Not feeling up to cooking, Stacy ordered pizza. Roger was pleased to see dinner waiting when he walked through the door.

He worked on a slice of pizza and asked Nephi how he was doing. Stacy explained what happened with Bradley. Roger offered his condolences, and gave Nephi a hug. Nephi knew that Alex would be working, so he sent a text asking him to call when his shift was over.

After they had watched a couple of movies, Stacy could see that Nephi was still upset, and in no condition to drive, so she invited him to spend the night there on the couch. He accepted the offer. After family prayer and scripture study, Nephi gave Chloe a hug and a kiss goodnight, and kissed Wyatt on the cheek, before they went to bed.

Stacy and Roger stayed up talking with Nephi until about 10:00, when they headed to bed themselves, leaving him alone in the living room with the TV, and his thoughts. Nephi had prayed so hard for a different outcome, but it wasn't in God's plan. He knew that God always hears prayers. For whatever reason, he had chosen not to answer this one, at least not in the way that Nephi wanted him to. He had to learn to accept God's will, and in this case, it wasn't easy. He distracted himself with some Bonanza reruns while he waited for Alex to call.

A little before midnight, his phone rang. It was Alex.

"Hi Alex."

"Hi, am I calling too late?"

"Not at all, I've been waiting for your call."

"Is everything okay?"

"Not really," he said. "Bradley passed away this afternoon."

"Oh, sweetie, I'm so sorry! I don't even know what to say. How are you holding up?"

"I'm hanging in there. Stacy was at the hospital with me when it happened, so I spent the afternoon with her family and I'm spending the night at their place."

"I'm so glad you're not alone."

"Sorry to spring this news on you after work. Are you okay?

"Bradley was a great guy and I'll miss him, but I had kind of prepared myself for this outcome. Unfortunately, it's not the first time I have lost a friend like that."

"I'm so sorry. Do you want to talk about any of it?" asked Nephi.

"Not right now. What can I do for you?"

"I think I'm okay for tonight. I just wanted to let you know. I would love to see you tomorrow morning, though."

"Oh, I would love that. I work in the afternoon, so we can spend more time together if you come to Salt Lake."

"No problem. What time do you want me there?"

"Be at my place around 11:00."

"Sound good! I'll see you then. Bye, baby."

"Goodbye."

Having spoken to Alex, Nephi drifted off to sleep. Deep sleep provided his mind some time to process the loss. He was distraught, but not to the point where he could not function. Stacy got up early, and made Belgian waffles for breakfast. Nephi didn't feel much like eating, but at the insistence of Stacy, he forced down half a waffle and some strawberries.

He thanked Stacy for everything, and went home for a run and a shower before seeing Alex. Clean and refreshed, he felt he could move forward. The truck was nearly out of fuel, so he made a quick pit stop on his way to Alex's apartment.

Alex opened the door and gave Nephi a tender hug, and a sympathetic smile. To this point, they spent most of their time together in Utah County, and this was Nephi's first time inside Alex's apartment. The front door opened into the space between the living room and kitchen, where the dining table sat, with the living room to the left, and the kitchen to the right. Bookshelves lined the living room walls in a zig-zag pattern which intrigued Nephi. He had never even considered that anything othr than straight bookshelves existed.

He noted that most of them were cookbooks, with a spattering of historical fiction, biographies, and thrillers mixed in. In the corner was a functioning traffic light, with the green circle illuminated. A sectional sofa lined the wall opposite a large, flat screen TV. The coffee table was made from wooden planks, supported by wagon wheels.

"Pardon me, while I stand here, and fawn over your decorations," stated Nephi as he gazed around the room.

"I'm glad you like it. Have a seat. Can I get you anything to drink?"

"I'm good for now, thanks," replied Nephi, taking a seat

on the sofa.

Nephi noticed that Alex was wearing a black hoodie that said "Amsterdam" on it with a dragon crest emblem on the chest. He complimented Alex, letting him know how much he liked it.

"Oh, thanks," said Alex. "I got it on my trip to Amsterdam. It's my favorite hoodie. A bit big for me, but very comfortable."

"I love it! When did you go to Amsterdam?"

"Years ago. It's the only place I've ever been other than here, but it was amazing. I'll tell you all about it later, but right now, I want to talk about Bradley."

They sat on the sofa, holding hands and sharing memories of time spent with Bradley. They laughed, and they cried while remembering their friend. After about an hour, Alex invited Nephi into the kitchen, so they could continue talking while he made lunch.

"Macaroni and cheese okay with you?"

"I've always loved mac n cheese," replied Nephi. "Ever since I was a kid, the store bought kind with the powdered cheese has been my favorite."

"Honey, don't speak that blasphemy in my kitchen. I don't do powdered cheese."

He continued preparing lunch while they talked. He used high end elbow macaroni with real butter, heavy cream, and two kinds of cheese that he shredded himself. Once he made the macaroni and cheese, he moved it to a baking dish and topped it with a mixture of panko crumbs, and parmesan cheese, and then sprinkled smoked paprika on top. He placed it in the preheated oven to bake while they talked about life.

"So, how far do you plan to take the whole Mormon thing," asked Alex.

"I'm not sure what you mean. You know I'm Mormon and that it is important to me."

"I know that, and I admire that you stick to your convictions. I really love that about you. I'm just curious as we get more serious, where you will draw that line, intimacy wise."

"That's a fair question. I fully intend to follow all the commandments, including the law of chastity. I love making out with you, but I won't go any further until marriage."

"You realize that the church views sex with a man as a sin, whether you're married or not, right?"

"Yes, I fully realize that, believe me. It's more of a commitment that I have made to God, and to myself, rather than anything to do with the way the leadership of the church views it."

"Sweetie, I can't say that I understand that, and I'm not sure how long I can hold out in such a relationship, but I care about you, and I love being with you, so I'm happy to walk down this road with you, at least for now."

"I understand your hesitation, and I would love to go further as much as you would, but I need to stay true to who I am in every sense, and that is who I am."

"I'll be damned if I'm not in love with you, Nephi."

"Please watch your language, and I love you, too."

Alex laughed and moved toward Nephi, placing his hands on the back of his neck while they kissed. The kissing intensified, and they made out with Alex sitting on the kitchen counter, and Nephi standing against it, straddled by Alex's legs. They kissed until the oven timer intruded on their moment. Alex removed the dish, and placed it on top of the stove.

Sitting at the dining table, they enjoyed the macaroni and cheese. Nephi agreed that it was far better than the powdered cheese to which he had grown accustomed, and he even ate a second helping, which is something he never did.

After lunch, Alex had to get ready for work. They shared another sweet kiss, before Nephi returned to Utah County. His first stop was Gene's ice cream shop, to break the bad news to Gene and Jodie. They had a good cry, and thanked him for stopping by.

The next two days were a blur as Nephi let the reality of Bradley's death sink in. Monday evening, he received a call from Rob, announcing that Tiffany had just given birth at the hospital in Riverton. Nephi's healthy new niece weighed seven pounds, nine ounces. She measured twenty inches long, and they named her Ella Mae. Nephi welcomed the good news, and drove to Riverton to meet her.

Nephi was nervous walking into the hospital, as it brought back memories of his many visits with Bradley, but this would be a happy visit. Little Ella Mae was beautiful. Nephi sat in Tiffany's hospital room, rocking her in his arms, while her dark eyes stared up at him. He sang her a lullaby, and put her to sleep. A new niece was the best therapy he could have asked for after losing his friend. He dreamed of having children of his own one day.

While he rocked Ella Mae, Jacob and Camille arrived at the hospital. It was an awkward moment, after the blow up at Thanksgiving, but they were civil to each other. Nephi handed Ella Mae to Camille, and then walked over and gave Jacob a hug, and told him he hoped he was well. He then gave Tiffany a gentle hug in the hospital bed, and wished her well before kissing Ella Mae and leaving the hospital. The last couple of weeks brought a whirlwind of emotions. Life had thrown Nephi so many curve balls, and he hoped he was about due to hit one of them.

Back in Pleasant Grove, Nephi read scriptures, and said a prayer, asking God for strength to get through Bradley's funeral, and to handle whatever might come next in his life. He prayed for inspiration to understand God's will for him, and to have the courage to accept whatever it might be. He fell asleep that night, dreaming of holding baby Ella Mae in his arms.

CHAPTER 19

On Saturday, December 7th, the sun came up over Mt. Timpanogos, casting light on the city of Pleasant Grove. It provided a hint of warmth on a cold day. The church kitchen buzzed with the women of the Relief Society, who were busy preparing ham and funeral potatoes for the family of the deceased.

At a Mormon funeral, it is customary for the Relief Society to provide a meal for family and friends after the service. There is typically an open-casket viewing prior to the service, but in Bradley's case, his family couldn't afford a burial plot, or a casket. They opted for cremation, and without a body, there could be no viewing.

They scheduled the funeral for 11:00, with the luncheon to immediately follow. While the women of the relief society prepared funeral potatoes, Nephi set up tables and chairs in the cultural hall.

Bradley was his friend, and he wanted to assist with his memorial service in any way that he could. He set all the tables in place, carefully covered them with white tablecloths, and surrounded them with chairs. A few of the young men from the ward were helping, but Nephi was doing most of the work.

With the cultural hall all set for the luncheon, Nephi checked on the kitchen to see if they needed any help, and then moved to the foyer, where he found the program for Bradley's funeral. It featured a nice picture of him on the cover.

The opening hymn for the service was "Come Follow Me", followed by a prayer offered by Bradley's brother, Todd. Brother Carmichael, the Elders Quorum President would then read Bradley's obituary, followed by a talk from Brother Baker, First Counselor in the Bishopric. The congregation would then sing "How Great Thou Art". Bishop Thompson was the concluding speaker. The service would conclude with everyone singing "God be with you till we meet again", and Sister Garnsby would offer the closing prayer.

Nephi found it odd that nobody from Bradley's family would speak at the funeral, but was glad for a chance to say goodbye, and to serve him by setting up the tables for the luncheon.

While Nephi read through the program, he heard footsteps behind him, and turned to see Bishop Thompson who had just entered the church.

"Good morning, Bishop," he said.

"Good morning. I was hoping to find you. Can you step into my office for a moment?"

"Sure thing, Bishop."

Nephi followed Bishop Thompson into his office, and Bishop closed the door.

"The cultural hall is all set for the luncheon," Nephi reported. "What else can I help you with?"

"The thing is, Nephi, Brother Hanson has requested that you not attend the service. I know he was your friend, but as his father, I have to respect his wishes, and I'm sorry, but I need to ask you to leave."

"What on earth? Why? Why would he do that?"

"I understand that Bradley was staying with you prior to his passing, and Brother Hanson blames you, in part, for his death, and thinks that your example contributed to turning him gay, and he doesn't want to see you at the funeral."

Nephi almost fell out of his chair.

"Blames me? I mean, if I had been there instead of hunting, maybe things could have been different, but he wouldn't have even taken those pills in the first place if it wasn't for his father. And turning him gay? Really? People don't 'turn' gay. We are born this way. If he wants to blame someone for that, he has nobody to blame but God." Nephi's voice was elevating as he grew more upset. "The nerve of that man…"

"Nephi, I have to stop you right there. I really am sorry, but you will need to leave before the service begins."

Nephi just sat there in disbelief. He was speechless.

"Nephi?"

"The last thing I would want is to disrupt Bradley's funeral. He was my friend, and I loved him. I will need to find some other way to say goodbye."

"Thank you for understanding, Nephi. I have one more thing to discuss. Your brother, Jacob, called me this week, and I understand that you have started dating. Is that true?"

"What business does Jacob have calling you? He hasn't been in our ward for years, and my personal life is none of his business, or yours for that matter."

"Your brother was just concerned for your spiritual welfare, as am I. I just want to warn you before you do anything stupid."

"Warn me?"

"I don't want you to make any choices you will regret. I know that you suffer from same sex attraction, and if you commit a homosexual sin, the road of repentance will be difficult. Even if you repent, you will lose certain privileges."

Nephi sat, shaking his head in disbelief.

"Privileges? Such as?"

"Such as the ability to serve in any capacity with the youth of the church. Once you commit homosexual sin, you can never serve in a calling with the youth again."

"For real? I have heard of convicted child abusers that the church excommunicated, and then re-baptized, who later served in a calling with the youth. Is that policy real? Just because I am gay, I can't serve with the youth? I love kids and I'm good with them. What are you afraid I'll do?"

"I'm not saying you would do anything. I know you. I just want you to be aware of the church policy, so you understand before you do anything that would put you in that situation. Suffering from same sex attraction does not disqualify you from such a calling, it's only if you give into those feelings, and commit a homosexual sin."

"Thanks, Bishop. I understand what you are saying. I guess I best be on my way."

"Thanks again for understanding, Brother Willard," said the Bishop, as Nephi fled his office.

He exited to the foyer where he ran into Alex, who was just arriving for the funeral. He explained to Alex that he was not welcome, and the two of them headed out the door. Gene was in the foyer, and overheard the conversation and followed them.

"Nephi, hold up," he called.

"I overheard your conversation, and I am very sorry. You don't deserve that. I'll tell you what, I'm not one for these churchy services, and I know Jodie would love to get out of here, too. How about the two of you meet us at the ice cream parlor and we can give Bradley a memorial service of our own?"

With tears of gratitude, Nephi hugged Gene, and thanked him. "We'll head over there now," he said. "See you in ten."

Leaving his truck in the church parking lot, he rode with Alex in the Prius. They arrived at the ice cream parlor, which had not yet opened for the day, and waited for Gene and Jodie to arrive.

"I can't believe that guy," cried Alex.

"You don't know the half of it. Let's give Bradley the service he deserves. In the last few weeks, we were the closest thing he had to family, anyway."

Gene and Jodie pulled up next to them, and they walked together into the ice cream shop lobby. Gene went into the back and returned with four cups of ice cream, handing one to each of them.

"Mint chocolate chip," he said, "Bradley's favorite. Let's eat his favorite ice cream while honoring his memory."

Nephi placed a spoonful of ice cream into his mouth. He had never been particularly fond of mint ice cream, but it he didn't mind it today. Thinking of Bradley brought a smile to his face.

"Do you mind if I offer a prayer to start our service?" asked Nephi.

"Go right on ahead," replied Gene.

Nephi bowed his head, folded his arms and closed his eyes. Everyone else did the same.

"Dear Heavenly Father, we come before thee at this time in remembrance of our friend, Bradley Hanson. Please bless his family, and all those who loved him with comfort and peace. Please help them remember him as the beautiful soul that he is, and celebrate the goodness he brought into our lives. We thank thee for the opportunity that we had to know him. Now that he is in thy arms, please let him know how much we love and miss him. In the name of Jesus Christ, Amen."

"Amen," they all repeated.

"Now let's go around the room while everyone shares a memory of Bradley," suggested Gene.

"I'll start," offered Jodie. "The guy that worked morning shift before Bradley was such an ass..."

Gene chuckled to himself as she continued.

"He always barked orders at me, and made me do his cleanup work at the end of his shift. He was so condescending and rude that I was a day away from quitting. It made me so happy to hear that he had given two weeks' notice. Gene told me he hired a new guy, and I was nervous, but the first time I met Bradley, he put me completely at ease. I was struggling to lift one of the large ice cream pans up into the sink for washing. He took it from me, placed it in the sink, and washed it while asking if there was anything else he could help with. He was always so willing to help, and so optimistic. He always seemed happy to be here, except for that day his family came in, that is."

She continued, "I always encouraged him to enroll at UVU. He was so smart, and I know he could have done anything he wanted, but he wasn't confident in himself. He worried that he hadn't learned the right things in home-school. I thought he was coming around to the idea before he passed. I guess what I really want to say is that Bradley was super nice. He was my friend and I'll miss him."

"Thank you, Jodie," said Gene.

"I'll go next," offered Alex. "I first met Bradley at the Trunk or Treat at Nephi's church. Everyone was being rude to Nephi because he invited me to the activity. The adults wouldn't let their children near us. It hurt my feelings, but I could tell that it crushed Nephi. Bradley came and told us that his family had kicked him out, and he didn't know where to go, and we all went to Nephi's apartment, where Nephi offered Bradley a place to stay for as long as he needed. I thought he would end up mooching off of Nephi's hospitality, but that wasn't the case. He cleaned and cooked, and pulled his weight, even when he was at his lowest. The kid had a good heart. As far as I can tell, he brought out the best in Nephi, and Nephi brought out the best in him. I never knew him to be anything but kind, which is more than I can say for myself."

They all sat in silence for a couple of minutes, reflecting on the words of Alex and Jodie, and their experiences with Bradley.

Gene broke the silence as he began to share, "I'll never forget my first interaction with Bradley. He walked into my shop off of the street. He was quiet and timid. At first, he struggled to work up the nerve to talk to me. When he started to introduce himself, I had to ask him to speak up. He told me his name, and asked if I was hiring. I told him I had an opening coming up, and he could come back in two days for an interview. He seemed excited, and went on his way. I wasn't sure that he would be a good fit. When he came back for an interview, I was busy helping customers at the counter."

"There was a mother seated at a table struggling with her four young children. One of them dropped her spoon, and started to scream. Bradley took a new spoon from the counter and handed it to the child with a smile. She calmed right down. He picked up the spoon off of the floor, threw it away, and then grabbed a towel off of the counter, and wiped off a dirty table. It was just part of his nature, he did it all before I interviewed him, and he didn't even know I was watching. I knew right then he was the man for the job. He was one of the best employees I ever had. I'm just sorry his time was so short. I loved that boy."

"We all did, Gene," replied Nephi.

They sat in silence for another moment, and then all looked at each other.

"Well, I guess it's my turn now," observed Nephi. "I don't know where to start. I grew up in the same ward as Bradley, and worked with his dad in my calling. I saw Bradley all the time, but didn't know him well. I honestly didn't even care to get to know him. I wasn't especially fond of his father, and assumed he would be the same."

"I'm sure that the only reason he approached me on Halloween is because I have been openly gay for quite some time. At church, they say I 'suffer from same sex attraction', even though I tell them over and over, I'm not 'suffering' from anything. Bradley must have assumed that I would understand, because I am like him in that way."

"Looking back, I had no idea that he was gay. My gaydar must be broken. When he told me what happened that night, I felt for him. I could see that he needed me, but I needed him more. I had been so lonely. I needed a friend, someone to talk to, and just share how my day went. Bradley was that friend, and so much more."

"I hope sometime in eternity he can forgive me for leaving him alone to go hunting. I really don't know if I'll ever be able to forgive myself. I love Bradley. I miss him, and I would do anything to bring him back. Life won't be the same."

Now silent, the ice cream parlor filled with reverence and peace. It was almost as if they could feel Bradley there with them, smiling as they enjoyed mint chocolate chip ice cream in his honor, and spoke fondly of him. Nephi wasn't sure how the funeral was going back at the church, but he knew it couldn't be any better than this.

The four of them finished the ice cream in silence, and let the weight of the hallowed occasion sink in. Slowly they all stood and exchanged hugs. It wasn't a traditional Mormon funeral, but for Bradley, it was a fitting farewell.

Nephi and Alex left the ice cream parlor, grateful to have known Bradley, if even for a short time. Alex took Nephi back to the church to retrieve his truck, and then headed back up north to get ready for work. Nephi spent the rest of the day remembering Bradley while binge watching their favorite show until he fell asleep.

In the morning, Nephi readied himself for church, put on his coat, and made the walk through the snow to the church building, being careful not to let his slick bottomed shoes fall victim to the icy sidewalk. Upon arrival, he took a seat on the pew next to Mike and Darla. His mind still in a fog, the words of the Sacrament meeting speakers didn't stick. Sacrament meeting ended, and he headed toward the Gospel Principles class, but Bishop Thompson intercepted him and asked to meet in his office.

Nephi was surprised to see President Miller, the leader of the Stake, sitting in Bishop Thompson's chair. President Miller stood and shook Nephi's hand.

"Please take a seat, Brother Willard," he requested.

Nephi sat in the chair across from the desk, while Bishop Thompson took a place beside President Miller. Nephi looked across the room at President Miller, confused at the purpose of his visit.

An older gentleman with dark gray hair, and a round nose that held his horn-rimmed glasses in place, President Miller had a kind face that smiled back at Nephi. He asked Bishop Thompson to offer a prayer. Bishop Thompson prayed for the Spirit to be present during the meeting, and for a positive outcome. He concluded the prayer in the name of Jesus Christ. President Miller looked Nephi directly in the eye.

"Brother Willard," he said, "I am here to invite you to take part in a disciplinary council. We are hoping you will meet with us at the Stake Center on Saturday at 10:00."

"A disciplinary council?" asked Nephi.

"Yes, I have received some reports alleging that you have

violated church standards. A disciplinary council is somewhat of a church court, where we will review the facts of the allegations, and give you the opportunity to speak on your own behalf. You are also welcome to bring witnesses, if you wish. If you confess to the allegations, your defense and the witnesses will not be necessary."

"I am confused. What are these allegations, and what does a disciplinary council look like? I'm not familiar with a church court."

"Don't worry," replied President Miller. "It's not like a regular court. The purpose of the trial is not to punish. I want you to think of it as a court of love. The whole reason that we hold disciplinary councils is to save the souls of transgressors, protect the innocent, and maintain the good name of the church. We are holding the council because we love you, and are concerned about the eternal state of your soul."

"And the allegations?"

"We received information that you might have committed homosexual sin, and also that you are guilty of apostasy. We will review the evidence and discuss each allegation with you, and any witness you bring forward. The details are in this letter."

President Miller handed a sealed envelope to Nephi across the table. "Read it at your leisure, and we can discuss everything on Saturday. Are you available at that time?"

"I am available, but I'm still confused. Why is this being done at the Stake level instead of in the ward, and what does the church court process entail?"

"Because you hold the Melchizedek Priesthood and are accused of grievous sin, the Stake administers the disciplinary council. You will meet with myself and my two counselors, along with the twelve members of the High Council. We will present you with the details of the allegations, and give you a chance to reply. We will ask questions of you and any witnesses you present. We will then excuse you, and assign half of the High Council members to defend you, while the other half will support the allegations against you. I will solicit their feedback, and then decide. Later, I will meet with you to explain the decision."

"I see. How long does it take to make a decision, and what will happen to me after that?"

"There isn't a timeline on the decision. I may need time to fast and pray for God's guidance. It could be a day, or several weeks. There are several potential outcomes of the disciplinary council. I may take no action, in which case, you would carry on as usual. I could decide on formal probation, where you could not partake of the Sacrament, hold a church calling, or attend the temple until your repentance is complete. Another option is disfellowshipment. If we opt to disfellowship, you will still be a member of the church, but will not be in good standing. The restrictions of probation apply and it also restricts you from speaking at church meetings, offering public prayers, and sustaining church officers. The final option is excommunication. In that case, you are no longer a member of the church. It carries all the restrictions of being disfellowshipped, but also prohibits you from paying tithing, and revokes your temple blessings and priesthood."

"Okay," said Nephi, fully depleted. "What do you foresee happening in my case?"

"I can't say until we hear from you and your witnesses, but if we find the allegations accurate, the most likely outcome would be disfellowshipment or excommunication. If that happens, understand that those outcomes are not the end, but the beginning of the repentance process. Any time we take such action, it is difficult, but we do it out of love. It offers each soul the best opportunity for repentance and salvation."

President Miller's face told Nephi he was sincere. He really believed every word he said.

"Okay, President Miller. Thank you for explaining everything to me. Where will we meet on Saturday?"

"Please come to the Stake Center with any witnesses. We will meet in the High Council room."

"I'll be there," replied Nephi.

"Thank you, Brother Willard. I appreciate your attitude and cooperation in this matter. I'll see you on Saturday."

Nephi shook the hands of both men. Church was nearly over by that time, and Nephi walked straight home. Sitting at the kitchen table, he read through the letter that President Miller provided. It accused him of living with another man in a homosexual relationship, and apostasy by means of promoting doctrine contrary to the church.

The reference to living with another gay man had to mean Bradley. He couldn't believe someone was accusing him of that, especially the day after Bradley's funeral. He called Alex to ask if he was available Saturday morning, and if he would be a witness.

Alex did not at all want to meet with LDS church leadership, but reluctantly agreed to witness on Nephi's behalf, because he knew that Nephi had nobody else that knew all the details of the situation. Nephi thanked him profusely.

Nephi's next call was to Stacy, who also agreed to show up to the disciplinary council as a witness. Nephi feared the events on the horizon. His faith meant everything to him. He believed in Jesus Christ, and His gospel, with all his heart. The prospect of excommunication terrified him, but he was glad for friends he could call on for support, even in the most difficult of times.

CHAPTER 20

Along with a new work week, Monday delivered more snow. A blanket of white covered Pleasant Grove. The icy temperature matched the reception Nephi received from Mark, while the disciplinary council loomed. As a member of the Stake Presidency, Mark would be an active participant in the court of love, and he already seemed to have formed a judgement.

Despite Mark's startling glares, and unusual avoidance, Nephi kept it together at work, and pushed his team to improve both 'Handle Time' and 'Idle Time'. Their monitor scores were better than every other team in the call center.

Each morning and night, he spent more time than usual on his knees, pleading with God for a positive outcome at the church trial. He prayed for God to bless the leaders of the Stake, that they might understand him and his intentions, and that the Holy Spirit would be present during the meeting.

Nephi spent Wednesday and Thursday evening in Salt Lake with Alex. The first night, they went to dinner and a movie as Nephi did his best not to think about the disciplinary council, but the distractions were short-lived. The second night, they hung out at Alex's apartment, playing board games until late.

Stacy met Nephi for lunch on Friday. He played tic-tac-toe with Chloe while he talked to Stacy about the potential outcomes of a church court. By that time, his anxiety had the better of him, and he couldn't bring himself to eat much. Right after lunch, he started fasting for a positive outcome and to allow the spirit to be present when he pleads his case with the church.

Waking early on Saturday morning, Nephi read the Book of Mormon for an hour, and spent just as long on his knees. Reading and praying brought him comfort as he felt the Spirit calm his heart, and felt that everything would work out. Around 9:00, both Stacy and Alex arrived at his apartment. He invited them in and they kneeled together while Nephi offered a prayer aloud that there may be love and understanding present in the High Council room during his disciplinary council.

They rose to their feet, and each gave Nephi a hug and wished him luck with the church court. The three of them went to the Stake Center together in Alex's car. Nephi couldn't remember ever feeling so nervous. They walked through the doors into the foyer and waited for the meeting to begin. They sat on the couch with Nephi in the middle. Alex was holding his right hand, and Stacy his left. They were about fifteen minutes early, and the High Council room door was closed. Nephi figured they must be meeting about his case.

Right at 10:00, the door opened and President Miller emerged. He shook each of their hands.

"Come on in, Nephi. Your witnesses can wait here for now."

Nephi followed President Miller into the room where fourteen other men waited for him. Nephi took a seat and scanned the faces in the room. Each of them carried a look of contempt. It sure didn't feel like a court of love. He recognized a few of the men, President Stone was his boss at work, and Brother Mendenhall was the High Counselor assigned to his ward. He also recognized Brother Tanner from his ward, who was a member of the previous Bishopric.

Nephi smiled, trying to calm himself. President Miller returned a grin, but smiles were not forthcoming from anyone else in the room. President Miller informed Nephi of the charges - homosexual sin and apostasy.

"The first allegation," he stated, "is substantiated by two witnesses. Brother Bevan Hanson told us you had a homosexual relationship with his son, Bradley. He said the two of you lived together in the same one-bedroom apartment. Brother Jacob Willard reported that you shared a tent with another gay man named Alex during a recent hunting trip, and that the same man also slept in your apartment recently."

Nephi shook his head in disbelief as they presented the allegations. President Miller studied him carefully.

"Brother Willard, after hearing the witness statements, do you confess to the sin of homosexual relations?"

"No," replied Nephi, "I have never had sexual relations with anyone before. I am a virgin."

Nephi noticed that many in the room were shaking their heads. It was clear that they did not believe his statement.

"Very well," said President Miller. "Please explain the events to us from your perspective.

"Bradley Hanson lived with me prior to his death because his family kicked him out of the house when he told them he was gay. He didn't have anywhere else to go, and I took him in. We never had a sexual relationship. I offered him the bed, and I slept on the living room sofa."

"So you never had intercourse with Bradley?" asked President Stone.

"No, never!"

"What about oral sex? Did you have oral sex with him?"

"No, we had no sexual contact of any kind."

"Did you ever touch his penis either above or underneath the clothing?"

"No, I did not. As I said, we had no sexual relationship. We were just friends."

"You never even kissed him?"

"He kissed me once, and I let him know that I wasn't interested in that type of relationship, and that was it, we were good friends and nothing more."

"Do you masturbate while thinking about men?"

"No, I don't masturbate at all."

Nephi felt intimidated and horrified as they barraged him with terribly personal questions, as fifteen men in suits stared on. It was a horrible feeling that he wouldn't wish on anyone. He couldn't even imagine how women who take part in a church disciplinary council must feel. A court of love it was not.

"Is there anyone who can substantiate the story the way

that you tell it?" asked President Miller.

"Yes, my friend Alex is outside, and he can verify everything. My friend Stacy is also here. I confide everything in her and she can also speak on my behalf."

"Is this the same Alex," asked President Stone, "who went with you on the hunting trip?"

"Yes, it is."

"And what do you have to say about the allegations from your brother concerning him?"

"Jacob and I are not what you would call close. Just like Brother Hanson, he is making assumptions about my actions without having firsthand knowledge of the details. I have never had sexual intercourse with Alex and yes, that includes oral sex and petting. We have never had sexual contact."

"Did he share a tent with you and stay in your apartment?" asked President Miller.

"Yes, we went elk hunting the week before Thanksgiving, and after Bradley died, he stayed at my apartment to avoid the long drive back to Salt Lake but nothing sexual happened."

"Did you kiss him?" asked President Stone.

"Yes, Alex and I are dating, and we kiss, but nothing more."

"Can anyone substantiate things about Alex?" queried President Miller.

"Alex and Stacy are both here and they can speak to the relationship."

Brother Mendenhall raised his hand to get Nephi's attention and said, "Brother Willard, you know that while suffering from same sex attraction is not a sin, acting on that attraction is. Given that, why are you in a dating relationship with a man?"

"I have lived as celibate my entire life. I am, in fact, still a virgin. That life is lonely. I crave human interaction on the same level that you experience with your wives. I believe that is natural. I have struggled with that loneliness, and recently started exploring the option of dating. Alex and I have become good friends. Can I ask a question of you?"

"Yes, go ahead, Brother Willard," replied President Miller.

"Can you imagine how it would feel if loving your wife was a sin?"

"But it's not," said President Miller.

"I understand that, but I am trying to gauge the level of empathy in the room. Can you imagine yourself in my place? What if God made you to be attracted to a gender forbidden for you to love? How would you feel?"

"I'm sorry, Brother Willard, I'm afraid this line of thinking is detracting from purpose of the meeting. I can't put myself in your place and will never understand what it's like to be attracted to a man."

"I'm not asking you to do that. All I am asking is for you to imagine what it would be like if having a marital relationship with a woman was a sin."

"But it's not a sin. This conversation is becoming circular and I'm cutting it off right here. Let's get back to the details of the alleged sins."

Exasperated, Nephi resigned himself to the fact that empathy was not to be found among this group.

"Okay, what else would you like to know?"

"So just to confirm," said President Stone, "your version of the facts are that you spent nights alone with both Bradley and Alex, but did not have a sexual relationship of any kind with either of them. You kissed both of them, and are now in a courting relationship with Alex. Is that correct?"

"Yes, that is correct, more or less."

"Before we proceed with the second allegation," said President Miller, "I would like to hear from your witnesses regarding the first. Brother Tanner, please step into the lobby and ask Alex to join us."

Brother Tanner stepped out of the room and returned with Alex. President Miller directed him to sit on the opposite side of the table. Sweat beads formed on his forehead and dripped down his face. Nephi had never seen him so nervous.

President Miller told Alex of the accusation against

Nephi. He explained that they would ask questions related to people Nephi knew, and places he had been. He then proceeded with the questions.

"Are you familiar with Nephi's apartment?"

"Yes, I have been there many times."

"Were you there while Bradley Hanson lived with Nephi?"

"Yes."

"Are you familiar with their sleeping arrangement, and if so, can you describe it?"

"Yes, Nephi gave his bed to Bradley, while he slept on the sofa. I thought it might be only for the first night to make him more comfortable, but that arrangement continued and until Bradley died, he slept in the bed, while Nephi slept on the sofa."

"Are you aware of whether there was a sexual relationship between Bradley and Nephi?"

"You're kidding, right? Do you even know Nephi?" He shook his head in disgust. "No, there was never any sexual relationship between them."

"Okay, thank you. We understand that you went hunting with Nephi. Is that correct?"

"Yes, we went into the Uinta Mountains. It was snowy and beautiful. We saw deer and elk, but Nephi didn't shoot anything."

"What were the sleeping arrangements when you went hunting?"

"We slept in a tent, and we each had our own cot near the stove."

"Was there any sexual touching, or sexual intercourse between the two of you while you were there?"

"Despite my best efforts, no. We kissed, and that's it. You guys sure don't seem to know your boy Nephi, at all. He's a good Mormon. He has boundaries, and he firmly let me know where they are. He doesn't cross them. I've known a lot of Mormons, and most of them aren't like Nephi, most are weaker. I'm telling you guys, Nephi is the most Mormony

Mormon that ever did Mormon. I've never seen anyone follow your rules better than him."

"So you're saying, there was no sexual interaction at all, including no oral sex?"

"Are you even listening to me? No, there was nothing. Nephi doesn't do that."

"We understand that you and Nephi are now dating, is that correct?"

"Yes, we have been dating ever since the hunting trip."

"In the time that you have been dating, have you ever had sexual intercourse?"

"Again, no, we have never had sex or anything remotely close to sex. We have made out. Kissing. That's it."

"Thank you for your time in answering our questions. If you wouldn't mind waiting in the foyer, we will let you know if we have any further questions for you."

Brother Tanner opened the door and escorted Alex back to the lobby. He then returned and closed the door.

President Miller resumed questioning Nephi. "Brother Willard, your story and Alex's are remarkably consistent. Either you have collaborated and rehearsed your story, or you are telling the truth."

"We are telling the truth," replied Nephi.

"If that is the case, I am still very disappointed in you. You musn't only avoid sin, you must avoid the very appearance of evil. As an active member of the church, you must protect the church's good name."

"Are you suggesting that I should have refused Bradley a place to stay, and forced him to fend for himself on the street?"

"I'm saying that as a man who suffers from same sex attraction, you should not cohabitate with another man under any circumstances."

"When a human in need is kicked out of their home because of something they cannot change or control, I will not force them out on the street. That's not in my nature, and I am not sorry for giving Bradley a place to live when he had nowhere else to go. I'm not sorry for giving Alex a place to crash after a long, exhausting day when it wasn't safe for him to drive home."

"Okay, Brother Willard, thank you. I want to pursue the second allegation now, that of apostasy. Bishop Thompson reported that you disagree with church doctrine relating to the family. That you believe that doctrine may change at some point. Is that true? We know that God is the same yesterday, today, and forever. He does not change."

"I do not believe that the doctrine will change in the future, but I hope it will change. I pray for it to change."

"Please explain."

"There are examples in church history when the church declared a position to be doctrine and later changed its position. It is well documented and even acknowledged in the official essays that the church released. Once such example is the revelation given to President Kimball that all worthy men may receive the Priesthood, and enjoy temple blessings. Prior to that time, church leadership widely taught that men of African descent would never receive the Priesthood. Some of those leaders proclaimed that stance to be unchangeable doctrine, a position that later changed."

He continued, "Another example is the practice of polygamy. The church proclaimed the practice as revelation from God, but later forbade it. From then on, the church declared polygamy against God's law, and excommunicated those who practiced it. Given that precedent, my hope is that at some future point, the church position will change on same-sex marriage. I understand the church condemns same-sex marriage and declares that stance as doctrine from God that will never change. I do not claim that the church doctrine is anything different than what it is. All I am saying is that, as a gay man, and a lonely human being who longs for bonding with another human being, I hope it will change someday."

"I see," replied President Miller. "Who do you share this belief with?"

"It's not a belief. I don't believe it will change, or predict it will change. I have seen nothing from the church that makes me believe it will ever change, but I hope that it will."

"And who do you share that hope with?"

"I share it with God in my prayers. I share it with my closest friends, Stacy and Alex, and I shared it with Bishop Thompson."

"With whom else have you shared your hope that the eternal doctrine of God concerning same-sex relationships will change?"

"I have shared it with no one else. I don't have that many friends, and my family wouldn't care to hear it. I really don't have anyone else to share it with."

"So you know that church doctrine states that same sex marriage is detrimental to society, yet you still support same sex marriage?"

"That is correct. I support it."

"Thank you, Brother Willard. We have everything we need from you. I will now convene with the men in this room, and we will deliberate concerning your case. I will let you know when I have decided. Do you have questions before you leave?"

"Don't you want to interview Stacy?"

"We have all the information we need. Her testimony will not be necessary. If we feel that we need any more information, we will reach out."

"I just want you to know that I have a testimony of the truthfulness of the gospel. I know that Jesus Christ lives and that he is my Savior. I am so thankful for Him and His atoning sacrifice for me. I know that the Book of Mormon is true. I have read it and felt its spirit. I love this church and strive to live the way God wants me to live every day. I say these things in the name of Jesus Christ, Amen."

"Thank you. Brother Tanner will see you out."

"Do you have any idea when you might have a decision?"

"Not at the moment. I won't put a timeline on it, and these things can take time. I'll be in touch."

Brother Tanner opened the door and Nephi exited the High Council room and made his way to the foyer where Stacy and Alex waited for him.

"Well?" asked Alex.

"They said that they have all they need for now. Apparently, they don't feel like they need to hear from Stacy. They will discuss it, and President Miller will call me when he has decided."

The trio left the building to find that heavy snowfall had continued while they were inside. There were two inches on top of the Prius, and Nephi cleared it while Alex started the car to get the heater going. They stopped at the grocery store on the way home, where Alex bought the ingredients to make Rigatoni al Forno. They returned to Nephi's apartment where they talked while Alex made lunch.

Nephi was nervous, and wished that he already knew the outcome of the disciplinary council, but he realized the answer wouldn't likely come today. Alex's cooking seriously impressed Stacy and Nephi. They had never tasted better Italian food. After lunch, Alex had to leave for work, and Stacy stayed with Nephi for a few hours to keep his spirits up. They has been friends for as long as both of them could remember, and she hated to see her friend in pain.

When it came time for her to leave, Nephi walked her to her car, and cleared the snow for her. She gave him the biggest bear hug she knew how to give, and wished him luck with President Miller. Nephi returned to the apartment and closed the door. Alone in the empty room and overwhelmed by the emotions of the day, he lay on the couch and cried himself to sleep.

CHAPTER 21

Sunday morning, Nephi got up early. He prayed and started a fast. He fasted that President Miller would see into his heart and understand how much he loved the church and that he must also be true to himself, to the way God created him. The two sides of him had wrestled for his entire life. Until now, he always suppressed one part of him in favor of the other, but that only led to loneliness and misery. He could no longer ignore his true self. At the same time, he could not suppress his Mormon side. He fasted and prayed that President Miller would comprehend the gravity of his internal conflict.

After scripture study, he watched a church music DVD while he pondered and reflected. Feeling spiritually prepared, he bundled up and made the walk to church through the snow. He arrived early and helped the young men shovel and salt the sidewalks, and then went into the chapel where he sat with head bowed, preparing himself for the meeting.

Brother Hanson who sat in the pew directly in front of Nephi interrupted his reflection.

"I don't get it, Nephi," he said, "why do you keep showing up? You don't believe in church doctrine and you don't belong here. Just give it up."

"You don't know what I believe, and I don't come here for you or anyone else. I come here for me. I come because I want to be here, and that's all that matters."

"No matter, before long they will excommunicate you, and then we'll finally be rid of you."

"That's not set in stone, and even if I that happens, what makes you think I would stop coming to church? I come because I want to, and I don't foresee anything changing that so you'll just need to get used to seeing me."

"Why don't you understand that you don't fit in? You are an abomination. What do I need to do to make it clear that you shouldn't come to church?"

"That's not for you to decide, and nothing you can say or

do will change that. It is my decision where I worship God, and you have no say in the matter. Even your lies to the Stake President can't change that."

Nephi bowed his head and continued to meditate, blocking out Brother Hanson and all other noise. The sound of silence is all he could hear. He directed his thoughts to the Savior, and imagined Him on His knees in the Garden of Gethsemane, experiencing Nephi's own pain, blood dropping to the ground as he bore the sin, pain, and suffering. Nephi knew that Jesus understood him. He knew that more than any other being, Jesus had empathy and pure love for him, and that comforted him.

Darla's hand on his shoulder brought him out of his deep state of pondering, and the opening hymn began. Nephi sang exuberantly, enjoying the music of the organ and the voices singing in praise to God. He focused on every word of the prayer, and returned his mind to his Redeemer as he sang the Sacrament hymn and partook of the Sacrament. Nephi savored the moment, not knowing if this was the last time they would permit him to partake of the sacred emblems of Christ.

He enjoyed the speakers and the remaining hymns, allowing himself to be fully present in the meeting. After Sacrament meeting, he went directly to Elders Quorum and volunteered to give the opening prayer. He answered nearly every question during class, not knowing if those privileges would be available to him the following week.

That day, Nephi fully participated, and enjoyed church like he never had before. The prospect of losing it all was daunting, and he wanted to enjoy it while he could. On his way out, he stopped by Bishop Thompson's office, and handed him a tithing envelope while shaking his hand. It was his last tithing check of the year, and he was proud to be a full tithe payer.

He walked out of the church smiling, knowing that he had done everything he could to exercise his faith that day. If being true to himself meant he would lose most of those privileges, that is the way it had to be but he could no longer pretend to be what he was not. Somehow, some way, the two parts of him needed to stop wrestling and find harmony.

There is no stopping time, and the week marched on. Nephi was anxious to hear from President Miller, but he couldn't let that stop him from living. On Monday, he had to separate Angela and Brock again when he found them seated next to each other, playing footsies while taking calls. As always, he reminded them to be discreet at work. His team stats continued to be strong, and the silent treatment from Mark continued, but he decided it was best not to worry about things that he could not control.

Tuesday rolled by, and then came Wednesday. He was in his office in the middle of a call monitor when Mark knocked on his door.

"Please come to my office as soon as you score that call," he said.

Mark had barely acknowledged him for the past two weeks, and Nephi wondered what he wanted. Was it related to work or church? Mark had been known to mix them in the past. He directed his mind back to the call until he gathered enough data to assign a score, and then went to Mark's office.

"Come on in and close the door," Mark instructed.

Nephi took a seat and looked across the desk at Mark. The look on his face was almost one of excitement.

"What can I do for you?" asked Nephi.

"President Miller would like to meet with you tomorrow evening at 6:00. He knows I work with you, so he asked me to see if that time works for you. Are you available?"

"Yes, I am. I'll be there. Do you have any idea what he will say?"

"I'm afraid I don't, and even if I did, I wouldn't be at liberty to say."

"Okay, thanks. Is there anything else?"

"No, that is all for now."

Nephi left Mark's office and returned to his own, where he closed the door and called Alex. He explained that

President Miller wanted to meet with him Thursday evening and asked if Alex would accompany him for moral support.

"I'll be there," said Alex. "Anything you need. I'll meet you at your place after you get off work."

Now that he knew of the meeting, it was all Nephi could think of. The anticipation almost drove him mad. He finished the work day, and headed home for a nice long run on the treadmill to work off some of his nerves. He texted Stacy to let her know of his meeting. She wished him luck. After everything that happened recently, Nephi needed a win, and he hoped his meeting with the Stake President would provide it.

Work on Thursday was difficult to get through. Nephi went through the paces, but his impatience made each minute seem like hours. After several call monitors and coaching sessions with members of his team, the work day finally ended, and he headed out to the parking lot, excited to get back to the apartment to see Alex, and then to meet with President Miller, the holder of his fate.

As he walked to the back of the parking lot where he always parked, he noticed that something was on top of his truck. When he got closer, he could tell that the 'something' was actually a 'someone'. There, lying on his side across the hood of Nephi's truck, was Alex, holding a bouquet of flowers.

"Aww," he exclaimed, "that's just about the sweetest thing I've ever seen. Thank you."

He helped Alex down from the hood and hugged him tightly, and then kissed him passionately. The kiss was deep and long, filled with love and plenty of tongue. Both lost in the moment, they didn't hear the vehicle that was coming toward them.

The loud blare of a car horn interrupted their kiss.

"Be discreet!" yelled Brock out his downed window as he and Angela cruised by on their way out of the parking lot.

Nephi couldn't help but laugh. He looked down at the flowers, and then back at Alex, and resumed kissing right there in front of his truck in the Brower parking lot. He hugged Alex one more time, and then they got in their respective vehicles and proceeded to Nephi's apartment, where Nephi changed into a suit, and kneeled by his bed to pray while Alex waited in the living room.

They sat talking in the living room about the potential outcomes until a quarter to six.

"Looks like it's time to go," said Nephi.

"Honey, just know that whatever happens, I'm with you. I have your back."

"I know you do, and I love you for that."

They got in Alex's car, and together went to the Stake Center. Nephi told Alex to wait in the car, but he refused and instead, followed Nephi inside and sat in the foyer while Nephi went into President Miller's office.

"Brother Willard, thank you for coming to see me tonight," said President Miller.

"Of course, I've been waiting to hear from you," replied Nephi.

"May we start with an opening prayer?"

"Yes, please."

"Will you offer it?"

"I would love to."

Nephi prayed, "Dear Father in Heaven, we thank thee for this beautiful day and for the opportunity that President Miller and I have to meet here together. We pray that thy Spirit will be in our meeting, and that we may discuss things in a spirit of love, respect, and mutual understanding. Please bless that we may arrive at the outcome that is according to thy will. We thank thee for the church, and for our Savior, Jesus Christ, and we say things in Jesus' name. Amen."

"Amen," added President Miller. "Thank you for that beautiful prayer. I do hope we can discuss things in a spirit of love."

"So do I. Have you made a decision about me?"

"Yes, Brother Willard, I have made a decision. First, let's discuss the allegation of homosexual sin. While you have engaged in activity unbecoming of a priesthood holder, and failed to avoid the appearance of evil, I found the allegation of homosexual sin to be false. I do not believe that you engaged in any sexual activity, and I commend you for your firm boundaries. I cannot, however, condone your actions in kissing someone of the same gender."

Nephi smiled. Good news so far.

President Miller continued, "As for the second allegation, that of apostasy, I have found you guilty on those grounds due to your support of same sex marriage, combined with your declaration that God's doctrine has changed in the past and your hope that the doctrine regarding same sex marriage will change. Making it worse, you shared those beliefs with others. The Lord will not stand for that. Because you are a holder of the Melchizedek Priesthood, and you have been through the temple, you are hereby excommunicated from the Church of Jesus Christ of Latter Day Saints."

Nephi's head dropped. He was heartbroken, feeling as if they had violently ripped away a piece of his soul. Devastated, he listened to President Miller's words.

"You may appeal my decision to the First Presidency within thirty days if you wish. Details regarding that process are in a letter I will provide you. Excommunication lasts for a minimum of one year and we must reconvene a disciplinary council to agree on your reinstatement before you can be re-baptized. Being excommunicated means that you are no longer a member of the church. I revoke all of your temple blessings, your priesthood, and the terms of your baptismal covenant. You may not take the Sacrament, you may not pay tithing, and you may not pray publicly in the church, or speak in any church meeting. You may continue to attend church meetings, and I hope that you will, but you must remain silent in those meetings. You may not have a church calling or participate in any other manner besides listening. Do you have any questions?"

"No," Nephi said as he shook his head, still staring at the ground.

"Brother Willard, I want you to understand that this decision was difficult for me. I care about you and your spiritual wellbeing. I take this action out of love, and truly believe that excommunication is the right next step in your repentance process. This is not the end of anything, but a beginning to your repentance. I council you to cease all romantic relationships with persons of the same sex, and return to the righteous behavior you exhibited so well while serving as the executive secretary to Bishop Thompson. I love you Brother Willard, and this is all done out of love."

"Thank you, President Miller," replied Nephi, eyes still fixed on the carpet.

"Please take this letter. If you have questions, feel free to discuss them with your Bishop."

Nephi stood and took the letter. He limply shook President Miller's hand, and left his office, dejected. He sauntered through the foyer, moving right past Alex and heading out the door. Alex stood from his seat and followed him.

"Bad news, I take it?"

Without speaking, Nephi continued walking to the car, and sat in the front seat. Alex sat in the driver's seat.

"What happened in there?"

Nephi was in shock and didn't know what to say. Eventually he managed to find a few words.

"They excommunicated me."

"Oh, honey, I'm so sorry," replied Alex. "I know that the church means so much to you, and I have honestly never seen a better Mormon. It's not right."

Nephi made a half smile and gently squeezed Alex's hand.

"Thank you for being here."

"Well, look at the bright side, at least you just got a ten percent raise," said Alex in an attempt to cheer him up.

Alex realized he had made a mistake when Nephi shot him a death glare.

"How dare you say that? You don't understand. Paying tithing is a privilege to me, and I am beyond upset that I no longer have that privilege. How can you even joke about part of me being torn away?"

"I'm sorry. I didn't mean it that way. I was trying to lighten things up, and I see now that it was wrong and insensitive. I'll be honest, I have a hard time understanding it, but I'll try."

"Thank you. Sorry I snapped, I just feel so empty right now. Let's get out of here."

Alex drove out of the parking lot and steered toward Nephi's apartment. Nephi looked at his phone where he saw a text from Stacy asking how it went. He didn't feel like responding. When they arrived at his apartment, he handed his phone to Alex.

"I can't handle telling Stacy right now. Will you please reply and let her know what happened?"

Alex took the phone. "Stacy, this is Alex. They excommunicated Nephi and he can't bring himself to talk or text right now, but he will call you later, probably tomorrow." He hit send and the two of them went inside.

Alex put in a Gilmore Girls DVD, knowing it couldn't help but cheer Nephi up. Alex then scavenged around the kitchen for something to make for dinner. Finding olive oil, flour, a can of crushed tomatoes, and some cheese, he started in on some homemade pizza. He worked in the kitchen while he listened to Nephi do his best to hold back sobs as the show played in the background.

With pizza in the oven, Alex made his way to the sofa. He had no sooner sat down, than they heard a knock on the door. Alex opened the door to find Stacy with cheesecake in one hand, and a card game in the other. She walked into the apartment and placed her things on the table before plopping down on the couch next to Nephi, and wrapping her arms around his neck.

"Don't think for a moment you can shut me out when you need me," she said.

Nephi returned her embrace. With Stacy on one side of him, and Alex on the other, Nephi finished out the episode, and then turned off the TV. The ding of the oven told them dinner was ready and Alex cut the pizza in thirds. While they ate, Stacy dealt the cards, and they played and talked until late. Nephi still felt like a part of him died, but it helped to have his friends by his side while he processed it. After a few rounds distraction, they had polished off half the cheesecake. Then Alex decided it was time to corral the elephant in the room.

"Ok, sweetie, you have had some time to process it. I need to know how you are doing. Where is your head about this whole excommunication thing?"

The mood instantly turned somber as the room fell silent. Nephi thought for a moment. "I have never felt like this before. I feel broken, like something in me doesn't work anymore. It's like they fractured my soul and I lost one of the pieces. It's strange to no longer be a member of the church. Being Mormon has always been who I am."

"What makes you Mormon?" asked Alex. "Is it seeing your name on the attendance roll in Sunday School? Is that what makes you Mormon, or is it your actions and the way you behave every day?"

Nephi stared at him, stupefied by the profound point he was making.

Alex continued, "The entire time I have known you, you have lived the perfect example of what Mormons profess to be. You are compassionate and empathetic. You serve others just because it is the right thing to do. You don't drink alcohol or coffee. You don't watch porn or cuss. I have noticed you read the scriptures and pray every day. You never miss a church meeting. If I'm not mistaken, that's what makes a Mormon. I see others who are in 'good standing' in the church that break every one of the church rules, and who don't seem to care about it, but they still show up to church every Sunday. They judge others for sinning differently than they do, but you don't. If there ever was a Mormon, Nephi, you're it."

Nephi just sat and stared at him, still not believing that

the words came out of his mouth.

Alex continued, "Honey, you don't need a Stake President or Bishop to tell you whether you are Mormon, your actions speak for themselves. Excommunicated or not, you are the most Mormon person who I have ever met. You, Nephi, are the perfect Mormon, I mean other than the fact that you're gay, which by default makes you a bad Mormon, but there's not much you can do about that, now is there? And if it makes you feel better, you are welcome to pay ten percent of your income to me."

A smile started to spread across Nephi's face. It started in the corners of his mouth and grew until it forced dimples into his cheeks and then expanded to his eyes. The wrinkle in the middle of his forehead disappeared and he let out a deep belly laugh.

"I can hardly believe you," said Nephi. "Your words were beautiful and you're right. What matters is my relationship with God. My Bishop and my Stake President have never been the reason I go to church. If my testimony was based on the leaders, I would have stopped going a long time ago. I go to church to improve myself and to strengthen my relationship with God. What happened today does not take away the Mormon in me, it is just a part of my nature, just like being gay is part of my nature."

He gave Alex a hug and kissed him. Stacy smiled. "I'm sure glad to see that smile on your face," she said. "I have never been so worried about you before."

They played a few more rounds of cards before Alex and Stacy returned home. Alone, Nephi thought about the events of the day. Despite his epiphany during Alex's surprising speech, he was sad at the outcome of the 'court of love'. He didn't want to be excommunicated. He enjoyed church and the church community, even if they didn't seem to want him.

He found sleep difficult that night as he continued the struggle to get his mind around it all, to understand what it meant as the two parts of him continued their wrestle.

CHAPTER 22

Nephi's tired eyes made work difficult on Friday, but he powered through the day. He managed get through it with little trouble, other than some ribbing from Brock and Angela about the kiss they witnessed the previous day, and the occasional glare from Mark. After work, he headed to the mall. Christmas was only five days away, and he wanted to find the perfect gift for Alex.

What do you buy for a beautiful man who enjoys cooking, loves rock and roll music, lifts weights at the gym, and already has pretty much everything he wants? Finding the perfect gift proved more difficult than Nephi had hoped. He wandered from store to store, but couldn't find anything that spoke to him, although he found some candles and lotion for Stacy. Almost ready to give up, he found a jacket he thought would look sexy on Alex. He bought it, but he wasn't sure if it was more a gift for himself or for Alex.

On the way out of the mall, a kiosk caught his eye. The woman at the kiosk was demonstrating a sous vide cooking system. She sealed meat and vegetables into bags and then put the bags into a bucket of water along with a sous vide wand. The wand cooked the meat to perfection. As a chef, Alex could surely appreciate such a device. Nephi bought the entire system, bags and all. He hoped the sous vide system, together with the jacket, would be the perfect gift.

Christmas was Nephi's favorite holiday. He loved everything about it. Jesus held a very special place in Nephi's heart, and he was honored to celebrate His birth. Christmas music, the colorful lights, the snow covered houses, and the giving of gifts; Nephi loved all of it, and he really looked forward to spending his first Christmas with Alex five days from now.

On Saturday, Nephi drove his truck into downtown Salt Lake City, and parked in the Winter parking garage at the Gateway Mall. He had invited Alex to meet him there, below the movie theater. Alex arrived and found Nephi in the midst of the horde of Christmas shoppers, and wrapped his arms around him.

"I hope you don't want to see a long movie. I have work this afternoon."

"Don't worry, you'll be to work in plenty of time. We're not seeing a movie."

"Then what are we doing?"

"Follow me," said Nephi as he took Alex by the hand and led him away from the mall across the street. "This is one of my Christmas traditions," he explained.

Nephi and Alex entered a building that Alex had never noticed before. There were lines of people inside, eagerly waiting to fill their trays with food.

"Is this some kind of cafeteria?" asked Alex.

"It's a homeless shelter. I volunteer here several times per year, but Christmas time is my favorite."

He led Alex back into the kitchen, where they put on aprons, gloves, and hairnets, and replaced two of the volunteers serving food on the line. Nephi dished out the potatoes while Alex handled the corn.

Soul after grateful soul streamed by them as they served the meal. The experience humbled Alex. As time went on, Nephi continued to astonish him. Knowing Nephi, he was not at all surprised, but at the same time, this was unexpected.

Serving those who needed assistance made Alex feel good, and he was thankful that Nephi shared the experience with him. At the end of their shift, they headed over to Temple Square and walked around the visitor center and the life size nativity scene displayed on the lawn. Nephi preferred to see it at night when it was all lit up, but Alex's work schedule wouldn't allow it. After spending several wonderful hours together, Alex headed to work and Nephi went home.

While getting ready for church on Sunday morning, Nephi received a call from Alex.

"Thank you for spending time with me yesterday. I would love to spend the morning with you today, too."

"Alex, you know that I have church this morning. Maybe

I can come over afterward for a couple of hours before you have to go to work."

"Come on, can't you skip it just for today? They have made it clear that they don't want you there, anyway. Isn't it more about the way you live and your actions than going to a meeting every week?"

"It's really about both. Just because I'm excommunicated doesn't mean that I will get lax with my church attendance. It is important to me."

"Okay, I really don't understand why you want to be there when they don't want you, and why you would choose to be there instead of with me, when I want you, but I guess you're gonna do what you're gonna do."

"Come on, Alex, don't be mad. You know this is who I am."

"Alright, fine. Go to church. Don't bother driving up to see me today. I've got to work early, anyway. I'll talk to you later this week."

The way the call ended didn't sit right with Nephi. It bothered him. He thought Alex understood who he was, and it frustrated him that he now expected something different. He finished getting ready and went to church. Mike and Darla were already seated when he arrived and he took his usual seat next to them.

Mike leaned over across Darla's lap and motioned to Nephi, who leaned his ear toward his father.

"What are you doing?" asked Mike.

"I'm not sure what you mean. I'm doing the same thing I do every week."

"That was before they excommunicated you."

"Dad, I can still attend church, I just can't pray, talk, or partake of the Sacrament while I am here. President Miller even encouraged me to attend."

"You are so selfish, Nephi, don't you ever think about anyone but yourself? What do you think everyone else is saying? Just look around. All eyes are on us."

"I'm sorry I am such an embarrassment to you, Dad. I'll

find a different seat."

Nephi stood to leave, but Darla grabbed his hand and pulled him back down, before turning to her husband.

"Mike, he is our son and we love him no matter what. Of course he can sit with us at church. Who else would he sit with?" asked Darla.

"If you don't care what anyone thinks, then fine, you sit here next to him. I will find another seat," replied Mike, who moved to the other end of the pew, away from Darla and Nephi.

"Mom, I love you, and I appreciate what you are doing but there is no reason for this to come between you and Dad. He can sit by you. I will go sit over on the side. I really am fine by myself."

Nephi stood and started to leave. She pulled back on his arm, but he continued, and found a place alone at the side of the chapel. Mike returned to sit next to Darla. She stayed next to him, but turned her shoulder from him.

Nephi was sad and disappointed. He hadn't expected that reaction from his father, of all people. Today church lasted only one hour, since it was three days before Christmas. Nephi waived away the Sacrament when it was offered to him, knowing he could not partake. It felt as though every eye in the chapel was watching him as he refused it. The speakers focused on the Christ child, and the meaning of the holiday. Nephi sat and listened. At the conclusion of the meeting, he made a quick exit and walked home.

That evening was his family's Christmas party. Every year, they met together at Mike and Darla's place on the Sunday before Christmas. Darla prepared ham and homemade dinner rolls, and the family sang Christmas carols together and then had a white elephant gift exchange ripe with gag gifts and dollar store treasures. Nephi always looked forward to the party, but not so much this year. His mood was soured by the excommunication, his first spat with Alex, and his father's reaction at church in the morning. The only thing he was looking forward to was seeing his nieces and nephew. He was especially excited to hold little Ella Mae.

Nephi was the first to arrive at the party, and helped his mom prepare dinner. His father was nowhere to be found, most likely hiding out downstairs watching football. Tiffany and Rob arrived right after Nephi buttered the top of the rolls, fresh out of the oven. While they removed their coats, Nephi took Ella Mae out of her car seat and rocked her in his arms. He brought her close to his face and took a deep breath. Nephi loved that new baby smell. He gave her a kiss and handed her to Darla, who smothered her with kisses.

Ammon and Chelsea arrived next. Nephi gave Sophie a hug and listened while she told him all about her new Christmas dress with red and white ribbons, and how she built a snowman in the front yard.

Jacob and Camille arrived last. Nephi gave them both a hug, even though he didn't feel much like hugging Jacob after he made flawed assumptions, and took them to the Stake President. Dallin and Crystal told him all about their week, and he kissed each of them on the cheek.

Dinner was delicious, as always, and Nephi was glad that nobody made his excommunication a topic of conversation. The atmosphere seemed almost normal. Nephi washed the dishes after dinner while everyone else set white elephant gifts in place. While he washed, Jacob joined him in the kitchen.

Voluntarily washing dishes was out of character for Jacob, but Nephi was glad for the help. Nephi washed while Jacob dried.

"Dad tells me you went to church today."

"I go to church every week."

"I'm just curious why you insist on continuing to go. You are clearly not wanted there, and you have beliefs contrary to the doctrine of the church. I really don't get it. I'm not trying to be mean, I just really want to understand why you continue to go."

"I can't tell you how tired I am of answering this question. I get it from both sides, from people within the church and outside of the church. I'm either not Mormon enough or I'm too Mormon, not gay enough, or too gay. No matter what I do, I can't win. Does it really matter to you that much where I spend my time?"

"I'm just curious. I don't get it."

"I go because I want to go. It's as simple as that. Why can't that be good enough for everyone? Church is just where I want to be. Is there anything wrong with that?"

"No, there's nothing wrong with it, I just don't get it."

"Well, the thing is, that you don't have to get it. I get it and I do it for me and that's all that matters."

"Okay, okay, I was just curious. You don't have to bite my head off."

They finished washing the dishes in silence and then joined the others for Christmas carols. This was usually Nephi's favorite part of the party, but this year, he just couldn't bring himself to find any joy in it.

After the Christmas carols, came the white elephant gifts. This was the children's favorite part. They each ended up with a dollar store toy, while Ammon walked away with the toilet seat that had returned to the white elephant party every year for the past decade. It had become a trophy, of sorts. Nephi always got a kick out of it, but he just wasn't into it this year, and it seemed rather juvenile.

After the gift exchange, Nephi excused himself from the party early and went home to sleep. He hadn't slept well in over a week, and he needed to catch up. He slept for ten hours, waking up just in time to throw on some clothes and get to work. For the first time he could remember, we went to work without making sure his hair was perfectly in place. He felt on edge, frazzled, out of sorts.

Cutting it close on time, he parked near the entrance rather than taking his usual spot at the back of the parking lot. Once in the office, he got straight to work pulling reports and planning his day. With reports in hand, he made his way to Monica's office for shift hand off. Mark walked into the office, interrupting the shift change.

"Nephi, please come to my office. I need to speak with you."

"No problem, I'll be there as soon as I finish shift hand off with Monica."

"No, I need you to come now," Mark insisted.

"Okay, don't get all worked up, I'm coming now."

Nephi followed Mark into his office and took a seat.

"What's up, Mark?"

"What is up, is that we are letting you go. Your employment at Brower is terminated effective immediately."

"What? Why? My numbers are better than ever and turnover on my team is lower than any other team in the call center. What are the grounds for termination?"

"Utah is an at-will employment state, and I don't need to give you grounds at all. We can terminate you at any time, for any reason."

"You can't fire anyone in a protected class. It is illegal in Utah for you to discriminate based on sexual orientation."

"Who said anything about discrimination? I am terminating your employment for cause."

"What cause?"

"I have been documenting your violations for months. You have taken a long lunch four times in the past three months, and you held a joint verbal warning meeting with Brock and Angela, when you should have met with them separately. That is enough grounds for termination."

"Come on, Mark, that's nothing. You do more than that every day. What is this really about? Is this because I'm gay, or because I was excommunicated? Am I being fired because of some twisted religious conviction of yours?"

"How dare you assume that has anything to do with it? Of course this has nothing to do with any of that. You are terminated based solely on the documented violations. I have arranged for corporate security to escort you out of the building."

Mark opened the door where a security guard was waiting. The events of the last few days all ran through

Nephi's head. The excommunication, the fight with Alex, his father's refusal to sit with him at church, and Jacob's challenge to his church attendance. Now this, being fired for some vague, unjust reason. In a fog, he started walking along with the security guard toward the lobby.

Their progress was halted by Mark, who called down the hall after them.

"Nephi, wait a minute, I have one more thing."

Nephi turned around to face Mark.

"Ok, what is it?"

"You have to learn that the Lord will only bless you when you choose his side. When you kick against the pricks, the road is hard. There is a link between spiritual and temporal blessings. Things will get better if you repent."

Mark's words were the last straw. Something in Nephi snapped. "I'll show you the meaning of kick against the pricks," he yelled as he charged down the hall toward Mark as he said, "Only one of us will get out of here today."

Out of control, he neared Mark, who turned and ran the other way. Nephi was faster than him, and was about a foot from catching him when he was tackled from behind by the security guard, and dragged into the security office.

Security called the police and detained Nephi in the office. By the time a police officer arrived, Nephi had gathered himself. The officer interviewed Mark and the security guard, and then met alone with Nephi.

The officer was a handsome African American man who stood about six foot three, and must have weighed 250 pounds, not an ounce of it fat. He was built of solid muscle, with large arms and a broad chest. He spoke to Nephi in a gentle voice.

"Son, I'm officer Williams. What's your name?"

"Nephi Willard, sir."

"Do you want to tell me what happened here this morning?"

Nephi provided the officer with the background story including Bradley, the disciplinary council, and the excommunication. He described every detail of his interaction with Mark that morning, up until the time the security guard detained him.

"Thank you," said the officer. "I have already met with your boss and with security. Your boss gave me a story that doesn't exactly match yours, but lucky for you, the security guard's version of events matches yours perfectly. It seems to me that you are dealing with a Grade-A jerk there, a bully. But that doesn't make what you did right."

"I know, officer, and I'm sorry. I don't know what got into me. I just kind of snapped. I promise I've never done anything like that before."

"Well, that's what I figured. You don't seem like the type to do something like that. I am concerned about you. Losing a good friend is tough, and to follow it up with everything else that you've been through is enough to drive anyone to their limit. Have you had any suicidal thoughts lately?"

"I mean, I don't know, I've always been a happy person, and don't think like that but I guess lately, I have been asking myself where I fit in. I am Mormon and I am gay but I don't seem to fit into the Mormon world. They don't want me. And well, the gay world isn't a good fit either. Nobody in that world seems to understand me. They mock my morality standards and my insistence on attending the church I love. There just doesn't seem to be a place for me. I don't know about suicidal thoughts, but I have wondered an awful lot lately if there is a place in this world for me."

"Son, I'm very sorry about that. I don't know you from Adam, but based on my limited interaction with you, I can tell you that the world needs more people like you. There's a place for you here, of that I have no doubt. You just have to find it."

"Thanks, officer. So what happens from here?"

"Your boss wants to press charges, but I honestly don't see any grounds for it. Consider yourself lucky that you didn't catch up to him in the hall. However, I am going to place you on a 72 hour hold."

"What does that mean?" asked Nephi.

"Well, son, based on our conversation, I believe you can benefit from professional psychiatric care. I will commit you to the inpatient psychiatric unit at the hospital. They can keep you there involuntarily for up to 72 hours. I know it's not what you want to hear, but it is in your best interest."

"But tomorrow is Christmas Eve, and this will be my first Christmas with a boyfriend. Can't it wait until after Christmas?"

"I'm afraid not. You need to go now. I will call an ambulance to transport you there, but I will follow and make sure you get checked in okay. Am I going to have a problem getting you there?"

"No, sir, I won't give you any trouble."

"Ok, I appreciate that. I must take your phone, but is there anyone you would like me to call to let them know where you are?"

"Yes, will you please call my mom and my boyfriend, Alex?"

"Sure thing. Just write their numbers on this pad.

Nephi wrote the numbers and handed them to the officer. "Please ask my mother to call my friend Stacy," he requested.

"No problem, son. The ambulance should be here any minute."

When the ambulance arrived, Nephi followed the officer outside and sat in the ambulance. The paramedics checked his vitals and transported him to Greater Provo hospital where they had an open bed in the psychiatric unit.

CHAPTER 23

The hospital environment seemed foreign to Nephi. Not just the psychiatric unit, but the hospital in general. He had always been healthy, and this would be his first stay at a hospital. He was afraid, not knowing what to expect.

A nurse brought Nephi to an exam room. "Hi, my name is Craig," he said. "I will check you in and take your vitals. Change into these scrubs and I'll be right back."

Craig's build was stocky and muscular. He could pass as a football player or a security guard better than he could a nurse. He had curly brown hair and a goatee on his chin but no mustache under his nose. His eyes were a striking color of light blue. He was kind and confident. His manner set Nephi at ease. Upon returning to the room, he first took Nephi's blood pressure and heart rate, and then checked his temperature. With good vitals recorded, he proceeded with the questions.

"In the past two weeks, how often have you felt down, depressed, or hopeless?" he asked. "Not at all, several days, more than half the days, or nearly every day?"

"Two weeks ago, a good friend of mine passed away. Since that time, my church excommunicated me, and my boss fired me, so I definitely have to say nearly every day."

"Have you had any thoughts of suicide? Please choose from "never", "some thoughts of death", "some thoughts of suicide", or "some attempt at suicide."

"I would have to say some thoughts about death," replied Nephi.

"Thank you. How is your energy level?"

"Lately, my energy has been lower than normal. I have struggled with a lot of things since Bradley died."

"And how is your sleep?"

"I have hardly slept in the past two weeks, although I got a good ten hours last night."

"Have you had trouble finding joy in things that you typically enjoy doing?"

"Come to think of it, yes. I have had trouble enjoying a lot of things."

Craig's questions continued along the same line as he made detailed notes. Once all the questions were answered, Craig said, "Thank you. That's all I need for now. Dr. Montez will be with you shortly."

A woman with gray hair, that extended about four inches below her shoulders, soon entered the room. She wore a white coat and carried a clip board. With head tilted downward, her brown eyes studied Nephi over the top of the silver frames of her glasses. She looked down at the clipboard, and then up again before speaking.

"Hello, Nephi, I'm Dr. Montez. How are you feeling?"

"I'm doing okay. I would be better if I wasn't in here."

"I understand why you might feel that way. I am confident that you are where you need to be right now. I think we can make you feel better. It looks like you have had a lot going on lately."

"I guess I have," said Nephi.

"So many negative life events in such a short amount of time is enough to shake anyone. The way you are feeling is normal, given the circumstances."

"How long do you think I will be here?"

"Let's take it a day at a time and go from there. Based on the answers you gave Craig, I am diagnosing you with Major Depressive Disorder. I know it sounds scary, but it is treatable. Nearly ten percent of adults experience similar depression at some point in their life. I will start you on 20mg of Fluoxetine. It is an anti-depressant drug that should help you feel better."

"I'm not sure I want to do that. I have never really had to take medication and I don't know what to think about anti-depressants."

"I know there is a stigma when it comes to mental health and the medication associated with it, especially in this community, but there doesn't need to be. Just like a physical ailment like an upset stomach or a broken arm, mental ailments require treatment, and there is nothing wrong with that. It is better than continuing to suffer."

"I guess that makes sense."

"Good. Here is your Fluoxetine and some water. Take it now and we'll talk about next steps."

Nephi placed the pill on the center of his tongue and washed it down with a swig of water.

"Very good," said Dr. Montez. "You will need to take one of those each morning. Next, we will get you settled in your room. This is not a hotel and you will need to keep your room clean and tidy. For now, we are putting you on HRSA, which means that we consider you at high risk of self-abuse. There are a few restrictions that come along with that designation. If you have family or friends that bring you clothing, it can't have any drawstrings and you can't have shoes with laces. No lighters, cigarettes, or controlled substances are permitted, and you cannot have a cell phone or any other electronics with you. You also may not have keys, belts, cords, jewelry, or anything made of glass. Do you have any questions?"

"What will I be doing for the next three days?"

"You will have both independent and group therapy sessions. You are responsible for taking care of your room, you'll have the opportunity for recreation including games, puzzles, and short walks. You will learn skills to help you better cope with the challenges of life when you go home. Let's get you settled and a nurse will then review the full schedule with you. Sound good?"

Nephi nodded. Dr. Montez left and Craig returned to escort Nephi to his room. The room was small and plain. There was a bed with dresser drawers build in to the bottom, a small desk, and a chair. The padded white walls had no mirrors, and there was no way to open the plexiglass window that overlooked a courtyard. Nephi noticed that the doors were lockable from the outside. It felt more like a prison than a hospital, but he made the best of it and approached it with a good attitude.

"Welcome home," said Craig. "This place is all yours for the next few days, at least."

Nephi didn't like the sound of that. He would prefer to

sleep in his own bed. He hoped that if he did everything they expected, he would be home soon.

Craig continued, "Each day, you will wake up and shower before 8:30. You will go to the dining area for breakfast from 8:30 until 9:00. No outside food is permitted. From 9:00 until 9:30, you will attend a group meeting for goals, and then you will return to your room for cleaning and quiet time. At 10:00, you have individual therapy with Dr. Montez. At 11:00, you have recreation time. That is followed by lunch at 12:00 and then a life skills class at 1:00. You will then have therapeutic games at 2:00 and group therapy at 3:00. You have a walking break until 4:00, and one-on-one counseling with Dr. Wilmington at 4:30. Dinner will be at 5:30. You can have visitors from 7:00 until 9:00, but may have only two visitors at a time. Lights out at 9:30 and do it all again the next day. I will leave a copy of the schedule with you. Do you have questions for me at this point?"

"I have no idea what time it is," replied Nephi. "What do I have next today?"

"Sorry, man, I should have led with that. It's almost noon. I'll let you get settled for about ten minutes, and then I'll bring lunch into your room, but just for today. You will take the rest of your meals in the dining area with the other patients. You'll meet them in group today at 3:00. Any other questions?"

"Not for now."

"Alright then, I'll be back with your lunch in ten."

Craig left, locking the door behind him. Nephi sat on the bed and looked down at his hospital issued clothes. He didn't like what he saw. At least it would only be for a few days, then he could wear his own clothes again.

Craig returned with lunch. Dry chicken, green beans, macaroni, and jello. Nephi didn't have much of an appetite but choked down a bit of chicken and green beans. Tired, he lay down on the bed and closed his eyes. The next thing he knew, Craig was waking him to escort him to life skills class. He entered the room and looked around to discover that it seemed much like a high school classroom. The instructor was seated in the front of the room and the other patients formed a semi-circle around him.

Craig introduced Nephi to the class, and the instructor invited him to take a seat.

"Welcome, Nephi. My name is Jonah. Let's go around the room and let everyone introduce themselves."

There were five other patients, who told Nephi their names, one at a time. First there was Sampson, a heavy set man who appeared to be in his mid-forties. Next was Gemma, a blonde girl in her early twenties with a look of despair in her eyes. She was followed by Lilliana, a fidgety woman, who seemed about Nephi's age. The remaining patients were Jack and Ron, a thirty something man with a timid voice, and a man who must have been in his sixties, that reminded Nephi of his father.

"Okay, everyone, who can tell Nephi the essential life skills we are learning here?" asked Jonah.

"Self-care and cooking," said Lilliana.

"Very good. We must learn to take care of ourselves by keeping our bodies clean and exercising, and we must be able to plan and cook healthy meals. What are some other skills you are learning?"

"Setting goals," added Jack.

"Good, Jack. We not only set goals, but plan to achieve them, don't we? Nephi, as you'll learn, the other skills are maintaining a clean living space, managing your money, building healthy relationships with others, managing your time responsibly, and finding and keeping a job. Today we are talking about relationships."

In Nephi's view, he wasn't in dire need of instruction in any of those areas, but he gave Jonah his full attention anyway. Worst case, he would learn something useful. Nephi enjoyed observing the interactions between the other patients and Jonah. If nothing else, the people-watching in this place was great.

Life skills was followed by therapeutic games where Nephi worked on a puzzle while the others played a board game. The staff encouraged him to join the others, but didn't push when he insisted on the puzzle. They were impressed that he completed a 500 piece puzzle in less than an hour.

Game time was immediately followed by a group therapy session. Nephi had heard about group therapy in movies and books, but it wasn't what he expected. A therapist facilitated the discussion, which was attended by the same patients from the life skills class. He learned more about each of them in the session. They were each on HRSA like him. Gemma had been sexually abused by a church leader as a child, and her mind had blocked it out. Recently, she remembered everything. Overwhelmed, she attempted suicide, and they committed her to the psych unit.

Sampson was addicted to drugs and overdosed. The paramedics saved his life, and he was sent to the hospital. Lilliana's husband physically and verbally abused her for years. Her speech was now impaired and her uncontrollable fidgeting manifested. She was having suicidal thoughts. Ron's wife of forty years recently passed away from cancer, and Jack was just diagnosed with Bipolar I Disorder, and had recently experienced his first manic episode. Nephi shared about Bradley, the excommunication, and the events at work earlier that morning. It felt good to have people listen without judgement.

After group, Nephi had a break, and was glad to be able to walk. It was too cold to go outside, but there was a small recreation room with a climbing wall and a small walking track with colorful shapes painted on the wall. He felt like taking a nice, long run on the treadmill, but a leisurely stroll around the track would have to do.

Nephi felt better after his walk and had some time to rest in his room for a while before Craig led him to his therapy appointment. A fit young man with short, black hair, and stubble on his face greeted him.

"Hello, Nephi, I'm Dr. Wilmington. It's a pleasure to meet you. We'll be working together during your stay here."

Dr. Wilmington was nice enough, but he seemed way too

young to be a doctor.

"How are you feeling?" asked Dr. Wilmington.

"Well enough, I guess, considering everything."

"I have a few basic questions for you before we talk more. Since you met with Dr. Montez this morning, have you experienced any blurred vision or other changes to your eyesight?"

"No," replied Nephi.

"Are you having any headaches or dizziness?"

"No, I feel fine."

"What about hallucinations?"

"No, none."

"Have you felt light-headed, like you might pass out?"

"No."

"Excellent. And how is your mood?"

"Surprisingly good."

"Thank you."

Dr. Wilmington then asked Nephi all the same questions that Craig had asked in the morning. He was annoyed at answering the same set of questions, but answered them just the same. Dr. Wilmington then asked Nephi about his upbringing, and then about Bradley, the church, and his job. The topics were painful for Nephi to discuss, but he somehow felt better after talking about it. They then talked about Alex, a topic that Nephi didn't mind discussing at all. Before he knew it, their time was up. He couldn't believe an hour had gone by.

Dinner came next. This time, Nephi ate in the dining area. He sat with his new friends from group, and enjoyed the conversation while he picked at the hospital meatloaf and vegetables. Nephi knew that visiting hours came after dinner. Without his phone, he had no idea if Officer Williams was able to get in touch with anyone. He didn't know what to expect.

While sitting in his room, thinking about the day, a knock came to the door. In walked a nurse with big brown eyes and hair pulled back in a ponytail.

"Hi, my name is Tess," she said. "I'll be your nurse this evening. You have some visitors. I will escort them in, two at a time."

Nephi was glad to hear that someone had come to visit him. He came to the hospital just this morning, but it seemed like much longer. He felt like he was living in a different world, and looked forward to a connection from the old one.

Darla and Stacy came through the door. They both hugged Nephi, and then his mother sat next to him on the bed, while Stacy sat in the chair. He told them of the encounter with Mark that landed him in the psych ward, and of his experiences in the hospital.

"I brought some of your old clothes from the house," said Darla. "They said you might want them. I also got you some new slip-on shoes and slippers. Hopefully you can use them."

He gladly took them from her. "Thanks so much, Mom. I can't tell you how much I appreciate it. These hospital clothes are just hideous."

"I'm sorry that Dad wasn't able to make it tonight. He wanted to be here, but the union Christmas party is going on and he is in charge of it this year, so he couldn't skip out. He'll be here tomorrow."

"I understand. I'll only be here for a few days, anyway."

"What can I do to make this better for you?" asked Stacy. "I feel just awful that you are stuck here for Christmas."

"There's nothing you can do except be here. I'm so happy to see you. I have a Christmas present for you at my apartment, but I suppose you'll have to wait until after Christmas to get it."

"Oh, Nephi, I'm not worried about that. I just want you to be well."

He spoke to them for the better part of an hour. It did his heart good to see them and to hug them. Of everyone in his village, they were two of the most important. They left him with a hug and a kiss on the cheek.

Soon after they left, Nephi heard another knock at the door, and then it cracked open.

"Knock, knock," said the voice on the other side as the door swung open.

"Alex!" exclaimed Nephi. "What are you doing here? You have work tonight."

Alex ran to Nephi and embraced him, squeezing him tightly like an orange being juiced. Alex then stepped back and looked Nephi up and down, studying him.

"You look good," he said, sounding almost surprised. "I traded my shift tonight for lunch shift on Christmas day. Unfortunately, I wasn't able to find a replacement for my shift tomorrow, but I'll be here Christmas night. Here, I brought you something."

Alex extended his arms toward Nephi revealing an article of clothing. Nephi took it and looked closer.

"Your favorite Amsterdam hoodie… I can't take this."

"Nonsense, I know how much you like it. I'm sorry, but I had to remove the drawstrings from the hood."

"Thanks so much for coming. I'm so happy to see you. Do you think you can still love me after they threw me in the looney bin?"

"Oh, honey, this is nothing," replied Alex.

"Nothing? They have me on crazy pills. I have to take Fluoxetine every day."

"Big deal, I've been on Paroxetine for almost ten years. It's not that abnormal. You'd be surprised how many people take antidepressants. I don't even know who I would be without them anymore, and I hope I never find out."

"I never knew that."

"That's because I never told you. After all, you just said things like "looney bin" and "crazy pills". Talk like that perpetuates the stigma around mental illness. That's exactly why I didn't tell you."

"I'm sorry, I didn't mean it like that, I was trying to be funny."

"Kind of like when I tried to be funny about your ten percent raise?"

"Ha! I guess I get your point. I'm sorry, I shouldn't use those words."

"There's nothing wrong with being here. It is just a tool to help you manage everything you are dealing with right now. Your mind is sick, and needs treatment. It's nothing to be ashamed of."

"Thanks for the reassuring words. I am understanding that now," said Nephi.

"I was in the psychiatric unit at the behavioral hospital in Salt Lake for two months after my episode," confessed Alex.

"You had an episode? What happened?"

"You know I have been hesitant to talk about my family. That's because it is painful to talk about. Hell, I don't even think about my family anymore."

The swearing bothered Nephi, but he figured it best to ignore it this time. He just listened as Alex continued.

"As I told you, I grew up on a farm in Jensen. My father is a white farmer from Utah, who met my mother when he was serving a LDS mission in Mexico. After his mission, he brought her to Utah and married her. When I was little, he beat her regularly, while I watched helplessly, not knowing what to do. My father always hated me. I was too feminine for him. He hated the way I looked, the way I dressed, and the way I talked. I loved to cook with my mom in the kitchen, but he forbade it, allowing me only to do "manly" work on the farm."

"So you were raised in the LDS church?"

"Yes, we had family prayer every day, read from the Book of Mormon together, and attended weekly meetings. I heard the teachings at church, but they didn't match what I saw in my father's behavior at home. My father reminded me of Corianton in the Book of Mormon. He was the son of the prophet, Alma. He abandoned his mission, and spent all of his time hooking up with the harlot, Isabel. When the people saw his behavior, they wouldn't believe the words of his father, Alma. My dad was like that. When I saw his example, I couldn't believe any of the things being taught at church. He preached goodness, but didn't live it."

"I never would have guessed," said Nephi. "You even know the Book of Mormon."

"Honey, don't get too excited. If I'm honest, I relate more

with the harlot, Isabel, than any of the rest of it."

Nephi laughed. It felt good to laugh. It felt even better to be with Alex.

"So what happened with your parents?"

"Long story short, I came out to them when I was seventeen. My dad was furious. He flipped out and went ballistic on me. He pinned me in a corner and beat the shit out of me, and I mean that literally. I thought I was going to die, and I probably would have, if it wasn't for my mother. She called the police, and then hit him with a frying pan. He turned his anger on her, and started beating her. The police arrived in time to save us both, and I spent two weeks in the hospital recovering."

Nephi listened in horror as Alex continued the story. "When I was finally well enough to speak, I told the county Sheriff what happened and told him that I wanted to press charges. That Sheriff looked at me straight-faced, and told me that if he was my dad, he would have kicked the shit out of me too. He said that he would not help me press charges. I didn't know what to do, but I knew I couldn't go back home if I wanted to survive. I talked an acquaintance from school into driving me to Salt Lake, where I started living on the streets. I was arrested for theft, and they committed me to the psychiatric unit at the hospital. Involuntary three day hold, same as you. Well, I ended up staying there for three months. It's the best thing that ever happened to me. I learned how to manage my own life. After that, I ended up in state custody for a few months, until I aged out."

"Alex, why didn't you tell me any of this? I'm so sorry."

"Don't be. It made me who I am. I didn't tell you because I didn't think I could get through it, but maybe I'm stronger than I thought. From there, I ended up working low level jobs in restaurants for minimum wage and working my way up. Eventually, I put myself through culinary school, and now here I am, still working in restaurants and still on Paroxetine, but more or less a stable, responsible adult. And I'm still not fond of the church. Your recent experience did nothing to change that. You are about the only decent Mormon I have ever known, and they kicked you out."

"What happened to your mother?"

"I honestly don't know. I've never been back, and I never plan to go back. I hope she got out, but she showed no sign of desire to leave him. If I had to guess, based on the way things were going, I have to assume she is dead. I guess everyone in that town is dead to me."

Nephi wrapped his arms around Alex and held him, Alex's head against his chest, running his fingers through Alex's hair.

"Look at us," said Alex, tears in his eyes. "You're the one in the hospital, and yet here you are, consoling me."

They lay on the bed and just held each other until visiting hours were up. With visiting hours drawing to a close, they shared a tender kiss, and wished each other a good night. Alex left and Tess returned to check on Nephi. She repeated the same set of questions that Craig and Dr. Wilmington asked earlier in the day, and then she left, locking the door from the outside. Nephi found sleep quickly, and slept soundly through the night.

The coming days became routine for Nephi. He had some very good moments and also some terrible ones. The other patients in group became his friends, especially Gemma. She was so sweet and kind, despite the terror she experienced in her life. Nephi felt a connection to her. Through hearing their stories, and the secrets of Alex's past, Nephi came to realize that he had lived a sheltered life. All of the bad he experienced paled in comparison to the things that others had gone through. He didn't understand how they could stay so strong.

In this world, there is a great shortage of empathy. We get so caught up in our own lives and our struggles, that we can't see past them. All around us people are suffering, crying for help, but we don't notice their great problems because we are staring at the small ones in front of our face.

If we can see past our problems, and put ourselves in the place of another, we just might come to a new level of understanding, and be the means of lightening the load of another. As Nephi reflected, he realized that is what the Savior did. He put Himself in the place of each of us, in a way that only He could. Because of that, He truly understands us and is in a unique position to lighten our burden.

Christmas was Nephi's third day in the hospital. He met with Dr. Montez, expecting to be released that night.

"I am very pleased with your progress, Nephi. Your survey results are improving and you are making positive steps. I believe you could benefit from a few more days. I recommend that you remain here until Saturday."

"Another three days? But why? I feel ready."

"In my experience, three days is not enough. You are new to the medication, and I would like to observe you for a few more days so I am more confident you will be okay. I know it's not what you want to hear, especially on Christmas, but I really think it's for the best. I can't keep you here if you really want to leave, but I strongly recommend that you stay."

"Just three more days?" he asked.

"Three days."

Nephi thought about it. He wanted to go home badly. He reflected on his time in the hospital and how much he had learned and grown. Three more days really wasn't that long, and at least he would get to see Gemma every day.

"Okay, I'll stay," he said.

"Very good. I think you have made a responsible choice."

During his visit with Alex that night, Nephi expressed regret that their first Christmas was spent in the hospital.

"As long as you are getting the help you need, it's a good day for me," said Alex.

"I got you a Christmas Present. When I get out of here, I'll give it to you," said Nephi.

"Don't worry. We'll celebrate when you're home. I got you a present too but they wouldn't let me bring it in. They were afraid you would figure out some way to hurt yourself with it, I guess."

"I've been thinking a lot in here. I guess I haven't had much else to do," observed Nephi. "You know how you keep asking me why I insist on going to church even after being excommunicated?"

"Yes, I have wondered that."

"Well, you're not the only one who has asked me. People inside and outside of the church ask me that all the time. It's quite tiring, actually. Anyway, I have thought about it a lot while I have been in here. Like I told you, I want to be there, and it is about my own growth, and my relationship with God. But after further reflection, I realized it is more than that."

"How so?"

"There are others like me. Others who are gay, lesbian, transgender, bisexual, aro, ace, or otherwise queer. All of us feel like misfits and outcasts in the church. We don't know where, or if we belong. It feels like there is no place for us. We are stuck between two worlds, a Mormon world that we love, and a queer world inherent to our nature… to the way God created us. I need to go to church not only for me, but for the others. If someone else like me or Bradley comes to church, I want them to feel welcome. I want them to have someone to sit with so they know they belong. They can sit with me."

"Honey, you have been doing a lot of thinking, and everything you just said makes all the sense in the world to me. I'm sorry I have pestered you so much. I get it and won't ask again. The more I get to know you, the more I love you."

"I feel the same way about you," replied Nephi.

The couple held each other, not wanting to be apart. Since it was Christmas, Tess had compassion for Nephi, and let Alex stay an extra thirty minutes before she made him leave.

Each day in the hospital, the highlight for Nephi was the interaction with family and friends. Alex visited every day that he could, and called on the days that he couldn't get out of work. Stacy, Darla, Mike, Ammon, and Tiffany also paid him visits. By Saturday, he felt stronger, and better equipped with tools to handle the stress dealt by life. He was glad that he took Dr. Montez's recommendation to stay the extra time. He felt healthier than he had in a long time, and he had a better understanding of himself.

Nephi thanked all the doctors and nurses on his way out. He was grateful to have his belongings back, especially his phone. It would allow him to talk to loved ones whenever he wanted. That was something he would no longer take for granted.

Alex found someone to cover his Saturday shift and met Nephi at the hospital to take him home. Nephi's mental state was much improved. He would continue to take Fluoxetine each day and meet with a counselor twice per month, but he was free to go home.

CHAPTER 24

Upon leaving the hospital, their first stop was the Brower parking lot to retrieve Nephi's truck. Alex then followed Nephi to his apartment. Nephi unlocked the door and walked in to discover that his apartment had been decorated for Christmas. Colorful lights hung on every wall, and a tree covered in white lights and tied with golden bows stood in the corner of the living room with wrapped gifts below. A stuffed stocking hung from a hook on the wall. Nephi hadn't experienced such Christmas magic since he was a young boy.

"Merry Christmas!" shouted Alex.

"Merry Christmas to you, Baby," he replied. "Can we sing Christmas carols?"

"Honey, of course we can sing, as long as you don't mind hearing them out of tune."

They sang "Jingle Bells" and "Deck the Halls," followed by "Silent Night" and "Away in a Manger." Nephi smiled the whole time, as the joy of the season touched his soul.

Nephi retrieved Alex's gifts from the bedroom and watched eagerly as he opened them. The jacket was a perfect fit, and looked as sexy on Alex as Nephi had hoped. He determined that gift was actually for himself, after all. Seeing Alex's face light up when he opened the sous vide system was priceless.

"I've been wanting to get one of these," he declared. "Thank you."

Alex kissed Nephi and smiled at him. Then he kissed him again before retrieving a small present from underneath the tree.

"This one's for you," he said, extending the gift toward Nephi.

Nephi took it and examined the wrapping of the small, thin, square package. It must be a disk of some sort, maybe a computer disk, CD, or DVD.

"Well, aren't you going to open it?"

Nephi gently tore the wrapping paper, taking his time to

enjoy the moment. This was the first Christmas he had spent with someone he loved, and he wanted to savor it. He peeled back the paper to reveal a picture of Tommy Page wearing a wool winter coat, head leaned forward resting on his arms. His hair was mussed, and he looked to have a bit of stubble on his face. He was gorgeous. Nephi opened the cover, where he saw a CD. The name of the album was 'Time' and he had never before heard of it. His eyes lit up, and appeared as if they were ready to pop right out of his head.

"But, how?" he wondered aloud.

"I found it at Wallaby Record Store in Salt Lake. It's an old school music shop that sells vinyl and CDs. This album was in the import section. Apparently it was only released in Asia."

"Will you listen to it with me?" asked Nephi.

"Of course I will."

Nephi stood and hit the eject button on the DVD player next to the TV.

"What are you doing?" asked Alex. "That's a DVD player. The album is a CD."

"It plays CDs too. I do it all the time," he replied as he inserted the disk and turned on the TV.

The album began to play and Nephi extended his arms toward Alex. Taking him by the hands, he lifted him off of the sofa, and placed his hands around Alex's waist. Dancing to the music, they glided across the living room floor. Nephi almost wondered if he was in heaven. He loved every song, but especially the title track, and also his favorite of the album, "Spend Tonight with You". The song was so beautiful, and the words seemed as if they could be his own as he moved to the music with Alex.

As the last few songs played, they moved from their dance floor to the couch where they kissed, gently at first and then passionately. They were both lost in the moment until Alex pulled away abruptly and looked at his watch.

"Oh no, we're late," he exclaimed.

"Late for what?"

"We're supposed to be at your parents' house right now."

They kissed one more time and then went to Mike and Darla's house where Nephi's entire family was waiting for them along with Stacy and her family.

"Merry Christmas, Uncle Nephi," said Chloe when Nephi walked through the door. She ran to him and hugged him around the leg.

"Merry Christmas, Chloe Bear."

Dallin, Crystal, and Sophie, soon joined her, all clamoring for attention, which he was more than willing to give. Nephi had missed the children, particularly on Christmas. His favorite part of the holiday was seeing their faces in awe at the lights, and the mystery of a wrapped gift.

They spent the night talking, exchanging gifts, and enjoying eggnog, hot cocoa, and hot apple cider, along with a Christmas feast prepared by Darla. Even though it was December 28th, it was the best Christmas that Nephi had in quite some time.

After the family party, Nephi and Alex returned to Nephi's apartment where they talked late into the night. Nephi told Alex all about his experience in the hospital, while Alex shared the events of his life in the past week. The conversation then turned to Nephi's employment.

"Have you given any thought to what you want to do for work?" asked Alex.

"I don't really know anything except call centers and hotel reservations. I'm not sure what's out there."

"Have you ever heard that it's not what you know, but who you know that matters?"

"Yes, I've heard that before, but I'm afraid I don't have any connections."

"Well, I just might know someone who can help. It's not a guarantee, but it's worth a shot."

"Who is it?"

"My old boyfriend, Jerry. He is the General Manager at the High Palace Hotel reservation center in Salt Lake."

"Aren't those the fancy, high-end hotels?" asked Nephi.

"Yep, those are the ones. Jerry has worked there forever. I don't know if they have openings at the moment, but I can find out."

"That would be great. Are you still on good terms with him?"

"Yes, we weren't good for each other in a relationship, but we are still friends and talk every once in a while."

"Thanks, I appreciate it. I can use all the help I can get."

"Hey, Nephi," said Alex. "Speaking of Jerry, I have been in a lot of relationships. Do you have questions, or want to know about anything in my past? I'm not proud of everything, but I'm an open book if you are curious."

"Sweetie, none of that matters to me, and I don't care to know it. Whatever happened in your past made you who you are today, and led you to me. All I care about, is that we are here together now, and I love you. Rather than worry about your past, I look forward to our future."

"Oh, be still my heart, Nephi Willard, where on earth did you come from, and how did I ever get so lucky?"

Alex positioned himself directly in front of Nephi, face to face, and gazed deep into his eyes. In that moment, Nephi could see right into his soul. He saw love. They kissed and held each other, both feeling something burning deep within them.

"It's getting late," observed Nephi. "Do you need to get going soon?"

"Honey, I'm not going anywhere tonight."

"Ok. You take the bed. You know I'm fine on the sofa."

"Come on, won't you join me?" pleaded Alex. "Just for tonight."

"Okay," replied Nephi, "just for tonight. But just sleeping."

"Yes, just sleeping," laughed Alex, a smile on his face.

They both moved to the bed where they cuddled and held each other until morning. Nephi felt safe in Alex's arms, and he never slept as well as he did that night.

In the morning, Nephi got ready for church while Alex slept. Before leaving, he went into the bedroom, leaned over, and kissed Alex on the forehead, which roused Alex from deep slumber.

"Wait," said Alex. "I have something for you."

From a small paper bag on the nightstand, he pulled a small rainbow emblem, and pinned it on Nephi's lapel.

"So the others know they can sit with you," he said.

Nephi kissed him and made his way toward the door. "Will you still be here when I get back?" he asked.

"I don't work until this afternoon. I'll be here."

Nephi proceeded out the door, and walked to church with the rainbow pin on his lapel. He took his seat alone, at the far side of the chapel, and bowed his head while he listened to the organ music.

Just before the beginning of Sacrament meeting, Nephi felt someone sit next to him on the bench.

"A little bird told me you're willing to sit with people like me," a voice whispered in his ear.

Nephi looked up to find Alex sitting next to him, dressed in gray dress slacks, a light pink shirt, and a tie, with a tie tack that matched Nephi's lapel pin. Nephi smiled and put his arm around Alex as gasps echoed behind them.

They sat reverently and listened to the service, singing each hymn joyfully. Nephi sang in tune next to Alex, who was dreadfully off key. After Sacrament meeting, they both sat and listened in Gospel Principles class before returning to the apartment for lunch. Alex then returned up north to work, while Nephi enjoyed his apartment. It seemed extra spacious compared to his hospital room.

On Monday, Nephi ran on the treadmill until he couldn't run anymore. He had missed rigorous exercise. He spent the rest of the morning searching for jobs online. Alex called around 2:00 to let Nephi know he got in touch with Jerry and scheduled an interview for Nephi on Monday, January 6th at 11:00. The opportunity excited Nephi since he only had enough savings to last a month.

Alex had to work on New Year's Eve, so Nephi spent the night with Stacy and Roger, playing board games and watching the apple drop on TV. He and Alex rang in the New Year the following night, going out to dinner and watching two movies at The Gateway in Salt Lake.

The week passed and Nephi either saw or talked to Alex every day. Monday arrived, covered in ice and snow, and Nephi prepared for his interview with Jerry. He dressed in a suit and tie, gassed up his truck, and drove to Salt Lake to the High Palace Hotels reservation center. Fine paintings and gold trim adorned the lobby, obvious signs that High Palace was several grades above Brower.

"Hello, I'm here for an interview with Jerry Kerby," said Nephi, as he approached the reception desk.

"Very good, Mr. Willard. Please have a seat. Mr. Kerby will be with you shortly."

Nephi sat on a comfortable chair in the lobby and waited while rehearsing the facts of his job experience in his head.

Jerry soon met him in the lobby and escorted him to his office.

"Welcome, Nephi. I'm glad to meet you. Alex told me all about you, including what led to the termination of your position at Brower Hotels. It sounds like a terrible ordeal."

"It was terrible but I would rather not focus on that. I have a lot to offer High Palace Hotels, and I would like to discuss any opportunities you have available that might match my experience."

"I'm glad to hear that. It's the kind of attitude we need around here. You should understand that High Palace is not Brower. Here, we are "the refined serving the refined". Our guests are cultured and so must be our employees. Our manner of speaking and presentation must be elegant so we convey the brand image. Would you have difficulty with that?"

"I don't believe so. I enjoy refined things, and am very serious and professional by nature. People relate well to me, and I can coach others and help them perform well."

"I understand you were a shift manager at Brower. Is that correct?"

"Yes, I managed a team of twenty five reservations agents. I validated the team statistics every day, monitored and scored agent calls, provided coaching, and managed the career progression of the employees that reported to me. The day shift was my responsibility. I worked from 7:00 until 4:00."

"That's excellent. Tell me about the statistics you measured."

"We kept track of 'Handle Time', 'After Call Work', 'Call Abandon Rate', and 'Time in Queue', among others. I found that you have to be careful which metrics you emphasize because the measurements on which you focus will change the behavior of the agents, sometimes in ways you didn't expect."

"Interesting. I have also found that to be the case. It sounds like you will fit in well here. When are you available to start?"

"As soon as you're willing to have me."

"Great! We have a new agent training class that started today. You can join them tomorrow. I propose that you complete our two week training course with this batch of agents, and then take calls for a month before I move you to a shift manager position. How does that sound?"

"That sounds perfect."

"I'm afraid that I don't have a manager position open in the day, though. Your training for the next two weeks will run from 9:00 until 4:00, but when you start taking calls, I will move you to the evening shift. You will work from 3:00 in the afternoon until 11:30 at night. Will that work for you?"

"That works."

"Wonderful. I recently had a night shift manager position open up, so one of my shift managers is pulling double-duty. You can take that spot."

"That sounds great to me. I'll see you tomorrow at 9:00."

Nephi thanked Jerry, and went to his truck, doing a little victory dance and pumping his fist on the way. He called Alex to let him know the good news, and thanked him for the introduction.

Alex took him to lunch in celebration. After several difficult weeks, Nephi found himself with a new love, a new job, and a new appreciation for his very nature. He couldn't wait to delve into his new world.

CHAPTER 25

Nephi rolled out of bed and kneeled to pray. Sunlight streamed in his window, causing him to squint before closing his eyes. He thanked the Lord for the many blessings in his life, and then sat on the bed, and read from the Book of Mormon. After a hot shower, he put on his gray dress slacks, buttoned his Olympic blue shirt, and headed out the door.

The sun stood high in the sky, warming the green trees and flowers below. A nice walk in the 67 degree weather was the perfect way to start the first Monday in May. Nephi walked two blocks from his one bedroom Salt Lake apartment to the TRAX light rail station, where the train would take him to work. Ten short minutes later, TRAX stopped one block from the High Palace Hotels reservation center.

Nephi couldn't believe only four months had passed since he started at HPH. So much had changed during that time, he could hardly remember what his life was like before.

The Salt Lake singles ward he attended was more progressive than his family ward in Pleasant Grove. A growing group of queer Mormons joined him each Sunday, each wearing a rainbow pin on their lapel, tie, or dress. Many in the ward were not comfortable with their presence. They were subject to occasional derogatory remarks, but they had each other for support, and responded only with kindness.

HPH fit Nephi better than he had hoped. Unlike Mark, Jerry led by example. There was no job beneath him. He was willing to get on the phone and take customer calls, and help with monitoring associates when the managers were overwhelmed. His leadership set the tone for the entire call center.

Nephi made each person on his team feel valued. He listened to them, and took action based on their feedback to improve the work environment, which resulted in better service for their guests. In a few short months, Nephi's team had gone from the lowest performing team in the call center to the highest, and Jerry took note, even offering Nephi a choice of shift. Despite the offer, Nephi stayed on the evening shift. Nephi liked his team, and even better, he worked on the same schedule as Alex. Instead of a shift change, he talked Jerry into letting him split his days off. He took Sunday off because it was the Sabbath day, and Wednesday because it matched Alex's schedule.

Now that the distance that separated them was blocks, rather than miles, and given their similar work schedules, spending time together wasn't so difficult.

Alex and Nephi spent time together every day. The strongest bonds don't happen all at once. We form them over hundreds of shared moments. Those bonds are strengthened as people rely on each other through trials. After everything they had been through, Nephi and Alex shared a special bond. They were inseparable.

Though weekly lunches with Stacy were no longer possible, Nephi still spoke with her often. He continued to attend the monthly family dinner at his parents' home every Fast Sunday. He was in a good place physically, spiritually, and emotionally.

The changes in his life ran through his mind as he walked from the TRAX station to the office. He badged in and smiled at the receptionist on the way back to his office, where he kicked off his daily stats report process, and went to the break room to put his lunch in the fridge.

Walking the floor to check in with his team, he thought about Brower, where he had to fight to keep Brock and Angela separated. He didn't have that issue at HPH, and he hated to admit it, but he kind of missed them.

Nephi went about the work day monitoring calls and coaching his team. He liked working at HPH and felt connected to their motto - 'The refined serving the refined.' While he came from a blue collar background, and was proud of that, he also enjoyed the theater, fashion, and fine food. Nephi related well to the guests, and enjoyed interacting with them.

Promoting the people on his team was his favorite part of

the job, though. He loved helping others to succeed, and celebrated their success. So far, he had already promoted two agents to level two, and another to level three. Nephi's team respected him, as did his peer managers.

At the end of his shift, Nephi walked along the streetlight-illuminated sidewalk to the TRAX stop, and caught the last train home. He still wasn't used to the darkness when he left work, but it became more normal as each week passed. He walked from the stop to Alex's apartment.

Alex brought food home from work - Tagliatelle Genovese and Stuffed Porchetta. They enjoyed the meal while they talked. It was excellent, as always.

"So, Honey, tell me about your day," said Alex.

"My day was good. Normal, but good. My team is doing really well, outperforming every other team at the reservation center. How about you?"

"Mondays rarely get too crazy, but my sous-chef called in sick, so I had to pull double duty. Nothing I couldn't handle."

"You're amazing at what you do. I can't believe how good this pasta tastes. It surprises me every time."

"Don't forget that you need to get time off for Pride. It's four weeks from this weekend."

"Don't worry, I'm already approved for Saturday the 6th. I'm all yours for the entire day."

"Ooh, I like the sound of that. And you have Sunday off anyway, so we're good."

"Yes, I have Sunday off, but I have church from 11:00 until 1:00."

"Not that day, you don't. The Pride Festival goes all day on Saturday and Sunday, but the parade is the main event, and that overlaps with your church time. You can't miss the parade. I need you there with me," insisted Alex.

"You know that church is important to me, and that I go every week. You've never had a problem with it before. We have a group that all sits together. Is it really that big of a deal if I miss the parade?"

"Are you kidding me right now? Pretty much everyone in

your group will be at the parade that day anyway, so you don't need to worry about that. You can be so selfish sometimes. I have supported you and even showed up at church when you needed it, even though I hate that place."

"I know that, but…"

"But nothing," Alex interrupted. "Pride for me is every bit as important as church is for you, and it only comes once per year. You can go to church every other week. It's not just a parade, it has meaning. In June of 1969, New York police cracked down on Stonewall Inn, a gay bar in Greenwich Village, for no good reason. It was blatant targeting and discrimination. Those in the bar resisted, and a riot broke out. Ever since then, we have celebrated Pride during the month of June, as a symbol that we are proud of who we are. We are part of the community and have rights, just like everyone else."

"Well," started Nephi.

"Be quiet and listen. I'm not finished," replied Alex. "In Utah, the celebration used to be a small, informal gathering at Tanner Park. It has grown into a large, well-organized event. It is important to me, and to others in the community, and it should be important to you, too. There is a lot of history behind it. I support you going to church, and I will continue to support you. But Honey, I need you there with me at the parade."

"But I have to set an example. I really feel like I should be at church."

"You are so damn self-righteous. It's sickening, really. Just one week! You stay home if you're sick don't you?"

"Yes, but it's not the same. I wouldn't be skipping church because I'm sick, I would be skipping it to have fun."

"What would you be missing out on? They won't let you talk, pray, or take the Sacrament, anyway."

"I would miss out on being there, and singing from my heart, and showing my commitment to God."

"What about showing a little commitment to me? I have given you everything. I go along with your commitment to the law of chastity. Believe me, I wouldn't do that for just anyone.

You are all take and no give. I really need this. Please, do this for me."

"I need time to think about it," said Nephi, as he headed for the door.

"Time to think?" Alex called after him. "This should be a no-brainer."

The door closed, and Nephi walked toward home, frustrated - their argument replaying in his head. Why didn't Alex understand? Why didn't anyone understand? It always had to be either, or. Why couldn't it be both? He wondered if it was impossible to be gay and Mormon. He thought he had found a way to strike a balance, but maybe he was wrong.

This was the biggest fight that he and Alex ever had, and he wasn't sure what to do about it, or how to make it right. Nephi loved Alex, and wanted to make him happy. He thought he had shown commitment, but apparently, Alex didn't feel it.

Even though he wasn't in the mood to pray, Nephi kneeled at his bedside and spoke to God to ask for guidance. That night, he went to bed angry, and woke up still angry the next day. He still needed to think, to figure things out.

He went to work and started his day. He had a one-on-one meeting scheduled with Jerry at 4:00 to discuss his team. Nephi reviewed the stats with Jerry, discussed the agents that were getting close to a promotion, and planned for the gaps they needed to work on. After the business of their meeting concluded, Nephi asked Jerry if he had some time to speak regarding a personal matter.

Nephi knew that Jerry and Alex had history, and thought maybe he could lend some insight into their current situation. Jerry was happy to talk with him, so Nephi recounted to him the history behind it, and the details of their fight.

"What do you think?" asked Nephi.

"I admire and respect your religious convictions," said Jerry. "But to be honest, Nephi, I think you should think really hard about what Alex is asking for in this situation. From what you have told me, I can tell that he is really into you. He has jumped through hoops for you that he wouldn't have done for anyone else. He certainly never went to such lengths for me. I know that your religion is important to you, but you should think of Pride almost like a religion for Alex. I mean, we all love Pride and it is important to us, but Alex takes it to another level. When he went to his first Pride, for him, it was like being born again. I really don't think you understand how important this is to him."

"So, what do you think I should do?"

"Oh, no, I'm not letting you pull me in that deep. I can't tell you what to do. You must decide that for yourself, but you should do a lot of reflecting. You obviously understand your own perspective, but try to put yourself in Alex's shoes. Imagine you had gone through everything he has in his life, and you discovered Pride and a place where you belong, a place where you don't feel ashamed of who you are, where you are free to be yourself. Then imagine celebrating that moment one time per year. Do that, and then look at it again from your own point of view, and compare them. Then you'll just have to make the decision that's right for you. Sorry, but that's all I got."

"Thanks, Jerry. That's good advice. You've been very helpful. Thanks again for everything."

Nephi left his office and continued the work day, thinking about Jerry's words in the back of his mind. He made some good points, and Nephi really hadn't done a deep thought exercise, putting himself in Alex's place, and viewing it from a different point of view. After his shift ended, he went home to further ponder his dilemma.

Jerry's words made sense, but Nephi's feelings were getting in the way. Hearing Alex call him selfish brought to his mind the words that his father spoke at church after his excommunication. It hurt and he just couldn't bring himself to get past it, so he pushed the feelings down, and did his best to ignore them.

Two weeks went by while Nephi wrestled with his own thoughts and feelings. He hadn't tried to contact Alex, and Alex hadn't reached out to him. He missed Alex, and wanted the fight to end, but also didn't want to abandon his own stubborn pride. Nephi had been telling himself that he followed Jerry's advice, but deep down, he knew that he had only done so half-heartedly. On a Wednesday a little over two weeks before the Pride Festival, he thought more on Jerry's words, and realized that he had been a hypocrite. He expected others to show empathy, but had not done so himself.

He kneeled at his bedside, and prayed for help in humbling himself, and sought direction. Nephi then imagined what it would be like to be a young boy in a home where his father abused his mother, and didn't accept him. He imagined the horror of being beaten nearly to death by his own father, and then being alone on the streets, with no concept of how to care for himself.

The daydream continued as he placed himself in the psychiatric ward for months, getting help and learning valuable skills, before ending up in state custody. There, he waited to age out of the system, just to find himself all alone again. He pictured finding a community where he could be himself without fear of harm or judgement and what that acceptance meant.

Through his thought exercise, Nephi felt that he understood Alex better. He compared that to his own desire to attend church, and then Alex's words played back in his head. It was only one week. Why couldn't he give up only one week for the man he loved? Church was there every week, but the Pride Festival was only once per year.

The reality slapped Nephi in the face. Alex was right. He acted rigid and selfish. He was a hypocrite, and his holier-than-thou attitude was ruining the best relationship he ever had. Alex had given up so much for him. He had been so understanding about everything with the church. He took work off to be with him in the hospital. He had done everything he could ask, but Nephi still made it all about himself.

Still in his pajamas and with mussed hair, Nephi slipped on a pair of shoes, and ran several blocks to Alex's apartment, and banged on the door. With no answer, he knocked again. It seemed that Alex wasn't home. Nephi started walking away, when he heard the door latch. He turned around to see Alex standing at the door.

"Alex, I need to talk to you."

"Who the hell do you think you are? I can't believe it has taken you this long to come back. Nothing for over two weeks, and now you show up expecting me to just open the door and let you in? What if I don't want to talk to you?"

"I couldn't blame you for that. Everything you said is true. I have been selfish and self-righteous, only caring about what I wanted. I'm sorry. Can you forgive me?"

"What's the matter, aren't you going to lecture me for swearing? I honestly don't know if I can forgive you right now. There is no doubt that I love you, and part of me wants to forgive you, but the other part of me wonders what comes next. What else will you choose over me?"

"I'm sorry. I know I was wrong. You will have me to yourself for the entire Pride Festival, parade included. I understand how important it is for you, and I'll be there for you - for whatever you need."

"Honey, I appreciate that, but it might be too little, too late. For this relationship to work, things need to be equal, but it always seems that I'm way more committed to you, than you are to me. There has to be give and take, and I just don't see it."

"That's because I haven't shown it. I see that now, and I'm sorry. I love you and I want to be with you. What do I have to do?"

"I wish I knew."

"Let me come in to talk about it."

"You have said what you came to say, and I've heard you. Now it's my turn to think. I just need a little space. I'll be in touch."

With that, Alex disappeared behind the door, and Nephi returned home, hoping he hadn't blown it for good.

Over the next week and a half, Nephi texted and called

Alex every day without a reply. He apologized every way he knew how, but just didn't know how to get through. Alex seemed to be ghosting him, and he was growing concerned. He had to figure out a way to let Alex know that their commitment was on the same level.

With only one week until the beginning of the Pride Festival, Nephi started to panic, and racked his brain, trying to come up with a way to make Alex understand. Something popped into his head that seemed insane, but Alex had to know he was serious. He set off for the mall to make preparations to carry out his plan. After several hours of searching, he found the perfect items. That night he had work, but tomorrow would be Sunday, the perfect day to execute his plan.

Work came and went and Nephi, nervous about what might happen the following day, did his best to sleep. He woke in the morning and went through his normal routine, preparing for church. Just like every Sunday, he attended church, sitting with the rainbow squadron, singing the hymns joyfully, and listening to the talks. After church, he talked to Stacy for a while, and then called and spoke with Darla to distract himself from the anxiety building in his belly.

Six o'clock rolled around and Nephi figured La Bambolina should be starting to get busy. It was go-time. Wearing his nicest suit, and the new tie he bought at the mall, he grabbed the bouquet, and took the light rail to the restaurant with strangers staring at him the entire way.

Upon entering the restaurant, he approached the host.

"Hey, Billy, are you ready with the table that we discussed?"

"Sure am, Nephi. Right this way."

He led Nephi to a table in the center of the restaurant. Nephi took a seat with his back to the kitchen and waited while the host headed back to have a word with the chef. A few minutes later, Alex emerged from the kitchen and approached the table.

"Is there a problem, sir?" asked Alex.

"There certainly is," said Nephi, as he scooted his chair

backward a few inches to use it as a stepping stool to climb on top of the table. He turned to face Alex.

"What are you doing here?" Alex demanded to know.

"I'm here to let you know I'm committed," came the reply.

Nephi then took a deep breath, and burst into song, singing "I'm Sorry" by Brenda Lee, at full voice. The restaurant patrons all turned and stared. Alex's face turned red.

"What are you doing? Get down from there."

Despite Alex's protest, Nephi kept singing. He really got into it, gesticulating wildly, and using the flowers as a microphone. As Alex watched, he couldn't help but smile. As the song continued, his smile grew into a laugh. He wondered if Nephi had gone insane. Maybe it was time for another trip to the hospital. Alex wanted to stay mad at Nephi, but he was now finding that very difficult, which only added to his anger.

He was intent on staying mad to teach Nephi a lesson, but by the end of the song, his anger had nearly vanished. The restaurant erupted in applause, and Nephi took a bow. He then started singing "Turning Me On" by Tommy Page.

"Nope, I'm done. I'm stopping you right there," said Alex before Nephi could get through the first line. Alex grabbed him by the hand, and helped him down from the table. Nephi presented Alex with the beautiful flower bouquet, and then dropped to one knee and pulled a ring from his pocket.

He took Alex by the left hand and looked into his eyes.

"Alex, you are the best thing that ever happened to me. The past few weeks have been miserable without you and I never want to go through that again. I want to spend this Pride and every other Pride with you. Will you marry me?"

Nephi slid the ring onto his finger and looked to his face for an answer. Alex smiled, love beaming from his eyes. He couldn't help but let out a squeal, before composing himself enough to answer.

"Oh, Honey, of course I'll marry you."

Nephi stood and kissed him, to the delight of the patrons, who cheered as they recorded the proposal with their phones.

CHAPTER 26

Saturday, June 6th marked the beginning of the Utah Pride Festival's main events. The festival kicked off at 1:00. Alex had looked forward to this day all year. The forecast called for clear skies, and 82 degree weather. Nephi walked to Alex's apartment. They drove down State Street and parked off of 400 South across from Washington Square, home to the Pride Festival.

This was Nephi's first time attending the festival. The size and coordination of activities impressed him. Tents topped with colorful canvas lined the streets. The booths offered food and drink, LGBTQIA+ merchandise, and opportunities to connect with community organizations.

It astonished Nephi to see some of those organizations, not officially sponsored by the LDS church, but made up of Mormon individuals seeking equality and positive relationships with the LGBTQIA+ community. He noticed booths sponsored by Mormons Building Bridges, Mormons for Equality, the Provo Pride Council, Mama Dragons, and more. There were even booths set up where Mormon mothers and fathers offered hugs to anyone who felt the need to receive one.

Nephi's face lit up to see the outpouring of love and acceptance. It made him feel giddy inside, a feeling he hadn't expected. Alex saw the look on Nephi's face, and knew that he had caught the bug. He leaned in for a kiss, and then took Nephi by the hand while they explored the festival together.

Alex led them to the Pride Center Zone first, and then through the History Zone. While Nephi had been out for quite some time, he had never really participated in the community, and knew little of the history of Pride. Alex aimed to change that. Nephi was surprised to learn the long, proud history of Pride in the nation, and in Utah. He had no idea that so many people had fought for so long, at a time when society was even less accepting of queer people than now.

Together, they sat through a Cultural Competency presentation, where Nephi learned about the cultural characteristics, beliefs, history, behavior, and values of various LGBTQIA+ individuals. Through the presentation, Nephi better understood the cultural differences and similarities between individuals. It was eye-opening, and more importantly, mind-opening.

The day continued as they visited the Pride Store to pick up some merch. Nephi found more rainbow pins for church. They also bought Pride Festival t-shirts.

Alex wanted to check out some musical performances. It was the dance performances that caught Nephi's eye. They spent time enjoying both. Nephi appreciated the day much more than he expected. Until today, he didn't understand how much he had to learn.

Nephi's favorite part of the day came late in the evening. After grabbing a bite to eat, they made their way to the karaoke stage. It disappointed Nephi to see that there were no Tommy Page songs available on the karaoke machine. Instead, he rocked a trio of boy band songs. It surprised Alex how natural he looked on that stage. His pitch was perfect, and he even did the dance moves. The crowd was eating out of his hand, clapping in unison as he sang.

When Nephi finished, they went crazy, calling for an encore, but he disappointed them, and left the stage to give a chance to whichever poor soul had to follow him. He found Alex and begged him to get up and sing.

"Honey, you know I'm tone deaf. If I get up there, it will be so bad. I'll totally embarrass both of us."

"I don't care if you're off key. You love to sing and you shouldn't let the fear of judgement keep you from doing something you love. Besides, you can't be much worse than this guy," said Nephi, pointing to the show queen singing some song from Wicked on the stage.

"I seriously can't. I would die from embarrassment."

"Come on, Baby! I love it when you sing. Don't sing for everyone else, sing for me."

Against his better judgement, Alex agreed to take a turn on stage for just one song. He waited his turn, and when the time came, walked onto the stage and grabbed the mic.

"I want to dedicate this song to my fiancé," he said. "If it weren't for him, I never would have known what "redneckin' it" is all about. Nephi, your favorite country song…"

Alex lowered his head and extended his arms to the side, fingers fully extended. As the music started, his arms crept downward until they were near his knees before bending at the elbows and moving upward across his chest. He grabbed the mic, bringing it to his mouth. "Cotton Eye Joe" by Rednex started pumping out of the speakers while Alex sang his heart out. While he sang, he did his best version of a country line dance, which from the crowd, just looked awkward.

Nobody could tell for sure which key he was singing in, but they knew that the notes that came out of his mouth did not belong together. Small children could be seen covering their ears as Nephi stood front and center, doing his best to sing along between fits of laughter.

The song ended, and the crowd roared, more a celebration that the performance was finally over, than a sign that they enjoyed it. Alex took a big bow, and ran off the stage to find Nephi. They looked at each other and laughed and then hugged. They walked around the festival, hand in hand. It felt good to hold hands in public without worrying about where the next ignorant homophobic confrontation would come from – something straight couples take for granted.

When the night was over, they returned to Alex's place where Alex sipped coffee and Nephi drank hot cocoa while they talked. Nephi thanked Alex for opening his eyes and showing him such a great time. He had gained a better understanding of why this annual event was so important to Alex. He apologized again for being an idiot.

"Enough apologizing," Alex told him. "We're past that now. From here, we only look forward."

Nephi thanked him again and gave him a warm, lingering kiss before he returned to his apartment for the night. He couldn't wait until they were married, so he wouldn't have to say goodnight. He looked forward to a continuation of the festivities in the morning.

Sunday morning came early. Having worked the night shift for several months, Nephi was used to more sleep, and had to force himself out of bed. He changed into shorts and his favorite workout shirt, and went for a run, and then returned home for a cool shower.

He dressed in black Capri pants and the Pride Festival t-shirt he bought the previous day. He then walked to Alex's apartment. Alex had made Nephi a breakfast of hot cocoa and beignets, which they enjoyed together before making their way to 200 South to watch the parade.

It amazed Nephi to discover that the Pride parade was the second biggest parade in Utah, after the Days of '47 parade that takes place in July. He also came to an appreciation of the diversity in Salt Lake City, and the size of the LGBTQIA+ community. He hadn't previously realized the extent of the community, since it was right in the middle of the conservative stronghold of Utah.

Large crowds of people lined 200 South for over a mile, waving flags and cheering while they waited for the parade to begin. Nephi noticed people who had set up canopies, and others who brought colorful umbrellas to shade themselves from the sun. He could see the procession approaching in the distance.

Nephi looked over to see Alex bouncing up and down, clearly excited by the atmosphere. A large group of motorcycles came through first. The bikers wore helmets in the colors of the rainbow, with rainbow flags attached to the back of their bikes.

Next came a contingent from the transgender community waiving their light blue, pink, and white flag in the air as they marched. The parade was just beginning, but it stretched back as far as Nephi could see. As each group passed, the crowd cheered.

With many in their group wearing flags around their neck as a cape, the Utah Pride Center came next. As they passed, Alex explained each flag. Nephi already knew of the Pride rainbow flag, but many of the others were new to him. There was a lesbian pride flag, a pansexual flag and many more flags representing individuals from the asexual, transgender, non-binary, bisexual, genderfluid, agender, aromantic, and intersex communities. Nephi was getting an education, and he enjoyed it.

The Mormons Building Bridges group came next, a group with no official affiliation with the Church of Jesus Christ of Latter Day Saints, but who are members of the church supporting inclusion of those in the LGBTQIA+ community. They were followed by a group carrying large colorful arches made from balloons.

Then came a man wearing only a rainbow speedo and a headdress reminiscent of a Las Vegas showgirl. He sped by on rollerblades, dancing and singing as he went. Nephi wasn't entirely sure that he was an official part of the parade, but he enjoyed it just the same.

There were baton twirlers, cheerleaders, a marching band, and parade floats. Clubs from the University of Utah, Weber State University, Utah Valley University, and Salt Lake Community College each provided a float. There was also a float decorated to commemorate Stonewall. The local news stations and brewing companies joined the fun, as did a guy that had fashioned some amazing rainbow colored butterfly wings for himself from balloons.

The parade went on and on. It took two full hours to watch it from beginning to end, and Nephi loved every minute. He was glad he came to support Alex, but also glad that he hadn't missed an event that felt life-changing.

After the parade had gone by and the crowd dissipated, Nephi and Alex made their way to the Pride march. They marched to the State Capitol building and took part in the Pride Rally on the steps of the Capitol. Nephi was proud to be there and felt an affinity to those with whom he marched.

That evening, Alex surprised Nephi by taking him to the Pride Interfaith Service held at the Methodist Church in Salt Lake. Alex knew that Nephi skipped church that day, and didn't want him to miss his weekly dose of churchiness. It was a sweet gesture that endeared Nephi to Alex even more. He enjoyed the service, where individuals of all faiths joined in celebration, and worship of God.

Alex had one last surprise up his sleeve. At the end of the service, instead of heading home, he drove to La Bambolina where he had a private table for two and a candlelight dinner waiting for Nephi. Alex had pre-arranged everything. Bruschetta and calamari for antipasto, Fusilli alla Napolitana for primo piatto, and Chicken Parmigiana for secondo. The meal was complete with sparkling apple cider and cheesecake.

Each course was perfect, and the company was even better. They talked about the events of the past two days while they ate, and played footsies under the table, much like Brock and Angela had done all those times in the office.

After two amazing days together with Alex, the dinner was the perfect way to end the weekend. Nephi liked the way the candlelight brought out Alex's beautiful brown eyes. Ever since he was a teenager, he dreamed of finding a love like this. At the time, it seemed impossible, and even now he had a hard time believing it.

After dinner, Nephi excused himself to use the restroom. When he returned, he found Alex down on one knee, holding a ring box, with a bouquet resting on the table.

"I figured it's only right that you have an engagement ring, too," he said.

Nephi extended his hand, and Alex placed the ring on his finger, and then stood, sliding into Nephi's arms. They held each other and kissed. Alex wrapped his arms around Nephi's waist and slowly slid them down, firmly gripping his butt cheeks, and squeezing briefly before returning them to his waist.

"Honey, have I ever told you what a hot ass you have?"

he whispered.

Nephi leaned in closer and whispered back into Alex's ear, "Language, mister! And also, thank you. Yours isn't so bad either."

They kissed again, before returning to their seats, where the conversation turned to their engagement.

"What are you thinking about the wedding?" asked Nephi. "Big? Small? Location?"

"None of that matters to me. I don't have any family to speak of, and don't have many friends, either. For me it's just about the two of us, so I'm good with whatever you want. What are you thinking?"

"I don't have many friends either. You and Stacy are about it. That's okay though, I have found that you don't really need all that many. Having one or two good friends is better than a hundred surface friends, or a thousand social media followers. As for my family, I'm afraid they will be nothing but drama, especially my dad and Jacob. Honestly, they would probably end up ruining the whole thing."

"So what do you want to do?"

"I just want to get married."

"Honey, I know that. You know what I mean."

"No, I mean I want to get married now."

"If you're ready, I'm all for it, but the county building isn't even open right now. We need a license before we do anything. Want to go tomorrow morning?"

"No," replied Nephi. "We can be to Vegas in five and a half hours. Let's go now."

"It's late, and we have work tomorrow afternoon."

"You're at work now. Surely you can work something out. See if tonight's chef will cover for you, and don't worry about me, I have unused sick days, and I feel a cold coming on."

"I'll be right back," said Alex as he headed into the kitchen.

After a few moments, he returned to the table with a smile. "Let's do this," he exclaimed, offering Nephi his hand.

Nephi took his hand and kissed it gently before standing and walking with him out the door, hand in hand, with a skip in their step.

The Prius made its way south toward Sin City, transporting the sweethearts to a place where they would be legally and lawfully wed. They passed the Salt Lake suburbs, and went over the Point of the Mountain. They moved through Pleasant Grove, Orem, and Provo, eventually passing Spanish Fork, and waving goodbye to the judgement of Utah County, as they continued south.

The exits for the cities of Santaquin, Mona, and Nephi flew by the passenger side window as they drew closer to their destination. With Scipio and Fillmore in the rearview mirror, Alex noticed that his gas tank was running low. A full tank from this point should be enough to get them all the way to Las Vegas. He pulled off the next exit with fuel service, in the town of Beaver, Utah.

Nephi pumped gas while Alex got some road trip snacks. Feeling ironic, Alex returned to the car wearing a t-shirt that said "I ♥ Beaver".

"I got one for you, too," he said, tossing a shirt toward Nephi. "Something to remember our wedding trip by. We can wear them to your next family dinner so Jacob will feel more at ease."

"You're terrible," Nephi replied, with a wide grin, while pulling the shirt over his head. "But if truth be known, I prefer otters."

With the Prius full of gas, and a bag full of snacks, they continued their journey to the City of Lost Wages. For one Nephi Willard, it would soon become the City of Lost Virginity.

The road trippers arrived at the Las Vegas city limits around 3:00 AM on June 8th, the day that from now on, would be celebrated as their wedding anniversary. Tired, they pulled into the High Palace, Las Vegas where Nephi's employee discount landed them a suite with a hot tub for under a hundred dollars per night.

They went to the room and soon fell asleep in each other's arms. There, they slept soundly until almost 11:00 in the morning, when they woke up and ordered room service. The eggs benedict and croissants really hit the spot before they showered and hit the town.

Their first stop was a mall to pick up some clothes that were more appropriate for their wedding than the "I ♥ Beaver" t-shirts on their backs. Alex ended up with navy slacks, a light blue button-up shirt and a tie, while Nephi opted for gray slacks and a pink shirt with a bowtie.

Now looking more like a wedding party than ill-mannered teenagers, they headed for the county clerk's office to get a wedding license. An hour later and eighty bucks poorer, they entered the first wedding chapel they saw on the strip – the Marry U Wedding Chapel, positioned between a go-go bar and a casino.

It wasn't much to look at from the outside. One could easily mistake it for a Chinese buffet. Alex led Nephi inside, where they discovered a beautifully decorated building. The marble floor led from the front office into a chapel with white pews lining both sides. Three arched windows at the back let ample light into the room, and the vaulted ceilings gave it an air of grandeur.

There was nobody else there at mid-day on a Monday, and the woman behind the reception desk smiled and asked them to take a seat. She verified their marriage license and reviewed the wedding packages.

With no guests, the basic package was perfect. She pinned a boutonniere on each of them and summoned the wedding officiant and photographer.

With the chapel doors closed, Alex and Nephi walked, hand in hand, from the rear of the chapel to the front, while the traditional wedding march played. The photographer snapped away as they approached the officiant.

There they stopped, smiling at each other as she started the ceremony. She glanced down at her paperwork, double checking their names before proceeding.

"We are gathered here to join Alex Jones and Nephi Willard in the union of marriage. This contract should not be entered lightly, but with thought and acknowledgement of its obligations. Would the two of you like to exchange vows?"

They looked at each other, puzzled. In their spontaneity, neither of them had thought that far ahead.

"Sure," said Nephi. "Alex, I love you and don't feel complete without you by my side. I vow to love you and cherish you forever. You have me, all of me."

Alex returned Nephi's loving gaze and replied, "Nephi, you are everything to me. I have never been with anyone who makes me feel like this, someone who makes me want to be a better partner and companion. No words are enough to describe the depth of my love for you."

Love welled up inside both of them at the sweet sound of the other's words.

The officiant continued, "Alex, do you take Nephi to be your husband, and do you promise to love, honor, and cherish him, forsaking all others and holding only unto him, forever and ever?"

"I do."

"And Nephi, do you take Alex to be your husband and promise to love, honor, and cherish him, forsaking all others, and holding only unto him, forever and ever?"

"I do."

"You may now exchange rings."

"We already did," replied Alex, holding up his hand for her to see.

"Very good. To build a lasting relationship will require love and patience. I suggest that you continue to date. Dedicate time to your marriage, and do something every day to show your husband that you love him. It doesn't have to be big, but it must be consistent. Trust each other, love each other, and be patient with one another. Let the little things go before they develop into larger irritations. If you do those things, you will build a marriage that lasts."

The officiant paused and looked over each groom. With a

wide smile, she resumed the ceremony. "And now, by the power vested in me by the State of Nevada, I am honored to declare you legally and lawfully married. You may seal this declaration with a kiss."

Alex and Nephi faced each other and kissed. The kiss started gentle and sweet. It lingered and grew in passion as they embraced. They slowly decoupled their faces, and thanked the officiant for the ceremony.

"Hey, look at us," said Alex. "Another Snuzzle success story. Maybe we should be in their next commercial."

They laughed, and then joined hands and made their way back to the High Palace, Las Vegas as husbands.

They arrived at the suite, and opened the door. Alex carried Nephi over the threshold, something he had always wanted to do. He set Nephi down gently, and closed the door behind him as they started to kiss.

Their lips didn't separate as they moved from the door to the bed. They somehow managed to remove their shoes and ties before they lay down, lips still locked. They kissed for several minutes before Alex moved down to kiss below Nephi's bottom lip and then his chin, lingering for a moment while he gently sucked it. Continuing downward, he kissed Nephi's neck, driving him wild.

Ready to take it to the next level, they undressed. Nephi sat on the bed while Alex stood on the floor next to him. This being the first time Nephi had seen a fully naked man, other than himself, he looked Alex up and down, studying his body. He admired the definition in his arms and his abs. He loved the little ridges that formed just below Alex's abdominal muscles, where his torso met his pelvis.

Alex moved to the bed, where the kissing resumed. Nephi had already given Alex everything else, and was now ready to offer up his body. As they made love, Nephi gave himself fully to Alex, and Alex to Nephi. Alex was so gentle with Nephi, and the joy Nephi felt was like nothing he had experienced before. The unbridled expression of physical love moved his heart in a way he hadn't anticipated, and he began to cry.

Alex noticed the tears in his eyes and looked at him with love. "Is everything okay, Honey?"

Nephi smiled, gazed into Alex's eyes, and ran his fingers through his hair. "Everything is perfect," he whispered.

They nestled up to each other in bed, and basked in the emotion of the moment. The couple had been through so much together, and it seemed this moment would never come. But here they were, a happy married couple with their entire lives ahead of them.

In that moment, Nephi reflected on how far he had come. He was in touch with his feelings, and realized that he had never been more content than right now. He understood that one can't be truly happy while living a lie.

There was a time when Nephi was ashamed of who he was, when he prayed fervently for God to turn him straight. That time had passed. Nephi now understood that real happiness comes only from living true to your nature. Nephi accepted himself, just the way God made him, and was glad to be gay. He wouldn't change it for the world.

CHAPTER 27

Having driven all morning, Nephi was back in the office Tuesday afternoon. Normal life demanded his time, and the honeymoon would have to wait. On the drive home, they discussed their living arrangements and decided to live in Alex's apartment since Nephi only had two months left on his lease.

At work, fresh batch of trainees had finished orientation, and they assigned three of them to Nephi's team. Wanting them to form good habits early, he spent the first half of his shift monitoring their calls. It was obvious that they had paid attention to training, but each of them had some minor things to correct. He coached them on the needed improvements, and had them shadow experienced agents for the rest of the shift.

After work, he took the train to his apartment to gather his toothbrush, and pack a bag with necessities, before walking to Alex's apartment, their new shared home. Alex had arrived a few minutes earlier, and was dishing up food from the restaurant for dinner. They ate and watched a movie together, and then made love and fell asleep in each other's arms.

When Nephi woke up late Wednesday morning, he called Stacy to share the news.

"What? You're married?" she asked. "Why didn't you tell me? I totally would have come to Vegas with you."

"I figured you would want to be there, but with complicated family situations and all, we figured we should just go for it, just the two of us. No judgement, no stress."

"I can't blame you and I seriously want you to know that I'm happy for you. You deserve to be happy."

"I didn't know how I would feel, but I am happy. I'm happier than I've ever been."

Nephi told her all about the road trip, the stop in Beaver, the hotel, and the wedding chapel. Stacy filled him in on Chloe's preschool group, and all the trouble Wyatt was getting into with his newfound mobility. One or two good friends, Nephi thought to himself, that's all you really need.

Nephi's next call was to his mother who congratulated him, although the tone of her voice showed some hesitation. He enjoyed catching up with her just the same. Nephi let her take care of sharing the news with the rest of the family.

Before long, Alex woke, and the newlyweds spent their day off the way you would expect them to – having a lot of fun while hardly leaving the bedroom. So far, married life wasn't so bad.

The following day, Alex begged Nephi to take one more sick day to stay home with him, but between Pride and calling in sick to get married, Nephi felt obligated to work.

Soon after Nephi arrived at work, Jerry came into his office.

"I have a favor to ask. An emergency meeting came up, and I can't get out of it, but I have a shift manager candidate here for a job interview. Will you please handle the interview for me?"

"Right now?" asked Nephi.

"Yes, right now. I'm sorry about the short notice, but like I said, it's an emergency."

"I haven't had a chance to review a resume or anything. How do you want me to approach it?"

"Just ask behavioral interview questions about past job experience. Get a feel for cultural fit and call center management competency. If he does well, I can have him back for a second interview."

"Ok, sure. I can do that."

"Thanks a lot, Nephi. He's waiting for you in the small conference room."

A little annoyed at the lack of notice, Nephi went to the small conference room and opened the door.

"Good afternoon," he said with a smile.

"Nephi?" replied the voice.

Nephi's heart sank when he realized that the shift manager candidate was Mark Stone. Seeing him brought a flood of memories of the bullying and abuse at Brower. Visions of the security guard and Officer Williams flashed through his mind, requiring him to direct focus to his breathing to collect himself. Once he was over the initial shock, he took a seat.

"Mark, what brings you here? A shift manager job seems like a step backward for a General Manager."

"I should leave," said Mark as he started to stand.

"Sit down, let's talk for a minute," requested Nephi.

"The truth is, I'm no longer at Brower. I'm looking for something new. After some false allegations about gender discrimination and harassment, they forced me out."

"Oh," smiled Nephi. "That's a shame. It's terrible when false allegations cost you your job."

"Listen, I know that there is history between us, but I want you to know I'm not above stepping down to the shift manager level. I would be good in this job."

"It's good to know you're not above stooping to my level," said Nephi. Alright, I will ask some questions to assess your fit at HPH, but I'm curious, who is running the reservation center at Brower now?"

"They gave my job to that Monica. Can you believe that? They'll be sorry when she gets pregnant."

"Actually, Mark, I can believe that. Monica is good at her job. I hoped that the loss of your job might have humbled you, and that maybe you would have changed, but I see that you're the same old Mark."

"What does that mean?" asked Mark.

"It means that I will escort you out of the building now, and we'll be in touch if we determine you are a good fit."

"But I…"

Nephi interrupted him mid-sentence, "Let's go." He opened the door and led Mark toward reception.

"Oh, Mark, I also want to let you know that I am now married and yet somehow, the Lord still blessed me with this job that pays nearly twice what I was making at Brower. Funny how things work out."

They arrived at the lobby where Nephi said goodbye and wished him luck. Mark left, and Nephi turned around to find Jerry standing there with a satisfied smirk on his face.

"You knew who that was all along, didn't you?"

"Maybe I did," Jerry replied. "I just figured that would do your heart good. You know that karma, she really is a bitch."

They had a good laugh before returning to work. Nephi smiled through the entire shift.

The week wore on while the newlyweds settled into their new routine, getting used to living together. They were happy and in love. Sunday morning came and Nephi prepared for church.

"You're still going, huh?" asked Alex.

"Did you expect me to stop?"

"No, I know who you are, and I love you for it, but part of me maybe hoped you would stay home with me."

"You're welcome to come with me."

"No, I'm good, enjoy yourself."

"Thanks, I will," replied Nephi.

Rainbow pin on his lapel, Nephi went to church and sat with his friends in the Rainbow Squadron. He thought it strange to attend a singles ward now that he was married, but he was never really there to meet people in the first place, and it's not like the church recognized his marriage, anyway. In their view, even though he saved himself for marriage, he was committing homosexual sin and violating the law of chastity.

He sang his heart out and listened to the talks, same as every week. After Sacrament meeting, a member of the congregation that he didn't recognize approached him.

"What are you and your friends doing here?" he asked. "You clearly don't believe in the doctrine of the church. Why even bother showing up?"

"You know," replied Nephi, "that question used to bother me, but I don't really mind it anymore. I now understand that I am who God made me to be. He wants me to be happy, and who am I to argue with God? I used to reject a part of myself, but I now embrace every part of who I am. I love myself. Why do I come to church, you ask? What it comes down to is that I know who I am. I am a son, I am a brother, an uncle, and a friend. I am a gay man. I am a husband. I am all of those things, and I am also a Mormon. That, my friend, is why I come to church."

"Okay, well, have fun in hell I guess. I just don't understand why you can't follow the counsel of the apostles to trust in the Lord with all your heart. Trust that if you obey all the commandments, and stay celibate that he will take care of you in the end."

"See, the thing you don't understand is that I do trust in God with all my heart. In fact, I trust him more than that. I trust that he made me the way I am, and I trust that he won't hold that against me when I am judged. I trust God more than you will ever know."

The man shook his head and walked away. Nephi raised his head high and walked toward Sunday School class.

While he walked, Nephi thought about how everywhere we look, people are stuck in boxes. Active and inactive, gay and straight, twink and bear, liberal and conservative. There are too many boxes to count. He wondered if anyone really fits into a box. We are all God's children, individual members of the human race, with complicated thoughts and feelings, and restless souls.

Nephi thought that maybe if we forget about the boxes, and look for opportunities to include one another, to compromise, and to love, we might find more peace. That maybe, just maybe, if we focus on love, and leave the judgement to God, we would all be better off.

He continued to Sunday School, where he found the class discussing the Book of Mormon. The teacher explained that the Zoramites wouldn't believe any of the words of the prophet Alma because his son, Corianton, was consorting with a harlot. It reminded Nephi of Alex and he smiled.

Church ended and Nephi returned home to the apartment he shared with Alex. There, waiting for him in the kitchen, were a sandwich, a cup of cocoa, and a kiss.

Printed in Great Britain
by Amazon